The Two Lives of Grand Duke Michael

The Two Lives of Grand Duke Michael

The Last Tsar of Imperial Russia

1878 – 1918 dead or alive 1878 – 1947

Michael Roman

This book is a work of fiction with a background of historical fact. The author has created
a 'what if' scenario in the life of the main characters, Grand Duke Michael Romanov and
his secretary Nicholas Johnson using a time line in the first half of the 20th century.

He introduces political, armed forces and other peoples of that time to enhance the parts
played out by the main characters, whilst endeavouring to portray a largely fictional
novel. He would stress that any inclusion of a historical person has been shown to the best
portrayal of their characteristics, avoiding harm to their historical lives and descendants.
Fictional characters are also introduced and any resemblance to any real people or
incidents are purely coincidental.

Matador
9 Priory Business Park,
Wistow Road, Kibworth Beauchamp,
Leicestershire. LE8 0RX
Tel: 0116 279 2299
Email: books@troubador.co.uk
Web: www.troubador.co.uk/matador
Twitter: @matadorbooks

ISBN 978 1788034 517

British Library Cataloguing in Publication Data.
A catalogue record for this book is available from the British Library.

Printed and bound in the UK by TJ International, Padstow, Cornwall
Typeset in 11pt Adobe Garamond Pro by Troubador Publishing Ltd, Leicester, UK

Matador is an imprint of Troubador Publishing Ltd

Quotes

'Writing a book is an adventure. To begin with it is a toy then an amusement. Then it becomes a mistress, and then it becomes a master, and then it becomes a tyrant and, in the last stage, just as you are about to be reconciled to your servitude, you kill the monster and fling him to the public.'

'The truth is incontrovertible. Malice may attack it, ignorance may deride it, but in the end, there it is.'

'Continuous effort – not strength or intelligence – is the key to unlocking our potential.'

Winston Churchill

Dedication

To my life long buddy and solumate…

who died just before this book went into publication. A
man of immense presence, persuasion, whilst offering
sound advice, and whose life became a mantra to my own
aspirations. A Churchillian figure in bulldog looks and
attitude with points of view sometimes challenging but
often enlightening. His life was inspirational of these two
quotations from Winston Churchill.

*'Never give in, never give in, never, never, never, never in
nothing, great or small, large or petty – never give in except to
convictions of honour and good sense.'*

And

*'If you have an important point to make, don't try to be
subtle or clever. Use a pile driver. Hit the point once. Then
come back and hit it again. Then hit it a third time, with a
tremendous whack.'*

Malcolm Horsfall, September 1946–November 2017.

With Thanks

Hannah, who is a very beautful woman inside and out, for her support and inspiring me to use her as a role model for one of my main characters... Olga Bystrovia.

Colin my brother, who provided the opportunity to make for him a 'Fabergé Egg', which was the catalyst of this novel.

Adrian my friend, who listened with enthusiasm and encouragement to my first expounding of the content of this novel.

Malcolm, my life long childhood friend, who provided a peaceful platform at his log cabin in the Rockies to help me create a bucket list which kickstarted this novel... and at this precise moment of penning these thanks to him, I received the most awful news from his wife Shirley that he had died.

Colin Sidaway, a fellow author I had a chance meeting with whilst admiring our classic cars in a Motorway service station. He encouraged me with these words... 'Just get on with it yourself and self-publish, in spite of your many refusals from publishing agents.'

Acknowledgements

Wikipedia and Wikimedia, for supplying the free encyclopedia platform to the public that anyone can edit. Started in 2001, it currently contains over five and a half millions articles.

Rosemary and Donald Crawford for the historical facts they have re-produced in their book, *Michael and Natasha*. A historical account of a true love story combined with tragedy, in the last days of the Romanov Dynasty.

Contents

Author's Preface

There are no other books which have taken a slice of history and manufactures an historical event of a member of the Russian Imperial Royal family to produce a hero from semi-obscurity. Numerous historical high ranking political and armed forces figures are set within an audacious plot during the background of WW1.

Lenin, in 1918, encouraged the assassination of the only Romanov who undoubtedly could have changed the shape of 20th century history. The weaving of history into a credible 'what if' of the brother of the assassinated Tsar Nicholas II, which could have changed the whole order through his perilous two week round trip to the UK in 1918... and but for his assassination, the dream of freeing Russia from the early days of Communism... was ended.

It fulfils the readers need for a powerful story that transports us into the life and world of a tragic yet heroic figure in history. He was the very first of the Romanov Dynasty, preceding the fate of the ex-tsar Nicholas II and his family, to be assassinated...

Rumours, theories and tales of torture have echoed through the years, inspiring wild speculation, and fantastic claims of the 'truth' of the final days of Grand Duke Michael

Alexandrovitch Romanov.

The Two lives of Grand Duke Michael is a unique epic novel that takes place in the first half of 1918 and challenges fact over fiction in this interplay of a historical drama, a tragic love story and an account of espionage and shocking state duplicity. It questions the accepted views in a compelling and entertaining read.

This novel draws on historical fact and imaginative thinking which creates his two lives and two wives in a 'what if' drama. The Grand Duke's heroic attempts to defeat the emergence of Bolshevism and his subsequent assassination whilst under house arrest in the near Siberian city of Perm are a tragic ending to a life which could have changed the world order and avoided millions of deaths in those dark decades to come. Now this, the first comprehensive account, draws attention to the Grand Duke, who is understood to have briefly reigned as the last Tsar of Russia.

According to contemporary accounts, Michael was seized from a hotel in Perm where he was sent into exile, and bundled into a carriage along with his secretary, loyal friend and confidante, Nicholas Johnson. They were then taken to a clearing in a forest outside the city. There they were assassinated.

Crucially, the only undisputed fact is that no remains have ever been found, despite extensive searches in this century. The novel challenges the accepted account and paints a much different picture, with a careful and detailed revealing of Michael II's survival against the odds, helped by British secret service officers, including Sidney Reilly of MI6 – the 'Ace of Spies' – and the new life he built in the United Kingdom. He was given a new identity, and closely monitored by MI6, for whom he eventually worked at Bletchley Park.

Drawing from historical documents and extensive research, the author makes interesting, controversial challenges to commonly held beliefs. He reveals the duplicity of Michael II's first cousin, King George V of the United Kingdom and the government headed by David Lloyd George. The vivid narrative uses the author's imagination, to construct a credible and exciting story of one of the greatest adventures in history.

Antecedent

Winter 2016. I am sitting at the bay window of a caravan which is sited on the east coast of Yorkshire, overlooking one of nature's most beautiful bays. To the right I can see the rugged thirty four metre high limestone cliffs of Speeton towering over the rock-strewn beach below. To the left I can see the charming and unspoilt old fishing town of Filey, which today is a haven for thousands of discerning tourists each year, often accompanied by children and dogs.

The two hundred metres of soft golden sands at low tide, bordered by cobalt-coloured waters and blue skies from the left… scanning towards the right and seeing the thrashing waves on the defending Speeton Cliffs is a dichotomy of vibrating senses which excite the spirit.

I am holding a pen in one hand and a 1912 nickel silver egg-shaped wristwatch in the other.

I am about to reconstruct a story of monumental proportions, revealing events that took place in the early part of the last century which held the balance of fundamental and radical changes of the world order, played out by the younger brother of Tsar Nicholas II, the emerging fledgling Bolshevik regime and the Western Powers of the First World War.

My mind is slowly transported to the year of 1917… one hundred years ago.

Prologue

Russia in the New Year of 1917 was in anarchy and the threats to the existence of the Romanov Dynasty were becoming greater each day. The Russian Front in the war with Germany was collapsing, and food and munitions shortages were causing the people to demonstrate in the streets and outside Imperial buildings.

A provisional government was formed in March 1917, due to the rising unpopularity of the Tsar and the Romanov Dynasty, and the consequence of Soviet and Bolshevik tendencies for a change of power in Russia. The intention was to exert sufficient pressure on Tsar Nicholas II to abdicate.

He did so on the evening of 15 March, in favour of his younger brother Grand Duke Michael who was at that time the commander of a very successful fighting division on the German–Russian Front. Michael awoke the following morning to this news and was very concerned, as he had no previous knowledge or consultation with his brother Nicholas about any transfer of power. He firmly rejected this title, but did qualify this: he would only accept and carry out the duties of becoming the new Tsar if he were supported by a vote from the people and the acceptance of the interim government under the leadership of Alexander Kerensky.

Michael was a popular choice as could be seen by the early rumours which quickly circulated the streets of Petrograd and filtered into Russia and the world. He was loved and feted by the population at large, especially as he had the confidence and support of the army and some other armed factions appearing in the discontented Russia. He was a unifying force for good even outside Russia; many Western Governments would have approved of his accession and certainly deemed him a man with whom they felt they could do business with.

Events however that day overtook the implications of Michael's proposed accession, as the new government would not accept the handover of royal authority. Michael was relieved of his command in April 1917 and spent the rest of the year under surveillance or house arrest with his wife Natasha and their son George, always assisted by his faithful friend and secretary of the past five years, Nicholas Johnson, who was also a British citizen.

APPENDIX I

Introducing the characters

Sir George Buchanan

The British Ambassador to Russia 1910–1917. Sir George Buchanan had developed a strong bond with Tsar Nicholas II and attempted to convince him that granting some constitutional reform would stave-off revolution. Buchanan actively supported the Duma in its efforts to change Russia's stately system during wartime. He also facilitated activities of British spies, Reilly and Lockhart, in Russia..

Tsar Nicholas II

Nicholas II or Nikolai II was the last reigning Emperor of Russia, ruling from 1894 until his forced abdication on 15 March 1917 in favour of his brother, the Grand Duke Michael. His reign saw the fall of the Russian Empire from being one of the great powers of the world to one of economic and military collapse. Nicholas approved the Russian mobilization in 1914, which led to the causes of the fall of the Romanov Dynasty. He eventually took command of the armed forces after a series of catastrophic defeats. However, his influence had a negative effect, as he was neither a tactician nor a popular leader, and shortages of arms and food supplies soon led to the near-destruction of the forces in the field. Their saviour was the suing for peace with Germany at the hands of Lenin in 1918.

Following the Revolution of 1917 and his abdication, the tsar and his family were imprisoned. In the summer of the following year, he and his family were eventually executed by the Bolsheviks on the night of 16–17 July 1918 in Ekaterinburg, a remote town in Central Russia.

Tsarina Alexandra Feodorovna

She was Empress of Russia as the spouse of Tsar Nicholas II, and a granddaughter of Queen Victoria of the United Kingdom. Alexandra was the last Tsarina of Russia. She was appalled at the declaration of war in 1914 and foretold that this would be the downfall of the delicately balanced Russian state, which had been fraught with revolutionary attempts to overthrow imperial rule. When Nicholas became head of the armed forces, he entrusted his wife with the governing of Russia in his absence.

Alexandra had no experience of government and constantly appointed and reappointed incompetent ministers, which meant the government was never stable or efficient and led to the troops and civilian population being denied essential supplies of food and material. She paid attention to the self-serving advice of Grigori Rasputin, a Russian mystic, and their relationship was widely, though falsely, believed to be sexual in nature.

Her reputation for influencing her husband's resistance to the surrender of autocratic authority over the country severely damaged her popularity and that of the Romanov monarchy in its final years. This resulted in the Bolshevik revolutionaries murdering her, her family and her entourage in the summer of 1918 during their captivity in Central Russia.

Albert Stopford

Albert Henry Stopford, known as Bertie Stopford, was a British antiques and art dealer, who also specialised in the manufactured jewellery from the houses of Fabergé and Cartier. He was well known to the three British monarchs of the first part of the twentieth century.

He was an emissary for the British spy organisation M16 becoming the eyes and ears of Petrograd during the First World War. During the years leading to, and the war, he forged friendships with several high-ranking members of the Russian royal family, becoming an intimate friend of the Romanovs. He carried out many courier activities under the guise of his diplomatic immunity, transporting out of revolutionary Russia, vast quantities of wealth in antiques and jewellery.

He also assisted the British MI6 in intelligence gathering and supported Sidney Reilley in his clandestine Russian endeavours, implementing the Churchill plan to invade northern Russia.

Bruce Lockhart

Bruce Lockhart joined the British Foreign Service and was posted to Moscow as British Consul-General in early 1917, but left in October that year. He soon returned to Russia as the United Kingdom's first envoy to the Bolsheviks in January 1918 and was also working for the Secret Intelligence Service. He set up a secret service agents system in Petrograd working with Sidney Reilly, his MI6 colleague where both were paving the way for the Allied invasion of Russia.

In 1918, Bruce Lockhart and Sidney Reilly were dramatically alleged to have plotted to assassinate Bolshevik leader Vladimir Lenin. He was arrested but he escaped trial due to an exchange of 'secret agents'.

Alexander Kerensky.

When the February Revolution broke out in 1917, Kerensky was one of its most prominent leaders in the newly formed Russian Provisional Government.

Alexander Kerensky was a Russian lawyer and politician who was also serving as the Minister of Justice in the Provisional Government. He eventually became the Minister of War, and leader of the Socialist Revolutionary Party. Kerensky was a key political figure in the Revolution of 1917, but later in that same year his government was overthrown by the Lenin-led Bolsheviks during the October Revolution.

Grand Duke Michael Alexandrovitch Romanov

He was the youngest son and fifth child of Emperor Alexander III of Russia and youngest brother of Tsar Nicholas II. In 1912, Michael shocked Nicholas by marrying the unpopular Natalia (Natasha) Wulfert, who had two previous marriages behind her. Nicholas, in anger, accused Michael of disloyalty to the pledges of the line of succession and exiled Michael to England and removed him from the line of succession.

After the outbreak of World War I, Michael returned to Russia, assuming command of the 'Savage Division', which was a cavalry regiment. When Nicholas abdicated on 15 March 1917, Michael was named as his successor instead of Alexei. Michael, however, deferred acceptance of the throne until ratification by an elected assembly. He therefore became emperor for twelve hours. Following the Russian Revolution of 1917, he was imprisoned and murdered in Perm in June 1918.

Nicholas Johnson

Nicholas Johnson was born in Russia in 1878. His father, a British citizen, was a captain in the Imperial Army being posted to the Royal Courts. He shared a love of music with the Anglophile Grand Duke Michael, who, like Nicholas, was also a graduate of the Mikhailovsky Artillery School. These connections and shared interests led to a deep friendship with Michael and he was given the nickname 'Johnny'.

Speaking three languages, he was sociable, smiling, and an accomplished pianist, and would accompany the very musical Michael, who played several instruments, notably the guitar. In late 1912 the Grand Duke Michael chose Nicholas as his private secretary. He devoted himself to serving his master, and even in the face of certain death his loyalty never wavered. Thus, after the Revolution, Michael pleaded with his faithful servant to flee to Britain, as he was a British citizen, but Nicholas refused to leave his side.

Arrested at Gatchina outside St Petersburg on 7 March 1918, both were soon exiled to the city of Perm. On 13 June 1918, they were shot by a bloodthirsty rabble, probably by order of Lenin. As Nicholas lay dying, the wounded Michael went to his aid, begging the execution squad, 'Let me say goodbye to my friend.' Moments later, he too was dead, killed at point-blank range in the head. Their remains have never been found. Michael and Nicholas Johnson were canonised in 1981.

Countess (Natalia) Natasha Brasova

Natalia Brasova was a Russian noblewoman who married Grand Duke Michael Alexandrovitch of Russia. They were both exiled from Russia in 1912 and eventually, after a year of living in

European hotels, went to England and lived there until the start of the war.

At that point Michael asked his brother if he could return and partake in duties of the war. This was accepted and in September 1914 he left Paddockhurst in Sussex and returned with Natasha and their son George, eventually settling back in the family home at Gatchina.

Natasha founded two military hospitals and embarked on a mission of caring for wounded soldiers during her husband's absence at the warfront. Now people in Russia started to accept her as a member of the Royal family. As the war began to go badly for the Russians, Natasha was dismayed by the change in Michael's appearance; he abandoned his smart uniforms and decorations and wore a plain uniform with his muddy boots. Michael was upset by criticisms of his decision to be in the frontline of the war. He wrote to her, 'the present time is so hard for Russia that my conscience could not allow me *not* to join the frontline service – and I am convinced that having done that, I also brought you some good in terms of public opinion, which, unfortunately, we can't totally ignore.'

During the Revolution in 1917, she endured the hardship of deprivation, house arrest and imprisonment from time to time with her husband. She continually fought Lenin for her husband's release from house arrest in Perm, but was unsuccessful. After his murder in June 1918 she went into exile in England and then France to look after her son George and daughter Tata. Natasha never accepted that her husband had been murdered and chose to believe the accepted reason at that time for his disappearance in that he had escaped from imprisonment in Perm and was formulating plans to oust the Bolshevik government. Later in the early 1920s she at last accepted that he had not survived the imprisonment.

She died in poverty in 1952.

George Mikhailovich, Count Brasov

George Mikhailovich, Count Brasov was a Russian noble and a descendant of the House of Romanov through a morganatic line. His parents were Grand Duke Michael Alexandrovitch of Russia and his wife, Countess Brasova. He endured a great deal of movement and disturbance during the early Bolshevik years due to the harassment of his parents. He fled Russia in 1919 with his mother into exile in England to escape the dangers of the Revolution.

He was educated at Harrow. As he matured, many remarked at his strong resemblance to his father, and became heir apparent to the throne of Russia upon his father's murder in 1918.

On a holiday in France he was involved in a car accident where he crashed into a tree. He sustained massive internal injuries and died without regaining consciousness in 1931.

Although he had no succession rights due to the morganatic marriage of his parents, George was the last male-line descendant of Alexander III of Russia.

Sidney Reilly 'Ace of Spies'

Sidney George Reilly, commonly known as the 'Ace of Spies', was a secret agent of the British Secret Service Bureau, the precursor to the modern British Secret Intelligence Service, MI6. He is alleged to have spied for at least four different powers. Reilly was heavily involved in the revolutionary years, in the main to facilitate and support the overthrow of the Bolshevik regime via the planned invasion of Russia by the Western Powers.

Reilly was a Russian Jew originally named Georgi Rosenblum and born in Odessa in 1873. He arrived in London in 1895, and was recruited into secret intelligence work for the Special Branch of the British Police. When Rosenblum married a wealthy heiress in mid-1898, he crafted a new identity for himself as Sidney Reilly.

Reilly was soon put to work spying in the Far East and in Russia, and after over twenty years of service he was formerly inducted into the Secret Intelligence Service, the forerunner to MI6, in 1918. During this period of secrecy and subterfuge Reilly very much fed into his own legend, claiming to have spied for several different countries across four continents and listing numerous supposed wives and mistresses. He certainly loved the high life, fast women, adventure, deception and gambling, and as such he became a very talented spy, in spite of his fabrications and exaggerations.

During his covert operations and important information gathering, he also helped the Imperial families to escape whilst securing a wealth of their treasures. He was imprisoned with his colleague Sir Bruce Lockhart, but escaped. He was murdered on the orders of Stalin in 1925 in Russia.

Later Ian Fleming used Reilly as a model for James Bond. Today many historians consider Reilly to have been the first twentieth-century 'super-spy'. Much of what is thought to be known about him could be false, however, as Reilly was a master of deception, most of his life is shrouded in legend.

The Grand Duchess Maria Pavlovna

Grand Duchess Maria Pavlovna of Russia was a cousin of Grand Duke Michael. She was a prominent hostess in St Petersburg in Russia and lived at the Vladimir Palace. Socially ambitious, it was there that she established her reputation as being one of the best hostesses in the capital. A family friend, Albert Stopford, rescued the jewels from her palace safe and smuggled them out of Russia.

The Grand Duchess held the distinction to be the last of the Romanovs to escape revolutionary Russia, as well as the first to die in exile. She made her way from Venice to Switzerland and then to France, where her health failed. Staying at her villa, she died on 6th September 1920 aged sixty-six.

The Grand Duchess had a passion for jewels, and her collection was renowned of which many were favoured pieces and some being owned by Catherine the Great.

After the Duchess' death, many were sold by her children to support their lives in exile. Amongst the new owners of distinction were Queen Mary of the United Kingdom and Queen Elizabeth II. Some of her emeralds were purchased by Barbara Hutton, and later by actress Elizabeth Taylor, who had them recut.

Joseph (Novel Character)

Joseph was a very trusted and long-serving member of the Vladimir Palace where the Grand Duchess Maria Pavlovna resided during her married life. When the palace was vacated after Maria fled to the Crimea, the palace was put under guard and Joseph was required to stay on as caretaker. He noted that the palace was being used as a secret store for the Bolsheviks misappropriation of Imperial treasures, and assisted Albert Stopford in his quest to rescue the jewels of Maria Pavlovna.

Peter Polotsov

Senior officer in the Savage Division of the Russian Imperial Army and a close friend of Grand Duke Michael. He was transferred to the new Bolshevik-controlled army and posted to Petrograd as a commander in 1917. He arranged Michael's exile with full permits for himself and family to travel to Finland. They packed valuables and prepared to move, but their escape was seen by Bolshevik sympathisers and they were placed once more under house arrest. He continued to help the family during 1918.

Winston Churchill

Parliamentary Minister for Munitions to the British Government, Secretary of State for War and Air during 1917–1919. A major preoccupation of his tenure in the War Office was the Allied intervention in the Russian Civil War. Churchill was a staunch advocate of foreign intervention, declaring that Bolshevism must be 'strangled in its cradle'. He created a plan to organise an Allied invasion of Russia in 1918.

He secured, from a divided and loosely organised Cabinet, intensification and prolongation of the British involvement in Russia, beyond the wishes of any major group in Parliament or the nation and in the face of the bitter hostility of the Labour party.

David Lloyd George

British Prime Minister from 1916. He was the last Liberal to serve as Prime Minister.

Lloyd George welcomed the fall of the tsar in a message to the new Russian Prime Minister Kerensky. Lloyd George gave a cautious welcome to the suggestion of the Russian Foreign Minister Pavel Milyukov that the toppled tsar and his family be given sanctuary in Britain. In April 1917, the British Government withdrew its consent under royal pressure. Eventually the Russian Royal Family were moved to the Urals where they were executed in 1918. Lloyd George was often blamed for the refusal of asylum.

Ethel Voynich

Ethel Lilian Voynich was an Anglo-Irish novelist and musician, and a supporter of several revolutionary causes. She was born in Cork, but grew up in England. Voynich was a significant figure, not only on the late Victorian literary scene, but also in Russian émigré circles. She is best known for her novel *The Gadfly*, which became popular in her lifetime, especially in Russia. It is said that she had an intense relationship with Sidney Reilly in 1895, and subsequently wrote the book with him as the main character in 1897.

However, a noted biographer of Reilly, recalls that these were romanticised versions of such events and very doubtful, and counters instead that Reilly was perhaps informing on Voynich's radical, pro-émigré activities to the Metropolitan Police Special Branch.

The novel was hugely popular in Soviet Russia, Communist China and Iran, and its study by educationalists and its compulsory reading exerted a cultural influence on these countries. By the time of her death, around 2.5m copies had been sold. An opera was created by a Russian composer, and later in 1955 Dmitri Shostakovich wrote the score for a major Russian film based on the novel. In Italy where the plot takes place, the book and opera are by and large unnoticed.

She died in New York in 1960 and was very much unaware of the popularity of her book until 1955 when she was visited in America by a Russian diplomat.

Peter Carl Fabergé

When Peter Carl took over the House, there was a move from producing jewellery in the then-fashionable French eighteenth-century style to becoming artist-jewellers. Fabergé's production of the very first so-called Fabergé egg, the Hen Egg, given as a gift from the tsar to his wife Maria Fyodorovna on Easter of 1885, so delighted her that the Emperor assigned Fabergé the title Goldsmith by special appointment to the Imperial Crown of that year.

In light of the Empress' response to receiving one of Fabergé's eggs on Easter, the tsar commissioned Fabergé to make an Easter egg as a gift for her every year thereafter. The only stipulation was that each one should be unique and each should contain a surprise.

Upon the death of Alexander III, his son, the next tsar, Nicholas II, followed this tradition and expanded it by requesting that there be two eggs each year, one for his mother (who was eventually given a total of thirty such eggs) and one for his wife, Alexandra (who received another twenty).

In 1916, the House of Fabergé became a joint-stock company with a capital of three million roubles.

The following year upon the outbreak of the October Revolution, the business was taken over by a 'Committee of the Employees'. In 1918 the House of Fabergé was nationalised by the Bolsheviks and the stock was confiscated. The House of Fabergé was no more.

After the nationalisation of the business, Carl Fabergé left St Petersburg on the last diplomatic train for Riga in Latvia. The Revolution soon reaching Latvia, he fled to Germany and later travelled to Switzerland.

Peter Carl Fabergé never recovered from the shock of the Russian Revolution. He died in Switzerland on September 24, 1920 in relative poverty and ignominy from his past status. His family believed he died of a broken heart.

Collenius Johannsen aka Grand Duke Michael

This was the undercover name used by Grand Duke Michael during his travels around Europe in disguise with Sidney Reilly and Olga Bystrovia. His disguise was complemented by wearing a wig which altered his receding hairline and dark glasses to subdue glare (and hide nerves) He was posing as a Finnish diplomat working with the new Bolshevik regime. His papers were forged and supported that covert guise.

Boris aka Nicholas Johnson

This was one of the names used by Nicholas Johnson during his travels around Europe in disguise as a low-ranking soldier with little or no papers; he took the guise of a support and 'gofor' to Reilly and Olga Bystrovia. It was important that he seemed to have no connection with Michael as, if it was discovered by the Cheka, Russian State Secret Police that they had left Russia, then the lookout would be for two people, tall and short. This dissemination of the link between both would aid the deception they were casting.

Orlov Volkov Revieski aka Sidney Reilly

This was the undercover name used by Sidney Reilly during his exploits in Russia in aiding Grand Duke Michael and Johnson to escape from and return back into Russia in February 1918.

Olga Bystrovia (Novel Character) aka Hannah Chudasama

She was working for MI6 in 1917 and her guise was that of a Senior Commander Commissar possessing authority based on party ideology with powers to arrest from suspicions of non-conformity to ideology and doctrine.

She was an expert in several European languages, and

was adept in mathematics and creative thinking. Known for her coolness under stress she could marginalise aggression in opponents through her wit and charm. Together with her planning and strategic thinking, Hannah was key in assisting Sidney Reilly in his Russian theatre of operations and post settlement of Imperial families in exile. In her post-war years, after decommissioning from MI6, she chose to continue using her covert operational code name, Olga Bystrovia.

Olaf (Novel Character)

He was a chief engineer with a team of contractors from Sweden. The revolutionary government employed them to supply and install the very latest development of marine engines into the reconstruction of the Royal Yatch *Standart*. This boat was misappropriated by the Bolsheviks to destroy any reflections and emblems of Imperialism, but also to convert the boat into a minesweeping frigate.

Able Seaman, Basil Baldric (Novel Character)

This was his name as an undercover agent with MI6 who was commissioned to travel with Jack Blackman on board the HMS *Iron Duke* to rendezvous with Grand Duke Michael in the Barents Sea.

Baldric was a very intelligent strategist and his unassuming character, as a low-ranking navel recruit would disarm Michael and Johnson. His understanding of several languages also allowed him to listen in on the bugged cabin which they shared.

His prime responsibility was to monitor their views and intentions. A major issue was to discover if they had been able to bring with them the quantity of Romanov treasure which Reilly and Stopford had reported on, as a contribution to the prosecution of the coming invasion by the Allies at Archangel.

Jack Blackman – Adderley (Novel Character)

This was his name as an undercover agent with MI6 who was commissioned to travel with Basil Baldric on board the HMS *Iron Duke*. He was the official face of MI6 and attached to the Royal Navy and Royal Flying Corp. He could discuss in open conversation with Michael the role of MI6 and the secretive activities and disguises that were required to get him into Great Britain and safely back into Russia.

Admiral of the Fleet, Sir John Rushworth Jellicoe

Jellicoe, commanded the Grand Fleet at the Battle of Jutland in May 1916. Both sides claimed victory, but history shows the battle was drawn as each side lost many ships and thousands of men. The German High Seas Fleet retreated to port, but the British public were disappointed that the Royal Navy had not won a victory on the scale of the Battle of Trafalgar. Jellicoe later served as First Sea Lord, overseeing the expansion of the Naval Staff at the Admiralty and the introduction of convoys.

Robert Blackburn

Blackburn was an English aviation pioneer and the founder of Blackburn Aircraft. He was born in Kirkstall, England, and built his first aircraft, a monoplane, in 1909, making his first short flight on the sandy beach on the East Coast of Yorkshire at Filey Bay in the spring of 1909. In 1914 he created the Blackburn Aeroplane & Motor Company, establishing a new factory at Roundhay, Leeds.

He built a two-seat seaplane, the Type L, and was to be used in the Circuit of Britain race due to start on 14 August 1914, hosted by the *Daily Mail*. The First World War was declared on 4 August, and the race was abandoned with the aircraft being impounded by the Admiralty.

He introduced the first scheduled air service in Great Britain, offering half-hourly flights between Leeds and Bradford. In 1919 he set up the North Sea Aerial Navigation Company, using surplus World War I aircraft.

Blackburn was interested in not only building aircraft but also flying them. He offered flying lessons and established passenger flights between Hull, Leeds and Hounslow with summer trips to Harrogate and Scarborough. This enterprise was short lived and the business moved to freight only flying between Leeds and Amsterdam via Lympne and London.

He had a grandiose scheme to fly from Hull to Copenhagen and onwards to Stockholm, Helsinki and Petrograd.

Captain Laker (Novel Character)

Laker was an army officer adjutant assisting in administrative work and attached to the RFC. He was designated as liaison officer to Michael and Johnson during their visit to Yorkshire.

Captain Anderson

He was an officer of the RFC No. 47 Squadron based at Beverly East Yorkshire which was formed in 1916, as a home defence unit, protecting Hull and East Yorkshire against attack by German Zeppelins.

The presence of a representative from this unit at the Scarborough Conference was important to the invasion plans as they were designated to provide aerial support and training of White Russian forces during the invasion period. The squadron was eventually sent to Russia to help General Denikin's White Russian forces in their fight against the Bolsheviks in the Russian Civil War.

Woodrow Wilson

Thomas Woodrow Wilson was an American politician and academic who served as the 28th President of the United States from 1913 to 1921.

Wilson found it increasingly difficult to maintain neutrality in World War I, due to Germany's commitment to unrestricted submarine warfare and their promise to the Mexican Government that if Germany was victorious, she would support them in winning back the southern states from the USA. On April 2 1917, the USA declared war with Germany.

The overthrow of the Russian Monarchy brought the war with Russia and Germany to an end. This relieved the Germans, and allowed them to dedicate more troops to the Western front, thus making U.S. forces central to Allied success in the remaining battles of 1918.

Wilson dedicated military resources to an intervention in Russia against the Bolsheviks, as he was convinced of the potential benefit to assist the Allies on the Eastern Front and bring Russia back to war with Germany.

General William Edmund Ironside

In 1918 he was promoted to command the Allied intervention force in northern Russia. This was his first independent command and he threw himself fully into it; for over a year, he travelled continually along the Northern Dvina River to keep control of his scattered international forces.

In late 1919 he was forced to abandon the White Army to their fate and the success of the Red Army under the control of Lenin and Stalin.

Major-General Sir Alfred William Fortescue Knox

In 1911 General Knox was appointed the British Military Attaché in Russia. A fluent speaker of Russian, he became a liaison officer to the Imperial Russian Army during First World War. During the October Revolution in Russia he observed the Bolsheviks taking the Winter Palace on 25 October 1917. He was aware of the plight of the Romanovs and was on hand at any moment to intervene in the safety of Grand Duke Michael on behalf of the British Government. He had met Michael on several previous occasions, especially during the combat years of the Russian and German armies.

First Sea Lord, Rosslyn Erskine Wemyss

Returning to the Admiralty from Commander of the Dover Patrol, and following the decision to dismiss the First Sea Lord Admiral Sir John Jellicoe, Wemyss was appointed in December 1917, First Sea Lord. He was political advisor to operations for the invasion of Russia.

Admiral Sir Edwyn Sinclair

Sinclair was a Vice Admiral of the fleet at the time of the Scarborough Accord meeting. Earlier in 1916 he was the first to sight and engage with the German High Seas Fleet at the battle of Jutland. In December 1918, he was given the role to take his 6th Battle Squadron to sail into the Baltic and with Danish collaboration, via the de-mined straights of Denmark, and up to Estonia to assist in their war of independence against Bolshevik Russia, where he delivered large quantities of armaments. He also captured a number of Russian warships and handed them to the fledgling Estonian independence leaders. He gave further assistance in blockading the Russian naval base at Kronstadt, thus aiding the British campaign to liberate Petrograd (Leningrad).

In November 1918 he was given the honour of leading the surrendered German Fleet into internment at Scapa Flow.

General John Joseph Pershing

General of the Armies, most famous as the Commander of the American Expeditionary Force on the Western Front in World War I during 1918. Pershing was of the opinion that the war should continue and that all of Germany should be occupied in an effort to permanently destroy German militarism.

He, with British forces, sent his troops to prosecute

the invasion of Russia at Archangel in 1918. He assembled an expeditionary force of around 4,500 enlisted troops in England and sent them to Archangel and Murmansk to engage with Bolshevik forces, the fledgling Red Army. This was an Allied campaign with the cooperation of General Ironside who was commanding the British contingent, and joined by France and Serbia.

Adrian Woollaston

Woollaston was head of maintenance at Knebworth House near Luton when Michael was in residence during 1913/14 and was his personal chauffer. He retained this position with Lady Lytton, who was acting as caretaker, and was on hand to receive Michael and Johnson when they returned to Knebworth House in 1918 to retrieve their hidden stash of jewels.

Edith Villiers, Countess of Lytton

She became Queen Victoria's Lady-in-Waiting in 1895. After the Queen died, she then continued in the employment of Queen Alexandra until she retired in 1905, starting a retirement of more than thirty years. She lived at Homewood, a 'dowager house' on the family estate at Knebworth Hertfordshire, where she managed house affairs.

Louise (von) Kreisler Johnson

Louise was the mother of Nicholas Johnson who was the faithful secretary of Grand Duke Michael, and was married to Nicholas A. Johnson, a Captain in the Russian Imperial Court. She accompanied Michael to England in 1912 and resided with him and her son at Knebworth House near Luton, and Paddockhurst in Sussex. She remained there after Michael and her son were recalled to Russia at the start of World War I and was in-residence until the end of the war. She gave refuge to Michael's wife Natasha at her new home in Wadhurst when she fled Russia in 1919.

King George V

George V was King of the United Kingdom and the British Dominions, and Emperor of India. When Tsar Nicholas II of Russia, George's first cousin, was overthrown in the Russian Revolution of 1917, the British Government offered political asylum to the tsar and his family. However, worsening conditions for the British people, and fears that revolution might come to the British Isles, led George to think that the presence of the Romanovs would be seen as inappropriate. Advanced planning for a rescue was undertaken by MI1, a branch of the British Secret Service. But because of the strengthening position of the Bolshevik revolutionaries and wider difficulties with the conduct of the war, the plan was never put into operation. The tsar and his immediate family remained in Russia, where they were murdered by Bolsheviks in 1918.

Queen of Denmark, Alexandrine Auguste of Mecklenburg-Schwerin

Alexandrine Auguste of Mecklenburg-Schwerin was Queen of Denmark as the wife of King Christian X. She was also Queen of Iceland. Her mother was Grand Duchess Anastasia Mikhailovna of Russia, a granddaughter of Emperor Nicholas I of Russia.

King Christian X of Denmark

Christian started a military education before his ascension to the throne as was customary for princes at that time. He married Princess Alexandrine in 1898, who was a daughter of Duchess Anastasia Mikhailovna of Russia. In 1912, his father King Frederick VIII died and he then acceded to the throne as Christian X. Denmark was neutral during the First World War, but were persuaded to assist the Allied powers if an invasion of Russia took place as planned in 1918.

Carl Theodor Zahle

Zahle was Prime Minister during World War I and the main objective for his administration during the war was to keep Denmark neutral. Although Denmark was neutral, the war meant a scarcity of goods and materials and regulation of the economy became necessary.

After the war the government was accused of having been too friendly towards Germany and the economic regulations limited the profits of business life. On top of that came the question about northern Schleswig and in particular Flensburg. A referendum was held on the return of parts of Schleswig to Denmark from Germany and it was demanded that Germany should cede the city of Flensburg.

Admiral Otto Kofoed-Hansen

In 1918, he was head of the Danish Naval High Command in neutral Denmark as a result of the First World War. He was an able, energetic, dedicated and authoritative naval officer with a talent for strategic understanding. He played a crucial role in the decision to shut the Danish Straits with mines. A lockout would primarily benefit Germany, but would ensure that they would not invade and occupy Denmark. This was the only realistic option for Denmark and so avoiding war with Great Britain.

However, he could be persuaded to join a force of combined Allies with American help if the conditions were right, to aid the planned Allied invasion in Russia to remove the Bolshevik threat.

Captain Heinrich von Nostitz Janckendorff

Janckendorff became the new commander of U-151 in early 1918. After having undergone a refit in Flensburg, he was commissioned to take the boat into the Baltic for sea trials. The U-151 was a cargo-carrying vessel which was designed to import valuable supplies which were being denied to Germany by Allied blockading and the mining of the straights of Denmark. Also, similar valuable exports were carried out reciprocally.

However, in 1917 the submarine was converted into a highly effective and menacing war machine, which was able to stay at sea for many months and was instrumental in the sinking of a large tonnage of Allied shipping, mainly on the American Eastern Seaboard

Admiral Reinhard Scheer

Reinhard Scheer was an Admiral in the Imperial German Navy during World War I. In 1916 Admiral Scheer took command of the III Battle Squadron, which consisted of the newest and most powerful battleships in the High Seas Fleet. Scheer led the German fleet at the Battle of Jutland on 31 May–1 June 1916, which was one of the largest modern naval battles in history.

Scheer joined those calling for unrestricted submarine warfare against the Allies, a move the Kaiser eventually permitted. In August 1918, Scheer was promoted to the Chief of Naval Staff and retired after the end of the war.

A strict disciplinarian, Scheer was popularly known in the Navy as the 'man with the iron mask' due to his severe appearance.

Admiral Alfred von Tirpitz

Tirpitz took the modest Imperial Navy, starting in the 1890s, and turned it into a world-class force that could threaten the British Royal Navy. His navy, however, was not strong enough to confront the British successfully in the First World War. The one great engagement at sea, the Battle of Jutland, ended in a draw with both sides claiming victory. Tirpitz turned to submarines, which antagonised the United States, and called for the most extreme use of weapons, especially unrestricted submarine warfare.

Commander Francis Cromie

Francis Cromie, was a distinguished British Royal Navy Commander, and chief of British Intelligence operations in northern Russia for the British Naval Intelligence Division. In the early part of World War I from 1915 he assumed command of the British submarine flotilla in the Baltic. The British Admiralty had inserted several C and E class submarines into the Baltic to tie down the German fleet in any attempt to break out into the North Sea. They were based eventually in Finland which had some sort of neutrality in the war under the command of Francis Cromie

Later during the war and Russian Revolution, he was naval attaché to the diplomatic staff of the British Embassy in Petrograd, Russia. There he met his death, at the hands of murdering Bolshevik thugs, while defending the British Embassy.

Captain Jenner (novel character)

He commanded the fated British submarine which he scuttled during an action with the U-151 in the Baltic. Reilly managed to persuade Von Tirpitz not to sink the British submarine and avoid the resultant wanton loss of life. Instead he confused Jenner into allowing their heaving to with the U-151, thinking that they were being rendezvoused by another British submarine. Reilly's efforts were rewarded when Tirpitz agreed, and the submariners were taken captive on the cavernous U-151 with no loss of life.

Otto August Strandman, Estonian politician

He was an Estonian politician, who served as Prime Minister. He was one of the leaders of the Centre-left Estonian Labour Party, and Minister of War (1919). Strandman a supporter of autonomy, was chosen to compose the draft of self-government reform that eventually created the Autonomous Governorate of Estonia. He was to be a key member of the Estonian attempt to invade Russia, striking at Petrograd with the help of the British and American navies and using arms which were supplied from Britain.

Konstantin Päts, Leader of the Estonian Independence movement

On 19 February 1918, Päts became head of the Estonian Salvation Committee that issued the Estonian Declaration of Independence on 24 February. He was also Minister of War that left him organising Estonian troops for the War of Independence against Russian Bolsheviks. He was to be a key member of the invasion force and would strike at Petrograd with the help of the British and American navies.

Patriarch Tikhon of all Russia Orthodox Church

Saint Tikhon of Moscow was the 11th Patriarch of the Russian Orthodox Church during the early years of the Soviet Union. During the Russian Civil War, the Patriarch was widely considered as anti-Bolshevik and many members of the Orthodox clergy were jailed or executed by the new regime. Tikhon openly protested against violent attacks by the Bolsheviks on the Church. He was concerned that the Russian people were being forcibly coerced to abandon their faith. Church closures were becoming commonplace together with imprisonment and murder of clerics. His support for an Allied invasion was a key factor in encouraging an uprising against the Bolsheviks to preserve his Church.

Kaiser Wilhelm II

Wilhelm II was the last German Emperor and King of Prussia. He was the eldest grandchild of the British Queen Victoria and related to many Monarchs and Princes of Europe. His support for Austria-Hungary in the crisis of July 1914, led in a matter of days to the First World War. Bombastic and impetuous, he dictated policy during the First World War with little regard for the civilian government. He abdicated in November 1918, on the signing of the Armistice and fled to exile in the Netherlands.

Vladimir Lenin

Russian Communist revolutionary, politician, and political theorist. He served as head of government of the Russian Republic from 1917 to 1918, of the Russian Soviet Federative Socialist Republic from 1918 to 1924, and of the Soviet Union from 1922 to 1924. His main concern during 1918 was the possibility of a resurgence of support for the return of the Imperial Throne. His only certainty of retaining control was the ultimate permanent removal of the imperial families.

Joseph Stalin

Stalin was one of the seven members of the first Politburo, founded in 1917 in order to manage the Bolshevik Revolution. Thereafter, civil war broke out in Russia, pitting Lenin's Red Army against the White Army. He ordered the killings of many counter-revolutionaries and former Tsarist officers in the Red Army and burned villages in order to intimidate the peasantry into submission and to stem mass desertions in the war against the White Army. Stalin had deserters and renegades publicly executed as traitors. He had a particular vengeance against the Imperial Royal Family.

Anastasia Kosygin Peasant farmer (Novel Character)

Anastasia was a widowed peasant farmer in Estonia living not far from the Russian border. She was a keen member of the Orthodox Church and experienced the murder of her husband two months earlier because he would not supply livestock to the Russian military and keen to help reinstate peace through the re-establishment of Imperial Rule.

Andrei Kosygin Peasant Farmer (Novel Character)

Twenty-one-year-old Andrei was the only child of Anastasia and now had the responsibility of managing the small holding and eking out a living for himself and his mother.

He had his own personal score to settle with the ruthless Red Army, who had murdered his father and kidnapped his fiancé.

Commissar Olga Pushkina (Novel Character)

Pushkina had risen to power during the early years of the revolution and was embittered towards imperial rule from her childhood days of peasant farming and food shortage. She was a tough and ruthless Commissar and her rule was authoritarian. Her posting at the borders of Estonia was due to her specialty in uncovering escapees with her sharper observation of human characteristics.

Sergei (Novel Character)

Sergei was the commander of a small guard of six Red Army troops which were commissioned to escort Michael and Johnson to Perm. He was a veteran of the Imperial Russian Army, which fought the Germans at the Russian Front from 1914. He had certain sympathies for the Romanovs and, especially as he saw that they were not confrontational, eventually developed a leaning towards assisting in their comfort on the journey to Perm.

Major Nicholas Andropov (Novel Character)

Major Nicholas Andropov was a loyal member of the Savage Division, which Michael had commanded with great effect against the Germans in 1916. He understood Michael to be a true leader of men in his simple and non-autocratic approach to leadership. Michael would often lead from the front and share with his men a like-for-like existence without ceremony. Andropov went into hiding when the Bolshevik Revolution began taking its toll on Imperial sympathisers. With money he had saved during the war, he erected a café in a small township along the Trans-Siberian Railway.

O'Brien and Hess

They were British Intelligence agents sent to Perm to monitor the position and safety of Michael and Johnson. Sidney Reilly had requested a backup of intelligence gathering as he was planning to rescue Michael and bring him back to England so that he could still become the figurehead of the planned invasion. They remained in Russia after rescuing Michael with Reilly and continued covert surveillance and intelligence gathering in preparation for the Allied invasion in 1918.

Gavril Ilyich Myasnikov

He was an early member of the Russian Revolution. The Tsarist police arrested him for those activist roles he played against Imperial Russia, sentencing him to over seven years of hard labour in Siberia. In 1917, Myasnikov was active in factory committees within the Soviet and Bolshevik parties in his hometown of Motovilikha and in Perm. He was particularly hardline and wanted revenge on the Imperial Family because of the seven years of hard labour he had to serve under Imperial Rule. Myasnikov is known as the execution initiator (under the apparent orders of Lenin) of the Grand Duke Michael Alexandrovitch Romanov.

Group of Militant Perm Bolsheviks

The group of Perm Bolsheviks who took Grand Duke Michael and Johnson from their hotel, 'The Korolav Rooms', in Perm and forced them to travel to a forest near the town of Motovilikha; there they murdered them. Their bodies have never been discovered.

Andrei Marcov

He fired the fatal shot to the head of Michael. As a token of the work they had carried out for the Bolshevik Revolution, Marcov stole a watch from Johnson. He kept it until his death in 1965, claiming it had never needed any repairs and had kept perfect time.

Natalia Mamontova, (Tata) Grand Duke Michael's Daughter

Natalia was the daughter of Grand Duke Michael's wife, Natasha, from her first marriage. Natalia was persecuted like her mother by the Bolsheviks and fled to England in 1919 with her mother. These dramatic events and disconnected life with her mother, unsuccessful marriages and liaisons, may have led to her own tragic life. She was married three times and died in comparative poverty.

Sir George Mansfield Smith-Cumming

He became Head of the Secret Intelligence Service. His foreign section became MI6 or the Secret Intelligence Service. Cumming came to rely heavily on Sidney Reilly (aka the 'Ace of Spies'), a secret agent of dubious veracity based in Saint Petersburg. There he laid plans with Reilly to rescue Imperial Families and help, with the aid of Albert Stopford, to sneak out of Russia vast amounts of treasure and valuables belonging to the Imperial Family. He also instructed Reilly and Lockhart to undermine the Bolsheviks, prepare for the Allied invasion and sow propaganda and confusion. In 1914, he was involved in a serious road accident in France, in which his son was killed. Legend has it that in order to escape the car wreck he was forced to amputate his own leg using a penknife. Later, he often told all sorts of fantastic stories as to how he lost his leg and would shock people by

interrupting meetings in his office by suddenly stabbing his
artificial leg with a knife, letter opener or fountain pen.

Admiral Sir Hugh Sinclair

He became head of operations at SIS, MI6.
Sinclair entered the Naval Intelligence
Division at the beginning of the First World
War, and later Director of Naval Intelligence
and Chief of the Submarine Service in 1921.
He became the second Director of SIS
in 1923. Beginning in 1919, he attempted to absorb the
counter-intelligence service MI5 into the SIS to strengthen
Britain's efforts against Bolshevism.

In spring of 1938, using his own money, he bought
Bletchley Park to become a wartime intelligence station.
From there he was able to build up a network of intelligence
gathering and brought in Mathematicians, Linguists, and
Genius thinkers.

Aretas Akers-Douglas
2nd Viscount Chilston

The 2nd Viscount, served as British
Ambassador to Russia from 1933 to
1938.

Boris Legran

He was a Director and Curator of the Hermitage Museum in Leningrad. During his time at the helm, Legran was busy with the Socialist Reconstruction of the museum. In other words, he oversaw that the works on display were being presented in keeping with the new principles of the country's life and new policies. Legran supported the creation of an exhibition imbued with ideology, that modern observers consider to have been vulgar. His goal was to turn *objets d'art* – for instance, the Fabergé jewellery – into a kind of evidence to the oppression of peoples under the Tsarist regime.

Legran's three years in office are remembered for the scandalous sale of the highlights of the museum's collection to the West. With his connivance, clandestine auctions were held abroad, to raise additional money for the ongoing industrialization of the Soviet Union. Legran believed that antique furniture, magnificent jewellery, and paintings on religious subjects were of little interest to the Soviet people.

Sir Stewart Menzies

Menzies, after being seriously ill following a gas attack in the First World War, recovered and then entered service with MI6 and was soon promoted as second in command to Sir Hugh Sinclair. He became an associate of Sidney Reilly and through Reilly's skulduggery became allegedly involved in the downfall of the Labour Government. After the death of Sinclair, Menzies was made Chief of SIS in 1939.

When the Second World War began, SIS expanded greatly. Menzies insisted on wartime control of codebreaking, and this gave him immense power and influence, which he used judiciously. Menzies kept Prime Minister Winston Churchill supplied daily with important Ultra decrypts, and the two worked together to ensure that financial resources were devoted towards research and upgrading technology at Bletchley Park to keep pace with Nazi coding refinements, as well as directing talented workers to the massive effort, which employed nearly 10,000 workers by 1945.

Menzies was certainly adept at bureaucratic intrigue, a virtual necessity in his position, but his efforts as Chief had a major role in winning the Second World War, as evidenced by his nearly 1,500 meetings with Prime Minister Churchill during the war.

Lois Maxwell aka Miss Moneypenny

Moneypenny's name was created by Ian Fleming in his James Bond novels and based on Kathleen Pettigrew, the personal assistant to MI6 Director Sir Stewart Menzies. She was noted for giving a warm and friendly reception to senior officers who visited her office to view confidential papers. Lois Maxwell pictured here was the first screen actress to undertake that role in the series of James Bond adventures.

Xenia Barkov (Novel Character)

Xenia was a good friend and colleague of Olga Bystrovia at the MI6 branch in Madrid during the Second World War. She lived in Odessa and became an émigré from Russia in escaping the Bolshevik Revolution. Before the Second World War, she became a friend of Albert Stopford whilst in Paris, who gave her some jewellery shortly before he died.

King George VI and the Queen Elizabeth

George VI was King of the United Kingdom and the British Commonwealth from 11 December 1936 until his death on 1952. He married Lady Elizabeth Bowes-Lyon in 1923 and they had two daughters, Elizabeth and Margaret.

British Prime Minister Stanley Baldwin advised his elder brother Edward that for political and religious reasons he could not marry a divorced woman and remain King. Edward abdicated in order to marry, and George ascended the throne.

Queen Elizabeth accompanied her husband on diplomatic tours to France and North America before the start of World War II. During the war, her seemingly indomitable spirit provided moral support to the British public. In recognition of her role as an asset to British interests, Adolf Hitler described her as 'the most dangerous woman in Europe'. After the war, her husband's health deteriorated and she was widowed at the age of fifty-one. Her elder daughter, Elizabeth, aged twenty-five, became the new Queen of England.

PART I

MICHAEL'S FIRST LIFE

1

Albert Stopford and Romanov Treasures

George Buchanan put the phone down after a private conversation with Nicholas, distressed to learn that Nicholas and his whole family were to be transported out from the Alexander Palace and into the central Russian city of Tobolsk. This was an attempt by Kerensky, who was the interim leader of the provincial government, to keep them safe from the lawless revolutionaries who were constantly trying to gain access to the family to persecute and probably execute them all.

A stiff and formal character, Buchanan was a career politician and loyal government servant with a keen eye for what worked, who considered his judgement to be the 'best' and was unafraid of making his point for the betterment of society.

They had discussed how they might be able to secure some of their transportable wealth out of sight of the guards and secret service, the Cheka, as it was essential that they could financially fend for themselves, or even barter for their lives should that become a reality. Buchanan told Nicholas that he would send his envoy Albert Stopford (who Nicholas knew of) to advise them and provide some comfort with an official farewell from the British Government.

Albert Stopford had a well-founded reputation as an expert in antiques and jewellery and had created a lucrative business in dealing with European heads of state in sourcing and supplying antiques on the European and international stage. He was a tall, wiry, middle-aged gentleman with an aristocratic countenance and an engaging smile, possessing an air of authority, and spoke several languages. He moved very easily in royal and diplomatic circles, gaining people's confidence very quickly, and was trusted for his integrity, honesty, and more so for his bravery in the face of adversity

He was driven into the Alexander Palace grounds by ex-Tsar Nicholas's chauffeur in his beloved Prince Henry sports tourer to meet Nicholas and the family prior to their pending move to Tobolsk. He carried a large briefcase which contained an 8-inch diameter canister and three smaller Gladstone bags. The canister was a modified naval gun shell casing, as he knew the purpose of this final farewell was not just a commission by George Buchanan, the British Ambassador to Russia, to offer official farewells.

As he entered the Palace, Stopford was taken aback by the chaos in evidence as much of the staff at the Palace were engaged in the rushed, manic packing of many family belongings and personal items, together with essential furniture.

He was met by Nicholas in his private office, together with his wife Alexandra. Tsar Nicholas was generally a poor judge of the moments, and was bullied into decision-making behind the scenes by his wife for her own agenda. He was a man-pleaser and had no real grasp of practicalities, being too engrossed in preserving a status quo from the realities of revolution, being locked into the past Romanov autocratic style of control. He was faultless, however, in his devotion to his family and saw that as the only reality in his life.

The conversation switched from the niceties and condolences to the main purpose, which was to advise the family on how they might secrete many items of jewellery in their packing cases and upon their private clothing. Their daughters were chosen to be the main carriers, as it was clear that all their possessions would be searched. The girls would at least be sure, out of protocol, not to undergo a body search. This was the surest way to hide the jewellery, and was essential so that they would have some form of financial support over and above the fast-declining value of the rouble currency. They would be allowed to take Russian currency, but the inflation they were encountering in Russia would soon use up much of that, to impoverish the Royal Family.

The new home at the Governor's Residence in Tobolsk would provide few of the home comforts they had enjoyed all their lives, but at least they were assuming some kind of safety and peace, as they would be ensconced so far away from the daily troubles and threats to their lives.

Stopford was taken to a small anteroom and presented with the sight of a huge suitcase lying on a table which contained a vast array of jewellery of all shapes and sizes. Stopford, using his extensive knowledge in antiques in this genre, started to sort from the huge cache of assorted jewellery what they should take, and indicated how it might be sown and secreted into the clothing and shoes of the family, notably their children, whose undergarments were to prove a safe hiding place.

As it would not be possible to secure more hiding places other than the secret compartments constructed in the many trunks they were taking, Nicholas announced that Stopford should take the remaining items out of the Palace in the smaller official diplomatic bags he had brought into the Palace in the large Gladstone briefcase.

Stopford was pleased that Nicholas had mentioned this; it seemed his conversation with Buchanan earlier may well have persuaded him that any remaining items of jewellery were better taken under the protection of the British Government. He filled the three small Gladstone bags with whatever he thought was of most value, and placed them in the 8-inch shell casing and closed the briefcase.

Nicholas instructed Stopford to take the surplus jewellery to Gatchina Palace and give it to his brother Grand Duke Michael, for his own use and furtherance of his life, in the hope that he would be able to escape to a neutral country. Nicholas recognised that the Romanov Dynasty was quickly disintegrating and it was a means of Michael's and his wife Natasha's survival beyond the current crisis of Russia becoming a communist state under Bolshevik rule.

Stopford was then given the keys to the Prince Henry Tourer and he drove out of the Palace, heading for Gatchina where he would garage the car at the Palace which was the family home of Michael and Natasha and hide the three Gladstone bags stored in the canister. Stopford had in the recent past smuggled other Romanov valuables out of Russia in vehicles, and had used to great effect for this purpose modified 8-inch shell casings which were designed with a hinged end cap, and chassis attachment lugs which could be screwed to the oak chassis of most limousines which were built at that time.

He knew of the Rolls-Royce half-track that was lying somewhat forgotten at the rear of the Palace garage, and thought that if Michael were to make any serious attempt to escape Russia, then when that time came the best vehicle to use would be the half-track, as it was an all-terrain vehicle. He slid underneath the Rolls and fixed the canister to the oak chassis very securely, pleased that the jewellery would be securely concealed and in the best place to transport it out of the country.

2

Michael and Johnson

That July morning in 1917, Nicholas and his family with their entourage and baggage boarded a train in Petrograd, from where they were to be taken to an out-of-the-way city called Tobolsk in Siberia to be kept under surveillance in a more secure environment. They were supervised by the Prime Minister of the provisional government, Alexander Kerensky, who was also Commander in Chief of the armed forces.

Shortly before the train pulled out of the station, Grand Duke Michael appeared on the platform and met with his brother under the watchful eye of Kerensky whilst waiting for the train to leave. Michael was a very tall, slim and imposing figure and had a healthy tan. He wore informal summer clothing as it was a typical hot Russian summer day. He was usually a very relaxed and jolly member of the Imperial Family and had an attractive ease in his gait and in his handling of people. Everybody loved his easy character, especially as he took interest in all whom he met. He was not of a typical royal manner and was not aloof nor unapproachable. He loved fast cars, excitement and 'derring do' and had no interest in government and politics, and cared little about writing and understanding administration.

He was caring and easily fell into romantic love, but was seemingly prey to those who were engaging with him for prestige, or were not worthy by the standards of royal protocol, which often influenced him towards rejecting his choices. He eventually fell in love with a twice-divorced (with children) commoner and married her against the wishes of his brother Tsar Nicholas II. For this act of treachery, he was exiled to the UK, but brought back to Russia when the First World War broke out, when he was given command of a cavalry regiment.

He was deeply loved and appreciated by all who fought under him: he did not glorify himself in glitter and status. His position as Commander of the 'Savage Cavalry Division' on the German front since the outbreak of war ranked him to the status of hero, and he was adored by many of his army comrades as a concerned and caring leader who would join them in the thick of battle. His presence amongst them was a rallying point which contributed to some measures of success. World politicians thought he would make a great alternative to Nicholas and wanted to install him on the throne after the abdication of Nicholas.

But today was different, as he shared the anguish of his brother and the uncertainty of his family's fate at the hands of the Bolsheviks. The conversation between the brothers was stilted and awkward, but pleasantries were exchanged with a fearful foreboding of the future for the whole of the Dynasty. Few words were spoken of much importance as both were under scrutiny from Kerensky. However, the gaze between them was sufficient to confirm the love and loss to each other that this malevolent affair was invoking in their thoughts as they clasped hands in silence. Nicholas managed to pass to Michael a note, which he would read when back in the safety of his villa in Petrograd.

Nicholas re-joined the family in the coach and leaned out of the open window to embrace Michael for the final time. They kissed in brotherly love.

Nicholas whispered to Michael, knowing his wealth would now be in his control and the future of the Romanov Dynasty. Make a mental note of this very important secret information I tell to you now. 'The secure future of Russia and our Imperial Dynasty lies in your hands and you will be supported with the coming Allied landings in Archangel in 1918 to aid our war with Germany. Be ready to take my place.'

As the train pulled out, Michael was joined by his secretary, Nicholas Johnson. As they walked towards the waiting Rolls, Michael explained to Johnson the enlightening conversation he had had with his brother, and sought the wisdom of Johnson, as he knew his views were sound and reasonable and he had relied upon him in the past on many occasions. Johnson's advice to Michael had become an important factor in their long friendship and in the fulfilment of his role as personal secretary.

They had grown to become good pals as teenagers and shared much fun in their lives together. Johnson's mother was an employee of the court and taught music, and her husband was an army Captain and based within the security of the royal household. Johnson was also a pianist of note. He was the gap-filler to Michael: he was very conscientious and did all Michael's paperwork, and was a very astute advisor to him as he was a person of high pragmatism and intelligence, and was able to arrive at no-nonsense conclusions with clarity and ambition on behalf of Michael, who was too relaxed and laid-back. His physique was in stark contrast to Michael's, being much shorter and rather rotund. He had a pleasant smile and a rather disarming unimportant presence which allowed him to melt into the background of social gatherings with Michael, thus disguising his sharpened mind and value to his master and dear friend. They were a perfect pair, and the bond between them was resolute.

Upon hearing of the conversation between Michael and Nicholas, Johnson was circumspect as he realised that Nicholas was under enormous pressure from the state, his family, and in coming to terms with the new order imposing a massively reduced lifestyle. Johnson concluded that this was the reaction of one man trying to save the *Titanic* and that it was delusional. However, he was keen to see what Nicholas had written in the secreted note and reserved his judgement.

Michael was intrigued by the suggestion that there would be an Allied invasion to save Russia from the Bolsheviks. He wondered where Nicholas had come by this information, and whether it was in fact a proposal of reality, or just an illusion and dream of Nicholas and his family to salve their feelings of shame and dishonour. The thought, however, was one of possible credulity and he mused over the prospects.

Arriving back to the safety of their villa in Petrograd, Michael and Johnson were greeted by Michael's wife and their son, young George, and they all sat down for a light lunch Natasha had prepared. Over lunch the day's events

were discussed and Michael pulled out the note Nicholas
had passed to him. It read:

My dear brother Michael.

*I am deeply distressed at what may await us in
Tobolsk and with only thoughts for my dear family,
which now extends to our entourage as they themselves
are vilified each day they remain with us. Their own
lives are becoming precarious and I commend them
for their loyalty.   God will provide for us in the way
in which he deems our lives to progress from this day
forward, as we are entirely in His hands as to our fate
and the future of Russia.*

*Michael, I earnestly ask you to deal with the
following so that you may save for yourself the family
treasures and who one day I pray will reclaim the
throne of the Tsars. My abdication in your favour still
stands as my Royal will, and if you are not able to take
my place then I pray that one day your lineage will
prevail and our line of accession will unify Russia once
more in the coming future. I predict dark days ahead
for us, and you my brother, but God will deliver the
throne back to you or your descendants.*

*Within the last few days I have come to understand
that our safe futures are in peril. I have contacted Albert
Stopford for his assistance, and you will find that in
your much-loved family home in Gatchina Palace, I
have had transported from our Alexander Palace much
of our wealth in easily transportable items of value.*

*Please, at your earliest convenience make haste and
seek for yourself the support of Stopford and discover*

*and guard our treasures in the Gladstone bags which
have been deposited there in secrecy for your own
benefit.*

*Finally, I wish for nothing better for the future of
our country that you should reinstate our fortunes and
I know that your rule will be just and rewarding for the
peoples of Russia. I am confident that you will be able
to implement all the changes that in my foolish attitude
I refused to accept as being the saving instruments of
our Dynasty.*

*In God and my love for you my brother, I bid you
farewell and would ask for your prayers daily for our
family as I fear the forebodings which are besetting us
as a family.*

Farewell
Nicholas. X

After reading this, Johnson and Natasha were confused and
confounded, and were conscious of what a grave mistake
Nicholas may have made in trusting an unknown British
person with a massive fortune of jewellery which should have
been passed to Michael in other ways rather more directly.

Johnson, concerned, thought it wise to contact the
British Embassy and spoke with the Ambassador, George
Buchanan who was a close and major supporter of the ex-
Tsar Nicholas. Buchanan knew of the movement of the Tsar's
valuables to Gatchina and Stopford. He assured Johnson of
his credentials leaving him with the most important message
that Michael should be ready to engage with the future
now being drawn up by the Allies to save Russia from the
Bolsheviks.

Two weeks later, Buchanan set up a meeting at the Embassy for Michael and Johnson, to discuss the future now that Nicholas was effectively imprisoned and out of the equation for the current future of Russia and the Imperial rule.

Buchanan also introduced Sidney Reilly and Bruce Lockhart to Michael and Johnson as British Government officials. Other than formalities, both agents said little during the meeting, as they were circumspect towards Michael's intentions and preferred to keep much of the purpose of their involvement within their own counsel to avoid any undue exposure.

Michael was particularly concerned to know more about the jewellery which had been stashed at Gatchina Palace, and where it was hidden. Michael had lived at Gatchina throughout his childhood, and more recently on and off as it was now his family seat. As Stopford had been instrumental in secreting the hoard, it was arranged that he would show Michael where the three bags were hidden in due course.

Buchanan then turned to Michael and presented him with the idea of an invasion by the Allies, and asked what views he might have of that. Michael was careful not to mention that Nicholas had earlier mentioned that same idea in a note. He felt that he could express surprise, thus allowing Buchanan to fully identify the means and reasons of such an exploit.

Johnson then intervened and asked rather bluntly what the purpose and end game was as far as Russia was concerned. Buchanan had a rehearsed reply: they wanted to restore the Imperial Throne to Russia and defeat the

Bolshevik revolution which was gathering more support day by day.

Johnson was rather concerned at such a shallow reply and wanted to know more details. Buchanan responded in that it was early days, and the precise planning and influences required to ensure success were being sought. Johnson persisted and asked Buchanan who he thought would become the reinstated Tsar. Buchanan was rather evasive, and responded finally that it was a matter for the members of the Romanovs to come forward in the next few months and declare an interest.

The meeting ended, and Michael and Johnson returned to their villa in Petrograd. However, within hours of that meeting Michael and Johnson were put under house arrest by Kerensky at the villa. It seemed at first view that they had been under surveillance and that the interim government were now more concerned about the influence which Michael may have in state affairs now that Nicholas had been exiled to Tobolsk.

3

Grand Duchess Maria Pavlovna Treasures

There were now further concerns over rescuing Romanov jewels from the advancement of the Bolshevik revolutionaries, who were becoming braver in the systematic ransacking of vacated palaces in search of negotiable riches. Upon news of Michael being placed under house arrest in his Petrograd villa reaching the Grand Duchess Maria Pavlovna, now residing in the Crimea out of reach of the Bolsheviks, she contacted her son Grand Duke Boris Vladimirovich. She instructed him to seek the assistance of Albert Stopford, who was a friend of the family and with his envoy status and immunity with diplomatic bags may be able to retrieve the huge hoard of jewellery which was in a secret safe in her Vladimir Palace in Petrograd, which was now abandoned.

Boris paid Stopford a visit at the Embassy compound and consulted him over how he might assist in the retrieval of the jewellery and secretly transport it out of Russia so that it was safe from further theft by the Bolsheviks. His plan was to ask Stopford to place the jewellery in a safe UK bank vault. Then, when and if the time came to escape from Russia and the Bolshevik threat, it could be easily recovered.

Stopford agreed to help, as he was a good friend of Maria Pavlovna. The best plan was that Stopford should go alone in disguise as a Red Army Sergeant to the Vladimir Palace, and after retrieving the jewellery he would take it to Gatchina where he knew of a safe hiding place. From there, the treasures could be taken out of the country when the timing was right. It was planned for a dark and moonless night, to gain as much protection as possible from discovery.

Choosing the best evening of darkness for cover, Stopford left the British Embassy by foot in the disguise of a Russian Red Army Sergeant and walked through the streets of Petrograd and found a taxi. He requested the driver to drop him off at a local hotel near the Palace, and told the driver to wait for at least two hours for his return.

Making his way on foot to the Palace he found his way to a side door. He was once more carrying his large Gladstone briefcase with three smaller Gladstone bags inside in the same way as his previous mission at the Alexander Palace for ex-Tsar Nicholas. There he was met by a loyal and trusted member of the old household, Joseph, who had been expecting him through the advice of Boris. He had two half-shielded hurricane lamps to assist in the quest of retrieving the treasures. Joseph was very helpful and showed Stopford to the location which had been described to him by the Grand Duchess's son, Boris.

Joseph left Stopford with one of the hurricane lamps, in the private quarters of the Duchess which consisted of several rooms. He wanted to minimise his possible incrimination of being involved with the events, as he knew the palace was under surveillance by the Cheka.

Stopford searched for a while and then came across the room where the safe would be hidden in a false oak-panelled wall in the bathroom of her maid's annexe. He soon found the panel described to him, which had her motif stencilled in the centre. Pressing the left-hand side twice, it sprung open, revealing the safe.

Having the unlocking codes, he discovered that the contents were so numerous that they filled the whole safe. The bags he had brought with him, he soon realised, were not quite large enough to bring out all the items undamaged, as he had to stuff and press them down to an extent that he had noticed a tiara was being bent a little dislodging some of its pearls. There were also several bonds and share certificates. He thought that these were not very negotiable, but just in case he stuffed those which he thought were of value into his shirt, locked the safe door and closed the oak panelling secret door in the bathroom.

Stopford retraced his steps with the aid of the lamp and met Joseph at the foot of the grand winding staircase. As he was about to thank him, Joseph mentioned to Michael that he knew of another secret hiding place within the palace where there could be other valuable items waiting to be discovered. He particularly wanted Stopford to investigate that, as he hated what the Bolsheviks were doing to destroy the fabric of Russian royalty and society, and he would much rather see the fortunes of the Royals being repatriated for their own disposal for any future use in destroying the Bolsheviks.

Joseph led Michael to the side of the grand staircase

and showed him a secret doorway into the underbelly of the stairs. Upon opening it, the space was empty, but Joseph, an old man who could not investigate the intricacies of the structure, had always felt that there was something special hidden there. He had seen from time to time, over the past months, certain high-ranking army officers enter that space and not emerge for several minutes, and each time carrying in bags and sacks, and coming out empty-handed.

Stopford, being lithe, energetic and slim, started to investigate with the help of his hurricane lamp and looked for the tell-tale signs of cavities and joints. He was struck by the panelling on the rear wall supporting the first landing and thought it unusual to install such detailed panelling in a place where it would never be seen or appreciated. Tapping the surface, he heard a hollow sound and thought that it was an ideal place to begin his search.

He guessed that it would be an easy entry for practical reasons, and that there would be a pressure device somehow which would release an opening mechanism. Looking around and above his head into the treads and risers of the staircase he spotted an innocuous metal bar running from the riser of the tenth tread towards the supporting wall. It would have been readily recognised as a tension bar to hold tight the staircase, but it could also be an instrument of release. He rattled the bar and found it to have a circular free movement, and upon twisting it several times he was pleased to find that suddenly a hollow panel sprung open.

Moving towards the gaping 2 metre by 1 metre opening he found a space which was stacked with an odd assortment of briefcases, sacks and small bags. Stopford spent around twenty minutes in utter amazement at the discoveries whilst opening the bags. He realised that the sheer volume could not be easily transported away and thought that he should take what was easily transportable. He was an expert in high-value jewellery and so chose that which would be most beneficial to retrieve. The remainder would require an alternative strategy of removal and could wait for a later visit. The source was very secure. Joseph had discreetly disappeared as he felt that if he had no further knowledge of Stopford's visit, then he would be safe under any questioning by the Cheka should they become suspicious.

After quickly identifying and sorting the smallest and best-valued items, Stopford chose two briefcases from within the hideaway which on inspection seemed to have a good selection of high-value items. He then closed the door, and reversed the winding on the retaining bar to secure it, locking it tight.

Now, with the extra jewellery which was in the two briefcases, he thought for a moment and tried to rationalise any future ownership. Maria had been specific in what she wanted Stopford to recover. What he had discovered was beyond her knowledge of what was stored in the house, and he wondered then who were the rightful owners. He could only assume that it was other Romanovs and perhaps high-society members who had been using the secret hiding place. Therefore, trying to track down the owners during these times of great danger would be impossible, and not only futile but a very foolish action.

He decided impulsively that the wealth he had extracted should be used as an inducement and reward, given the costs to the Allies of the rumoured invasion plans. That would therefore be an honourable and acceptable use of the wealth, and if the invasion objectives were successful then its owners would reap the rewards in other ways due to the re-establishment of their former way of life.

Stopford was now faced with carrying out three briefcases and three Gladstone bags, which had some considerable weight. He made his way to a cloakroom just off the main entrance and hoped to find a more appropriate means of transporting the haul. He was relieved to find several large suitcases stored there on a shelf. He chose two of them and quickly placed the haul in the two suitcases. These, he thought, would not attract much attention as there was a lot of coming and going in revolutionary Russia due to the current chaos.

He met Joseph in the kitchen area at the rear of the Palace and thanked him for his helpfulness and his loyalty to Maria. Joseph, now an old frail gentleman and having no family, as he had devoted his life to serve the Romanovs at Vladimir Palace, felt an urge to take off from around his neck a pendant which he had received from the Palace to mark his twenty-fifth year of service. Stopford quickly recognised it as being a Fabergé-produced miniature egg, which had emblazoned on it the cypher of Maria and an Orthodox Christian cross. Joseph gave this to Stopford as a gift towards the anti-revolutionary forces, saying that it should be sold for their cause. This, he explained, was all he had of any meaningful value, and it was his contribution to the cause of destroying the Bolsheviks.

Stopford was suddenly made aware of the love and respectful feelings that so many ordinary Russian folk still had for the Imperial family. This act of support reminded him of the Biblical tale of the 'Widow's Mite'. Stopford, taken by this generosity, embraced Joseph and said that the selfless act would be retold to many, of his very moving love and loyalty, especially in the light of his own poverty and very uncertain future as a servant of the Royal Family.

It was still dark and dawn would not break for several more hours, so Stopford set off, carrying the two suitcases, into the darkened streets of Petrograd in search of the taxi which should be waiting for him. He found the taxi parked only 100 metres from the Vladimir Palace, close to the hotel where he had left it a while ago. The driver was sleeping at the wheel and Stopford awoke him with a prod and with a well-paid offer to take him to his new destination, Gatchina.

Arriving in Gatchina just before the break of dawn, he ordered the driver to take him into the Palace grounds and directed him towards the Palace garage. Driving past the two dozing guards in the sentry boxes, he shouted at them to stand up and present arms as he swept past. They recognised him as a Sergeant and thus obeyed his command. Alighting and paying the driver a month's wages of roubles, Stopford bade him farewell. He lugged the suitcases to the garage door and opened it with the key that Boris had obtained for him. The Palace was deserted, other than a skeleton assembly of staff, since Michael and Natasha were in Petrograd under house arrest in their villa.

Stopford now had to act quickly to hide the bags. He decided that the new discoveries should be hidden in the half-track Rolls-Royce. Knowing that the canister of Nicholas's treasures was safely bolted to the chassis, he now thought an excellent hiding place would be to take out the rear seats of the car. He was delighted that the well under the seats were just the right size to carefully hide the two suitcases and reinstal the seats, knowing that they were hidden in plain sight, in a safe place that people would be unsuspecting of.

He now walked out of the deserted Gatchina Palace and towards the guards, who saluted him as he marched past. His Russian language was very unsure and he did not want to engage in any conversation. He strode off into the town of Gatchina and ordered a taxi, as it was now daylight and the town was awakening for a new day.

4

Rolls-Royce Treasures

Buchanan, knowing of the need to get Michael re-ensconced into his home and birthplace at Gatchina made strong representations to Kerensky to have Michael released from his house arrest in his villa in Petrograd. Michael was suffering from ulcers and needed complete rest in familiar surroundings for the benefit of his wife and child, and should be allowed to return as soon as possible. By the first week of September, Michael and his family were allowed to go back to Gatchina, whilst still under house arrest.

Shortly after that, Buchanan arranged for Stopford to visit Michael. A splendid dinner was arranged for him and it became a time of bonding and friendship between the parties towards a common cause. Michael, whilst being gullible and inclined to trust anybody on face value, entered this friendship with the approval of his secretary Johnson and his wife Natasha, and he was sure Stopford would be proven to be worthy and very helpful going forward.

Michael and Natasha were splendid hosts and took the opportunity to reveal to Stopford their past life together. They explained that they had met at the end of the last decade and found in each other kindred spirits and a love which neither had experienced in the past. Natasha was previously twice married, and had borne a daughter, affectionally known as Tata, who was now a bright teenager and trying desperately to come to terms with the new style of austerity living being imposed upon her and her mother.

Michael explained that Natasha was not accepted into the royal circles when they met, and was soon ostracised since she was not of noble birth and was mother to a daughter of her first marriage. Their son George, born in 1910 whilst Natasha was still married (though for technical reasons the divorce which soon followed was backdated), was deemed illegitimate and with no claims to the throne. However, they chose after some years of clandestine meetings and awkward circumstances to secretly marry in Vienna whilst on holiday in 1912, much against the wishes of Michael's brother Tsar Nicholas. Michael, as a member of the Imperial Family, could not marry without the consent of the ruling monarch, Nicholas II. Nicholas would not grant permission for Michael to marry Natasha.

After the ceremony and meeting up with their children in Cannes, Michael wrote to Nicholas with the news of the marriage. He and Natasha were disappointed and taken aback by the venom of Nicholas, and especially of his wife, the Tsarina Alexandra. In a rush of fury Nicholas branded Michael and Natasha as *personae non gratae* in abandonment of his royal duties and exiled them from Russia together with their family.

Michael, confounded by this extreme action of hostility, then chose to travel with his wife and children around Europe and enjoy a lifestyle of high living for a while. Then in 1913 he decided to take up residence in England and took out a one-year lease at Knebworth House near Luton.

They lived there quite happily with their son George and created a family home of some affluence and presence. All three spoke good English and were readily accepted into British society, and Natasha with her household made Knebworth into a warm and endearing place to live and entertained at every opportunity. Natasha was a petite and slim lady having beguiling beauty and an easy and charming personality. Her elfin face and engaging gaze made her an attractive partner for Michael, and she soon became a favourite amongst their many growing band of friends.

They then decided to move on at the expiry of the lease, and Johnson, who was in constant attendance with his mother Louise, created a lease for a new residence at Paddockhurst in Sussex. This was a smaller residence but much nearer London and the coast, and made for easy access to both. The lease was drawn up just before the outbreak of war. At that point Michael asked Nicholas if he could return to Russia and take up war duties. Nicholas agreed, with some limited forgiveness of Michael and gave him a command of a cavalry division. Natasha would absorb herself in the creation and sponsorship of field hospitals for the wounded and dying.

So, whilst many of their belongings were transported to the new house at Paddockhurst, some were still in storage at Knebworth. The lease on Paddockhurst was transferred to the use of the British Army, and Michael and his entourage left to return to Russia in the hope of taking up residence in Michael's seat at Gatchina Palace. However, they were refused, as Nicholas had decreed that Natasha could not live at any Imperial Palace, so they settled into a villa in Gatchina.

Stopford was amazed and outraged at the refusals of Nicholas to acknowledge the marriage, and more so at the fact that they were treated so badly and exiled from Russia. However, he could at least identify with much of the unrest and disappointments of life, as he himself had undergone so many adventures, mishaps and close shaves in his personal life and in working undercover for MI6.

After dinner Stopford took Michael into the garage and showed him where the bags were hidden. Stopford had chosen well in a place where there would be very little suspicion of the jewels ever being found as they were, in a sense, in plain sight. The garage had three cars parked in the centre and each was in pristine condition. However, in a dark corner and covered with stored bits and pieces, was a Rolls-Royce half-track which had been re-engineered for winter cross-country use by Adolphe Kégresse, a chauffeur of Tsar Nicholas and a keen engineer and inventor.

Michael was shown the half-track Rolls-Royce which was languishing in the corner of the vast space of the Gatchina twelve-car garage. Stopford, had had the bright idea some time ago of transporting valuables from place to place without detection by bolting to a car chassis a steel cylinder having the appearance of an exhaust silencer, which was sufficient in space to stuff the Gladstone bags in.

Both Michael and Stopford disappeared underneath the Rolls and Michael was shown the container and the opening mechanism. This was a device which was brought from the UK also had a Beretta gun so placed inside the cylinder.

Stopford emerged with the three bags and each one was

opened for his inspection. To the amazement of Michael they were stuffed with loose jewellery of all descriptions: pearl necklaces, tiaras, brooches – and much of it unrecognised by Michael as he was not in favour of the royal parties and balls and would never have noticed what incredible wealth was being worn.

Stopford, as an antique expert with a solid understanding of jewellery and values, announced that the value was worth several million pounds sterling (today possibly £50–100 million). These he explained were from the private collection of Nicholas, but there were other treasures also stashed in the Rolls. Stopford then told Michael that there were also two suitcases hidden under the rear seat wells which he had retrieved from the Vladimir Palace.

He mentioned to Michael that one of the suitcases contained the treasures of his aunt Maria Pavlovna and that he had to take these out of Russia and back to the UK for her safe-keeping. The other suitcase contained treasures which were from a secret hiding place unknown to Maria in the Vladimir Palace, probably placed there because of the continual thefts from other Royals by the Russian Secret Service, as their homesteads and palaces were being systematically looted. However, he assured Michael that there would now be no possibility of trying to return these valuables to any of the rightful owners, due to the dangerous prevailing circumstances. There were more valuables still left under the grand staircase, but he had only time and space to be selective in what he extracted. He said he felt the jewellery should be at Michael's disposal for his own reinstatement and additionally to aid the Allied war effort in the coming invasion.

Michael was extremely thankful to Stopford and realised this jewellery might well still be safe, even if the Palace was ransacked in search of any valuables, as the days were very uncertain. Angry mobs were on the streets seeking revenge for the state of the country due to the Romanov rule, and the Palace would always become a target at some point if law and order were not reinstated.

The Rolls was also a perfect hiding place, as if Michael needed to leave in a hurry and for any distance in winter weather, then the half-track was an excellent means of escape across country and he need not bother about preloading the car with valuables, only essentials. Even if he was stopped and searched only personal effects would be found.

Shortly after the dinner with Stopford, Michael was relieved to hear from a messenger that the house arrest had been lifted by an old army friend, Peter Polotsov, who had been with Michael during his war campaigns at the German front and had now been promoted to Army Commander in Petrograd. He and the family were also to be given a permit to travel to Finland.

Several days later, great joy was prevailing in the household and it was with vigour that the whole family and entourage packed and prepared to board the train in Petrograd, taking with them the half-track vehicle for Michael's winter use in Finland. Things were looking up, and Michael and his family could now look forward to enjoying the future in some comfort, knowing that the Rolls-Royce half-track was the key to their economic survival.

They loaded up the useful household furniture and personal affects in several wagons and with Michael driving the half-track, proceeded to the station. On the way, they were met by howling mobs of Bolsheviks who would not allow them to escape the justice of the state and were set to wreak terrible revenge on any Romanov. Whilst being attacked, they were rescued by Peter Polotsov, Michael's friend and old colleague, who escorted them back with a troop of men to the Palace for safety until he could arrange a safer passage later that day.

When they arrived at the gates, escorted by Peter, they saw Bolsheviks driving around the Palace grounds in the three remaining cars. When they saw the mounted guards returning they drove off in a hurry with the last of Michael's cars. Michael was so thankful that he was driving the half-track and that for the time being it was safe under his control. It was hardly worth anything in terms of great prestige and value, as it was a sad-looking vehicle without refinement.

They were placed under house arrest once again, with much apology from Peter, who thought it was for the best now due to the wild antics going on in Petrograd. At least there was a guard patrol to protect them.

5

Winston Churchill and David Lloyd George

Winston Churchill was becoming more concerned than ever before at the activities of the Bolshevik influence, and at hearing of the unpopularity of the government overseen by Prime Minister Kerensky. He had hoped that the neutralising effect of the interim liberal government, since the demise of Imperial Rule, would have been a bulwark to the ambitions of Lenin.

Churchill was known to be a gadfly, an upstart, political adventurer, a warmonger, and British to the core, born into wealth and power created through the family's political history stretching back two centuries. He had experienced political and wartime planning failures to this point in his career, trying to assert himself to levels of success matching his predecessors.

He could be summed up in character by two of his many quotes: 'Never give in, never give in, never, never, never, never – in nothing, great or small, large or petty – never give in except to convictions of honour and good sense.' From his experience of scant love and affection he experienced as a boy he wrote: 'Solitary trees, if they grow at all, grow strong; and a boy deprived of a father's care often develops, if he escapes the perils of youth, an independence and vigour of thought which may restore in after life the heavy loss of early days.'

Churchill's physical and emotional resilience were invaluable to him throughout his life, and especially during his conduct in war. Churchill also used his hobby of painting to relax and reinvigorate himself. He painted outdoor scenes often, to free his mind from the pressing events of his busy life. This relaxation allowed him to step back from events, to consider them in their historical context.

It was now becoming clear from the reports coming back from Russia, that the movement for ending the war in Russia was gaining momentum, and the reality of a peace deal with Germany was a strong possibility. So, in early November 1917 and after hearing of the overthrow of the Kerensky Duma by Lenin, he persuaded the War Office to meet with full participation of all the Allied Commanders and Governments in secrecy at Naval Headquarters at Whitehall.

The purpose in Churchill's mind was to set a course and road map for intervention. His scope and agenda was:

- To secure from any confiscation by Lenin, the vast amounts of military materiel and food stocks which had been convoyed to Archangel for the assistance of the Russian fight on the Eastern Front with Germany.
- To arrange an invasion plan at Archangel to link up with the 'White Army' using Allied forces and the troops of

the United States which had recently entered the war against Germany.

- To encourage the uprising of the Estonian and Finnish Armies to enter Russia from the west, upon an invasion from the north at Archangel by the Western Allied Armed Forces.

- To persuade the Danish Government to enter the war, not necessarily against Germany, but to force the Bolsheviks from power with a view of the reinstatement of the Romanov Dynasty to which they had close family links. They would assist with the Estonians to enter Russia from the west via the Baltic Sea.

- To reinstate the Romanov Dynasty via the Grand Duke Michael, brother of the abdicated Tsar Nicholas II.

- To aid Russia with war materiel, senior advisors to the Russian Army, and encourage a substantial army of sympathisers and defected Russian troops to rise up and bring to justice all the Bolshevik and Communist agitators.

- Assemble an effective force of modern equipment and fresh troops to re-engage the German Army and keep the Eastern Front alive.

The grand powers met in secret at Admiralty House in London and concluded after three days of initial planning and discussions that this was a very viable option and should proceed with the utmost urgency, and commence the build-up and redirection of essential materiels to the invasion project. A further resource was formulated beyond the Churchill manifesto, which was to encourage the Japanese Navy to bring in a taskforce into Vladivostok and cut the lines of Pacific supplies to the Bolshevik Government and to further discourage Lenin to a point of capitulation.

Buchanan would then be informed of the embryonic plans and to gather as much intelligence as possible to aid the planned invasion dates of summer 1918. However, one of the primary support issues to the plan was the enterprising idea to bring Grand Duke Michael out of Russia for a short period so that he could be dissuaded from going into the safety of exile and escaping the Bolsheviks, but to stay in Russia and become the rallying point of the invasion plans.

This was a difficult plan to enact but was vital as the Allied focus was on him and it was imperative that he understood the ramifications of the plot and needed to see for themselves his resolve and agreement to stand for his country. It was deemed that Michael would only take on this mantle himself if he in return could see and speak with the major Allies and the Royal Family in Britain about their own commitment and resolve to ensure that a pact could be cemented of the highest bearing and order. These were monumental life-changing arrangements and would have far-reaching effects on world events for the future, and of dynamics Michael or the Allied Powers could ever conceive.

Buchanan, in Petrogard and now informed on the basic structure mused on the enormity of this task and was seeking further advice on what his role would be, and how this might be accomplished. Churchill then arranged a meeting with Lloyd George and asked Lockhart, who was in London to join him to seek a way forward, and return to Russia in the New Year and inform Buchanan of the plans to date.

The British Prime Minister, Lloyd George, was a very popular man and spoke the language of the people to the people. He had a cynical side which was aimed at the establishment, but knew how to control his inner thoughts. Often taking the side of the obvious and pragmatics in negotiations, his charm would be the persuasive element of any engagement, allowing the other side wiggle room whilst they were unaware of his tactics.

He joined the meeting and was very specific that, whilst they should upgrade the spy network personnel and numbers, he was more concerned with the first major issue, which was to get Michael out of the country to meet with the Allied heads of state. Lockhart pointed out to Lloyd George that the British spy network was effective in Russia, but the absolute security of these people was not certain, especially as the Russian Cheka were an effective force and if too many British agents were engaged to assist in the removal of Michael, then it could compromise the whole plan should they get caught and be tortured to find out their mission.

Lloyd George was quick to appreciate this and suggested the assistance of Sidney Reilly who, whilst being known to the Russian secret service, was of such guile and quick thinking, and through countless other successful engagements he was a natural choice, and had the wherewithal to undertake the strategy that was desired to make this a successful outcome. Reilly was in London at that time and was called to the MI6 office to be consulted.

After a briefing, as Reilly was a person who kept his own counsel and was enabled to mastermind the operation, concluded that he needed the assistance of Albert Stopford.

This was to be his visible front, as Stopford was known and liked by many people in Russia and was seen as an eccentric art and antique dealer. He also had connections with the Russian Revolutionary leaders, as his expertise was called on from time to time by the Bolsheviks to examine and determine values of items of Russian heritage, and he had the connections to dispose of these on the world markets, the object being, of course, to bring into Russia much-needed foreign currency due to the tumbling value of the rouble.

Lockhart thought this was an excellent choice, as the plan would be least detected and had the advantage of Stopford being able to move around Russia much as he pleased, and to be released whenever he encountered any border or official difficulties, due to his persuasive personality and place in the society of Petrograd and Moscow.

Lloyd George was pleased with this pre-planning approach and left Lockhart to become a free agent in the matter, but warned him that this was a commission of the highest importance and that it was so secret that the British Government would deny any knowledge of the plot to bring out Michael should it fail. Lockhart returned to Russia under diplomatic immunity in January 1918, since the UK was committed to continue diplomatic relations.

6

Ethel

Whilst Reilly was in London his one-time lover and mistress, Ethel Voynich – who had had a significant book published in 1897, *The Gadfly* – got a note to him through her network of friends asking to see him. Reilly was intrigued and excited as he had not seen her for over 20 years and was eager to make her acquaintance once more. His own agenda was to rekindle the love affair if possible, but more so to discover if he really was the person who she was writing about in her novel, *The Gadfly*. Reilly was keen to discover the truth to the rumours as they were very strong, and it suited his ego. He fondly reminisced about the time they had spent in Italy for a brief affair in 1895. However, he did realise that Ethel seemed to have a pressing reason of her own to see him.

The Gadfly story majored on a beguiling romance with a self-assertive revolutionary, Arthur Burton, who spent much of his time of intrigue in Italy, where the action was set. A thread of a tragic relationship between Arthur and his love, Gemma, simultaneously runs through the story. It is a story of faith, disillusionment, revolution, romance and heroism.

Ethel was a significant figure not only on the late

Victorian literary scene but also in Russian émigré circles. She was a novelist and musician, and a supporter of several revolutionary causes. Her father was a famous mathematician and her mother was a feminist philosopher and author. In 1893 she married Wilfrid, who himself was a revolutionary, and an antiquarian who had a keen interest in books.

Ethel had created a book shop business with her husband in London, and it was there that she had invited Reilly to meet in the afternoon. The store seemed to be thriving as there were a good number of customers browsing through the orderly stacks on the shelves. Entering the store, he saw Ethel immediately, as she was looking out for him. She rushed over to him and they both warmly embraced as old friends. She grasped his hand and pulled him over to meet Wilfred, who greeted him formally, and Reilly was happy to note a certain warmth. Ethel then invited him to a backroom sitting room. Wilfred preferred not to join them as he knew this was a sensitive time, and was happy that Ethel was able to meet with her past.

Sitting comfortably, they exchanged details of their lives since the last time they had met over 20 years ago. After a while, when that part of the formalities was shared, Ethel gave Reilly a small package which she encouraged him to open only when he had left. Ethel drew the conversation of warm exchanges to a close after fifteen minutes and thanked Reilly for accepting her invitation to see her. As they stood up to offer each other a final embrace, she announced in a low voice that she had never worked against the interest of the British Government, as was widely believed. Reilly considered the truth in her eyes, and pulling his arms more tightly around her shoulders, replied that he believed her.

He then comforted her with the knowledge that he had not been informing the Metropolitan Police in London of her revolutionary radical pro-émigré activities, as was rumoured. Ethel had worked in Russia several years before she wrote her first novel, and it was thought his short affair with her was a mission purely to monitor her views and activities to inform the Special Branch. She was pleased to hear that from Reilly.

She embraced him and whispered that he was Arthur Burton and that the wrapped gift she had given him was a signed copy of *The Gadfly*. She asked him to look at the first page of Chapter 3 to discover her present peace of mind. She squeezed his hand and kissed him on his cheek, and bade him farewell. Reilly took one last look at her and noticed that tears were forming in her eyes as he turned and walked out of her life, knowing in his heart that it would be the last time he would see her.

Arriving back at his hotel in the Strand he sat in the lounge and over coffee and a cigar, settled down to read the book which he had been given by Ethel. Never having read it before, even though it was rumoured that he was the principal fictional character, he was eager to see what was written on the first pages of Chapter 3. From that, he understood just how Ethel was feeling and how she seemd to have become a settled and happier person, content with life. He saw the emergence of a person whom he had sincere feelings for, and was pleased that she had found peace and happiness, especially after such a long time since their previous romantic encounters. On the inside of the first page Ethel had written:

My dear Sidney

Thank you for the wonderful experiences of knowing you and the inspiration you gave me to express my own feelings in a novel way, allowing me to create my own gadfly in you, as a person who interferes with the status quo of society and authorities.

Ethel Voynich.

Reilly, entering a euphoric state of mind, settled back in the comfortable armchair in front of the warm dying embers of the lounge fireplace, and fell asleep with Ethel on his mind.

7

Sowing the Seeds of Ascendancy

A rriving back at the British Embassy compound in Russia, Lockhart was seeing more clearly the activities and worsening situations for the recently deposed Kerensky government officials and the Royal Families still left in Russia. Lenin was actively courting the prospects of a cessation of war with Germany and it was becoming evident that the Churchill agenda was now soon to become a necessary high priority.

Buchanan, before leaving his post for the last time and returning to England, advised Lockhart that it was now implicit that he meet with Michael at Gatchina to settle the question of him becoming the figurehead of the invasion plot. So, it was agreed that Lockhart would contact Reilly and to go with Stopford to meet Michael, with a mandate to discover his intentions by sounding him out about his becoming the future head of a reinstated Royal Russia. Buchanan arranged a casual dinner date at Gatchina being accompanied with Stopford and Reilly. The date planned was between the Christian and Orthodox Christmas celebrations, when it should be a lot quieter and less suspicious to have dinner. Michael had from time to time met with Stopford and had heard rumours of the resourceful Reilly, and was intrigued to meet him again for the second time.

Buchanan started the after-dinner conversation by sounding Michael out about his remaining in Russia to become a rallying point for the hopeful overthrow of the Bolsheviks. They discussed the recent formation of the White Army, which was having some success in regaining territories. Although this did not amount to much, it was now creating interest from the Allies in Estonia, Finland, and the Western Powers who were fighting Germany in France and Belgium.

Michael was concerned that the new Bolshevik Government was promoting a ceasefire with Germany, and that it would inevitably mean the loss of territories to Germany as they would be the victors over Russia. Buchanan announced that the bigger threat to the world was the cessation of the war on the Russian Eastern Front, which would allow millions of men and much ammunition to be diverted to the Western Front and thus possibly defeat the British, French and newly arriving Americans.

To this end, Buchanan continued, and to support the White Army and its Allies, the Western Powers were contemplating invading Russia at Archangel, where they had strong depots of food and ammunition which were being used to support the Russian Army on the Eastern Front. However, the distribution of these supplies had ceased due to the rise in Bolshevism and prospects of a peace treaty with Germany. Michael joined in and mentioned that landing at Archangel would be easy due to the footholds gained, which should allow a swift build-up of British and American forces. Reilly brought to the discussion that there was also a strong possibility that the Japanese would also invade at Vladivostok to pressure the Red Army further.

Johnson thought about this comment from Reilly, realising that it was a fact that the Japanese wanted to wrest control of the whole of the Eastern Seaboard from Russia, and may well be an unwelcome negotiating chip if the Tsars were to be reinstated to the Monarchy of Russia.

The dinner party ended and Buchanan was hopeful that the seeds had been sown successfully and that his next approach to Michael would firm up his interest and persuade him to visit England in the New Year. Upon parting, Lockhart mentioned with jocular but earnest intent, 'Michael, you should grow a beard as soon as you start to think that this venture has any meaningful implications for you and the future of Russia. Incognito will be key during the coming events.' Michael mused at the thought of pleasantly melting into the background and not having to hide his face to avoid the regular open conflict with the public due to the current views held against the Romanovs.

The day after the encounter with the British delegation, Michael considered these options with Natasha and Johnson, and tried to weigh up the responsibility of the Russian Royals, his destiny, and the possibility of failure and the total demise of his family.

It was becoming clear that the war was nearly lost and the future of Russia was increasingly coming under the influence of Lenin and the Bolsheviks. Matters were not improving and the safety of all Romanovs was becoming a desperate issue. Michael was wondering whether he would ever be able to protect his family and achieve a flight to freedom.

8

The Reilly Plan

I n the meantime, the three British participants, Lockhart, Reilly and Buchanan, had between them created a plan to extract Michael from Russia for two weeks, get him into Britain to meet with the Western Powers, and then return him back to Gatchina – without being noticed. Much of the planning was left to the ingenuity of Reilly, who had the daring attitude and thinking to make this work.

He was a man of devilish good looks and a penetrating stare which was as fierce as it was disarming. His attraction to females was legendary: courting constantly and marrying as needed several times, mostly influential women who fell for his elegance, dangerous spirit and charm. His countenance was severe, threating and confidently aloof, giving the impression that he could carry out any duty or favour you asked of him in complete confidence of success and without question. This description falls short of any true description of his true charisma, character and behavioural traits. The best description of Sidney Reilly is in the mind's eye of the beholder: knowing him and never knowing him; a master of deception, secrecy, and skulduggery; a true master spy.

The Expedition timetable as follows from D-Day:

Day Point to Point

Feb 1 Gatchina – Belomorsk

Feb 1 Belomorsk – Iron Duke

Feb 2 Iron Duke – Scapa Flow

Feb 5 Scapa Flow – Scarborough

Feb 7 Scarborough: *Meeting with state leaders and army commanders*

Feb 8 Scarborough – Knebworth

Feb 9 Knebworth – Paddockhurst

Feb 9 Paddockhurst: *Meeting with King George V*

Feb 9 Paddockhurst – Filey

Feb 10 Filey – Esbjerg

Feb 10 Esbjerg: *Meeting with Royals and Danish Government*

Feb 11 Esbjerg – Flensburg

Feb 11 Flensburg – Tallinn

Feb 13 Tallinn: *Meeting with Interim Government and Patriarch Tikhon*

Feb 13 Tallinn – Narva

Feb 14 Narva – Gatchina

Distance to cover approximately 7,000 kilometres

13 days and 23 hours, Gatchina to Gatchina round trip

Coordination and assets used in the journey to and from Gatchina Palace:

Gatchina to Belomorsk (a White Sea Port:)
The Kagresse converted Rolls-Royce caterpillar half-track with front mounted skis

Belomorsk to the Barents Sea:
 The Royal Yacht Standart
Barents Sea to Scapa Flow:
 The British Battleship HMS Iron Duke
Scapa Flow to Scarborough:
 Blackburn Type L Seaplane
Scarborough to Knebworth to Paddockhurst:
 Royal Train pulled by the Scotch Express
Paddockhurst to Scarborough:
 Royal Train pulled by the Scotch Express
Scarborough to Filey:
 Vauxhall Prince Henry GT
Filey to Esbjerg:
 Blackburn Type L Seaplane
Esbjerg to Flensburg:
 Car
Flensburg to Tallinn:
 U-151 Submarine
Tallinn to Gatchina:
 To be advised.

The timetable of the plan was constructed to last exactly 14 days, and would use the confusion which was bound to occur in Russia of the changeover from the Julian calendar to the Gregorian on 1 February (Julian) This synchronisation with the rest of the world would advance the start date from Julian 1 February to Gregorian 14 February.

It was clear to Buchanan, who had his finger on the pulse of general Russian feelings and attitudes, that there was a lot of disagreement in Russia about the introduction of the new calendar system. This was more to do with the confusion which was arising with the general public and what it meant to them. Indeed, a lot of public opinion understood the introduction as a loss of 14 days in their lives, and that their wages would suffer. A large faction thought that because of this loss then for some rather illogical, unexplained reasoning they would simply mark time for fourteen days on 1 February, and 1 February would become 1 March. They also argued that their ages could change, as some could lose the right to a birthday.

These much mistaken views, were promulgated by certain factions to confuse the public and thus make financial gain in some way or another, created an excellent opportunity to extract Michael for fourteen days. In effect, he might prove from the confusion that from a date perspective he may never have left Russia!

The route of the plan was a journey around northern Scandinavia, into Britain, and returning via the Baltic Sea. It was the safest route due to the general invisibility of movement. It was undoubtedly perhaps the most intricate and ponderously long route that they could agree upon, but it was by far the safest.

The military planning needed for this timetable involved using hardware which posed many logistical challenges, and of mechanical serviceability. It also required a great amount of audacity, charm, bloody-minded espionage and duplicity, which was a challenge more to the mind of Buchanan rather than Reilly. Reilly was the 'Ace of Spies' master tactician and the author of propaganda, lies and confusion. This was to be the pinnacle of his life so far and he being determined to avoid retribution from his past skulduggeries, was out to seek success on a grand scale. Reilly was especially key in the first and latter part of the journey back to Russia as, whilst in close assistance, he had to create false papers and identities and to engage in a complex subterfuge plot to board a German submarine for the penultimate leg of the Journey.

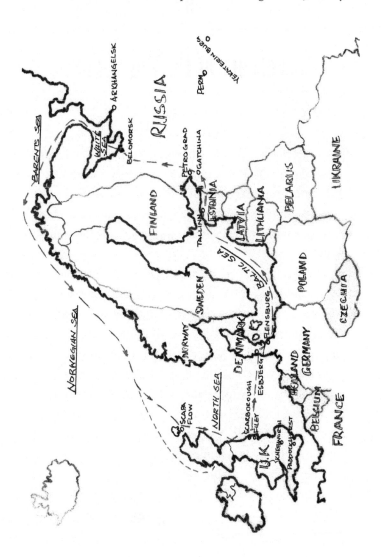

9

Acceptance of the Reilly Plan

On, 5 January, Michael, Johnson, Buchanan and Reilly had a dinner at the Embassy which was intended to discover the intentions of Michael with respect to the suggestion that he become the figurehead of the invasion, which was now in its final planning stages for the summer of 1918.

It was explained to Michael that if he undertook this role it would ensure the least amount of damage and loss of innocent life, as the success of the invasion rested on a peaceable transition of power. This, and public support being garnered from the Russian people and standing armed forces, were crucial and could only be accomplished if Michael was seen to be the embodiment of reason and the source of Russia regaining international respect and order. Also for the benefit of the continuance of the Russian Romanov regime, it was the only and best chance of that re-establishment to occur. The future of the world order rested with Michael, as it tipped a delicate balance between Western freedom and democracy, or enslavement under the tyranny of Bolshevism.

Michael understood very clearly the options and was left with little choice or freedom to express his concerns when faced with the consequences of his refusal. The further inevitable loss of life and world consequences could add more millions to those who had perished so far in this war. He mused also that this may well bring the German Kaiser to the negotiating table, as he would see that a war on the Western Front, especially with the USA now joining the Allies, and a serious Eastern Front being reopened with British, American and Japanese forces, would surely overwhelm the already strained and starving Austrian and German Armies. Also, Turkey was already suffering from war-weariness to a point where it would readily seek terms if this threat became a reality.

Johnson, who accompanied and advised Michael on all his official visits, especially at these difficult times of deciding Michael's position on this proposed world stage, asked Michael if he could disengage with him from the meeting so as to be able to look into finer detail of the consequences. He had noted that there was an appalling gap in the description from the British Government of the consequences for Russia and the endgame position.

They withdrew to a private office. Johnson put to Michael that it was patently obvious that if he agreed to all the proposals without securing a post-invasion governmental plan, then this could leave Russia as a puppet country under the complete control of the Western Allies. The question was: would Russia be any better off being under the yoke of Capitalism, or the enslavement of Communism?

The question was too huge to come to terms with and construct a coherent reply within the timescale of this meeting. Johnson was able to advise Michael that the terms of the Allied success and the effects upon Russia's future would be a question which must be raised in earnest with the Allies, which they reserved the right to bring as an agenda. They both, after ten minutes, returned to the dining room. Buchanan invited them to the drawing room. Michael announced he would indeed participate in the venture and become the head of Russia and a rallying point, with a caveat simply stating that the Allies should be aware that he would bring to the table his own terms.

Buchanan agreed, and said he would transmit that request to the War Office for consideration. Michael rebuked him and told him firmly that there was to be no consideration of this caveat, and that without confirmation that his own voice and terms would be heard then he would remain in Russia and at the disposal of the Russian Army should an invasion take place. Buchanan noted Michael's resolute stand and left the drawing room to transmit in code the details of the meeting.

Word returned from Churchill one hour later that he would agree to allow Michael a meaningful voice in the post-invasion plans for Russia. However, it was explained further that Churchill's plan was that he should be brought to Britain in the coming weeks for a meeting with the Western Powers' heads of state. This was to enable them to be confident on the principles and actions required, and to sign a treaty of intent with terms for the invasion policy and post-invasion influence of the Allies.

Michael and Johnson were shocked to hear of this addition to the meeting agenda and from the looks on the faces of Reilly and Buchanan it seemed obvious that they had been about to insert that caveat, had Churchill not made that announcement. Johnson exclaimed that it would be impossible to get Michael out of the country and back again without being arrested en route, and more to the point, that it would endanger Michael's family should they be discovered. There was also the factor that Michael would not be allowed into the country again and would be seen by the public as abandoning the Imperial cause.

Reilly, eager to convince Michael that plans had been made, took from his briefcase a set of documents and maps which he unfurled on the table, and he invited Johnson and Michael to join him so he could explain in detail exactly how the operation would be carried out. Michael was awestruck by the sheer audacity and meticulous planning that was presented to him, and taken aback by the scale and daring of the whole operation. The timescale seemed inconceivable, and his own participation was beyond what he had expected.

Michael himself was an unorthodox and playboy character and had a high degree of adventure built into his soul. The thought of trains, boats and planes – and submarines – were enough to capture his adventurous spirit, whilst filling him with trepidation. He could not turn down participation in such an adventure.

Johnson thought it was a mad adventure which could only result in disaster for Michael. However, he was resigned after counselling Michael on the dangers, that it was his choice. And, more to the point, he would not agree to Michael going alone, but had one non-negotiable caveat: he must accompany Michael, who relied on his counsel, and especially so given the forthcoming events of contract and politics. Michael saw the earnest desire of Johnson's expressions of loyalty and need to be with him, and agreed; especially as his company was important just to have a dear friend and confidante alongside him.

The D-Day date was agreed for midnight on 1 February 1918, Julian time; but became 14 February Gregorian time. Late in the night Michael returned to Gatchina and was met by Natasha who was on edge and very nervous about how the meeting had developed. Michael sat her down in front of a blazing fire and enjoyed a late Martini with her, whilst holding hands to encourage her in what he was about to say.

At that point, just before he expanded with the news of the invasion and him being required to journey to Britain, he reminded himself of the advice that Johnson had given to him on the journey back from Petrograd. He became quiet, remembering that she would be compromised if he told her everything. The Cheka might arrest her whilst they were away and force, by unimaginable means, the truth from her. He quickly switched his tack and simply told her that there were Allied plans afoot to rescue Nicholas and his family in collaboration with the White Army, which was gaining strength in the east of the country. From that, and with further Allied intervention, then within a few months it would be hoped that the restoration of the Monarchy would soon transpire.

Michael also explained that due to his ulcers becoming worse he had been advised at his meeting with Buchanan that there was a medical research and training centre in Tallinn (Estonia) and that they had perfected an unusual treatment for ulcers which required an examination and assessment prior to surgery. Michael had taken up the offer of this new treatment and was due to travel to Minsk for assessment studies and then onwards to Estonia. He would travel on the evening of 31 January (Julian) and go under disguise and false papers so that he would not be missed. Essentially, then, Natasha was to say that his ulcers had become a lot worse and that he had gone to see a doctor in Minsk and was unsure of his return date.

In the intervening days, Michael and Johnson had concept meetings with Reilly, who was the visionary and architect of the plans, to work out some of the finer details.

10

Carl Fabergé

Two days before they were due to leave Gatchina on the journey to Britain, Stopford arrived at the Palace with an old friend of the Romanovs. Michael greeted them in the Great Hall and immediately recognised the Royal Family jeweller, Peter Carl Fabergé. They embraced in some warmth of friendship and were invited into Michael's office. Johnson joined them, as he too was a friend of Fabergé.

It seemed, as the conversation unfolded, there was an express reason why Fabergé wanted to speak to Michael. He explained that just as Michael and the whole Romanov families were under surveillance by the Cheka, so he too and his family were under daily threat of being questioned and searched. His strong connection with the Romanovs and the other royal households in Europe was anathema to the Revolutionary Bolsheviks, as he was seen to be an epitome of all that was evil in Russia due to the wealth of treasures he supplied to the Romanovs.

He went on to say that a few weeks ago, his factory had been taken over by a so-called Committee of the Employees of the company, and it was threatened that very soon it would become a nationalised company. That meant the very little control he had now would be eliminated when the full nationalisation of his company began. He was almost crying when he mentioned further that the company, being the most renowned in Europe and worth three million roubles to him and his family, would soon be worthless.

Johnson then gently enquired whether he and Michael could be of any help to the family. It was a fact that it was not only the Romanov family who had been so badly smashed by the Bolsheviks: he had heard so many similar stories of wealthy industrialists being treated in the same way, to destruction and loss of livelihood.

Stopford then intervened on behalf of Fabergé, who was now sitting with his head in his hands and softly weeping. He took Michael and Johnson to one side and produced from his winter greatcoat a plain and simple cardboard box which was around 200 mm square. He opened it, and inside was a beautiful but simple Fabergé Easter egg of the kind which the Tsars had been receiving from him for the past three decades at Easter. Michael was surprised at receiving a gift in this secretive and sad manner, and he cast an eye back at Fabergé, still sobbing. Johnson thought more about it and put his hand on Michael's arm to subdue his thoughts of it being a gift.

Stopford then took the egg out of the box and with a twist and a push of a hidden mechanism, the lid of the egg rose about 10 millimetres. He then swivelled it around and unscrewed it, revealing that it was full to the brim of diamonds, rubies, emeralds and pearls.

Michael gently took the egg from Stopford, and was

shocked at how heavy it was. 'Why has he brought this to us?' he enquired.

Stopford lowered his voice and told Michael and Johnson that he wanted to ask them if they would take the jewels out of Russia and into the UK for safe-keeping in a London bank vault. Over the past few weeks Carl had been going to work as usual, but with the real endeavour being to get safely out of the factory as much of his treasure as possible. He would do this by each day filling the hollow heels of his boots, and had even resorted to swallowing gemstones in a steady flow each day.

Carl had been creating the egg at home with the help of Henrik Wigström, who was the head work master at the House of Fabergé. This was not of the usual standard, but originally he wanted it to be a final gift for Nicholas and hoped that the egg could be taken to him in Tobolsk. Stopford earlier had to advise Fabergé that this may not be possible due to the unrest and dangers in Russia, but he would try, and thought the best person to receive it in the meantime was Michael whereby the egg and jewels could be smuggled into the UK

Michael wondered if he would be able to carry this off as he already had a large stash of treasures in the half-track Rolls, and it would mean unpacking them again to store the loose jewels securely. Stopford then suggested that they should be kept in the egg, as it was best transportable that way. He explained to Carl that it would be placed in a London bank vault together with his jewels, and the egg could be given to Nicholas once he was freed. It was agreed as a good solution and Michael was only too happy to help an old friend who clearly was in as much distress with his life, business, and family as he and many other people in Russia were at these times.

Fabergé was now becoming anxious about the time as he knew he was under surveillance. He had been away from his factory for too long and did not want to be missed and interrogated. With that, Stopford left to take Fabergé back to Petrograd where his famous factory of jewelled art was located in Kuznetsky Most, which was 'the' street of fashion and expensive shopping.

Johnson thought for a while about the Fabergé egg and its treasure trove inside. He felt that Carl's final agreed wish for it to be taken to England was a risky solution. He was wary about the responsibility he was undertaking, especially as they were also carrying Maria Pavlovna's jewels to the UK. He also felt that it could be a further burden on their timetable to negotiate the depositing in a bank in the UK, as they already had a seemingly impossible timetable of a round trip in 14 days.

After careful thought, he decided that he would not take them but would secrete them in Gatchina and then work out a better solution when they returned. He thought that it might be better to get them to the Crimea where Carl himself could deal with the transportation out of Russia. At least they were out of his factory, and were in the first phase of movement.

Michael, some time ago, with the help of his chauffeur had hidden his favourite Rolls-Royce in a barn on the edge of the walled gardens. Johnson knew about this and that the barn had been in disuse for around ten years; it was overgrown and hardly recognisable as an outbuilding. Michael had done this as a last resort to retain a working car should Gatchina be stripped completely of all his possessions. So, that would be the best place to hide the egg, inside the leather lining and horsehair seating of the rear compartment.

Later that day, Reilly came to see Michael at Gatchina with two trunks to be attached to the rear of the Rolls half-track. Reilly explained that they contained essential changes of clothing and, more importantly, were uniforms of the New Revolutionary Brigades to form disguises for certain parts of their journey in and out of border checkpoints.

Most importantly, he showed Michael his forged ID papers which announced him as Collenius Johannsen, who was a resident of Helsinki in Finland and carried dual nationality, also being of Russian birth. He was known to be a sympathiser and activist of the Bolshevik regime and was on clandestine duties under the protection of the Cheka. He was at the outset to be dressed in a governmental dress style of lounge suit and stiff starched collar and tie, and was designated as being a member of the Bolshevik Party.

Johnson was to be simply known as Boris, and because of his peasant heritage from Siberia, he had no official papers but was under the complete control (enslavement) of the Commissar Orlov Volkov, which was the alias of Reilly. Johnson was to become a low-ranking army Corporal who was a personal assistant to Reilly and could be used as a fetch-and-carrier to enhance the position and power of Reilly in the face of any confrontations.

Reilly also had Russian nationality papers and was known to have been born in Odessa, the Russian Black Sea port. He carried a rank of Commissar and was senior to Michael. His role was to teach party principles and policies to ensure loyalty. His papers showed him to carry the name of Orlov Volkov Revieski, a Commissar Captain in the New Russian Army. This rank and attachment to military units was vital to give Reilly an air of authority which would put any person who chose to question their presence on the back foot, and place fear into them so that they may be persuaded to act as instructed.

Regarding the plans, which had been meticulously detailed with time, transport and place, Michael was instructed to learn these off by heart so that the document could be destroyed without leaving any evidence of what they were about.

The day before D-Day, Reilly, now dressed as a Commissar, brought to Gatchina a mechanic who serviced the half-track Rolls-Royce. Michael kept out of the way until he had finished, and in the meantime he and Natasha spent their last hours together. Natasha packed a backpack for Michael which contained basic food items and a change of clothes. He explained that he was travelling to Minsk using the half-track as the roads were unstable in winter, and they would probably have to travel overland and off-road in certain circumstances.

He used the excuse that he was taking Reilly with him as he wanted to travel incognito, and Reilly had connections with military who might wish to intercept and question them. This ensured his safety to a large degree, especially in these dangerous times. Johnson would also go with him again under some form of disguise.

11

D-Day

Around midnight on 14 February (Gregorian), the intrepid three, fully dressed in disguise, stepped into the Rolls which was purring away in the Gatchina garage, and set off fully laden with fuel, luggage and the secreted valuables from the Romanov families. The Rolls rattled out of the gates of Gatchina on the first part of a hazardous and very eventful journey to Britain.

Johnson knew his way around St Petersburg very well and chose the least obtrusive routes through the streets. He advised Reilly, who was taking the first stint of driving, on the best route, which he had been reconnoitring over the past few days to discover what nocturnal activities were prevalent among the angry mobs which roamed the streets in lawless pursuit of banditry and instant executions should they think fit.

Upon reaching the outskirts, and seeing the dim lights of Petrograd disappear, they took guidance by the half-lights of the Rolls and the full moon, with clear skies showing a bright star-laden umbrella which shone down on the snow-covered roads. Vision was magnificent due to these celestial aides.

The mood became jubilant between Johnson and Michael, but the redoubtable Reilly remained stony-faced and lacked any conversational spirit. He knew he had the most important commission of his life, and any failure could have dire consequences for the future of the world. He held onto this grim mantle for the rest of the journey north to Belomorsk, where they would rendezvous with the Royal Yacht *Standart*. Reilly thought to himself that Michael would more likely break down in confusion and tears when he clasped his eyes on the stripped-down remains and empty hull of the Yacht, recommissioned for the Bolshevik Navy.

After an hour of light banter between Johnson and Michael and some reminiscing of their childhood and early teens spent together, Johnson being the pragmatist suddenly exclaimed to Reilly in a shriek of horror that the Rolls was known to be a gas-guzzler and that a full tank would not get them even one-quarter of the journey. Reilly was not unnerved by this explosion of fear and simply smiled at Johnson with a wink. Johnson, now realising that it would always be better not to question the master planner, sat back and wondered what solution he had masterminded for refuelling.

After four hours, with Johnson nervously looking at the fuel indicator, Reilly slowed and veered off the road into a forest clearing. There the answer was awaiting them as they saw a 100-gallon bowser on wheeled skids parked in the open clearing.

Johnson was instructed to get out – knowing he had better get used to being the 'gofor' – and start filling the Rolls with the hand pump on the bowser lid. When the fuel tank was full, Reilly reversed the Rolls up to the tow bar of the bowser and told Johnson to insert the pin which he had stowed in the footwell of the car. Johnson duly did so, and climbed back into the Rolls, giving Michael a look of peace and happiness knowing that this first piece of logistics was well in hand. It boded well for the journey north.

Joining the road again, after a further four hours' driving it was becoming clear that the roadside marks were blurring into the landscape and it was becoming difficult to negotiate. Just as Michael was thinking that it would be a timely opportunity to stop and take stock of the difficulty they were encountering, Reilly pulled off the road and guided the car into a small track between the forest trees and negotiated a course purely by the absence of the dense undergrowth. After 2 kilometres, they came across a small cottage which had an illuminated lamp in the window. The Rolls pulled up to the very inviting shack, which promised warmth and respite and Reilly announced that they should join him in a hearty meal prepared for them by his accomplice Olga Bystrovia .

Immediately a half-naked woman came rushing out and shouted, 'Sidney! Sidney! Come quick!' as she threw herself against him in deep distress and urgency. She dragged him by his wrist into the shack, amid terrible cries of anguish.

Reilly came back out to the car with a threatening look on his face and immediately Michael and Johnson knew that something terrible had happened inside the shack. He beckoned Michael and Johnson to come into the shack. Lying over the kitchen table, which had been prepared for a substantial meal, lay slumped the decapitated body of a man. The woman was sitting by the fireside with her head in her hands, weeping uncontrollably.

Reilly gave firm instructions to take the body outside, wrap it in several layers of coarse sacking, and bury it. The ground would need hacking away with picks, but it was a clear instruction to which neither would give a second thought due to the distressing circumstances.

Reilly explained what had happened. Four Red Army Russian soldiers had forced their way into the shack about thirty minutes ago. They had discovered that Olga and her friend were supporters of the Russian White Army, and in their drunken state had murdered her friend who was a woodsman and raped Olga. Reilly then said he was going onwards to apprehend the murderers and bring revenge and justice for this reprehensible act of inhumanity. He would be back in two or three hours. They should rest and eat, and give some comfort to Olga.

Reilly searched outside looking for tell-tale footprints in the snow-laden ground. He quickly discovered tracks of what he thought belonged to the four men, imprinted in the snow. He saddled up the woodman's horse which was stabled at the rear of the house.

He saw by the direction of the footsteps that the men were heading towards Maselgskaya, a village which he knew to be about 5 kilometres north of the shack. If he was to catch them before they entered the village, then he would have to be very quick.

Reilly was soon pleased to see his quarry just ahead, and around 1 kilometre from the village. They were staggering along, and well under the influence of vodka. He could see, as he slowed the horse to a soft trot, that they were still carrying rifles.

He decided to call them from a distance and announce

himself as a keen supporter of the revolution and wanted to share vodka with them. They slowed, thinking that this was a genuine greeting, and that they would be able to brag of their earlier rape and murder of the family at the shack. Reilly put on a very pleasing face of happiness and dismounted to join the drunken party. They quickly realised that he was a Commissar and that as they were in army uniform, they had to be very circumspect in how they presented themselves.

Reilly slapped each on the back in typical Russian style and complemented the men on being revolutionaries and not members of the hated White Army. They relaxed and were quick to point out the gallant deeds of the murder of a suspected Romanov sympathiser and the rape of a lady who was also in the shack. One private announced that he had personally decapitated the woodsman. Reilly braced himself, expressing false joy and supressed his anger and hatred. He congratulated them again and took a swig of their vodka.

He then announced that he was going to the village and that they should join him, but first they should present themselves as best they could for inspection, and tidy themselves as being worthy representatives of the revolution. He lined them up after instructing them to lay their rifles against a tree. He walked slowly in front of them, his eyes penetrating, and took on his inimitable stern countenance, impressing them with a high order of rank. He made the odd remark as he walked slowly past, and then proceeded to inspect from the rear.

At that point he silently took out his revolver and within the space of four seconds had fired a bullet into each of the skulls of the three murdering beasts to whom he had brought retribution. The young private who had decapitated the woodsman was hysterical as Reilly grabbed him around the throat and slowly reminded him that the old man had died in agony.

Reilly wanted the screaming young man to shut up so he clubbed him to the ground with his revolver, rendering him unconscious. He then took out his bandana from under his fur hat and tied it tight around the soldier's mouth, gagging him to ensure his silence. He was now out of unconsciousness and Reilly bent down and administered the pain as he had earlier performed on the old man. He shot off the knee caps of both his legs. He then whispered to him that the wolves were hungry in that part of the forest and how he might like to be eaten alive at the pleasure of Tsar Nicholas and the White Russian loyalist army.

He then left a note tucked into the breast jacket of the private who had decapitated the woodsman. The note read, 'In furtherance to the continued success of the White Army commandoes, here lie the remains of four debased and violent murderers and rapists.' He signed it Orlov Volkov, which translates as Eagle Wolf.

Reilly then mounted his horse and rode off back to the shack, knowing that he had achieved revenge, but not knowing how he could ever make up to and console Olga, who was his stablemate in espionage for the British Government.

Michael and Johnson were still in shock when Reilly arrived back at the shack. However, in contrast it seemed that Olga was very near back to her normal intelligent and alert self as she had come through the grief, and knew that her stance had to be on a par with Sidney's to overcome and get on with the task at hand. Olga had packed her shoulder bag just hours before the Rolls had arrived, and was ready to join them. She quickly made Reilly a dish of food and both soon made ready with Michael and Johnson to embark in the Rolls once again for the final and longest leg of the journey.

Reilly introduced Olga Bystrovia as a member of the British Secret Service. This shook Michael, as he was unaccustomed to seeing such a beautiful, slim lady involved in the rough and tough life of espionage. This was her undercover name, used by Hannah Chudasama whilst she was working as a British spy in Russia. Her nature was very quiet and charming, and showed a softness of human nature. However, she was a self-assured survivalist and had a determination to succeed. When engaging in her MI6 affairs, then her knowledge of languages, quick learning, quick thinking and icy cold posturing drawn from her contrasting depths would put her in a controlling position in varied engagements.

They were now in fear of losing momentum and it was agreed that Olga would take the next driving stint and Michael would take the final leg of the journey. The first five-hour stint passed in a degree of silence as all were shocked to the core by the events that had suddenly changed the moods and lives of the travellers. Olga settling down into an even driving rhythm and cruising at a steady pace over the snow laden track, seemed to have put aside the trauma which befell her at the now distant woodland shack. Johnson was sat at the back with Reilly who was waking from a slumber he had slipped into for 30 minutes after taking some respite from the first driving stint. Quickly regaining his alertness and seeing that Johnson was still pensive, spoke to him with some encouragement and tried to take his mind off the shocking experience of the murder of the woodsman.

After engaging in small talk, Johnson hoped to discover a little more about Reilly and his clandestine operations in Russia. Reilly was most obliging and took some delight in recounting his recent commission and his endeavours to help the cause of bringing down the Bolsheviks.

He explained that he had been on assignment in Russia for several months and was seemingly attached to an RFC squadron which had arrived in the summer as a training wing to the Russian military. However, this was merely a cover to his special purpose which was in monitoring the Kerensky government that was showing signs of collapse with the rising menace and popularity of the Bolsheviks after Lenin's return to Russia in April 1917. But the primary task in his posting was to report on the German activities in wanting to secure with Lenin a treaty and cessation of hostilities due to a foreseeable and imminent collapse of the Russian armed forces. If this were to happen then this would be a disaster for the Allies as the transfer of German military from the Eastern Front to the West could provide them with a quick victory.

In fact, even his posting with the RFC training wing had little paperwork to show his assignment and service records, and most if not all the training crew never knew or saw him. His cover was so oblique and shrouded in mystery that he had become a ghost and officially did not exist in Russia, but was covered by SIS as being in America, Canada and finally in England as seemingly authenticated through various levels of official documents, using subterfuge and gamesmanship. To help support this cover he had re-appeared from time to time to show his face and provide some substance in documentary evidences to help disguise his Russian mission.

However, after this mission to get Michael to England and then a return back to Russia, he was due to officially surface and be on hand to operate on a more visible footing with SIS.

He closed the conversation by saying that if he did not survive this commission, then his official death had been meticulously planned as `missing in action without trace`. `Morte en Absentia`

Up to that point Johnson had been listening intently, but on that final chilling note he fell silent, and thought deeply about the massive risks that Reilly was undertaking on behalf of his country, his cause and Michael. He became humbled at how a person could speak of failure and death in such an unflinching and detached manner which was not reflective of humanity. He then glanced at Olga who was driving quite capably and wondered if she too would be under the same ghostly exitance on this mission. If so, then she may well have the same traits of shocking coolness and command of dangerous situations without fear for her own death. They could not possibly have any close family to care about and thus allowed them to take on a such a dangerous assignment. However, he noted the difference in outward expression between Reilly and Olga as she seemed to portray a very caring, assured and comforting persona which was very much at odds with Reilly. He hoped to discover more of this intriguing Asian lady during the journey.

Michael took over for the final leg and was surprised at

how well he could handle the Rolls, but of course this was much easier now as they had abandoned the fuel bowser at the last changeover and the steering was much more responsive.

12

The Royal Yacht *Standart*

Reilly told Michael to stop about 2 kilometres outside Belomorsk and took over the driving as he needed to negotiate any checkpoints, which he and Olga had arranged in the weeks earlier. The first checkpoint was on the outskirts of the town and Reilly announced the names of the occupants and showed the two guards the forged papers. The senior guard observed that there were now four occupants and the papers only showed that three were expected. Reilly explained that Olga was a senior Party member, and senior to himself. He asked Olga to produce her papers and asked her to announce herself.

'Olga Bystrovia, Commandant Commissar,' she rasped back at the guard, who was taken aback by her authoritative stance. She then loudly instructed Reilly to carry on to the port, snatching her ID papers from the hands of the startled guard.

The town and roads were in a poor state of repair and whilst cleared of snow to some degree, it was an unpleasant and bumpy journey towards the quayside of the fishing port. Reilly pulled the Rolls up on the quayside next to a very large hulk of a ship, and beckoned for the occupants to get out and start offloading the luggage.

Several engineers came down the gangplank of the ungainly ship and approached Reilly where intense discussions took place. After what seemed like angry bargaining and raised voices, Reilly pulled out a large package from his great coat and handed this to the guy who seemed to be the boss. The package was opened and the contents of high-denomination US dollar notes were counted. With a beaming smile, the boss grasped Reilly with a bear hug and shouted his delight to the other members of the group.

Three engineers then left the group and ran towards the Rolls and helped to carry the luggage to the gangplank. Reilly took out the rear seat of the Rolls and brought out two suitcases which Stopford had secreted there only weeks earlier. He then slid underneath the car and detached the shell container, opened one of the cases and placed the shell case inside, and closed and locked it.

Michael exclaimed what was going on and enquired where the Royal Yacht was. Reilly bypassed that question and told Michael that the two suitcases and shell canister were stuffed with high-value jewellery, and were for him to take out of Russia. He advised Michael to retain them in the UK for his future use. He gave him a security key for each suitcase, and advised him that until he was safely on board the HMS *Iron Duke*, which was waiting in the Barents Sea for them, they should not be let out of his sight. He also produced two Beretta guns, for Michael and Johnson, so that they should have some protection should they need to defend themselves and the valuable content of the suitcases. Only they should handle these items, and they should not let them into the hands of any other person.

Looking around he could see the workers taking the other luggage up the gangplank and onto the ugly hulk of a boat. Michael again enquired what was going on and why were they not taking the items onto the *Standart*. And where was it?

Olga joined in at that point and with a caring arm around Michael's shoulder began to explain that this was the *Standart*. It had been stolen by the Bolsheviks and was being converted to a minesweeper/layer to help keep the Baltic clear of mines and allowing goods to be shipped into Petrograd. Michael fell into deep shock and was angry, speechless, and on the verge of tears. Johnson consoled him and reminded him that this was a minor event in the huge culture change which was under way, and he should come to terms with this now as the world in Russia had changed. Johnson had been made aware of the demise of the `Standart` by Reilly during planning meetings before they left Petrograd and had chosen to keep Michael in the dark. He was carrying enough responsibility and felt that burden of loss would not help his delicate peace of mind.

Michael and Johnson then grasped a suitcase each, laden heavily with treasures, and trudged despondently up the gangplank to behold a site of utter emptiness. They were face to face with a makeshift wheelhouse providing limited vision over the bows and some form of attached accommodation shed made from corrugated iron just forward of the engines. On entering the shed they were relieved to see that this structure was on two floors and had been sectioned into three compartments. The first being the mess room and kitchen, with an office next door and below these rooms there were bunks set out to sleep ten people. It seemed that the engineers who were doing the mechanical installations used these as a home from home.

Michael and Johnson were introduced to the boss, Olaf was from Sweden as were his crew of engineers. Olga explained that they were employed by the Russians to fit out the *Standart* propulsion systems with the latest Western Marine engineering which had been developed in Sweden for their own navy. His spoken English was poor, but understandable.

The use of the *Standart* for the next leg of the journey was chosen as it was too dangerous for the *Iron Duke* to attempt to get that close to the Russian mainland; secrecy was required, and relations between Britain and Russia were disintegrating fast. The *Standart* was the best option as the Swedish guys were easily bribed for the two-day round trip, mostly in the dark, as they had not been paid by the Russian Government for several months and were in desperate need of payment. They did not ask too many questions but had no loyalty either way to Britain or Russia; the only loyalty they had was payment, and in this case it was in dollars.

Michael and Johnson were shown to their bunks and made comfortable with sandwiches and hot coffee. They soon thawed out over a well-lit open stove and Olga came to them and bade farewell announcing that they would meet again in Flensburg in a few days time for the final leg of the journey home.

Soon after Reilly and Olga had disappeared back into the Rolls, Olaf introduced himself and made sure that the two Russian gentlemen were comfortable, and assured them of a speedy journey to the next rendezvous point. With that, amongst shouts and commands in Swedish, which neither Michael nor Johnson could understand, they felt the first movement of forward thrusts from the twin diesel steam turbine engines. They remarked to each other how quiet they were and guessed that the huge coverings which had been placed over them by the crew were sound attenuators.

After an hour of sailing, Michael and Johnson were invited by Olaf to the wheelhouse and were surprised to see that their speed had increased beyond what they had thought. The quietness of the engines seemed out of step with the speed which was increasing steadily all the time.

Within one hour of negotiating the shallows and inlets around the bay, Olaf then declared in broken English, 'Now, gentleman let's see what our baby will produce in our second sea trial.'

With that the engines took on a more powerful sound and the feeling of a surge which ensued left Michael and Johnson reeling back slightly and looking for support from each other. There was a dial like a speedometer on the bridge and its needle was steadily moving forward, reaching the astonishing speed of 40 kph. The engines and the smoothness of the ride were a strange coupling with the rusting old ship. The engine noise then became secondary as the wash and sea turmoil took over.

Olaf now became more excited and mimicked having a whip in his hand, theatrically driving the horses forward. He shouted, 'Come my black beauties, show us what you can do!' With that, and a tug on the throttle lever which took it down to the last notch, the boat suddenly lurched forward and sat back at an astonishing angle for such a huge hull, with the vertical triple expansion engines driving two shafts powered from four boilers thrust the bows of the *Standart* upwards. Sea spray was thrown up from curtains of water either side of the bow in response. Another look at the speed needle showed it climbing from 40 to 60 kph in the space of around 60 seconds. Michael was quick to note that these speeds were considerable but were entirely due to the stripped out nature of the yacht and its ultra-light weight to power ratio.

Johnson had read and recorded to memory the details of the timetable and itinerary for the whole journey, and had committed to memory even the minor detailing which Reilly had so carefully researched to support the strategy. After five minutes or so of this high speed, Johnson being the pragmatist, gently reminded Olaf that the planned cruising speed was for 50 kph and that there was an allowance of two resting periods of one hour each so not to extend the new engines, which were under sea trial. Olaf looked as though his candy bar had been ripped from him and he adjusted the throttle back to 50, which was still a high lick of speed for an old tub.

Michael looked at Johnson in amazement that he knew these details, and quickly deduced that he had been privy to the state of the *Standart* from the early plans and discussions with Reilly. Michael shot a quizzical look which brought Johnson a confession that he knew about the reconstruction of the *Standart*. He explained to a disappointed Michael that he had not wanted to break any bad news at the outset of the journey, as he knew he had enough on his plate to think about, and wanted to keep him in the best of spirits for as long as possible.

It was now the early hours and Michael and Johnson

thought they had better get lots of rest as they had been in a state of nervous tension for thirty hours without any sleep. They were thankful that the bunks created for them were very comfortable, and the cabin was warmed by the glowing stove. The hum of the engines was a further boost to sleep as it lulled them into blackness with a gently rolling feeling of security. Michael thought to himself as he drifted off that he would just love to get his hands back on to the *Standart* after his certain Coronation next year, and he would enthuse over the rebuilding of the boat around these fabulous two diesel engines.

After six hours of continuous sleep each was woken with a firm shake by Olaf who announced that a meal had been prepared for them both. Washing and shaving now seemed very inappropriate amidst the smells of the sea, diesel fumes and roasting venison, which should be relished as an adventurous new experience, and compliance with the order of the day amongst the genial, unwashed and friendly engineers.

Breakfast seemed more like lunch, provided early as the boarding onto the *Iron Duke* was due in the afternoon. The food provided was exceptional and they asked how these Swedish guys were able to provide such a delicious, whilst being simple, offering of abundance. The quality of the wine too was befitting of most tables of high rank. Olaf explained that the terms of the work were primarily the best in supplies of food and wine, or the deal was dead! Payment was promised, but being very late, had come via Reilly – together with an extra bonus to do an undisclosed sea trial to rendezvous with a battlecruiser in the Barents Sea. He had no idea of the ship and where it was from, but he did not care, as the bonus was commensurate with three months' wages for each of his engineers.

During the final engine rest period, three of the engineers and Olaf invited Michael and Johnson to a game of cards to while away the time. This seemed like an excellent choice, as the flowing of high-octane vodka lightened the mood. The crew were delighted to see that both Michael and Johnson were happy to use dollars.

On one hand, Johnson seemed to have an excellent set of cards and was determined to keep the stakes raised to force Olaf, who was last in the bragging ring, to throw. Johnson soon ran out of dollars and produced roubles. Olaf reminded him that they were unacceptable as the rules were in dollar dealing. Johnson looked at Michael, hoping to borrow some money, but Michael was rather too drunk to understand the current climax of this big bet, and disappeared back to his bunk. Johnson was faced with throwing his cards, but Olaf politely suggested that if had such a good hand, he might throw in the key to the one of the 'suitcase's' which he had been protecting with some enthusiasm.

Johnson being a quiet man, was also a serious brinksman. He placed the key into the centre and instead of announcing that he would 'see' Olaf, as was expected since he had no more dollars, he raised the stake (Olaf had made the mistake of not setting any limit) to the value of the key. Johnson announced that its value was $3,000. This angered Olaf and he cried foul play. Johnson grabbed his thick arm and pulled his Beretta and announced that it was in the rules and he should either match the bid or throw. Olaf had no choice but to throw his cards on the table, especially as he was faced with a Beretta pointing at his eyes.

Olaf bashed the table and stood up and was about to throw himself at Johnson, but the Beretta was still pointed at him. Common sense then prevailed and he thrust out his hand to acknowledge that he had been defeated. Olaf, however, could not rest on not knowing how his hand had fared, and asked Johnson to a show of cards, as the game had now ended. They agreed to show one at a time, to raise the suspense.

Olaf started and showed the 7, 6, 5, 4 and 3 of Hearts

Johnson followed with the 4, 5, 6 and 7 of Clubs, and the 8 of Spades.

It was appearing that Johnson was winning on each turn, and that Johnson's last card must be the 8 of Clubs which would have won the game. When Johnson turned an 8 of Spades, Olaf went into another rage as he did have the winning hand. But he could not help admire the guile of Johnson who had trounced him to the tune of the $1,400 dollars which was on the table. Goodness knows what he would have said if he had known the true value waiting for him in the case had he won the key.

Johnson realised that he had been very foolish in putting at risk the Romanov treasures, and he was a little depressed at how his gaming instinct had got the better of him.

Michael lying in his bunk was catching up on his diary, but he was not sure whether it was legible as he was recovering from too much vodka. Johnson joined him and retired to his own bunk to read his novel of *The Gadfly* which Reilly had recommended to him. He was glad that Michael had not seen the final hand of cards and the risked Romanov treasures. He found he was not able to read as he was feeling sick. He visited the latrines and relieved himself of the last meal. He tried to console himself that it was simply sea sickness, as he was not a good traveller, and this whole journey would yet prove to be the biggest challenge of his life in holding back sickness.

However, he still had one eye on the crew who were now filtering back to their station. Olaf had gone back to his wheel house full of discontent, but admiration for Johnson.

Johnson tried again to read and hoped it might tire him enough to get some sleep. He put the book down and looked at his watch and noted the time. In the hope that Olaf and his navigation skills were on target, then very soon he would expect the *Standart* to start slowing. After another gripping chapter of *The Gadfly*, he was pleased to hear the hum of the twin engines dropping in resonance, and to feel that the angle of attack of the bow had dropped. He then woke Michael, who was in such a sleepy state that Johnson had to throw a cup of water in his face to revive him.

They both then climbed to the wheelhouse to join Olaf, and were met by a huge blot against the moonlit night. It took the shape of an enormous battleship of the like Michael had never seen even in his extensive travels before the outbreak of war.

'Gentlemen,' Olaf announced, 'I give you your journey's end.'

13

The *Iron Duke*

The *Standart* pulled alongside the *Iron Duke* and the ships were roped together for the transfer of Michael. The luggage was brought to the deck and Johnson duly counted the items to ensure nothing was left below, giving special attention to ensure the two large suitcases containing the future finances of their return to power were in the heap.

Michael saw the *Iron Duke*'s Quartermaster standing at the starboard rail, looking sneeringly at the two unshaven and dishevelled Russians. He guessed he was wondering what the fuss was about to create this meeting with a rusting tub to receive these two very non-descript men. He thought that perhaps the QM might take a view that they were refugees of some importance, due to the high alert they were under.

A gangplank was secured between both ships and two Able Seamen came across to take the luggage which was peculiar as he would have thought that would have been the last to come aboard. Then Michael and Johnson proceeded up the plank and into the safe care of the British Government. For the first time, they both felt a feeling of euphoric freedom and relief after undergoing over a year of persecution and fear. Michael was a little disappointed that there was no form of official greeting or fanfare to show the arrival of a very important member of the Russian Royal Family. Both men wondered about this, in some disappointment.

They were then taken into the enormous superstructure and welcomed by the QM, who very politely asked them to follow him to their quarters which had been prepared for them in the safety and warmth of the belly of the battleship. They were pleased to see that their cabins were quite spacious, and it was a twin unit which would allow companionship for them. The QM announced that they had also a private dining area with a small bathroom leading off the sleeping quarters.

He invited them to take lunch, which was being now prepared for them. He mentioned that there was no menu but hoped they would enjoy the traditional British ship's offering. With that he left. Two minutes later he returned with a sailor who he introduced as being their personal assistant whilst aboard.

Able Seaman Basil Baldric was to be the manservant to Michael and would prepare all his food from the daily set meals from the officers' galley, maintain his wardrobe, and be his general guide around the *Iron Duke*. Baldric was a pleasant fellow with good manners and suited to his role, whilst having the added advantage of being fluent in Russian. He greeted them in perfect Russian, and his accent seemed to portray a higher education than would have been guessed at.

The QM also mentioned that Jack Blackman-Adderley, who was a Lieutenant, would visit them after they had eaten lunch, rested and dressed more formally. Jack, the QM pointed out, would be the personal assistant to both Michael and Johnson.

Baldric then turned to the question of dress and said that they should change from their Russian clothes into the fatigues uniform of general duties. These were in the locker together with higher ranking naval uniforms for when they were to meet with the ship's officers and others on board. He also asked them to leave out the clothes they were wearing so he could launder and return them to their cabin. With those brief formalities dealt with, the QM took his leave and left Baldric with Michael and Johnson to see to their immediate needs.

As the QM left there was a distinct rumbling sound from deep within the ship, a sign that the engines were turning to higher revs, and they felt the first signs of forward movement as the pace was gathering. Johnson peered out of the porthole and saw the *Standart* slipping away in the wake of the *Iron Duke*. As he gazed at the forlorn remains of the Royal Yacht he noticed that on the bow, roughly painted in large letters, was *Vosemnadtsate Martza*. He remarked upon that to Michael, who was stripping down to shirt and trousers and discarding the heavy and soiled clothes he had been wearing for the northern journey.

Upon hearing of the new ID markings on the *Standart*, Michael froze and a flash of hatred and anger swept across his face. This new name was essentially the date upon which the Duma took control of the Russian state two days after the abdication of his brother, Tsar Nicholas II.

Now having changed into fatigues, Baldric collected the clothes and left, mentioning that he would serve them dinner at 1900 hours and that they should make themselves comfortable after freshening up. Michael and Johnson declined, and decided that just a fresh supply of coffee would be welcome for the rest of the day as they preferred to sleep on as the journey up to then had been quite exhausting.

The following morning, they were both totally refreshed after a long sleep. Breakfast was served punctually and was enjoyed as being a very unusual mix of fried bacon, eggs, sausages and beans. This was reminiscent of the time they had spent in England, and was a meal particularly enjoyed by the workers on the estate at Knebworth House.

Johnson asked Michael to concentrate for a while and to listen to him very carefully, as later they would be introduced to the ship's Commander and perhaps other British dignitaries, with the discussion inevitably coming to the point of the invasion and Michael's role. Johnson explained that, beyond the grand offerings of the Allies and the euphoria surrounding the whole venture, Michael must keep his focus rooted in the future benefits of Russia and his own position, and be very wary of a hidden dagger in the velvet glove of friendship.

Michael asked Johnson to explain further, as he had no real idea of what he was trying to say. Michael suddenly realised that in all the pressure of getting this far, and the subterfuge taking place, he himself had not given any time to look any deeper than the first layer of the onion skin, and really had no concept of what lay at the heart of the matter.

Johnson had been putting his own mind to this question for some time and had realised that there had been no information being provided about the post-invasion campaign, of what would be what, and what shape the new Russian Empire would take. He had assumed that no invasion force would undertake such a huge gamble of life, materiel and prestige without working out the end game in detail. Therefore, it was safe to assume that the Allied Powers knew exactly what they were going to introduce into Russia upon succeeding. It was also obvious that these plans, for their benefit, should be kept from Michael as far as possible.

It was Johnson's understanding that they could be walking a dangerous path which could well see the future of Russia under the heel of the West, in just the same way as was happening now under Bolshevism for the Communist future of Russia. Johnson, in his own time in the weeks preceding the D-Day from Gatchina, had been working on his own manifesto for presentation to the Allied Powers, and now wanted to bring this to Michael for his consideration and views.

Johnson had dealt with all of Michael's private and personal affairs since 1912 with great efficiency. Michael was comfortable with almost anything that Johnson did on his behalf, and was intrigued to hear of what he may now have prepared in draft for presenting alongside the discussion which would inevitably soon take place. With Michael's enthusiastic agreement to discover the details, he invited Johnson to reveal his draft manifesto.

Prometheus
Plan for the interim future of Russia, 1918

Upon any Allied force entering the state capital of Petrograd then immediately they would re-establish the interim government of the Duma under the leadership of Kerensky.

To secure the immediate release of any Romanov family who has been incarcerated or under house arrest by the outgoing and defeated power base.

Ditto with any political persons in the same way.

Food and medical aid to be distributed to the population as needed and required to bring back order and sustenance.

To disarm immediately any of the public who carry weapons which would be used against the new regime, and to create amnesties for all who carried weapons and held revolutionary ideals pre the invasion.

Law and order brought back to the Empire under the authority of the current police force after cleansing of corrupt members.

The Kerensky Government will be given the full powers that were in place prior to the dissolution in November 1917.

Kerensky will have the power to appoint the Cabinet members and to be able to veto any members of the new government imposed by the Allied powers.

The Duma will accept that the main terms of the new Government would be to continue the war on the German Eastern Front and could accept that the Russian Army could essentially come under the main control of the Allies, but on the condition that food, equipment and training are implemented to secure a useful and dynamic battlefront.

The Allies would make efficient landings and take control of the Baltic Sea and extinguish the threat of the naval blockade. This would either require the sinking or surrender of the German High Seas Fleet. Any ships surrendered in the Baltic Sea would be given to the Royal Russian Navy for use in their home waters.

Full and effective employment to be created within the Russian industrial regime to manufacture sufficient war materiel and to rebuild its armaments stockpile in new and modern equipment.

Education for all from 5 to 14 at state expense.

State-assisted medical care.

A levy on all industries to provide a pension for workers.

The farming industry to undergo a revolution in trading and equipment and to be able to use modern techniques with the aim to become self-sufficient in agricultural produce.

The petrochemical industry to undergo the same and similar changes.

An agreed oil production volume to be established on an incremental basis to provide three main areas of consumption: A) to supply the needs of the industrial revolution and domestic needs; B) to supply the needs of the war machine; and C) to provide exports to Great Britain and France, and to be paid for in US dollars.

The reinstatement of all lost lands to the boundaries as enjoyed at the start of the War.

Elections to be held within two years of the takeover of power on a national basis to promote a stable government and to be set for re-election no later than the passing of five years.

A new Constitution to be drawn up under the authority of the new interim Tsar Michael, the new Duma, and the Allied powers.

Michael Alexandrovitch Romanov to be temporally reinstated as head of state with full powers as before enjoyed on an interim basis.

This interim period to be no longer than two years and to be voted at the same time as the expected general election.

*Terms and manifesto of the interim reinstatement of the
    Romanov Dynasty to be petitioned for towards the interim
    government and Allies for the approval and voting needs of
    the population.*

*A Coronation to be held in public at minimal expense with full
    public participation but on a low key to encourage the new
    order of austerity and equality.*

Michael took a while to comprehend the changes and
how this new order would possibly sit with the Romanov
families, the new government and the public at large. After
thirty minutes of very careful thought, he got up from the
dining table and announced to Johnson that this was a
masterpiece of strategy and was most welcome to himself,
and appealed to his own eclectic values of freedom, equality
and fraternity. He felt that the Allies would happily accept
this notion, and certainly, and more importantly, so would
the Russian people.

They embraced in delight and immense hope for the
future, and for the first time Michael could see his dreams
of a new Russian Empire being a shining light to the world
and other royal dynasties as the only way to go in the new
and emerging modern world. They retired to their bunks
in a state of happy silence which allowed both to reflect on
dreams of an interestingly better future for Russia.

Johnson, however, being the strategist and practical
idealist, knew deep down that these were just words, and
a long, long way was yet to go in gaining acceptance and,
more so, overcoming the difficulty of implementation.

At around 1300 hours, Baldric reappeared with lunch.
Again he apologised for there being no menu, but assured

them that a Great British roast was universally accepted as being the best of British cuisine. He then reminded them that after lunch they should change into the more formal Royal Navy uniforms, as Jack would be visiting them around mid-afternoon.

14

Meeting with Churchill

Jack Adderly-Blackman knocked and walked politely into their cabin at precisely 1400 hours and introduced himself as a member of the MI6 SIS naval attachment. Michael and Johnson welcomed Jack and a conversation was struck up between them regarding the journey so far. Jack was interested to know how they had been treated by his fellow agent, Sidney Reilly. Michael was quick to point out that the presence of Reilly had given them security, he felt impressed by him, and was astounded by his intricate preparations and the accomplishment of the journey from Gatchina.

Jack asked Michael of his views of the Reilly Plan, and the massive responsibilities that were intertwined with the success of the events yet to unfold. Michael commented that it was an amazing strategy and complimented Reilly on his abilities to create this. Jack then deflated Michael a little and said it was true it was a great feat of planning, but he was sure that the original outline was the conception of Olga Bystrovia, who was his key contact in Russia. He mentioned that Michael already may have met her en route.

Johnson then interceded as Michael may well say more than he should at the mention of Olga. He felt that the episode of the killing of the woodsman and rape of Olga would implicate Reilly and create some uncertainty for him. He slightly changed the tact and remarked on Olga's efficiency and the authority she held in that circle. He pondered the thought that she was an exceptionally beautiful and bright woman, of unknown ethnicity, and enquired about this with Jack.

Jack agreed that it was an unusual appointment to MI6 but it was solely based upon her major success in other theatres and her rapid rise within the ranks of the British Secret Service. Her ethnicity was rumoured to be from the Western Provinces of India, and she was the daughter of a humble shoemaker. This surprised both Johnson and Michael, as a person of such low cast and yet perceived high education, possessing such beauty and intelligence, coming from a non-white background, was astounding to them. Both mused at the concept of freedom that was seemingly prevalent in the Western world, and the open-door policies that must exist to allow other cultures into such high-ranking positions.

Jack then commented with some pride, that she was a master of languages and had taught herself German, Russian and French in nine months of intense learning at Nottingham University. Of course, this was on top of her English and native Gujarati language.

'Then her name is not Olga Bystrovia, by which she was introduced?' Johnson enquired.

Jack looked at him, and commented, 'Everybody who you would meet relating to MI6 will never be who you think they are. Especially their names.'

He closed that conversation with a wink and quickly moved on to the main point of his presence. He commented on how well they had dressed: Michael in a Commander's uniform bearing three rings on each arm of the naval jacket, and Johnson in a Lieutenant's uniform which bore just one ring. He then announced that they should follow him, as he now needed to introduce them to Winston Churchill, who was a key member of the War Office.

Johnson remarked to Michael that he was aware of the activities of Churchill during the war, and that he had conceived an ill-fated attempt to shorten the war by trying to knock out the Turks by invading the southern region of the Dardanelles. Michael's face screwed up with some trepidation, but did remark that he was aware of Churchill's ambitions and fairly commented that it had seemed a great idea at the time, and that he was treated unfairly by the British press and his parliamentary colleagues.

Jack then provided each with a briefcase which contained essential notepads and pencils, and invited them to gather any further papers they required. Johnson went to his locker and took out the Manifesto which he had agreed with Michael the previous evening.

All three then marched out at a quick and efficient pace and followed along the poorly lit but busy passageways of the ship. They had to climb up several companionways before they arrived at the bridge of the great battlecruiser *Iron Duke*. On the way, they were surprised to receive several salutes from various rating ranks, which to them was a thorough dislocation in their minds from reality.

They were met by Captain Eustace La Trobe Leatham,

who welcomed them to the bridge. Both were intrigued by the array of instruments and the apparent speed of the ship, with spray rising from the bows in what was seemingly a rough sea, but with little feeling of rolling or pitching, probably due to the mass of the battleship.

They were also pleased to see at around 200 metres a destroyer on each side of the *Iron Duke*, easily keeping pace with the battleship. That was a comfort, as the infamous U-boats had wreaked terrible havoc on the British merchant fleet, and the German Admiral Scheer was claiming an imminent victory in the starvation of Great Britain through merchant ship losses.

After five minutes of interesting banter between the Captain, Jack and the two VIP visitors, the Captain having had no idea of who they were, or what their mission was, gave Jack leave from the bridge and then he led them to a large boardroom. There they were met by two uniformed high-ranking officers. The first introduced himself as Winston Churchill, who took the rank of Acting First Sea Lord (his previous role in 1916) but was actually Minister for Arms and Munitions. Churchill then introduced them to the other, more senior and imposing figure of Admiral Jellicoe.

Michael was immediately impressed by these officers' names. He recognised Churchill as being the architect, and scapegoat, of the Dardanelle invasion of Turkey mentioned in the conversation with Johnson earlier. He also knew Admiral Jellicoe's name, as the Commander of the Grand Fleet at the Battle of Jutland, which had taken place in 1916.

Formalities were exchanged whilst standing, then all

were invited to take a seat at the round conference table where coffee and tea were offered and served accordingly.

Churchill took it upon himself to be the main voice for the purpose of the meeting, and after thanking Michael for accepting the chalice of renewal in Russia, he complimented him on him being the Western Powers' best man for the job, and at the right time to steer the course of history and to help bring the war to a speedy end. He said to Michael with some fervour that this would come with strong benefits to Russia, becoming a major player in the new world order arising after the defeat of Germany.

Churchill, reading from his papers, brought to Michael the remainder of the Reilly plan and enquired whether the activities were still within his scope, and if anything changed in his own mind of how they might accomplish these very dangerous and adventurous tasks. This was now the time to be clear, as the journey going forward was becoming far more complex, and the risks of exposure, failure and death were very real.

Michael's response was that he was enjoying the adventure so far and there being trains, boats and planes involved with the excitement and demands of a submarine journey was right up his street. However, there was one part of the detail he was not clear upon… Churchill gently demanded for him to disclose this.

'When we leave Flensburg in the submarine to negotiate our journey back into Russia, I would very much like Sidney Reilly to lead us.' He supported this by retelling the story of how efficiently they had been brought to the *Standart*, and how safe they felt in their command of control and secrecy.

Churchill smiled and said he thought that was a good

point, as it was apparent that the top British spy was as good as his reputation. 'That is in our plan, Michael,' he replied.

Now Churchill wanted to turn to the main point of the meeting. He set the scene of the invasion plans and stressed with great earnestness the ultra-secrecy of the endeavours by three major nations who would fund, develop and prosecute this invasion to an extent that it would change the whole nature of the progress of the war to date. There were very high stakes and monumental risks to be undertaken, and the success, whilst highly probable, could not be achieved without further loss of lives and attrition.

The catalyst for this intervention was the loss of the Romanov influence, the establishment of Bolshevism, (which was anathema to the Western Allies,) and the need to defeat Germany. Success would almost certainly be guaranteed by the upholding of the Eastern German Front, and further escalation which could cause a rapid collapse.

The Eastern Front was disintegrating and the peace negotiations by Russia with Germany could indeed be the first real sign that the Allies could lose. The recent entry of America into the war could not guarantee any Allied victory due to the unpreparedness of America, and the several months it would need to transfer sufficient trained men, munitions and assets to the Western Front. That delay, and the movement to the west of released troops at the Eastern Front would have dire consequences and could overwhelm the much-depleted French, British and Commonwealth troops already engaged.

The success of this endeavour was very much reliant upon the Russian people seeing the advantages of a Western establishment in the country; the popular choice of the reinstatement of a new Tsar could only proceed under the proposed leadership of Michael. He again emphasised to Michael that he was a popular choice with the Allied Commanders. He then pointed out that there would be no intent to reinstate Nicholas on the throne. Nicholas had many opportunities to change the Constitution and provide workers' rights, demanded for so long, but had squandered his chances for reorganising Russia with some social reform and power to the population.

Michael's reply was circumspect. He said he was a very willing participant of the new order but had concerns that none of the post-peace arrangements had been tabled, and insisted that he was made fully aware of these plans now. Churchill was taken aback by this direct approach and he had to admit that this was policy which was not under his control, but assured Michael that there would be a benign new order. The purposes would be to restore Russia back to greatness, join the Western alliances and go forward in peace, security and prosperity. This pro-Western pact would assure Russia that they would never again be under fear of invasion from any of the central powers, as a pact would ensure non-aggression in the future alliance.

Michael was not to be taken in easily by these grand words, and enquired whether these ideals would be incorporated into any official treaty terms, which would be agreed and signed before any invasion were to occur.

Churchill sought to comfort Michael in the knowledge that these would be discussions for the British Prime Minister and his Cabinet. The treaty in full would be dealt with at a meeting of the Western Powers at a secret rendezvous on the East Yorkshire coast, which was the next destination as agreed with Michael under the Reilly plan.

Michael then announced that he had his own agenda and manifesto of how he would see the improved conditions in the lives of Russians, the new government, and the roles of the Western Powers in Russia after the end of conflict. Churchill mused this point as a departure from where he wanted the discussion to move and asked Michael directly if he could see that manifesto and comment on the probabilities and possibilities. Michael then turned to Johnson who had the manifesto in his briefcase, and asked him to produce it. Johnson became alarmed and asked to retire to an anteroom with Michael to have a five-minute recess. Churchill looked at Admiral Jellicoe, who had remained attentive but silent to that point, and they agreed that this protocol was in order.

Michael and Johnson left and entered the anteroom which was adjacent to the board room. They sat down in a corner as far away as possible from the boardroom door, and began a conversation in hushed whispers. Johnson reminded Michael that there was nothing of substance in Churchill's words and that he was merely placating them. It seemed that Churchill was a master planner of the invasion and tactics, and had very little understanding of Russia or any idea of how the post-conflict stage would look.

He strongly advised Michael to hold his powder dry and not release any information at this stage, as it was obvious that Churchill, once seeing it, would take all the details and transmit them by wire to London as soon as they left the meeting. If any advantage was to be gained, then it was at Scarborough, in a face-to-face meeting with the Powers. Johnson, being the excellent brinksman that he was, would orchestrate a position to put Michael in the seat of power with their demands. He reminded Michael that he himself was the whole key to the success of the invasion and without him it was quite possible that the invasion would stall, or not take place at all.

Michael quickly understood what his long-time confidante and friend was saying, and that the game of poker had just started. However, it would be a poor show if they simply returned and rebuked Churchill, and they needed something of major importance to lay on the table as a concern so that it would blindside them from the real meat of the proposals yet to be laid before the Allied conference in Scarborough. Johnson thought quickly, and announced that the main question should be the intervention of the Japanese at Vladivostok.

This seemed like a logical concern of major importance, as it had not been too long ago that Russia was at war with Japan over Manchuria and, more to the point, that the Japanese Navy had trounced the Russian Navy into an ignominious defeat. Any participation of Japan would leave the Russian people in bewilderment as to the real intentions of the West, and no doubt be counterproductive to any invasion plan which relied upon the goodwill and support of Russia at large from all sectors of society.

Therefore, it was agreed that they should go back into the meeting and simply put that major concern to Churchill in the hope that he would see the danger of his own plan failing due to the huge mistake they could make in carrying out the invasion. Agreed. They then walked back into the meeting and took their places with a degree of confidence.

Michael then proposed that the main concern, amongst

other minor points which they would put forward to the conference, was the equation of the Japanese and Manchuria. After Michael had explained at length that he was very supportive of the invasion, he pointed out that it would be a serious mistake to include the Japanese at Vladivostok. He went on to qualify this would not be tolerated by Russia, due to the recent loss of a naval war with the Japanese. Therefore, for the sake of the success of the mission and the support of the Russian population from all sectors, he would be asking the Western Allies to abandon that position. Michael felt confident that the threat to the Bolsheviks being directly in the west of Russia would quickly bring them victory, and would render the invasion at Vladivostok pointless.

Churchill pondered that point in earnest and consulted openly with Admiral Jellicoe. Jellicoe quickly agreed, as he himself had deep reservations of that position taken by Churchill in his planning. Allowing the Japanese to gain a strong presence in eastern Russia would inevitably become a real threat to the British Royal Navy, which generally ruled the world and the waves through its massive power. After defeating the German Navy they would then be faced with a much strengthened Japanese Navy with an excellent power base in East Asia from where it could threaten not only Britain but the western seaboard of the United States. The raw materials which they would end up extracting from East Russia and Manchuria would feed their own aspirations of ship-building and the proven efficiency they had matured in the last few decades would become a worldwide threat.

Churchill was impressed at this inspired thinking from Michael and Johnson, and was ready to agree to that caveat, which had Jellicoe's approval. Churchill then volunteered to seek approval very quickly for that part of the plan to be omitted, and said he would wire London immediately, and provide Michael with the answer during the journey.

On that apparent bright note the meeting ended, and both Churchill and Jellicoe thanked Michael for his attendance and even more so for the insight he had given toward the alteration of the Churchill Plan.

Michael and Johnson were quite pleased that they had been able to conduct themselves with a certain amount of presence of mind, their main achievement being the non-disclosure of the Johnson Prometheus Manifesto.

They then left the meeting room and once again went to the bridge. The Captain, who was reading the latest weather reports, had a concerned look on his face as he had just been informed that storm-force winds were approaching and it would mean setting the ship in the next three hours to a storm condition. He explained that all hatches, portholes and companionways would be battened down, with most of the watertight doors locked shut. This would mean that all non-duty personnel would be confined to quarters.

They thought that the best thing for the rest of the day was a guided tour of this great leviathan they were in before lock-down. They lingered for another thirty minutes or so, just taking in the breath-taking views of the Arctic Ocean under calm conditions, but noticed a more definite swell developing and sea spray being more prominent on the bow. Jack arrived on the bridge and joined them in light conversation. Michael asked if they could be shown around the ship. Jack enquired with the Captain to seek permission and was told that the tour would be best made the following day due to the impending storm. Soon they would be required to return to quarters. That was agreed, and Jack then escorted them back to the cabin where Baldric would be on hand to provide a dinner from the officers' menu.

Baldric was in the dining room fettering around and remarked on his surprise to see them both return as early as they had, since they had such an important meeting that morning. Jack then bade them farewell and asked Baldric to come to his quarters after taking the orders for lunch.

Johnson then turned his attention to the two precious suitcases which were stored under the bed, which he noticed had been disturbed. Pulling both out he examined the locks and found that both had been forced open, as each lock mechanism had fresh damage around the metal keyholes.

He beckoned Michael and inserted the keys into each lock, and opened the cases to discover that the locked Gladstone bags, briefcase, and shell canister were still there. However, on closer inspection of one of the Gladstone bags, he found it to be unlocked and again with slight damage around the key hole, which suggested that the lock had been forcibly prized open.

He was astonished to discover that the contents were untouched and checked this against the inventory placed in each bag, which he had listed to the last diamond. The canister was still sealed and could only be opened with a hacksaw without knowledge of the secret opening mechanism. This was a relief but also a mystery and a concern, as the perpetrator was not a thief but could be a spy. That could only be Baldric, in his view, and Michael readily agreed. This meant that Baldric was in fact with Jack, working for MI6, and they would have to be very circumspect about what they said and how they acted during the remainder of the journey. It was clear now that MI6 were aware they were carrying a hoard of immense wealth, as the inspection of the opened Gladstone bag would have given a trained person a good idea of the value, and given the volume of the other bags, they would know the combined value.

Johnson had an idea which would flush out Baldric to some extent. Baldric arrived around 1900 hours with dinner and laid out the fayre on the table in front of them. Johnson had made a point of chatting to Baldric in a friendly manner and suggested that he join them at the table for a glass of wine whilst they ate. Baldric was more than happy to oblige as if he were a spy then it would be in his interest to communicate more with Michael.

The conversation then spun around to Baldric and his service history. Baldric being in his mid-fifties was quite likely to have had a previous life of some interest. He mentioned that he had started life as a diamond cutter in Amsterdam and had worked for a while with Cartier and Fabergé in Russia. That explained to some extent his gentle manner and his ability to speak fluent Russian.

Michael then stepped up the discussion, showing great interest, and pulled from his private leather wallet a very fine necklace with a single ruby attached as a pendant, which Natasha had given to him before he left Gatchina. Michael said he had the idea that he would try and sell it in Hatton Garden whilst in Britain, and sought the view of Baldric as to its value in the hope that he might reveal some expert view.

Baldric was utterly amazed at the quality and weight of the ruby which bedecked the fine gold handcrafted necklace. Now he was off guard and in his own world of jewellery, he mentioned that it was a Cartier piece and he would not like to put a value on it as it was worth far more than he had ever known a pendant necklace to be. However, he did mention that there was at least £75,000 worth of weight, and more when considering the very high quality of workmanship and the size of the perfect ruby and its cutting.

He asked how Michael may have got hold of such a piece. In fact, he knew exactly who Michael and Johnson were, but was still carrying out his disguise as an Able Seaman. Michael simply replied that it was rumoured to be of the Romanov Dynasty and with all the chaos and theft going on in Russia, it was likely to be true.

With that, Michael then put it back into his wallet and thanked Baldric. But he was amused at the high value Baldric had placed upon it, and thought that it was a correct valuation as he had previously brought it to the attention of Stopford at Gatchina, who was equally excited at the thought of it being made available for sale. He thanked Baldric as he left for being such interesting company during dinner.

Michael gave Johnson a knowing look, and thanked him for being ever vigilant. Now they knew they were being watched. They also knew that the Allies would be informed of the wealth that they were carrying and were now on their guard as to what might lay before them.

The storm was now setting in and so they decided to sleep through it and hope that they would not become too uncomfortable during the night. Michael slept very well, but for Johnson it was a night of misery and sickness as the continuing rolling and buffeting, together with the raging noise of wind and sea, were not to his liking.

Baldric arrived in the morning time, at 0800 hours, with breakfast. Johnson asked Baldric how he had fared during the storm and he declared that he was of such a constitution that he revelled in the rocking and rolling and had spent much of the time with the other off-duty seamen in getting merry and losing – as usual – his hands of cards; but he always made amends with chess and backgammon.

With the mention of chess, Johnson enlivened his interest in this fellow and challenged him to a game of chess later in the day. Johnson was good – very good indeed – and had been unbeatable for several years amongst his peers at the University of Petrograd.

After breakfast, Michael and Johnson dressed in fatigues in readiness for Jack to arrive to take them on a tour of the ship. During the tour, which lasted a full hour, they saw the incredible workings of a magnificent battleship and were utterly amazed at the power and prestige this ship could impose in both war and peace. The deck was a mesmerising area of weaponry and, not least, the massive array of gun turrets arranged in two banks each fore and aft carrying two x 13.5-inch barrels and a turret amidship, ten in total, which could deliver one hell of a broadside up to 5 miles with great accuracy. The sides of the ship were bristling with a multitude of 6-inch guns.

Michael's eye then noticed that there was a huge tarpaulin-covered frame to the aft of the rear funnell and asked Jack what was beneath that covering. He replied it was a very fast seaplane which had been designed at the outset of war to race. Michael became excited as he had developed a passion for air racing when he was in the UK, and had been set up to co-pilot a Blackburn Type L in a Circuit of Britain race, but this had been abandoned at the outbreak of war in August 1914.

Jack listened with interest to Michael reminiscing, and let him continue, as he knew of Michael's love of sea flight. Michael went on to tell him that he had become a friend of the designer Robert Blackburn and had conducted several sea trials at Filey Bay on the east coast of Yorkshire.

Jack then said rather excitedly to Michael, 'Come with me!'

They disappeared into the cavern of tarpaulin and Michael suddenly was standing underneath the port wing of his beloved Type L. This took his breath away and before he could say much more, Jack had climbed into the co-pilot's seat and had invited Michael to join him in the pilot's seat. Michael rushed after him and was suddenly engulfed in feelings of adventure and nostalgia, once again sitting in the cockpit which took him lovingly back to the halcyon days of freedom. Michael explained to Jack that he had become quite expert in the Type L's flying and handling characteristics and it was planned that he would be flying with a sea plane during the journey back to Russia.

Jack then told Michael his flight plans may change in rather different circumstances. He explained that should at any point the *Iron Duke* not be able to make it to Scapa Flow, or be delayed beyond the critical timetable which had been set, then he would be invited to continue the journey in the Type L, either to mainland Britain or, in the worst case scenario, to Norway, where he would be contacted and sent to Oslo and be taken over to Scarborough by the Royal Norwegian Navy. Michael was taken aback by this amount of detailed planning, and was excited to realise that he was such a vital part of the journey action plans.

'That is why we are carrying the Type L instead of the usual Sopwith Baby, as we knew of your exploits with Robert Blackburn and that you could handle this situation if it arose. Should that case arise, then she will be offloaded by crane onto the lee side of the ship for best protection with you and Johnson on board', Jack explained.

15

Unescorted Home Run

They were then invited to the bridge. When they arrived, they could see that they were approaching land fast, and wondered why they were heading so close to shore. The captain explained that they had lost the attendance of one of the destroyers during the storm, due to a reduction in engine power, and were now seeking shelter in a fjord to await the arrival of the slower destroyer. The remaining destroyer still alongside would patrol the mouth of the fjord, on the lookout for any submarine activity. It was naval policy (especially under these circumstances when they were carrying VIPs), that they would only make steam again when they had a two-destroyer escort, meaning that they had to wait for the other destroyer to catch up.

Once the *Iron Duke* had found shelter in a safe fjord it would anchor and hope that within two hours the second destroyer would have made repairs and be back on station, protecting the *Iron Duke*.

As soon as the anchor was dropped a portly gentleman arrived on the bridge in unidentifiable naval fatigues, wearing a greatcoat and a woollen cap pulled over his ears.

He was carrying a box of oil paints and an easel, which he began to set up on the port side of the bridge. Michael and Johnson wandered over to the artist, who stood up to greet them.

He pulled out a cigar wallet from his inside pocket and announced, 'Gentlemen, please join me in a cigar and a glass of port.'

They then recognised the man in disguise as being Winston Churchill. They relished the thought of a cigar and port on the bridge of the *Iron Duke*, and in the company of a First Sea Lord. They chatted for a while and were interested at how expertly Churchill was applying the scenery to canvas.

After two hours had passed it seemed that the concerns on the face of the Captain had deepened. Jellicoe was asked to come to the bridge. Then a signals officer rushed onto the bridge, saluted the Captain, and thrust a decoded Morse message into his hands.

The captain showed a vivid turn of colour from ruddy red to sallow yellow. He turned to Jellicoe who was now anxious to read the same message. He then requested that Churchill, Michael and Johnson should return to their cabins with haste. Churchill in his inimitable style of forthright demands insisted that he must know the reason why. The captain announced that the lame destroyer could still only muster half-speed and was now actively being tracked by two U-boats.

This meant that the remaining escorting destroyer must go to her aid, and they would wait until darkness in the next hour and then break anchor and carry on the remainder of the journey under cover of darkness alone. Fortunately, the sea was still strong but was due to quieten when they entered the North Sea, where there would be clearing skies. The *Iron Duke* was seemingly well hidden in the fjord and it would remain until dark, where they would raise anchor and make a dash for home.

Jellicoe decided that radio silence from now on was imperative, as a triangulation from any submarines in the area would easily pinpoint the *Iron Duke* and more than likely give clues to her route into Scapa Flow. So they dare not signal for assistance by requesting the arrival of any destroyers from Scapa Flow.

It was a further fourteen hours or so before daybreak and the final part of the dash for port in daylight unprotected was a serious risk. Michael and Johnson were led back to their cabin for the remainder of the day.

Johnson felt that the next few hours should be spent engaged in chess, which would exercise his mind in a leisurely victory over Baldric. There was something about this chap which was deep and sinister, and well disguised, and he wanted to crack him open a bit further to discover what inner strength of intelligence he possessed. Baldric duly joined Johnson with some eagerness, as he had taken a similar view of Johnson and was suspecting that he could be a worthy adversary in chess warfare.

Johnson and Baldric sat down at the dining table to commence battle, whilst Michael lay back on his bunk to catch up on his diary and spend the rest of the time in boredom, as he had no interest in chess whatsoever. His thoughts soon turned to Natasha and his son George, and he suddenly realised that if anything were to fail on this journey than he may well never see his family again.

The first game was easily won by Johnson, who had been concerned that the opening phase of the battle suggested that he could get trounced by Baldric. However, as the game entered the final phase he was surprised to discover that elementary mistakes were being made by Baldric, and thus thought that this guy was a lucky fool who had by some means put him on the ropes in the main part of the game.

The second game was much longer, and again Johnson was worried that he would, for the first time in many games, be bound to lose. However, in a flurry of quick exchanges in the latter part when Johnson was certain that his defences were inevitably to crumble, he was surprised to see that he could take a queen and a castle in quick succession, and soon had a checkmate. Johnson felt now that he was being toyed with but would not admit it to himself as it was an attack on his ability. He thought about quitting whilst he was ahead but Baldric was insistent that he should be allowed to at least draw, and so another two games would follow.

The third game's opening gambits created the usual pressing and clever attacks by Baldric. Baldric on this occasion did not falter, and quickly and very expertly despatched Johnson. Johnson now dreaded the final game, as he was now convinced he was up against a grand master. Surely enough, in the opening gambit he was astonished to see how his defences were brought down with such speed, and the end came very quickly.

Johnson was relieved that he had at least made a draw of the game. However, he thought that with one last game he could deliver the final blow, so he challenged Baldric to 'speed chess', which meant that each player could take no more than an agreed three seconds to respond. He thought this might just give him the edge. Baldric obliged.

Johnson thought that the only way was to get him was in four moves in a 'fool's mate', thinking that this clever fellow would fall for that, it being so simple a procedure that he just might overlook it. The game started, and in less than thirty seconds of play Johnson banged the table and thrust his face into Baldric's and declared very slowly, 'Fool's mate. Mate!' Johnson ever the expert brinksman had again kept his cool and daring intact and was overjoyed that his reputation of being a winner in so many arenas had once again been retained.

Baldric rose slowly and complimented Johnson, and declared that he had indeed for the first time in years of never losing (other than purposely, as in the first two games, as his disguise) had indeed become a fool at chess. After Baldric left, he still wondered… did he let him deliver a fool's mate? He would never know!

It was now early evening and the *Iron Duke* had not yet pulled up anchor, as was expected for the home run. Baldric came to their cabin and informed them that they were still hopeful that the two destroyers would be able to return, and the Captain was being prudent as he was aware of Admiralty rules for a battleship under steam on its own. A few hours later they heard the anchor chains clanking to the fore of the ship, and became hopeful that the two destroyers had returned and that they would be relatively safe for the home run. Amidst the powerful throb of the engines, the crew once again held their breath as they pulled away from the fjord and into uncertain waters.

16

U-Boat Attacks

It was now the fifth day of their adventure and day was breaking in the northern winter waters of the North Sea. Michael and Johnson, after breakfast, and now knowing the route to the bridge, decided to join Jellicoe, Churchill and the Captain. They found all three in deep conference, discussing tactics should they become the prey of any submarine. Jellicoe and Churchill were both grim-faced. Michael and Johnson were surprised to see that there was no destroyer escort and wondered what had happened.

The Admiral, whilst small in stature, held strong beliefs in his own personality and wisdom. He had no fear, sought no favour with any establishment, and ruled by discipline and order. However, he became muted when his significance was set aside as he was brought to unfair account for his handling of the Battle of Jutland. Therefore, he was now more of a naval political figure, and would be wheeled out as occasions required. However, when opportunities arose for him to excel and put down the ghosts of past contradiction and failure, then he was the best around, in meeting the enemy head on.

Michael enquired why they were alone on the high seas. Churchill gave them a decoded message to read which had come in during the night from Scapa Flow, which was urgent and had broken radio silence. The message read that the two destroyers had been sunk, but one had been abandoned after extreme damage and the inevitability that she would sink. Scuttling charges had been set, but had failed to blow. However, whilst sinking slowly, she had been boarded by one of the U-boat's crew and vital secret documents had been extracted just before she sank. The papers would have told them of the presence of the *Iron Duke*, now alone. It was likely that there would be a surface attack awaiting them by a wolf pack. The final part of the message read that assistance was being sent.

It seemed that with full speed steaming they should make the Scapa Flow anchorage by mid-evening. The mood was becoming lighter, with some optimism as they now had a clear run and had the greater speed over U-boats. There was no chance that any submarine could chase the *Iron Duke* and catch her; the only method they had of interception was to lie ahead in wait.

At that moment, a klaxon sounded and the Captain's voice instructed all men to action stations as a submarine had just surfaced two miles ahead just off the port beam. Within two minutes of that warning there was another call to action: three miles off the starboard beam another submarine had surfaced. And within a minute of that warning there were two more subs sighted at 45 degrees to the *Iron Duke* on either side. A well-laid trap had been set and it seemed that to avoid any torpedoes the *Iron Duke* would have to turn about.

However, the closing speeds would not allow for that to happen in any measure of safety as this would show her broadside to those ahead, and as she turned through 60 degrees the same could be said of the boats to each side. All the forward and aft turret guns were now trained on each of the U-boats.

The *Iron Duke* shook from side to side as quick-succession fire commenced with guns pointed as low as possible, but at fast closing speed it was becoming more difficult to provide accuracy. Both forward U-boats were being drenched in plumes of water as explosives sent spray reaching twenty metres high, but the scoring was scattered around both boats and with no obvious hits. The forward U-boats were holding their course on what was becoming a suicide mission if they did not submerge. Suddenly, with half a mile remaining, both boats simultaneously dived, but not before unleashing four torpedoes which seemed to be skimming on the surface at high speed.

Jellicoe had anticipated that would be their tactic and had twenty seconds earlier swung the wheel hard to port. With a following wind which had increased in strength only an hour before, it was hoped to assist the turn of the swerve and hopefully escape the onrushing danger.

Fortunately, the torpedoes had not been set at a spread pattern, so they were concentrating on an inward arc which meant that the point of designated contact would be one focal point. It was clear that the U-boat Commanders had to decide whether the *Iron Duke* would go for a breakthrough and ram which would benefit a focused point of strike, or indeed try to swerve away.

The U-boat Commanders had chosen wrong, as the

turning arc of the *Iron Duke* was beginning to tell, and it was with relief that those on board saw the swing work out just in time. All torpedoes cleared the giant ship and sped through the churning water aft of her.

This swerve now put the *Duke* on course to negotiate the oncoming port attack from U-boat number three head on. Again, the closing speed was fast, and the same tactic was now left as the only option for the U-boat, hoping to have delivered its torpedoes as a broadside. However, there was a chance that the slight spread they had engaged in the settings might produce a hit if the *Iron Duke* were to turn at such a late stage in the attack.

Seeing the release of four more torpedoes, Jellicoe was left with the only option, which was to bear down on the U-boat and hope that the torpedoes would miss the target. The hope was that a narrow target would suffice for the torpedoes to slide by.

It was fortunate that the interval between firing each shot had been around fifteen seconds, as could be seen from the crow's nest lookout. The observer could see that the swell of the waves in the rising wind had caused a slight deviation of the sub whilst firing from slow speed, which had provided a bias on the shots. One torpedo would clearly miss, but the second was running true towards the bow, and it was clear that the *Duke* had to change course by a few degrees to allow that shot to pass by on the port side.

This information was quickly sent by voice tube to the Captain, who trusted his lookout who had been trained to a very high standard. Without any question Jellicoe ordered a five degree turn to starboard, and waited and watched through the remaining ten seconds to impact in deadly silence. The foam trail from the torpedo was now becoming clear. The closing speed was around 50 kph, and the fate of the *Iron Duke* was now sealed.

Number 1 torpedo had passed within 10 metres off the port bow, and number two was certainly going to hit head on. The course was set, and there was nothing to do for the next fifteen seconds as the *Duke* negotiated the remaining torpedo. Number 2 came head on and there was a thump dead on the bow, then a huge explosion which shot a plume of spray skyward. It was a direct hit, but the advantage was that it hit the ramming bow which was of high-tensile steel and plate some 12 inches thick. There were also four watertight doors on the bow bulkheads which could take a considerable impact with some safety from the ingress of seawater. It seemed that there was no deviation to the speed or direction of the *Iron Duke* as she progressed inexorably on the same chosen path to engage with number 3 torpedo.

Number 3 was now approaching, and it seemed there could be contact with one of the anti-torpedo bulges which had been fitted in 1917 as an extra protection against side-on hits which would blow the outer bulge and thus by and large protect the thick armour plating of the hull. Sure enough, it was a hit, and the ship heeled over to port with a deafening explosion. Again the *Iron Duke* was engulfed in a skyward plume of fire, steam and sea spray.

Torpedo 4 was seen to be passing by 15 metres abreast of the hull, and the *Iron Duke* was now safe from U-boats 1, 2 and 3. With all attention being turned to the attack by U-Boat 3, it now became clear that Jellicoe would need to deal with U-boat 4 which was astern of the *Iron*

Duke and attempting to close. U-boat 4 fired off four torpedoes at five-second intervals, and dived, as the guns of the Duke were finding their target and the U-boat was a sitting duck.

Because the *Iron Duke* had turned away from U-boat 1 and towards U-boat 3, it meant that the torpedoes from U-boat 4 were on a chase pattern, but could hit her rear starboard. The torpedoes not only had to gain 1 kilometre of travel, but also had to catch the fast disappearing aft quarters of the ship. The speed had now been cut to around 20 kph due to torpedo damage, and it seemed it would be a close chase to distance her from the four torpedoes.

The lookout focused his attention to the four oncoming shots, which were steadily gaining. Again, it was pointless to turn, as that would slow the ship and show the vulnerable broadside. There was no choice but to keep full power, even though she had been slowed by the hit on the bows, in the hope that the torpedoes would run out of gas before they caught up.

The lookout kept a running commentary shouting down the voice tube: 'Closing 100 metres 1, 2, 3 and 4. Closing 75 metres. Closing 50 metres 1 slowing. Closing 30 metres 2 slowing and 1 stopped. Closing 20 metres 3 slowing and 2 stopped. Closing 10 metres 3 stopped 4 running. Closing zero 4 running. Closing 4 running and passing. 4 running and 2 metres off starboard. 4 running and at bow. 4 running ahead. *The danger is past. 4 slowing and stopping.*'

Then there was a huge explosion and the superstructure of the port U-boat was blown to the surface. The torpedo which passed the battleship, having stopped had sank onto the third U-boat striking her and had created a Red on Red loss.

The Captain quickly asked for damage reports from both strikes. Fifteen minutes later the bow damage was reported as frontal armour blown off and two watertight compartments flooded, but with no further water penetration. This damage had influenced the speed and had crippled her to the extent of about 25 per cent loss of forward speed.

There was loud cheering through the ship, and it was agreed that Jellicoe had taken the correct tactical decisions and the *Iron Duke* had won through. The joy was reinforced later in the day when the lookout reported that there were smoke trails dead ahead, and the incoming Morse coded message revealed two destroyers were racing out from Scapa to provide a protective shield for the remainder of the journey.

The threat of the U-boats was no more, as they would need to regroup for any further attacks and this was now impossible. The only other threat would be from other U-boats in the area, and these would be easily dealt with by the fast incoming destroyers.

Everybody on the bridge was in a state of euphoria, hugging each other in relief at their escape and at seeing help on the horizon. Jellicoe was first to break off and resume his solemn stance. He coughed and said loudly, "Back to stations, gentlemen, and well done. God Save the King." From all ranks of sailors from the bridge downwards there was a unified rendition of 'Rule Britannia'.

Michael returned to his cabin very shaken and lay on his bunk in a state of deep depression. His thoughts were solely directed to the report that both destroyers had been sunk on

the northern cape of Norway, and he could only imagine
the huge distress that this venture had caused the families
of those sailors who had given their lives for the sake of the
re-establishment of the throne. How many more men would
die in this cause to create for Michael a comfortable future
life as the head of the Russian Empire?

Baldric joined Michael and Johnson in their cabin
with sandwiches and cocoa, with the intention to enquire
how they were feeling after the U-boat adventure. Johnson
was now of a mind to ask Baldric more directly exactly
what his position was in the crew, as he was absolutely
certain that he was not an Able Seaman. He was convinced
that his duties were covert, and he had been placed in a
position to monitor their activities and conversations and
report back to Jack.

Baldric turned to meet the enquiry full on, and was
rather proud to announce that he was an officer in Naval
Intelligence, and indeed his position on board was to keep
them under surveillance and report any unusual behaviour.
Johnson was pleased at this honesty and saw in Baldric
a kindred spirit of service and loyalty. Michael rose from
his bunk and announced to Johnson that, as usual, he was
again right in his assessment of people and situations.

Now that the three were more relaxed and open
together, Johnson ventured to dig a little deeper into the
life of Jellicoe, as rumours had filtered into Russia just
after the battle at Jutland over his abilities and the defeat
of the British at the hands of the Germans. At least,
this was the German propaganda, which seemed to be
carrying a great deal of weight in Europe; and to some
extent the abilities of Jellicoe were also being questioned

in British political circles. Now knowing that Baldric was in the hierarchy of Naval Intelligence, perhaps he could throw some light on this, especially as he had just witnessed a very bold, brave and imaginative encounter with the German U-boats, and wondered why this man had been branded a failure.

Johnson, being a very astute person, had realised during the battle that Jellicoe seemed to be relishing the engagement, and took direct control in an aggressive way which seemed to be at odds with his otherwise calm and patient characteristics. He also noted that Churchill as First Sea Lord was sitting at the rear of the bridge and appeared to be taking very little interest in the manoeuvres, and he had noted that there was a certain level of coldness and mistrust evident between the two men.

Baldric sat back and sighed with a concerned look on his face, as he felt Johnson should have a reply of some substance in view of the close position he held with Michael. A fudge was not appropriate, and Johnson was a man of intelligence and perception, so some degree of honesty was appropriate. Before he started to reveal the circumstance, Baldric asked Johnson to swear he would maintain a level of secrecy, as he was a party to most of the Naval Intelligence at the time of the action and could reveal his interpretation of the events. Johnson was eager to swear his confidence to whatever Baldric was about to reveal.

Baldric recounted that Jellicoe had effectively just been sacked two months prior to taking command of this journey, due to the mounting criticism being levelled at him for his apparent cowardice in not engaging with the German High

Seas Fleet in a sea battle which was fought off the Jutland peninsula close to Denmark in May 1916.

The British had been seeking a major engagement with the Germans to destroy their fleet in open waters, as the British Navy had a greater advantage in battleships, support vessels and a seemingly more robust and efficient navy. Admiral Scheer also felt ready to promote a similar battle for the same reasons, and was confident that he had the power to smash the British. So, the inevitable scene was to be played out and it was hoped that the winner would take all and the war would be won by the victor at sea, and the losing side would soon sue for peace.

The opportunity came in 1916 as the Germans were generally tied up at their anchorage at Wilhelmshaven, and they needed decisive action to release this bondage. After a successful campaign their purpose and strategy would be to engage with and sink cargo vessels, assisting in the U-boat campaign to starve Britain into submission. The British Navy was using the same tactic to do the same to Germany. A sea battle was inevitable as both sides sought the destruction of the other, which would change the course of the war.

Scheer started the opening moves when he decided to send Admiral Hipper's fast scouting group of five battlecruisers on a course of action to attack the British coastline, in the hope that he would lure Admiral Beatty's squadron towards the main German High Seas Fleet and a waiting pack of U-boats set in a picket line. If he could destroy Beatty, then knowing that Jellicoe was a rather more cautious tactician he hoped to either engage him on a more equal footing in numbers or to tie him up with the remainder of the British fleet at their home base and anchorage at Scapa Flow and turn the tables on the British, rendering them harmless. However, the German plan was altered due to bad weather and the scout group were ordered to the Jutland area, where they could attack British cargo vessels and perhaps open the blockade into the Baltic.

Unbeknown to the German Navy, British Naval Intelligence had picked up the scent of these manoeuvres and sent Beatty to intercept Hipper and bring him to battle, knowing that Jellicoe was leaving Scapa Flow with the remainder of the fleet to back him up. Beatty engaged in the only real battle and losses were heavy on both sides. Seeing that he was now at a disadvantage with weaponry and loss of capital ships, he decided to withdraw northwards and hope to lure Hipper into the path of Jellicoe who was steaming south to assist him.

Hipper took the bait and made chase. Hours later he was astonished to be met by the British main fleet which was directly in his path and was bearing down to attack. Hipper, seeing the trap, turned and laid mines in retreat. Also, he sent forward his fast destroyers which were ordered to cover his escape by using torpedoes to deflect Jellicoe from an effective chase. Matters were made worse for Jellicoe by poor visibility and the night drawing in.

Assessing the situation Jellico found that he would be at a distinct disadvantage if he gave chase, so he made the momentous decision to correctly play safe and withdraw his forces back to Scapa Flow with the remainder of Beatty's fleet. Following this regrouping, and contrary to the growing accusations he faced in the aftermath of being too cautious and even of cowardice, he in fact saved Britain's greatest assets and therefore could keep up the blockade of the Jutland peninsula, and maintain access to the North Sea, which helped to continue the policy of attempting to starve Germany to defeat by denying it a route to the importation of foodstuffs and war materiels. Effectively the German High Seas Fleet were back under lock and key after a break-out from prison.

This was a key decision and was honourably noteworthy. Instead, a barrage of abuse and personal attacks were his reward, generated by the Admiralty and politicians. Future history, in Baldric's view, would vindicate Jellicoe and raise him to a status more in keeping with his correct judgement in using the information he had at the time.

Churchill was one of his adversaries in promulgating these apparent failures, and was aided by Beatty. In fact, Baldric felt that Beatty should not have been so arrogant as to engage with the German fleet, as he had no knowledge of its size, and he should have shadowed Hipper and reported the positions and lain in wait for the main forces to arrive.

It seemed, then, that Beatty had failed, and he was reported to have blamed the quality of his ships rather than his own tactical command. Baldric's view was that this internal fighting was unjust, and it seemed that Beatty's continued grievance was somewhat of a cover to his own failure. He was a popular man and ingratiated himself as a hero in the political circles of society. By contrast, Jellicoe was a quiet and private man whose actions were always well grounded in balance of probabilities, and who would always prefer to be safe rather than sorry, especially as so many lives were at stake. Beatty's failure was at a high cost of lives on both sides, and it was very much inconclusive as to who had won the battle and what it had achieved. It seemed that the British had lost twice as many more lives and capital ships. Around 8,500 men from both sides were reported as dead and missing in the day's action.

Baldric concluded his account, with Michael listening impassively without much comment, and Johnson on the edge of his seat, showing great interest in the history of men and machines in that episode. Baldric proudly stated that the ship they were on, HMS *Iron Duke*, was the flagship of Jellicoe's fleet at the Battle of Jutland, and from that very same bridge he had conducted his battle campaign with the German High Seas Fleet.

Johnson was absorbed by this brief and apparently accurate account of the actions and motivations leading to the downfall of Jellicoe. His thoughts turned to how he must have been feeling during the earlier exchanges with the U-boats, and he may have been re-enacting his battle at Jutland, this time intent on proving to Churchill and the world that he was more than fit and able to carry the war to the enemy.

He replied to Baldric that what he had seen earlier that day in terms of the confrontation and astute tactics against the four U-boats should vindicate Jellicoe and underline his notable abilities, as he faced the enemy full on in beating off the attack. The damage sustained could have been a lot worse in the face of such aggression, and he fought on knowing he had to complete his mission of getting Michael to the British mainland to continue with the very important and world-changing plans that lay afoot.

Johnson thought to himself that, had Beatty been in

full command at Jutland, with his heroic and self-serving 'gung ho' approach to naval warfare under the prevailing conditions which did not favour such action, then had he attempted to get through the German mines and massed attack of torpedo carrying destroyers, his decision could easily have ended in the loss of the Grand Fleet. As it was then, it should be argued that Jellicoe's command was the saving of the Grand Fleet and could prove yet to be a war-winning outcome. 'Could Nelson have done any better?' he mused.

From what Baldric had described, it seemed clear now why Churchill wanted to take a back seat and to observe how Jellicoe would engage with the attack at first hand. Their coolness towards each other, which he had observed when they arrived on board and met for the first time, was now explicable.

Johnson thanked Baldric for his openness and assured him as he left that he would keep the confidence entrusted to him. Johnson begged one more question from Baldric. Why was Jellicoe in command of the *Iron Duke* now, when he had been removed from active service only a few months ago? Baldric was quick to reply that he was chosen as the best man for the job, for his intimate knowledge of the ship and the crew, together with his calculating care and caution which should ensure a successful outcome of what was a dangerous journey with only two escorting ships. Jellicoe had jumped at the chance as being his 'last hurrah' in command of his beloved ship. Maybe he was secretly hoping that this would be a journey of adventure, as it had turned out to be. However, whatever the outcome, even if it had resulted in complete failure, the annals of history would never record this event, and it would be lost in the mists of time at the hands of MI6.

17

Sea Plane to Scarborough

Approaching Scapa Flow, the timetable of the passengers was now in jeopardy due to the much slower speed from the damage at the ship's bow. An hour or so after the U-boat engagement, Jack came to Michael's cabin with a concerned look on his face, and asked how Michael felt about taking the seaplane to its final destination in Filey Bay.

He explained that they were now several hours behind schedule and further delays in docking and catch-up time could only be made up by taking a direct flight on the Type L. Another reason which was more to do with Admiralty pragmatism, was that the *Iron Duke* needed to dock in Glasgow to undergo urgent repairs to her bow. The route plan was to fly to an RFC base in Scapa for refuelling and overnight stay, and then onwards to Scarborough with a stopover for refuelling at RFC Acklington in Northumbria.

Michael was quite amazed at this turn of events and suddenly felt a rush of anxiety and trepidation at being asked to perform a duty which he was well versed in, but he had not been at the controls of a seaplane for four years. Michael saw the earnest look on Jack's face and knew his only answer could be 'Yes.'

'Thank you,' replied Jack, and asked Michael to pack only essential clothing. Michael exclaimed that he must take the two suitcases and would not leave without them. Jack reluctantly agreed, as he knew exactly what Michael was carrying, but was fearful of Michael crashing into the sea and perhaps losing his life. He rationalised that if that were the case, it would be likely that the whole invasion would be called off. So what about the jewels? They did belong to Michael.

Michael called Johnson from the Officers Mess where he was once again engaged in a battle of wits against Baldric, only this time it was backgammon. He informed him that they were about to become 'Heroes or Zeros', and the next leg of the journey was a critical calculation of Michael's flying ability. He asked Johnson if he wanted to join him, as the plan was that he would be in Scarborough for the meeting and his guile and intellect was needed to gain the best deal from the Allies.

Johnson, very aware of his friend's dire need of his presence, announced, disguising his fear totally, 'My friend and master, I have been close to you since childhood and your servant for the last six years. No circumstance could ever exist where I would not be at your side, and this circumstance you present to me is no exception.'

With that vote of confidence, they both packed small satchels and carried a jewellery-laden suitcase each to the flight deck where the Type L was ticking away having its engine warmed and pre-flight checks made. There they were met by two seamen who had a set of fur-lined trousers, jackets and goggles for each of them, which they put on, and finally a buoyancy vest each.

The seaplane was already hooked up to the crane and the engine was ticking over nicely. They were helped into their seats whilst Baldric was stashing the two cases into a compartment in the fuselage. They were given final instructions from the Flying Officer, who knew the plane well, and reminded them that the sea was carrying metre-high waves beyond the lee of the ship. They should take off into the waves and make due allowance for the extra weight of the suitcases as this would require an extra 50 metres of take-off space.

He asked Johnson to set course for Scapa which was due south-west. He explained the flight time was four hours and had sufficient fuel on board for five hours of flight. Daylight would cease around 1700 hours and so they had a good chance of making it safely. Landing at Scapa would be on a water lit runway in the harbour pool. At Acklington, there would be a set of burning oil barrels set out over a 200 metre strip on the airfield and the same at Filey Bay but on the beach, which was a short distance from the final destination of Scarborough. Landing at Filey would be a back-up plan should they consider that landing in the tight bay of Scarborough was impractical due to visibility. He explained that was the best he could do, other than to give them each a flask of 'Rosy Lee' each which had been spiked with a good measure of Glenfiddich.

The crane then lowered the Type L onto the quieted waters on the leeside and Michael pulled the throttle to show a bit of headway and pointed the nose in the direction of the oncoming waves. They looked up to see that the ship's port side was crowded with sailors, who were all shouting and cheering and waving their hats at the departing plane: whilst singing 'Land of Hope and Glory'.

Michael pulled the throttle back and felt the fine lady surge forward, skipping over the waves. When he felt that there was enough take-off speed he pulled back on the stick, and sure enough she lifted off in the most majestic way. Michael was awestruck by the power that was under the nose, and noted that there had been significant developments in the last four years of aeronautical engine speed and, he hoped, reliability.

The Battleship was fast becoming a distant object in the glistening sea, and he set course for South West. Michael then thought that they should set the time schedule and shouted to Johnson to keep the time. He askxed if he was wearing the tin toy watch which had been given to him as a present from the Woodrow Wilson Presidential campaign in 1912. Johnson shouted back declaring that the tin toy was the best watch ever and had kept perfect time in six years and had never been repaired. It was thoroughly reliable.

Johnson thought to himself that he recalled the day it was brought to Gatchina Palace by the American envoy as a gift so that Johnson might, as secretary, always be on hand to curry favour and respect for Wilson with Michael. Johnson had figured that the watch would be received with some derision if it had been given to any member of the Imperial family, as it was well below any standard of cost to be respectfully received by Michael.

The hours soon ticked by, even though they were rather monotonous, but were interspersed with a good swig from the flasks and the odd sighting of a fishing boat below. Their dead reckoning flight path took them to the Shetland Islands at around dusk. Flying over the rugged coastline they then steered South South West to make contact with the Orkney Islands, around an hour away. Soon the lights of Scapa Flow came into view, and the waterway landing strip was well lit up in anticipation of the arrival of Michael. After a smooth landing they were met on the quayside by the RFC Station Commander and given a hot meal and a billet for the night.

The following morning, after rising early, they found the Type L was fully refuelled and ready to undertake another gruelling three-hour flight down to RFC Acklington on the Northumbrian coast, there to rest the plane and re-fuel as there had been signs of overheating when the aircraft mechanics checked the engine at Scapa. The Type L was a fantastic plane, proven to be easy to fly and most reliable. The recently upgraded engine, which was fitted for sea flying, was perfect for a great aircraft and Michael hoped one day he would be able to return and take part in air races around Britain.

They were impressed to see the vast array of battleships and destroyers in the bay, and they knew this to be the Admiralty's main anchorage for the navy. Taking off from calm, sheltered waters was a joy and soon the bay was disappearing as they headed out to sea. This time the navigation was simpler as all they had to do in daylight was to follow the coastline.

About one hour away from their destination they were horrified to see that there was some untoward activity on the port side which seemed to be involving several fishing boats which were in close proximity to each other. Then it became clear that there was a grey shark-like U-Boat surfaced about 100 metres away from the group, which was firing its main deck gun at the boats. Michael's thoughts were to try to help the unfortunate sailors who were being seemingly systematically murdered in their boats. However, he then saw that there were lifeboats attached to the side of the U-boat and there were others rowing frantically towards it.

Michael thought to change course and circle the melee, since whilst he had no armament, he could at least report to Acklington RFC base what he was seeing when he arrived. After ten minutes or so of circling he then observed that the last of the fishing boats had been sunk and that the U-boat was surrounded by twelve or so lifeboats which were being towed in the direction of an oncoming tramp coastal steamer.

Michael kept watch, but at such a distance that he could not be shot at by the submarine anti-aircraft guns. It was now clear that there was an act of compassion being enacted by the U-boat Captain in that he simply wanted to sink boats and not kill the fishermen, who were innocent civilians. The final chapter of the event was seeing the U-Boat pulling alongside the stopped steamer and the crew of the twelve fishing boats being transferred to the boat, which Michael had identified as being Norwegian by her flag.

He felt relieved that the attack had been carried out in a way in which he highly approved; from his own military service he had seen from time to time inter-army compassion, and he himself had often arranged ceasefires so that the injured could be taken from the battlefield.

Time had been lost whilst watching the fishing boats coming under attack from the U-Boat, and the weather was becoming misty and murky. Finding the small airfield would be difficult, and they were to rely on flares being sent up around the ETA at five-minute intervals. The light would soon fade in this weather. They were expected at Acklington one hour ago.

They were fortunate, as hugging the coastline at low altitude proved to be the only navigational aid that was trustworthy in the poor light. They were becoming anxious at not having spotted any flares. Johnson was keeping a 360 degree watch and urgently tapped Michael on the shoulder and said that they had missed the airfield as he had just seen a flare go up directly behind them. Michael wheeled around and then they both saw a runway being lit up. It was a burning barrel runway and the ground crew were lighting the barrels one by one. Soon it became a clear pathway. Johnson then started to crank down the undercarriage for ground landing and they glided in to a welcoming, lit-up runway.

A lorry rolled up and mechanics were soon checking over the engine to see if the overheating was causing any damage. This was unusual attention, but it was probably due to the importance of Michael and the need to prosecute an invasion of Russia.

Michael and Johnson were given a lift to the airbase Commander's control tower where they explained why they were lost and what they had seen just an hour or two earlier. The Commander promptly sent a message to Admiralty HQ informing them of the position, in the hope that they would send a frigate to rescue the sailors from the Norwegian tramp steamer which they had noted was heading in a southerly direction when they had left the scene.

Time had now been lost and it was getting dark, and the Commander asked Johnson what he thought of the ETA at Scarborough. Johnson had been keeping meticulous calculations all the time and had noted that the interruption in flight had set them back around one hour and would require them to now land at Filey Bay, which had a safer landing strip on the wide sandy foreshore. This was always a best back-up plan if they were troubled by poor visibility.

They asked the Base Commander to relay this message onwards so that the strip could be prepared. The flight time remaining was around two hours, so it would be dark at that time. Michael was quite excited at the thought, as he knew the bay very well. That was the place where the Type L was conceived and constructed, and had used the sands on many occasions in the past with Robert Blackburn. Also, the thought of a night landing between burning barrels of oil was another great adventure for his diary.

They set off from Acklington on the final leg in darkness and were flying by instinct, the visible coastline and the seat of their pants in anticipation of the runway lights at Filey. Approaching Scarborough they could see it was in blackout and the only way to recognise the bay was from the emerging moonlight. In the distance, Michael, could see the long line of twin lights from the burning oil barrels on Filey Bay forming a corridor. Aiming the plane towards the runway he was overjoyed to be once again landing on British soil and in his favourite place: Filey.

As he glided in he knew exactly how to handle the Type L, and just loved the feeling of control and response by the fine lady which, in his mind during the flight, he had named Natasha after his darling wife who he had left back in Russia only a few days previously. Johnson was amazed at how expert Michael was with this machine. He had known of his many journeys to Filey just before the war but had paid little or no attention to his adventurous entertainment.

They were met by Michael's old friend Robert Blackburn who was delighted to receive his plane back in great condition, but also to embrace and receive Michael once again at Filey Bay, remembering the good times of their friendship several years earlier. Alongside him was Captain Laker of the RFC who had a car waiting in Hunmanby and was to take Michael with haste to the Grand Hotel in Scarborough.

Blackburn was a serial entrepreneur and risk-taker, using his skill in invention and design to promote his talents. His nature was quiet but robust, whilst being demanding of all those around him. His enthusiasm for pushing the boundaries was infectious and many would sit in awe and silence as he spoke of new ideas. He would encourage all his employees with advice and friendship, as he knew the importance of tactical interrelationships to achieve his own business goals. His Type L seaplane was rather old in design now, but robust and well tried out during the war years, and had proven reliable. He was again at the forefront of design and technology as the war effort had promoted his business and creative skills and led to the production of many new innovative ideas in aircraft design. They reminisced about the period in 1914 when the Type L was to take to the skies in a *Daily Mail*-sponsored Circuit of Britain air race. Unfortunately, it was cancelled due to the outbreak of war.

Michael was overjoyed to see that the vehicle was a Prince Henry Vauxhall, and perhaps one of the last of the line of 1914, with the fluted bonnet. These were also in his brother Nicholas's stable back in Russia, and he had driven them on many occasions. However, this was painted a drab green-grey and was not very well kept, but he guessed that as a forces field vehicle, only its speed and reliability would be of concern, and not its appearance. Laker apologised for the state of the car, but Michael could not care less as he was just delighted to be reunited with an old driving friend.

Scarborough was a short ride away and they soon reached their destination and were welcomed outside the imposing grandeur of the Grand Hotel by more senior staff, a Brigadier General and two Captains. They were shown to their quarters and were impressed by the stupendous size and fine fitments of the suite that had been prepared for them. This was possibly the largest hotel in Europe, and had a fine reputation. He had stayed there on several occasions just before the war, during his visits to Filey Bay.

The first thing they did was to take to the balcony and reflect on the beautiful moonlit bay whilst they drew on cigars and sipped fine port. Always Michael's thoughts at times of luxury would drift back to Mother Russia and the pain and agony its citizens were going through, and then of course to his beloved Natasha and son George. He always worried about how they were coping.

18

Top Brass at the Grand Hotel

After an hour or so of relaxation on the balcony, Sir George Buchanan visited them. They were astonished to see him as they had thought he would remain in Russia as Ambassador to be on hand for the coming invasion. Cordialities were exchanged and the three sat down and, over port, chatted about the events unfolding in Russia.

Buchanan explained that he had just been permanently recalled to the UK due to the appointment of Lenin as leader of the Bolsheviks. The government felt that he would be safer in the UK despite diplomatic immunity, as the Bolsheviks were a lawless lot, and if they were to discover the plot to invade, then he would become a target. Above all, he wanted to protect his wife, Lady Georgina (Meriel Bathurst), who had lived with him at the Embassy.

Buchanan commented on the remarkable mantle of responsibility that Michael had taken on, and was enthralled to hear of his journey so far that had brought him to Britain. Buchanan, now without portfolio, felt that this ambiguous situation might allow him to advise Michael unofficially. He lowered his voice and reminded Michael that he had been privileged to have provided advice to his brother Nicholas a year ago, when things were becoming very messy within the Royal Family and revolutionary trends were appearing. He acknowledged that Michael, too, had been voicing warnings, to which Nicholas paid no heed, simply sticking his head in the sand. In those times Nicholas's wife was becoming a pawn in the network of pro-German courtiers, and Buchanan expressed his view that 'Germany is using Alexandra Fedorova to set the Tsar against the Allies' and that the Empress was 'the unwitting instrument of Germany'.

He expressed his view that any British engagement against the Bolsheviks, to aid the White Army and rescue Nicholas and family, was a mighty task and had far more chance of failure than success. He advised Michael to press all the attendees at the meeting the next day on the evidence of possible success, how they would prosecute the war, and what military and armaments they would deploy.

Buchanan was concerned that the peace treaty between Russia and Germany would be signed within weeks, and there was a serious scarcity of able troops to deploy to counteract this emerging threat. America would feature in that invasion plan, but even after entering the war ten months ago, the fact was that neither the army nor the navy was still in shape for war and they did not yet have sufficient strength in transporting troops and munitions. They had made no real attempt at making studies of trench warfare, poison gas tactics or the use of heavy artillery and tanks, and were utterly unfamiliar with the rapid evolution of aerial warfare.

Both Michael and Buchanan were very concerned at

the future plight of the Royal Family in Tobolsk. Buchanan feared that the rapid movement west of the Czech and White Russian Armies would prompt either Nicholas and his family to be moved further towards Moscow, or their assassination, as Lenin could not allow them to be rescued and become a rallying point, which would undermine his revolution in its infancy.

Buchanan advised that Michael should press for a strong attack to the East towards the Urals and quickly meet up with the White Army. More to the point, a commando-type secret rescue was being planned for the spring and would be implemented as a precursor to the invasion. Indeed, Nicholas was being prepared at this moment for such an action, and was under advice to be ready.

Buchanan then turned towards the meeting and advised that he would be seeing Lloyd George, General Ironside, Major General Knox of the army, and the navy representatives would be First Sea Lord Wemyss and Admiral Sir Edwyn Sinclair. There would also be a senior member of the American Government, but that person was still unknown, and attended by General Pershing, who was the highest-ranking officer in the American Army and Commander of their expeditionary force in France.

Michael, for the first time, after listening to Buchanan was becoming fearful of the venture. Whilst the array of dignitaries he would be meeting impressed him, it would be a formidable task to direct the meeting towards his own agenda, he felt that the weight of power would render him as a simple pawn in the big game. It seemed that they might never consider Michael's priorities, which were primarily the rescue of his brother Nicholas and his family, and of equal importance, his own agenda in the Manifesto Johnson had prepared for him.

Buchanan left at around 1 a.m., wishing them the best of luck, and leaving his card, promising his support should they need to contact him at any time in the future.

That following morning at 0800 hours Captain Laker came to their room with two bundles of uniforms which they were invited to wear. Michael was aghast at his uniform, which was that of a Tsar in military dress. How they had manufactured it was a wonder. Johnson's uniform was equally impressive and was a morning suit of the highest finery worn by British diplomatic dignitaries, with hat to suit. Johnson had never been so well attired and it was obviously to reflect the importance and gravity of the occasion soon to engulf them. Captain Laker announced that breakfast would be served in their rooms at 1000 hours, and then he would escort them to the board room of the Grand Hotel at 1200 hours.

Over breakfast Michael and Johnson discussed their tactics. It was paramount that there should be agreement in the thrust to rescue Nicholas as a priority. Then the Johnson's Prometheus Manifesto should be unveiled.

At precisely 1200 hours, Captain Laker arrived and gave them an agenda and briefing. The agenda read as follows:

Day one commencing at 1200

Introductions
The Churchill Plan
The implementation

The resources to implement the strategy
Discussion to formulate an agreement.
Break for mid-afternoon lunch at 1330 and
resume at 1430
Financial planning to the invasion and estimated costs for a
three-month campaign
Preparation of an accord and communiqué
The preparation of a treaty to be implemented
Close of meeting and to retire to peruse the accord at 1730
Day two commencing at 1200
Discussion of the accord
Preparation and signing of the treaty
Close the meeting at 1330.

After they had absorbed the agenda, Laker took them to the boardroom where they were warmly greeted and introduced one by one. They were invited to share refreshments from the very well stocked bar; smoking was permitted. The room soon filled with genial chat and concerns for the Russian Empire, and more so the tragedies of the past and the probable discomfort and conditions of Nicholas and his family.

Michael, after ten minutes, noted the absence of the unknown senior American statesman who was to attend. On that observation, Lloyd George, the British Prime Minister, came to Michael and Johnson and invited them to follow him to the anteroom annexed to the boardroom.

Upon entering, Michael was staggered to discover Woodrow Wilson sitting comfortably in an armchair by a well-set log fire, leaning back in a very relaxed pose. He stood up and introduced himself, and then invited them both and

Lloyd George to join him around the fire. He immediately entered into small talk and expressed his concerns for Michael and the whole Royal Family.

Wilson had a reputation for being cold and disagreeable with men he felt were not sympathetic to him. In fact, his greatest fault was his inability to work with those who were not willing to follow his lead completely. He had absolute confidence in his own judgement. However, today he was different and showed his private, affectionate side to his character, being charming and generous of nature. Amongst friends he was a raconteur and a great imitator of people he knew. He sang well and he had a beautiful speaking voice. Above all, he loved good conversation, and clever, well-bred people who understood him, brought out the best qualities of his brilliant and witty mind.

Wilson was very conscious of the sensitivity of the whole Bolshevik affair and assured Michael that *the might* of the British and American forces were commited to the reinstatement of the Royal Family, the crushing of Bolshevism was paramount to them, and of course to secure all the borders and lands of the Empire.

Addressing Michael in a more poignant manner he assured him that 'the past and current leaders of Russia should take care to note that it was his heartfelt desire that some way may be opened whereby he would be privileged to assist the Russian people to gain their complete hope for liberty and ordered peace for generations to come'. This was an essential part of an accord which Woodrow Wilson had presented to the American Congress only days earlier and was in line with the thinking of David Lloyd George.

He went on to assure Michael that he was encouraged

by the bravery he was showing and the mantle of statesmanship and responsibility he had taken on, in that he had chosen to carry to the Russian people the assertions of freedom, peace and prosperity for the sake of his beloved Russia. In support of this principle Woodrow Wilson had made this perilous journey; on the one hand, to develop a peace strategy for the warring nations which he would be putting before Congress later that month, but equally to look Michael in the eye and know his mind, read his heart, and weigh his resolve in agreeing to head up the proposed invasion of Russia and his willingness to be reinstalled to the Monarchy.

On that note he finished by saying that any man who would undertake such a dangerous journey from Russia to seek the rescue of his motherland, was showing commitment of the highest order, and on that point he was more than satisfied that the success of the invasion was secure with Michael. The detail was for the politicians and generals to sort out between themselves, but for him the key was Michael, in whom he was well pleased.

Lloyd George backed up Wilson on all his comments and added that Michael was chosen due to his popularity in Russia among the politicians, the armed forces, and more so, the people, who loved him and his honest and simple approach to rule. He reminded Michael, however, that successfully freeing his brother and family was largely dependent upon the success of the invasion. He also commented that the secrecy of these meetings was of such importance that, should the whole process be subject to failure, the records of these interactions would become a mystery to future historians.

The mention of Nicholas was of great comfort to Michael, as this was the first agenda item that he wanted security for, and would allow a more congenial approach to the waiting senior Commanders in the boardroom. Lloyd George then interceded on the same front and promised Michael that as soon as they could rescue the Royal Party, they would be fast-tracked to the UK for safety, along with any other Royals they were to encounter in the invasion. He commented that they would be installed at Paddockhurst in Sussex, which Michael knew very well, for which Johnson had arranged the lease in Michael's name in 1914.

From there, and when it was safe to return they would be repatriated to Russia as time and appropriateness dictated; or not, as they could stay under UK protection indefinitely. However, essentially they would be free, and looked after by the UK government. Wilson chipped in and confirmed that should they wish to transfer to the United States then those same protocols would be in place, as outlined by Lloyd George. Michael was now feeling very relaxed and looking forward to seeing how the Allied Powers were to implement this new front to defeat the Bolsheviks.

Turning the conversation to a more genial tone, Wilson was most impressed to note that the watch which Johnson was wearing was one of his personal gifts to high-ranking world leaders at the time of his campaign to become President of the United States in 1912. Johnson was also eager to discuss that subject, as they were both aware of the provenance of the watch, and certainly Johnson was most gratified to know that he was wearing a gift from perhaps one of the most powerful men on the planet.

Johnson took the watch off and handed it to Wilson. Wilson looked at it with a great deal of warmth and nostalgia. He remarked that in all the past six years of his Presidency, he had never seen any one of the gifted dignitaries ever wear the watch, which was a disappointment to him. Wilson enquired how he had come by the watch. Michael became a little uneasy and was showing signs of embarrassment. However, Johnson quickly recounted the story of the American Ambassador choosing Johnson to receive the watch, and at the first opportunity to present it to Michael, who was spending a great deal of time away from Gatchina with his new wife Natasha and their son George.

Johnson then went on to explain that he had by and large forgotten to give Michael the watch, and it was not until a year later in Knebworth House in the UK that he had mentioned it. Michael then chipped in and helped him along and said that Johnson had become fond of the watch and always wore it. As he had been a great friend for so long, then he told him to keep it as a gift. Wilson was charmed by this generous act and was more than pleased that Johnson was a regular wearer of the watch and had such a love for it. Johnson then announced that it was very dear to him, and he was delighted that it kept perfect time and it had never needed any repair.

On that note Lloyd George stood up with a view to returning to the meeting. Wilson also rose and said to Michael that regrettably he would not be joining them as he had to get back to the USA while his absence had not been publicly noted. His journey was a perilous one, due to U-boat activity. He had been scheduled to return on the

Iron Duke and had heard of the encounter with four U-boats during Michael's journey to the UK and that the ship was now consequently under repair in Glasgow.

Lloyd George commented then that the new naval flagship, *Queen Elizabeth*, was now docking at Liverpool and awaiting Wilson's arrival so that he could sail onwards to the USA under escort of four destroyers.

With that they all shook hands and Wilson in true relaxed American style broke with protocol and hugged Michael, giving him his personal assurance. He then embraced Johnson and whispered that he was a lucky man to have such a watch, as only twenty-five had been made for the campaign, and it was likely that most of them were tossed away because of the low value of the design and casing. 'Look after it,' he said. 'And I wish the new owner in a hundred years time will have as much pleasure in wearing it as you have.'

Michael and Johnson returning to the meeting room, sat down opposite the attendees. The meeting commenced with an introduction to the Churchill Plan. The outline was presented in a dossier to each of the members, and were given several minutes read and make any notes. General William Ironside declared himself as the Chairman and brought the meeting to a formal start. He discussed each point of the plan with some precision.

William Ironside was a tall, athletic chap who excelled at sports and did not carry any complex in his personality. He worked well with the army chiefs and government and would undertake any role set before him. His compliance in matters had led him to be a useful member of teams where his personality, dignity, authority and bearing had brought

him to high office, where his charm and intelligence would
serve him well.

The Churchill Plan
Draft February 1918

Main Objectives.

*To land forces at Archangel with American aid and thrust these
forces south towards Moscow and occupy the city within
three months of the start of the campaign.*

To reinstate an Interim Government.

To stabilise the currency and banks.

*To bring Martial Law to the main cities under joint command
of White Russian forces and backed by the Allied landing
forces.*

*To promote the manufacture of war materiel and essential food
to feed the army.*

*To immediately send a combined force of troops to re-engage the
German Army.*

*To create sufficient pressure on that front to engage large portions
of the German Army and be a defensive force in the first
part and by the end of the year to launch a winter offensive
to strike at Berlin.*

*To force a surrender on both fronts and apply for war
reparations.*

*NOTE. An agenda item from the Plan has been omitted which
was to allow the invasion of the Russian eastern seaboard
by Japan to aid the Allied invasion. This was on the sound
advice of Grand Duke Michael and his secretary Nicholas
Johnson under the information that this would not be
tolerated by the Russian population, industrial masters*

and oligarchs due to a great deal of adversity that exists in Russia towards Japan.

Implementation.

To build up from May onwards further supplies and war materiel which were stockpiled in Scotland and was on reserve in case there should be any invasion of the UK, should it be defeated, by the German forces which were becoming a major threat on the Western Front due to the unofficial cessation of hostilities on the German Eastern Front with Russia.

Using approx. 30% of the northern fleet and 30 troop carriers and cargo vessels to provide a convoy to Archangel and a reserve force of men and materiel at Murmansk.

In June to progress the march south on the main highway and establish a force and equipment in Petrograd and control the city.

Simultaneously the Grand Fleet would in May, send a fleet of destroyers to sweep the Baltic of U-boats and attack any motor torpedo boat nests that would lie along the coast. In addition, the American Navy would bring in 30 destroyers to nullify any action considered by the German fleet.

In mid-May, 30% of the Grand Fleet to sail into the Baltic and join forces with Denmark, which would declare war on Bolshevik Russia.

The attacks would target all shore-based industry and U-boat production ports and pound them continually as they made their way up towards Petrograd.

A fleet of 50 motor torpedo boats to attack the German fleet at any quarter and support the destroyers to a point that the emergence of the German fleet into the Baltic would prove a disaster.

The Danish forces would be supplying mostly troop and food supplies to aid the incoming forces from Archangel and to provide mercy mission foods and medical supplies. The Danes would also be responsible for the Martial Order on the streets of Petrograd.

In addition, the Danish Navy would assist in neutralising the German Fleet alongside the British naval actions.

The whole of the northern Baltic coast to be closely mined to impede any breakout of the German Fleet.

The Grand Fleet to remain in the Baltic for at least six months to ensure full control and a neutralising effect of the German Navy.

The RFC to participate in the Baltic using air bases from Denmark, and fly regular anti-submarine patrols and use wherever possible torpedoes to assault any German shipping.

The land forces to then link up with the White Army and pursue a course for Moscow in August, and remove the Bolsheviks; by using a popular uprising this would be a swift and less bloody action.

The whole of the Bolshevik regime to be rounded up, tried and hanged for treason and crimes against humanity.

To achieve victory on all fronts by October 1918.

Ground Resources to implement the strategy:

British ground forces

30,000 in May to build to 100,000 by August.

American forces

20,000 in May to build to 50,000 by August.

White Russian forces

45,000 current and based in the east and the south.

Popular militia

90,000 to be raised on the invasion dates.

Hardware assets

A squadron of 20 tanks, 2,000 artillery pieces, 200 vehicle transports and coordination supplied by both American and British armies.

Air Support with observation and bombing capabilities with light fighter cover

To be advised, but first forward base to be established at Kotlas on the River Dvina.

General build-up of assets as required as the war unfolds and having control of the Baltic and routes into Archangel.

Agreement.

The agreement to be conducted under English Law and any dispute as to content and activation will become the vested powers of His Majesty's Government and that of the United States.

Financial contribution to the invasion and estimated costs for a three-month campaign.

It was noted that Michael had brought into the country a great deal of wealth from the Russian Royal Family and State. The cost of securing the Russian Empire would have to be borne by the Allies and Russia. To start this process, it would be necessary to impound the wealth that was carried into the UK to be solely used as a direct contribution towards the war effort in Russia.

Preparation of an accord and communiqué.

To be undertaken by the Secretary of State and War Department, which are on hand to interpret these discussions, and with the agreement of Grand Duke Michael.

The preparation of a treaty.
The Final Draft to be agreed upon for consideration and be signed by all parties present.

Lloyd George had been silent on most of the dealings as it was implicit that the Allied Commanders had thought this through in detail and it was pointless to add his voice to those of the British Commanders and Pershing, who joined with Ironside in much of the presentation. He then spoke towards the end of the meeting and announced that he had contact with Churchill, who had been in primary discussions with Michael on board the *Iron Duke*. He pointed out to Michael that he had been informed that he had created a Manifesto of terms which Michael would present at this meeting.

With that timely intervention, which saved Johnson the trouble of interrupting the proceedings, Johnson drew from his briefcase the Manifesto. He gave this to Lloyd George and politely mentioned that it was now late and they were tired, and invited him to read it with the other members of the party and discuss their terms in the morning.

The military and naval Commanders had been made aware that they would be presented with terms of some sort, but had no clue as to what they would contain. They had accepted the change in deleting the invasion plan by the Japanese at Vladivostok and complimented Michael on his foresight in requesting that they should be excluded from any plans. But they also knew that there were other matters which had been kept from Churchill.

The meeting was closed after an exhausting day of facts, figures and promises. Michael was in a daze and was quite unsure of all that had progressed. He felt inclined to just get the whole thing over with and rest, sign the damn thing in the morning, and go back to his wife and child as soon as possible. They returned to their rooms and immediately ordered dinner.

Johnson advised Michael that they should spend the remaining time, though exhausted, to look at the events of the day. He was more circumspect as he knew this was the one and only chance to get it right, and he knew he had to find the ace in the pack which put them in control.

They both agreed that it was pointless to enter the whys and wherefores of the military and naval aspects of the invasion, as it was beyond their comprehension of effecting success or not. So, Johnson directed the conversation to the main aims of the Churchill Plan. It was plainly obvious that it had totally ignored the plight of the people, industry, the future of the governments and the security of the population. There was little notice given to the new ruling parties and the formulation of the royal entity. It seemed that given the Allies had little regard, it was not only an invasion, but could well turn out to be the subjugation and a rape of the country and its mineral resources.

They discussed it in some detail, but could not decide what the best outlook was, and they knew they would be pushed for time and closure, with a lot of high-ranking people needing to get back to their civil and military duties. The wrangling could go on for hours, and they may get bulldozed into signing. This concerned them, up to the point where Johnson exclaimed that there was only one tactic, and he had found the ace.

All good tactics, should be simple to understand, he told Michael – and it was this: The ace in the pack was Michael. And it should not be underestimated, how important it was to have him heading up the propaganda campaign.

Johnson announced that they should simply go into the meeting and tell them that without the full inclusion of the points which he had raised in his Manifesto, Michael would simply refuse to comply. They should then leave the room and await the response, taking a view that there would be limited adjustment but in the main should stay on base.

Time was on their side and the Allies would be the ones fretting that an agreement had not been reached. Michael could simply announce that he would stay in the UK if required, or even never to return to Russia, as it was collapsing day by day. His own life and that of his brother and family were more in danger as each day passed.

Michael said, 'Eureka! Johnson, you have done it again. And with such elegant simplicity that I can now enjoy my dinner and sleep in peace.'

That following morning, after the same routine as the previous day, they were asked again to attend the meeting and Laker once more led the way. Walking briskly into the meeting, all the delegates shook hands, and immediately got down to business.

General Ironside opened the discussion with furrowed brows and looked at Pershing and Knox for approval as he opened the discussion. He was a tall, well-made man and of the Old School Tie Brigade. No nonsense, and formidable in negotiations and confrontations, he was very well versed in setting out the stalls to orchestrate his own round table victories. He brought to the table Michael's Manifesto and commented with as much courtesy as his position would allow.

'Michael,' he said, 'This is most admirable but is not in our remit or thinking at this moment in time. Of course we should address these concerns of yours, but they cannot be entered into a document which is principally about an armed invasion, as the politics and human plights and positions cannot be remedied here in this agreement.'

Johnson, who had guessed correctly that this would be the response, then stood up and announced, on behalf of Michael and the Royal Romanov Russia, that without the total inclusion of these terms then Michael would not become head of state and assist in the propaganda needs of the Allies. He asked the Allies to consider their position and said that they would be in the drawing room of the hotel should their presence be required further.

Ironside spluttered and Pershing almost broke out into a convulsion as he saw the two stalking off and bidding their goodbyes. They could not believe the effrontery they had experienced in being given an ultimatum. They were the power in the room, and could not have conceived such a response which had put them to such a disadvantage.

Lloyd George, who was sitting back in his chair calmly smoking his pipe, smiled at each of the high-ranking officers and remarked that this may have been a kick in the pants rebuff, but they should climb down from their ivory towers. He advised them to take a careful look again at the Manifesto. Indeed, he was off to the drawing room himself and was contactable, in just the same way as they might decide to contact Michael and Johnson. With that and a swish of his coat tails he sauntered out of the room with a pleasant, wry smile on his face. "Game, set and match," he thought.

After an hour or so, and realising by his absence that Lloyd George was implicitly onside with Michael, they decided to agree to the terms. However, they added the caveat that, come hell or high water, the war and its aftermath would be conducted under their own terms, and 'What will be, will be.' They were relying on the confusion and twists and turns of war to probably negate much of what Michael was insisting upon.

Michael and Johnson were invited back into the stateroom and were simply informed by General Ironside that their terms would be met, and the full Manifesto would be included in the treaty.

John J. Pershing had been rather unusually quiet during the second round of negotiations. He was a born leader, with extraordinary drive and determination. Insisting on his right to make up his own mind, he demanded freedom of thought and action, and would not let anything or anyone stand in his way once he was committed to his goal. Always seeking the forefront and the limelight, he needed to feel in command of important undertakings, and resisted supportive roles. Pershing was very impatient with the shortcomings of others. He assumed responsibility to be the protector and provider for those he loved, but demanded their respect and attention in return. With a good memory, he was intelligent, well balanced, with strong mental abilities; his thinking process was logical, and his problem-solving skills were outstanding. Against all his usual style of control and decision-making, he was respectful towards Michael and Johnson, as in his view, they had presented a good case for Russia.

'As a matter of fact,' Pershing interjected, 'what might we call this Manifesto?'

Johnson replied, 'Prometheus 1918. A Helper of Mankind.'

The treaty would be ready for inspection and signature in the stateroom and Michael and Johnson were asked if they would attend for the signing process. Michael agreed. All the delegates rose and shook hands in relief and gratitude that an accord had been struck.

Michael's mind then turned towards the next chapter in their visit to Britain, and the reclamation of valuables left at Knebworth House and Paddockhurst.

19

Retrieving the Royal Treasures

L aker then came to Michael's room and enquired whether they were ready to leave within one hour, as the Royal Train was now arriving at Scarborough station ready to take them on the first leg of their journey to Knebworth House in Luton.

He also informed them that they would not be allowed to take the two suitcases containing the valuables they had brought from Gatchina Palace. Johnson intervened and proclaimed that the contents belonged to the Romanov Family and were theirs, to cover the reinstatement costs and future well-being of Michael. Laker was insistent that it was imperative that the Romanov families should contribute to the enormous cost of the invasion, which was ultimately for their benefit.

It was plain to see that this was a strategically proper argument, and with some fair play attributed to the cause, Michael agreed on the condition that one of the suitcases did contain certain items which he would not part with, pointing out that one of the suitcases contained Gladstone bags which were a gift from Tsar Nicholas, and other items entrusted to him by his Aunt Maria Pavlovna from the Vladimir Palace. The other suitcase contained treasures that had been hidden under the stairs at the Vladimir Palace by persons unknown and were probably items misappropriated by industrialists and Bolsheviks. Laker agreed and took the remaining suitcase to Lloyd George.

Johnson proceeded to pack the remainder of the items, including the very important Bolshevik Russian Army uniforms. They still could continue wearing the British uniforms as they were yet to meet King George V and would form part of that protocol, and the journeys on the Royal Train. Laker had organised the trip to Michael's past residences and onwards to meet King George V at his request in agreement with Lloyd George via Sidney Reilly before they left Russia.

Laker then took them to the train waiting at Scarborough station and wished them a safe journey. The train was a huge Great Northern Railway 4-4-2 'green giant' and it was pulling just three coaches, to which Johnson remarked should make good time, as he could see from his own timetable that there was now slippage which would be best made up on a fast train. He noted that there was a name board on the front of the engine which read, '*The Special Scotch Express*'.

Boarding the train, they were met by two stewards who welcomed them and made them comfortable. One car was a lounge with an amply stocked bar, the second was their sleeping quarters and bathroom, and the remaining car was a kitchen and the sleeping area for the stewards. Johnson remarked to Michael that this Royal Train was being pulled by a famous engine which by its name was likely to have plied the north-eastern route from London Kings Cross to Edinburgh.

The journey to Luton would turn out to be rather quicker than expected as the train seemed to be doing a constant high speed and they guessed that they would have right of way, being a Royal Train. High tea was served to an extraordinary standard. It was not long after they were preparing to alight as they could feel the train slowing. The steward announced that they should be arriving at Knebworth Station in ten minutes.

Alighting from the train they were met by the Knebworth House chauffeur, Adrian Woollaston, whom they had both known some five years earlier when Michael, his family and entourage were leasing the house. They were both delighted to see Adrian again and spent an enjoyable ten minutes driving to the mansion, talking over old times.

Adrian Woollaston had a good and solid character, being approachable, friendly, and a reliable servant. His loyalty and friendships were held in high regard by those he was in service with. His often witty remarks were simple, sharp, but never cutting.

Johnson then broached the reason for the visit and enquired if the baggage they had left behind in August 1914 was still in storage. Woollaston gave them the news that the stored luggage was under lock and key, and controlled by the Lady Edith Lytton, who was residing at a dower house in the grounds as a retired person. It was explained that there had been some claim made upon Michael's estate by Lady Lytton as they had left the mansion in August 1914 towards the end of their tenure and they had not left the premises in a state 'as found'.

Lady Lytton would be waiting for their arrival and it was best that Michael should know about the impending problem.

On arrival, they met Lady Lytton in the Grand Hall where they were most graciously received and welcomed, with an invitation for them to stay for the evening, and join her for dinner. Lady Lytton would be best described as never having aspired to where she felt she should have been in society due to fate which led to lost loves and financial ruin. However, her fastidious and quiet attitude led to her becoming a Lady in Waiting to Royalty, and so her demeanour was of duty and charm. She was a forgiving person, an excellent hostess, and her attitude was inclined towards fair play and honesty. She always liked to help others, in her quiet way, as she had been helped in her own time of need.

Michael thanked her for her gracious welcome, declined the overnight stay, but accepted the offer to dine with her. He explained his reason for being in the UK, was simply that he was helping with the war effort and was engaging with the Allied forces to bring about the restoration of the Russian Monarchy

After dinner, served in the Great Hall on a huge table set for three, during which they discussed the worsening positions of the family and Russia at large, they withdrew to the small evening snug adjacent to the dining hall. Michael then engaged Lady Lytton with the reason they had come to visit: to collect some of the items they had left at the mansion before they were called back to Russia in 1914.

Lady Lytton then explained about the poor state they had left the property in and listed some dilapidations which had occurred during their tenure. Michael heard her complaints; Johnson came to his aid and explained that this was entirely his responsibility, and that Michael had to leave urgently with his family and entourage shortly after 1 August 1914, one month before the expiration of the lease. He had set in motion contractors to carry out the work, but due to the turmoil at the outbreak of war it seemed they had not turned up to carry out the work, as they themselves were naval reservists and had been called to action in the Merchant Navy.

Johnson then went onto explain in more detail why such a large amount of luggage had been left: it was contracted to be transported to Paddockhurst where it was well known that they were relocating, but for the outbreak of war. Indeed, contracts had been prepared and signed by himself, but alas it seemed that the full inventory of luggage was not transported as planned. Johnson then affirmed that they were ready to make reparation and that they had bought some negotiable items with them, but not cash.

This offer was pleasing to Lady Lytton who then showed them to the locked storeroom in which the many items left behind had been stored undisturbed for the past four years. Michael, seeing the great pile of furniture and housewares, realised that they could not yet have these items brought back into their possession.

Johnson then asked Lady Lytton if they could remain in storage until matters in Russia had stabilised; and at the earliest opportunity they would have them transported back to Russia. Lady Lytton was very gracious and said it was the very least that she could do in the circumstances, and she was delighted to help. She also announced that there were no bills to pay now or in the future, and that she just wished that they could return to normal life in Russia as soon as possible. With that she left; Michael and Johnson remained in the room and started the search for the trunks which Johnson had marked as being where the valuables were stored.

After a short time, they came to a trunk which Johnson recognised as being the one where he had personally supervised the placing of Michael's valuables and those of his wife, Countess Natasha Brasova. It was marked clearly with his own numbering as being 'GDMAR 008'. However, a second trunk was missing, which he knew was marked 'GDMAR 007'. Thinking carefully, he remembered it had possibly been transported to Paddockhurst with the main body of possessions which he knew had been moved before they had to leave for Russia.

The trunk was locked, and with no key available after such a long time, they had to force open the locks. The trunk contained mostly books and personal clothing of Michael's but at the bottom, and exactly where he remembered placing the item they were looking for, he came across a large Gladstone style briefcase, similar to the ones that were common at those times in Europe and used extensively by business men. He checked the code which had been stamped on the underside of the briefcase and it was as he remembered: 'GDMAR GB CD'.

This contained the personal treasures of Michael and Natasha. The key was located in a silk shirt placed close to the briefcase. Johnson opened it up and had a quick look at the contents, and was pleased that it was seemingly all present, as left four years earlier. Michael and Johnson were pleased to recover the items, especially as they had to leave behind a considerable amount of the wealth that they had brought from Russia, which was now in the possession of the British Government. It was a relief. Johnson closed the case and they both returned to the drawing room to join Lady Lytton.

Michael thanked her for her charm and hospitality she had shown them and asked if he could be excused from her presence to return to the train, still waiting on a side track at Knebworth station. He explained that it was imperative they continue their journey south for a meeting with King George V. Wollaston was on hand again to drive them to the station and they boarded the train for the final leg of that journey. They then retired to the sleeping car and in peace slept the rest of the journey to Sussex.

They awoke at 5 a.m. to discover that the train was stopped in a siding at Croydon, and seemed to be at journey's end. Johnson called for the stewards who both had arisen and were preparing morning coffee for them both.

They chose from a limited breakfast menu and were duly served after bathing and again dressing in the full regalia of high rank uniforms provided for them at Scarborough. Breakfast finished, they were met by the King's chauffeur and enjoyed a royal journey to Paddockhurst in one of the King's fleet of cars. Michael, being a keen motorist, observed that it was a Hooper Brougham Daimler Limousine which he knew had been in the King's ownership since early 1914.

The journey to Paddockhurst was short and uneventful, save to say that there was a lot of military activity on the roads and transporters carrying the new-fangled tanks that he had heard so much about that were causing havoc and fear amongst the German Army at the Western Front.

Arriving at Paddockhurst and seeing the gracious manor house, Michael noted that it was just as he remembered on his brief visit in 1914, where he, Johnson and Natasha were to make their new home after leaving Knebworth House. It was a darker and more imposing design, and a little sinister-looking he recalled, as it was today. However, he was happy in the fact that it was smaller and its upkeep was easier, and it was closer to London and the coast.

Johnson was hoping to meet his mother, Louise. He had the opportunity to send her a telegram when they were in Scarborough. There had been no response, but that may have been because of the pressure on the telegram service due to war and casualty activities.

They were welcomed by the site Adjutant who was responsible for the operations and servicing of the premises as Michael had released himself from the contract which Johnson had signed for a 12-month tenure at the mansion and put the premises at the disposal of the War Department. After introductions and a briefing of the morning meeting with King George V in the private lounge of the mansion, Michael enquired whether his secretary's mother was still in residence.

The site Adjutant at once confirmed that this was the case, and that she played a role in the personal welfare of the officers and was well regarded. He told Johnson he was pleased that he had met her son, of whom he had heard such positive comments over the past several years.

The Adjutant then took them to the private annexe of

Louise von Kreisler Johnson, as she was known. After several knocks, as it was still early morning, a smiling middle-aged lady opened the door and stood utterly shocked to see her son standing in the doorway with the Grand Duke Michael. She cried, 'Johnny, my Johnny!' (his royal nickname) and embraced him with ever-tightening arms as the full realisation dawned of seeing him again after four years and after deep worry for his safety. She burst into uncontrollable tears and Johnson led her into her lounge and sat her down with his arms around her.

The Adjutant left, with Michael standing there still in the doorway to the hall which led to the lounge. Watching, he himself, was overcome at this blessed reunion, and turned his own thoughts in desolation towards his own family, most of all his wife, Natasha, who had been left behind in Gatchina.

Louise broke away from the arms of Johnny and realised that she had not acknowledged Michael. She quickly arose and rushed over to Michael and cried 'Misha Misha!' (Michael's nickname). 'I am so so pleased to see you again and you are looking so fine.'

She was so surprised to see them both and wondered why they had not contacted her upon arriving in Britain. Johnson explained that he had sent a telegram two days earlier, but it seemed that it had not yet arrived and was caught up in the system delays.

Louise immediately thought about hosting the two inseparable mates and made tea and a bacon sandwich for her 'two boys' as she always referred to them. Misha had not had a bacon sandwich since he had lived in the UK, but Johnny had to admit that he had that pleasure many times at Knebworth and had visited the kitchens and made himself bacon, egg, and beans as his late-night secret indulgence.

Louise was very well educated, and a talented musician. She was a devoted mother to Nicholas and her two daughters and kept stability in the household when she was living in Russia, where she became a central figure alongside her son in the service of Grand Duke Michael. So, she always displayed an air of service, with a smile and a genuine intelligent authority which knew its place. Her motherly love was often sought after when needed in questions of personal advice and interactions, as she had a relaxed and soothing personality.

After they had exchanged news of the British in war conditions, and of life in Russia for her boys, Louise told them of her personal existance which she had created for herself whilst in Paddockhurst.

Louise then asked why they were in the UK. She hoped that they would not ever return to Russia, as it presented so many dangers for them. Micha explained in detail, as he very much trusted Louise, the full facts, and reasons for the visit, and the necessity for them to continue their journey that same day. They explained to Louise how confident they were of a successful outcome, and hid their own fears of the high possibility of failure.

The time was now approaching 10 a.m. and it was expected that King George V would now have arrived for his meeting with Michael. At that moment, and on time, the Adjutant arrived at Louise's door and asked Michael to accompany him to the private lounge to meet the King. Michael took his leave and Johnny continued to talk with his mother. After a while Johnny brought up the question of the luggage and furnishings which had been brought from Knebworth in 1914 in readiness for their occupation. Louise was quick to confirm that she was in full custody of all that first shipment, and explained that after repeated requests to Lady Lytton to return the remainder of the items, she was told they were being held against some dispute or other and their release was refused.

Johnny mentioned that he and Misha had visited Knebworth the previous day and it had now been resolved and Lady Lytton was on side and very helpful in these times of need. She was in full agreement to keep the remainder of the possession safely under her care until it was the right time to release them back to the royal household.

Louise was so thankful that it had been dealt with and was happy to show Johnny the several large rooms in which the furniture had been stored. She explained that the war office had asked her permission for the use of some of the furniture to which they had agreed, but that the rooms were under her personal care and they were happy to allow the continued storage ensuring the safety for as long as was appropriate. She confirmed that the War Department was still responsible for the lease at Paddockhurst and that she was safe in the knowledge if that was the case then she was comfortably housed in the foreseeable future.

Louise then helped Johnny to look for the items he sought. He explained that he was searching for a trunk marked 'GDMAR 007'. After a long search, it seemed that it was not to be found. Louise then remembered that there was a trunk in her cellar which at the time she had thought was rather personal in the way it was marked. She had completely forgotten about it. She then took Johnny to the cellar and there it was in the middle of the room, gathering dust and quite safe.

He opened it, again by force, and dug down to the bottom to discover that the briefcase has remained undisturbed. He found the key, as in the other trunk at Knebworth, in a shirt pocket placed next to the case. The case was identical to the first case they had retrieved from Knebworth, and again this was borne out by the stamping of the letters 'GDMAR GB CD' on the underside. He opened it in front of Louise and there was the remainder of the jewellery belonging to Michael and Natasha.

Johnny saw the amazement on his mother's face and suddenly realised that whilst they were securing their own future, he had not considered his mother. When the war was finished, and if he and Michael were brought to a sticky end when back in Russia if the Allied invasion failed, then he would not be around to help her. Johnny then grasped a handful of valuables, and not knowing what they were or having any estimation of their value, put them into his mother's apron pocket who was standing over him, and asked her to find a very secure place to hide them. He made her promise that should a time come when she needed financial help, then she should simply use the jewellery as a means of supporting herself in the future. Louis began to argue against his generosity but Johnny gently hushed her and would have none of it. With that he closed the case and went back to the warmth of the lounge and sat by the welcoming log fire and sizzling kettle to make himself a cup of tea.

Louise now needed to leave, to carry out her morning

duties with the serving officers in the main building. Johnny gave his mother a long embrace and a kiss, and said he would see her again shortly.

20

King George V

eanwhile Michael had been taken to the private lounge and invited to make himself comfortable by the fire, and told that the King would join him in a short while. Michael for the first time became uncomfortable as he was losing the words to say the things he had been rehearsing in his mind for the past year. He knew from conversations with Buchanan on several occasions in 1917 that the King had personally blocked the safe passage of Tsar Nicholas to asylum in Britain. These rejections had a very serious effect on their safety, and in Michael's mind this was the highest form of treachery, especially amongst close family, as they were.

The resolve to show his anger had been mitigated by the British intent and efforts to reinstate the Russian Monarchy. The intricacy, cost and effort of the invasion plans to defeat the Bolsheviks was to be considered. Certainly, the accord, extreme help, and organisation he had received so far since leaving Gatchina had been exemplary.

After five minutes the anteroom door opened to the private lounge and the King walked in, dressed in the full uniform of a Field Marshal. Michael, being dressed in the equivalent Russian uniform, was suddenly aware of his perceived equality with the King and felt that he could speak with him on equal terms as military and head of state – elect. It was unusual for Michael to dress in this manner as he was known to be a man of the people and always dressed without wearing braid, medals or honours.

Neither saluted, and there was a pregnant silence for a few moments. The King, being an excellent host with dignitaries, stepped forward to warmly shake Michael's hand and invited him to be seated, then the King joined him.

After a few formal niceties of small talk it was becoming increasingly obvious that this was not such a cordial meeting and that there was a more important conversation to be had between them. Michael's agenda was that he simply wanted to know why the King had abandoned Nicholas and the Royal Family to a fate of extreme danger, and possibly the extinction of the Dynasty. The King was aware that he would be faced with this question and knew that he needed to provide honest answers and take the blame where required for any ensuing tragedies which might unfold.

However, to soften the confrontation, the King graciously arose and walked toward the drinks cabinet and offered Michael a choice from a well-stocked bar. He chose a Martini cocktail and the King took a stiff-looking whisky. Cigars were taken and the scene was set for – hopefully – an understanding conversation between them.

Michael opened the first round, and as forcefully as he could muster, with limited grace, leant forward with a stern look on his face and in a polite raised voice said to the King, 'Why?' Michael leaned back and waited for his reply.

The King stopped in his tracks for a moment, by this abrupt approach then gathered himself. The first reason, he started to explain, was the pressure he was receiving from Queen Mary, which was to such an extent that he could not ignore her protestations about the receiving of Nicholas and family. She feared for the unpopularity it would raise amongst the British people in that they had become very aware of the nation's disgust that Nicholas had not ameliorated the situation in Russia. It was patently obvious that much-needed change was required in the handling of affairs for the common good, and yet he was blind to the desperation and plight of the Russian people.

Queen Mary had forcibly brought the point that they would be condoning the views of Nicholas and his wife, and that the British people would see that as a sign of complicity. This view may well, through cause and effect, create difficulties for the stability of their own royal standing. There was indeed a growing menace from British Communists, who wanted a cessation to the war and all its consequential fallout. The British Government, fearing a collapse of confidence, was so steeped in the war that they would not accept anything less than a complete surrender of the German armed forces. There had been some appalling casualties so far, and a peace pact without outright victory would not be welcomed.

The second reason, he argued, was that there was a possibility of defeat by the German Army and early on, just after the abdication in March, America had not yet declared war on Germany – this was not until the following month. Even when they did so in April 1917, it was not certain that this would be sufficient to turn the tide towards an

Allied victory. There was growing concern that Russia under the Provisional Government, and the rise of Bolshevism, and the poverty and shortages in the armed forces, could possibly allow the Russian state to pursue a peace policy with Germany and thus open greater reinforcement forces to the Germans on the Western Front. Already there was collapse in the Russian Army and German units were filtering away from the Russian front to reinforce the Western Front.

Communism may well triumph within the power vacuum left behind and it would be necessary to deal with Russia on whatever terms were thought benign to the UK. If, then, there were a continued presence of the Romanovs in Britain, this would always be a threat to the new Russian Government, whomsoever they were, as a move towards the Romanov reinstatement within Russia would lead to a continuance of the civil war in Russia and be an embarrassment to the British Government.

The third reason was that the British Government, which at the outset was prepared to have the family reside in the UK in exile, was becoming increasingly circumspect and let it be seen that the rebuttal was coming from the British Royals, whilst the Government hid behind a screen of smoke and mirrors. The Government had thought about the USA offering exile facilities instead, but as time progressed, and when the USA declared war on Germany in April, that idea was losing traction. It was certain that the UK's best interests were served by a status quo until things became clearer as the war progressed.

Finally, it then became obvious that the Russian Interim Government, prompted more by Lenin and the rising star, Stalin, was more of a view that it wanted to control and deal with the Romanovs. They felt they had a bargaining tool in their hand. The subsequent house arrest and imprisonments of Nicholas in Tobolsk placed him so far away into Central Russia that a rescue would be impractical for the British Government, and as the war on the Western Front was a high priority, there would be little appetite and no good reason for it.

The entry of the Americans into the war would not ease any of those tensions as they were very unprepared for a war campaign several thousand miles away which required huge coordination to prosecute any action, and it was becoming obvious that they would not be ready until 1918.

Michael sat in silence, taking all these reasonings into account in his mind. He had never thought to progress his thoughts in this way until today. They were viable reasons and if the boot were on the other foot then he may well have acted accordingly.

The King then offered his sincere apologies and was magnanimous enough to say that he should accept the blame as Michael saw it, and hoped that in the fullness of time that the family would be reinstated and that Bolshevik power would end. The King, then, in trying to close the meeting, commented that he had great admiration for Michael and his endeavours so far, and his involvement in the future invasion plans, and he felt fully confident that with the help of America, Denmark, the Estonians and the remains of the White Army, there would be nothing less than a success in that endeavour.

He confirmed to Michael that once he had been made head of state and the Royal Family had been fully reinstated, without Nicholas playing any further role of importance, that he would like other members of the European Royals, provide support to their futures, and welcome an invitation to the Coronation of Tsar Michael II.

Michael remained silent and gazed into the fire for several minutes, as did the King, each engaged in his own thoughts. Michael then announced that although George had accepted responsibility, had he approved very early on that they given asylum in Britain, then his brother and family would now be safe. He said it was conjecture as to how events would have turned out on the political stage, and that should have been secondary to the safety of the House of Romanov, who were now being attacked and ostracised throughout Russia and being stripped of their wealth and safety. Michael then coldly affirmed the position which George had taken, of full responsibility, and finished by saying that he would also hold him to account for events that led to the deaths of Nicholas and any of his family.

They both rose and shook hands. Before they parted, Michael stepped towards George and gave him a long embracing hug, and whispered, 'I know the difficulties of the choices you were faced with and I could not say right now that I would have acted in any other way, should I have been drinking from that poisoned chalice.'

Michael left the room without any further comment, and without looking at King George.

21

Return to Filey

The Adjutant met Michael outside the lounge and escorted him back to Louise's door, and informed him that the car was waiting whenever they were ready to be taken back to the Royal Train waiting for them in Croydon.

Michael knocked and entered to find Johnson sitting by the fire and snoozing. He looked at his friend and thought about insisting that he remain here in the UK with his mother, in total safety. He sat beside him and thought of all the good times they had spent together at university and military college, and the fun they had growing up and the early years of laughter in the Royal Courts. He was especially pleased at how Johnson had shown such efficiency in becoming his personal secretary and how he had received from him so much help in administration, and loyalty. He was particularly grateful of how his incisive thinking and wisdom had come to play such a great part of his life, even more so now in these very trying times of political unrest and change.

He started to stir in his chair and Michael gently woke him from his short slumber. Johnson was quick to recover his countenance and enquired with much interest on how his meeting with the King had progressed.

Michael said, 'As well as might be expected,' and no more. He felt that he should keep his own counsel on the reasoning of the King, and never to speak of it again.

Michael then turned to Johnson and gave him all the good reasons why he should stay in the UK. He thanked him for being the best friend he had ever had, and said he would miss him more than he would ever know, but his decision on him remaining with his mother was final.

Johnson smiled and stood up to embrace Michael, thanking him for his generous thoughts and well-wishing. He then stood back, still holding Michael's shoulders, and said in a determined voice. 'Get lost, my old mate. Where you go, I go.' He then brightly announced that he had the second briefcase, and that they should now quickly make tracks back to Russia.

Michael knew it was pointless arguing with his friend, even when he had a good case to argue, as he knew Johnson's resolve would not be broken. He reminded him of the great dangers that lay ahead, but thanked him deeply and sincerely, as he knew it would be a very lonely place without him in his life.

They made their way to the waiting car and set off to Croydon, carrying the second briefcase. Johnson then confessed to Michael that he had grabbed a handful of jewellery out of the case and given it to his mother as an insurance in case he may not be around to provide for her after the war.

Michael was happy that he had been so thoughtful, and thanked him for his wisdom. Michael then realised that he may not have said farewell to his mother, and mentioned that to him. Johnson simply replied that he had left his mother a long letter of love and hope, and that it was better that he just disappeared, as he would not be able to handle the emotion and heartache that both would experience on separating. It was best that way.

It was now early afternoon and they knew it would be dark when they arrived back at Filey Bay to meet Robert Blackburn. They also knew that a long and dangerous flight was awaiting them, to Denmark in the Type L floatplane in which they had flown off from the *Iron Duke* .

Upon boarding the train, they ate a light lunch and then slept during the whole of the journey back to Filey station.

22

Burial of the Treasures

A rriving at Filey Railway station they were again met by Captain Laker of the RFC in the drab and unwashed Price Henry Vauxhall. Laker asked Johnson if he would mind driving Michael onto Hunmanby, as he was instructed to take the train onwards to York where he had to interview new recruits to the RFC. He said the car could be left at Hunmanby, and to give the keys to Robert Blackburn for safekeeping. Michael overheard the conversation and gave his immediate approval.

Now, with all their luggage and the two briefcases retrieved from Knebworth and Paddockhurst loaded onto the Prince Henry, they drove off towards Hunmanby to meet Robert Blackburn and the Type L.

Nearing Hunmanby, they spotted a roadside café and thought it a good idea to stop and have a chat before they arrived. The reason being that Johnson was concerned about taking the jewellery stash back to Russia as he felt that it would become a burden to hide and it could at any point be stolen. Or even lost on the journey through some mishap or other. Michael felt that he had a good point and it would be a tragedy if either of those events were to occur.

They thought for a while over tea and sandwiches and then Johnson suddenly exclaimed, 'Got it! We bury them here in Filey Bay.'

He explained that if the Allied invasion was successful, then the jewellery could always be recovered in a trip back to the UK. However, if it was unsuccessful, then it was likely that they would be implicated in the failed invasion, and executed. So the jewellery would have no significance in their lives. They could create a coded message to be left for their loved ones and descendants in the hope that they would discover the whereabouts of the buried treasures.

Before they left the café, Johnson enquired whether he could buy a few large earthenware pots with lids, used for making stew. The proprietor was amused by this request and said that they would come at a price. Johnson agreed a rather excessive price for four pots. As they left the café, the owner, who had become a little suspicious of the surely posture of Michael and Johnson as they were certainly not local people, jokingly shouted out they may be jewellery thieves and were thinking about burying them.

Johnson replied, 'Got it in one!'

The proprietor and his wife thought that this just might be the case, and were more concerned when they saw them drive off in a rather expensive-looking but very drab motor car with RFC insignia markings. The lady of the house then exclaimed that it could be true, and that they should contact the Hunmanby police in the morning.

Michael and Johnson stowed the four large earthenware pots into the back of the car and sped off towards the cliffs at Speeton. This seemed like an excellent plan, especially as Michael could appreciate the dangers that Johnson was concerned about. So, they gave some thought as to where would be the best place. It had to be in an easy location for access, and that could be identified on an Ordnance Survey map.

Michael had noted in his many visits to Hunmanby in preparation for the Air Race in 1914, that there was a small settlement on the coast in a place called Reighton Gap, just one mile south of Hunmanby. There was a road leading directly down to the clifftop settlement, which had a useful carpark to the right on the cliff edge, used by occasional tourists to gain a viewing point of the magnificent cliffs of Speeton and Filey Bay towards the Brig. They thought it an excellent choice. They were disinclined to bury the cases in Hunmanby as they would be expected around now, and would be seen.

So, they drove onwards and turned left in the village of Reighton to take them to the cliff top. That road they noted was called Sands Road; it was essential that they picked as many landmarks as possible for future collection, which may be many years away. Travelling down the narrow lane they were thrilled to ride the steep folds in the road. It gave them a sort of childish joy as Michael stepped on the gas of the Prince Henry and drove quickly into the indulating folds and experiencing the breath-taking feelings with shouts of joy like being on a roller-coaster at the fairground. They certainly would not forget that landmark.

There were very few shacks in the settlement, and only some with dimmed lights. They entered a clearing at the end of the road without being seen. Michael pulled the Henry up quite sharply as they had not realised how close to the cliff edge they were.

Johnson jumped out and said, 'Perfect choice.'

They were helped by the clear night and a half moon which was rising over Flamborough Head; it provided adequate lighting without having to resort to a hurricane lamp, hence avoiding the possibility of being spotted by anyone.

The boot of the Henry had an array of tools and shovels (and hurricane lamps) to deal with such situations as were common in early motoring on unmetalled roads. Johnson selected a narrow spade and marched off, disappearing over the sloping cliff edge carrying two of the pots and the two briefcases under his arm. Michael was happy to let his friend do the hard work and was conscious of not really wanting to see the exact location, as Johnson would excel on his own in the place of his own choice.

Michael saw two benches on the cliff top and thought he would sit on one and take in the wonderful views and watch the moonlight reflection dance over the waves below. During this very quiet time he relaxed to a point that he fell into a dreamy state and thought entirely of his wife and child and how much he loved them both deeply and beyond words. He desperately hoped that he would see them again soon, and that all the possibilities of the invasion and return of Russia to Imperialism would work out for the best.

How he hoped that it would be a peaceful transition back to power and a complete surrender of the Bolsheviks. Surely they knew that there would be a reversal of their popular uprisings and see that the invasion was a force which they could not win against?

Michael's dreamy state continued and he was being embraced in a very warm and loving atmosphere which was pervading his body and mind. At that point he saw before him an illumination of an apparition of Natasha who was floating towards him across the glistening sea, growing in size as it moved ever closer to him until it became a full-size vision of Natasha. She was smiling sweetly, as she sat down beside him and snuggled her head onto his shoulder.

Michael knew in his mind that this could not be. But in placing his arm around the apparition his heart told him it was very true. He could feel her warmth and the firmness of her slight frame; he pulled her tightly towards him and gazed into her face.

In the meantime, Johnson, having found a suitable location, dug a hole in the soft brown clay. He opened the two briefcases brought from Knebworth and Paddockhurst emptying the contents into the two pots, and placed the excavated earth over them, firming it thoroughly with his feet. He then returned up the slope with the empty briefcases and put them into the boot of the car.

He now gathered the two remaining earthenware pots, and the suitcase brought over from Russia containing the items from Maria Pavlova's Vladimir Palace and the jewellery gifted to Michael from Nicholas. He soon found another suitable spot to bury the treasures, being purposely apart from the first location for security reasons. This was the best place to put Maria's treasures, as they simply had not found the time to deposit these into a bank vault in England. He quickly dug a pit of similar size.

He opened the canister using the secret mechanism,

took out the Gladstone bags and emptied each into one of the pots. Then the three Gladstone bags, which contained the jewels of Maria Pavlovna were emptied and put into the other pot. He placed the two earthenware pots into the pit and buried them as before. He brought the canister and the empty bags back to the car and left them in the boot.

What seemed like minutes was probably much longer, but Michael awoke from his dreams and saw Johnson standing over him looking rather pleased with himself. Michael snapped out of the vision with some annoyance. He really knew it had been a figment of his imagination, but he had enjoyed it while it lasted.

Johnson then made his way to the boot of the car and pulled out a small RFC sextant which he had spotted there earlier. He then announced that he was going to undertake some triangulation on the places where he had buried the two suitcases. He asked Michael to join him at the locations of the buried treasures. Michael watched Johnson, who was a keen surveyor in his early college days; he took various sightings by using the moon, Filey Brig and the sea edge of Speeton Cliffs. He noted the exact time and date from his trusty Wilson watch, and the bearings from compass north on the sextant. He also took a bearing on the horizon, and to the rear the coastguard houses which were perched on top of the high Speeton Cliffs in the background, all for good measure. He did this on both burial places and recorded them in his notebook. Later he would be able to calculate the exact positions using latitude and longitude coordinates. Michael observed other scenic objects, to fix in his mind. A little white red-roofed cottage on the cliff edge became a good point of reference, that he understood, and was baffled by the exertions of Johnson with his scientific mind. With that they were pleased and set off in the Henry back to Hunmanby to meet Blackburn.

23

Seaplane to Denmark

It was a short journey, and they soon found the road which led to Hunmanby Gap leading to the bungalow which Robert Blackburn had used next to the hangar and slipway. Michael pulled up outside the bungalow and Robert came out quickly to meet him, concerned that they were running behind schedule for the take-off as the tide was now turning and soon the sands would be covered in water. There was little time for a full catch-up of events in both their lives but long embraces and words of encouragement were delivered by Blackburn who had always been a strong supporter of Michael and his family.

Whilst the Type L could take off on water it was always desirable to use the sands as it gave them better lift and would not suffer any stalling from sea spray being flung into the radial engine. Quickly they packed the small amounts of luggage into the waiting craft on the slipway and dressed in the warm fleece-lined trousers and flying jackets, with goggles and life vests, which they had left in the Type L when they arrived in Filey a few days earlier.

Blackburn then turned to Michael and briefed him

on the journey. He told him that he should first head due south over the Speeton Cliffs and pick up the Flamborough lighthouse beam. The light beam had been fixed onto an eastern bearing and would remain lit for two hours after take-off, then it would return to shipping duties. Most of the sea traffic on coastal steamers had been put on stop and anchored in blackout, waiting until the lighthouse would again become active.

When they had lost sight of the beam, they would be looking to pick up the lights of ships from the Grand Fleet which would be sailing due east, line astern, and being spaced at 50 kilometre intervals.

'They will pick up your headlight beacon mounted on each wing tip and as soon as they see you they will illuminate the ship and fire two star shells for you to identify that they are indeed the Grand Fleet. This will be your guide to Esbjerg. When you arrive at Esbjerg the town and beach will be lit up, as Denmark is neutral in the war, and the beach landing will again be set by burning oil barrels to form a landing channel.'

'Your tanks have increased capacity and are full and will be more than required to carry out the journey which will take you an estimated five hours at a steady speed of 110 kph over the distance of 580 kilometres. You can increase the speed towards the end of your journey to make up any lost time by 50 per cent if you have the need, as there has been an engine upgrade since your flying days in 1914. However, your fuel consumption will increase, so be very careful as you only have a 20 per cent extra fuel load and it will be touch and go to get you there at an increased speed.'

Johnson took down all the details, writing them in his

notebook. With that, and the two flasks of hot drinks – hot coffee with a shot of whisky – they boarded the Type L and carried out the pre-flight checks. Everything being correct, they fired up the engine and let it warm for three minutes, then taxied off the slipway and onto the beach, facing south and towards the now menacing Speeton Cliffs.

The seaplane roared into life and Michael felt the increased surge of power from the upgraded engine which they enjoyed from the flight from Scapa to Filey bay just a few days earlier. Soon the plane was lifting and they were seeing the small settlement of Reighton Gap to the starboard side. The lift was not as expected; the wind was changing direction as they approached the cliffs and it was with concern that Michael had to provide more lift without stalling whilst giving the engine maximum power. As the cliff came ever closer it was at the last moment that they shot upwards and over the cliff with only 2 metres clearance.

The relief on the face of Johnson was palpable and Michael was smiling to himself at the adventure of danger. Johnson did not share those feelings, and was just relieved that his good friend was a great pilot in whom he had complete confidence.

Up, up and away they climbed, and soon saw the fixed beam of Flamborough lighthouse ahead. They raced towards it and then banked sharp to port and rode along the bright light which was directing them due east. The joy was immense and both shouted with glee at the feat they had just pulled off, excitedly riding a homeward-bound beam. The two pals chatted excitedly for the first half-hour.

The Flamborough light was now dimmed and the sea

mist had all but obscured it. They just hoped that the most dangerous part of the mission flying in total darkness would go to plan. The clouds had now obscured the moon and bearings were impossible should they miss the Grand Fleet. However, they were now due to pick up the first lights of the fleet. Michael decided to drop the height so that the low clouds enveloping them would not become an issue, and hopefully their navigation lights would soon become visible to the first ships of the British Navy.

After flying blind, using the inboard compass, they hoped that the rising wind speed would not be taking them off course, and were anxious about missing the first ship. Another five minutes passed, and then to their great relief they saw two star shell bursts on the port bow, 15 degrees ahead. They were off course, and so turned towards the diminishing light of the flares, and then could just faintly pick up the revolving searchlight of the first ship.

They soon came back on track and slid in behind the searchlight and overtook the ship directly from astern. The beam then turned eastward and stayed fixed allowing them to use that beam to ride to the next point of light.

Suddenly as they were leaving the ship behind, they unmistakably heard the British national anthem being played from the loudspeakers on deck. What a great feeling for two Russian Anglophiles to know that they were, in their hearts, part of the British Empire.

Losing the ship's eastward beam, again they relied upon compass bearings for the blind flying time between the ships' lights. After a period of nervous tension since losing the beam from the first ship, they were elated to pick up a faint light searching the western skies. They headed towards it and soon saw the welcome sight of two star shells bursting into the dark skies. This time, due to course corrections which Michael had made whilst flying blind, they were no more than 5 degrees off course.

As they flew over ship #2 they heard the loudspeaker very plainly burst into life and play the anthem of the navy, which was 'Rule Britannia', making the two pals chuckle to each other as they had not expected to be serenaded on their way to Denmark. Ships 3, 4, 5, 6 and 7 were met easily, and on each occasion, they were serenaded by sea shanties. The final rendition on ship 7, which brought them to tears, was the Russian national anthem.

Johnson noted that they were behind schedule by thirty minutes, as their journey had been too leisurely and not helped by headwinds. Michael had thought better of countering that with extra revs as he was concerned that his fuel levels should be become an issue, but he decided to give just a few revs more and squeezed the type L a little, enjoying the surge forward

The final leg was now in sight as they could see in the distance the lights of Esbjerg fully illuminating the coastline ahead. As they drew nearer to the port side they were pleased to see the oil barrel runway. As they approached it, Michael was not certain that they could land safely, as the run-in was complicated by an island which was too close to the lit runway and would need height to clear it, then a sudden drop down in height. The lit runway was on the end of the docks, and that presented more dangers for a run-in.

Michael circled twice and decided the best option was to use the harbour channel, which had very smooth waters. He could gain references of height from the glinting harbour lights on the calm sea channel which would give him an excellent opportunity for a safe landing. He circled one more time to assess his position and then set up for a water landing. Michael adjusted his height, and speed, which was favourable to the wind, and gently settled the Type L onto the water with a small amount of disturbance, then throttled back to idle the engine. When they had reached coasting speed he steered towards the harbour entrance and glided in.

The harbour was full of fishing boats and the odd tramp steamer, but he did spot an empty mooring in the Marina basin and gently pulled in to the side. A startled mariner, just tying up his own sailing boat, stared in amazement at the sight of an aeroplane which could travel on water.

The Harbourmaster was now running down to the moorings and waving at Michael, calling out to him in Danish. Michael responded eloquently in Danish as this was the language of his mother, the Empress of Russia Maria Feodorovna Dagmar of Denmark. The Harbourmaster was annoyed that Michael was late and had not used the oil-lit runway where there was a reception party awaiting him. Michael explained that the incoming tide had left very little width and he had spotted dunes further forward, and the island and proximity to the harbour would have meant that he would endanger the seaplane upon entry. That was why he had chosen the sea channel entry into the harbour. The Harbourmaster tied the seaplane to the marina platform and helped them unload their luggage from the plane.

Walking towards the Coastguard Office they were met by two people who had just alighted from a horse-drawn carriage. As they walked briskly over to them, Johnson became aware that he recognised the pair, who were dressed in black leather jackets and black trousers. Sure enough, as they drew close one of them called out Johnson's name with outstretched arms and it was Olga Bystrovia, who they had met on the first leg of the journey from Gatchina. The other person was already shaking hands with Michael and each offered an embrace, delighted to see each other safe and very sound. Michael slapped Reilly's back and shouted with joy, as the best vision he had had since leaving him at the dockside where they parted company before joining the *Standart*. Reilly, ribbing him, reminded Michael that it was the *Standart* no longer but the '*18 March*'. Michael coughed and choked with sadness at the thought.

'Gentlemen, please join us to the railway station.' They threw the luggage into the back of the carriage and trotted off to the station which was a short distance away.

Johnson's first thought was for the Type L which they had left behind in the marina basin. Reilly announced that it would now be cared for by the Danish Government and might find a role in service with them during the coming invasion.

After a short while they arrived at the station and boarded a second-class coach. This low-level exposure was seen to be best. It was imperative that Michael was not recognised as the country was neutral and teaming with German and British spies. He enjoyed the thought of once again being unrecognisable and in disguise.

Michael's enquiries now moved to the next step in the journey, and Olga replied that they would be meeting

King Christian X at the Garsten Palace, and he would be attended by members of the government and armed forces. Olga explained that there had been substantial talks with London and Washington and that Woodrow Wilson had made a quick stopover recently to reinforce the commitment to the invasion, and first-stage plans had been agreed.

The purpose of Michael's visit was to convince them of his determination to head up the invasion and to accede to the throne as and when the Allies had secured the safety of the Royals and the country at large. Michael was happy at this, as it would be an opportunity to speak with his cousin the King, and perhaps with Queen Alexandrine. The last time they had met was in 1910, after King Edward VII had died, at his funeral in London.

After three hours of stop and start they arrived at Sonderberg, from where the Garsten Palace was only 12 kilometres. Reilly mentioned to Michael that this was a very convenient meeting place as the Flensburg docks in Germany were only 20 kilometres away and were the starting point of the next leg of the journey by submarine. Johnson's thoughts hit a brick wall at the prospect of being submerged in a steel coffin, and he was predicting in the back of his mind a watery grave.

At Sonderberg they were met by a member of the Danish household who was chauffeuring a grand white Rolls-Royce from the Royal stable. After five minutes, they were entering the gates of the Garsten Palace, impressed at the formality of its design, and stark whiteness of the whole edifice. The grand courtyard, whilst small in comparison to Gatchina, was welcoming and had a certain feeling of safety and warmth within. Outside were parked several luxury cars and coaches and it was plain to see that their arrival was awaited.

24

Meeting the King and Queen of Denmark

They alighted from the car and were immediately met by King Christian bidding them a warm welcome. His wife the Queen was at his side and Michael and Johnson were taken aback by their warmth and total lack of protocol. This was so invigoratingly pleasing that they felt instantly amongst friends and supporters. They were more impressed that, at such an early hour, the King and Queen had arisen to greet them.

Queen Alexandrine was clearly a homemaker and servant to those in her presence. She would be as happy in the scullery with the servants or at the table with dignataries. Her welcoming attitude put all her guests at ease and her homes were formal, yet places of warmth without the usual pomp and ceremony of a royal household.

King Christian X was blessed with very similar personality gifts as his Queen and they made an engaging couple, who held their country in good balance in the world and in neutrality during times of war.

After a minute of small-talk the Queen asked Michael and Johnson to follow her to their chambers and suggested that they should rest, wash and change, and that lunch would be served at approximately one o'clock. Johnson was impressed with the down to earth nature of the Queen who did not feel it beneath herself to be a genial hands-on host. Such a difference from the snobbery and strict protocols of the Russian and British Throne and Government. Their bags were brought to the room together with light refreshments before they slept. Olga and Reilly were shown to separate rooms and made equally welcome.

After ten minutes Olga came to their room with a bundle of clothes which turned out to be more disguises for each to wear for the working lunch. Olga explained that from now on they would remain in these clothes until they were due to leave Tallinn. They unrolled the bundles and were surprised to see similar uniforms to those which they had left Russia several days ago. Michael was dressed as a Government Official and Johnson again as a lowly Corporal. Michael was back to being Colenius Johannsen, it seemed.

They slept for a few hours, bathed and then made their way down to the dining hall where they met the whole assembly and were shown to their seats by the senior butler. Johnson was quick to note that Olga was dressed again as a Commandant Commissar, as she had announced herself as being on the journey north to Belomorsk. The uniform, whilst generally plain, was rather more decorated than that of Reilly, and she also took on the air of a senior diplomat and officer. He wondered again what her background was in the British Secret Service.

The King met them at the foot of the stairs and greeted

them once more, and invited all into the dining room. There they were informally introduced to Carl Theodor Zahle, Council President and First Minister of the Danish Government, and Otto Joachim Moltke Kofoed-Hansen who was the Admiral of the Fleet.

Lunch was served where conversation quickly started and for the most part was of family matters between the Danish and Russian Royal Families. Michael was pleased to understand that the King and Queen were desperately concerned at the current fate of Nicholas and his family, and of the many other household members who were in equally dubious positions. They were quick to show support, and were contemplating making the final decision to enter the war against the Bolsheviks.

After lunch, they withdrew to the drawing room where there were several armchairs and sofas surrounding a blazing log fire. Cigars and port were offered around for the relaxation of all the guests. Michael was astonished to see Olga take a cigar and a huge slug of port.

The First Minister now became the main speaker, and he rather pointedly suggested that Michael may not have the stamina for the events lying before him, and said that it was a great responsibility he was undertaking. He asked, with some trepidation, about his wife Natasha: would she become Empress, and was she ready to take on the political and royal duties which would change her life? In addition, what of his son George? Whilst he was young, it would mean a life quite different from that he was living now, and for Natasha too. Was he indeed prepared to go the distance?

These were questions that Michael had raised to himself on many occasions in the past few weeks, but had never faced such questioning so succinctly presented to him by Carl. It was frightening, and suddenly he felt alone with the enormity of what he was about to undertake. He was not born for that role, as Nicholas was still alive and it would mean overturning his authority even though he had abdicated all responsibility. On that issue, he was comforted to accept that Nicholas had passed that mantle to himself, but it had never meant as much as it did now, as he had rejected that office eleven months ago.

Michael went into deep thought and silence pervaded the room for two or three minutes. At this point, nobody felt that there was any room for conversation. Johnson broke the silence and put his hand on the arm of his friend and quietly said that whilst an answer was needed, he himself would place his duty forever with Michael and Natasha. He comforted him in the view that, as he knew Natasha as well as Michael, he had no doubt that she would stand by him and become an excellent counsellor and consort, and that George would have the best of care in growing up and become the next in line to the throne.

Johnson also mentioned that there could be a complete change in the attitude of royalty, and that he could look to the Danish Royal Family and see how they were governing in open and concessionary terms towards the people. There could equally be such a devotion to the future Russian Royals as Michael made the fundamental changes that were being conceived in his mind.

Michael needed that insertion of wisdom from Johnson into his troubled thoughts, and after a moment he rose and addressed the audience. He raised his glass to a toast and said, 'It is my duty to serve the people of Russia in the terms of a referendum and manifesto which will bring peace and prosperity for generations to come.' He then added, 'Out with the old and in with the new. Long Live Russia and its new Royal Family.'

The delegates in the room rose in unison and loud cheers broke out and a round of handshakes and back-slapping were the order of the evening.

The Prime Minister sat down first and with head in his hands wept with joy that he had delivered these stark truths to Michael and found that he had seriously contemplated all the issues. He had made a monumentally important decision which would change the order of the world from this day forward. After they all had sat down, King Christian, with his wife's hand on his arm, announced that the Government and Crown of Denmark would support the invasion.

Then Admiral Otto Kofoed stood up and briefly discussed the agreed plans in which they would bring the Baltic Sea to an open territory for the British fleet, as the start of the war against Bolshevism. He would also have with him a fleet of American destroyers of a modern class with high speed capabilities, and these would be the main defence of the British battleships which would pound the shores and anchored ships of the German fleet, hoping to defeat them inshore.

He reminded the audience that with such a powerful flotilla of MTB boats, destroyers and submarines of the British Navy, the German fleet would be strangled, and would be foolish to enter open waters. The German fleet was already very nervous about coming out into action, and with the serious lack of morale in their navy and poor supply chains, it was likely that they might even surrender. Michael was pleased to hear all this talk and felt more assured of the outcome of the invasion being a success.

After two hours of further chat and confidence-building, Olga announced that it would soon be time to depart, to take Michael and Johnson on the next leg of the journey home. The royal car was loaded with their luggage and they set off to the German border bound for Flensburg.

They soon entered Krusa, which was on the border with Germany, and crossed with ease as the diplomatic papers were sufficient for them to move forward with the assistance of a signed letter from Admiral Sheer which granted them entry.

Michael was again impressed at how Olga had used her fluency in German and diplomatic authority to ease their way past the borders and achieve an official stamp of entry. The guards had paid little attention to the occupants of the Danish registered car as Olga's presence had a shrivelling effect on anyone who seemingly would want to challenge her authority.

They then quickly drove on to Flensburg and arrived at the dock gates. The Flensburg docks were of some considerable size and Michael could clearly see several battleships and cruisers in the distance. Once again, the security was quickly by-passed with another official document being withdrawn from Olga's briefcase, and again it was a signed instruction from Admiral Sheer to allow entry. This time they were escorted by a Mercedes truck with armed German guards sitting in the back, and they were asked to follow them.

Johnson was greatly impressed at the whole procedure as it was so seemingly simple and carried full authority. The fears they had contrived within themselves as they approached the German border were now totally vanquished. They felt that this was very much a 'mission possible'.

Within a few minutes, they were pulling up at a dockside which had a great number of U-boats moored alongside, and some were even three abreast. They all alighted from the vehicle and stood staring at the scene before them. Olga and Reilly strode off towards the U-boats and were met by a Commander who shook their hands and could be seen swapping papers and reading them with intensity. After a few minutes of discussions and the entry into the mix of a very senior-looking Commander, final handshakes were given and Olga returned to Michael and Johnson and briefed them.

25

U-151

O lga had met with Admiral Scheer in Berlin as Commandant Commissar of the Cheka. Reilly was also there. The Admiral was steadfast, respected, and used few words to convey his feelings and plans. He had commanded the German High Seas Fleet at the Battle of Jutland. His perfectionist tendencies, and the bold stance he took when faced with opposition, soon brought agreement with those he was engaging with. His strategies were as uncompromising as his nature but were well planned and usually brought success. This was a man of quick decisions and impatience.

Olga explained to Michael that they had forged papers from Lenin, so they could address him as a precursor to the meeting for a cessation of war between Russia and Germany, to be signed at Brest Litovsk in March. In doing so, she was supplying sensitive information about the Russian naval fleet and presenting an offer of control of key naval vessels which would be made available to join the German Grand Fleet as a bargaining chip towards the peace agreement.

The main purpose however was to obtain official papers

from Admiral Scheer which allowed the U-boat U-151, during its sea trials after its refit in Flensburg, to take a high-ranking Finnish diplomat to Russia. The diplomat, Colenious Johannsen, was visiting the Danish Government to persuade them to continue their neutrality.

This was to counter the British Government's recent diplomatic mission to Denmark to persuade the Danish Navy to engage in combined Allied actions to clear the Baltic Sea of the blockade set up by Germany. The Finnish Government, who were in the sphere of Russia, would recognise the peace deal between Russia and Germany, and therefore would not accept the control of the Baltic by British and American naval forces.

Colenious Johannsen was also keen to provide for Germany the bulk of the Russian fleet which was in anchor at Helsinki. Finland had been neutral for the best part of the war and did not have a standing army. They were of a view that they could gain full independence from the influence of Russia on the signing of the peace treaty. This would allow them to be able to trade independently with the adjacent nations and the world at large, and they would hope to see a strong trading treaty with Germany.

Admiral Scheer thought this was a very good position taken by the Finnish government, and had gained full approval from Kaiser Wilhelm to prosecute this in secrecy and to help Johannsen as much as he possibly could. From the Russian perspective, they were hoping that the help which they were to provide the German Navy with an increased volume of naval assets, would determine their retention of the governance of Poland.

So, unpleasant as much of the triangle of objectives

were, it did each government a favour in the outcome of the coming treaty of Brest Litovsk. For Germany, it could at a stroke add more power to their own Fleet and give them the confidence to break out of the Baltic and deal with the British Navy to the point of annihilating it, bringing control of the high seas into the hands of Germany.

However, this was a grand plot of subterfuge and smoke screens which Olga and Reilly had set up on behalf of MI6 in London. It really had one single purpose, which was to get Grand Duke Michael back into Russia and Gatchina under the utmost secrecy; and what better way than to use the enemy powers to assist that in plain sight? Michael and Johnson were in total amazement at the intricacy of all of this, and knew deep down that the sheer audacity of the plot was bound to win through.

They were then taken aboard the U-151 which was tied up in the docks, and introduced to Captain Heinrich von Nostitz Janckendorff who had recently taken command of the submarine. They were also introduced to the rest of the officers, and all four were taken into the belly of the super-large boat into quite comfortable quarters, given it was in a submarine.

Johnson remarked to Michael at the sheer size of the vessel and was amazed at the armaments which were clearly visible. Michael was also taken aback by the 'super sub' and gave due credit to the German design and technology in creating such a vessel. He wondered what damage this had already wreaked among the shipping of the Western Allies.

After they had settled down and rested for a while, they could hear increased activity coming from the ship's complement and then heard the gentle humming of the engines as they were brought into life. They were underway. Johnson's thoughts immediately turned to his earlier trepidation of being submerged and he felt sick at the thought.

After twenty minutes the Captain's voice came over the speaker system announcing that the sub had cleared port checks and was about to sail out of Flensburg for open waters. Michael was keen to join the Captain in the Comm. He knocked on Olga's door and mentioned that to her as a request. She strongly advised that, wherever he went, Reilly must accompany him. He had the quick wit to avoid any conversations which might prejudice the plan, and would keep Michael advised and under control. With that she spoke to Reilly, who to Michael's surprise was sharing her cabin, and he told Michael that he would have a word with the Captain and come back for Michael at the right time.

After an hour, Reilly appeared at Michael's door and beckoned him to follow. Permission had been granted. The journey to the conning tower was a tight squeeze in the passageways where they were often passing submariners at station or passing by with given right of way. The machinery and pipework was a maze of organised spaghetti and it seemed a monumental task to understand what was what.

They arrived at the Comm, and Captain Janckendorff was pleased to see them and advised them to dress in warmer gear from the Comm wardrobe. He then climbed the conning tower ladder, asking them to follow. At that point Johnson also joined them as this was a good opportunity to see the sights, and more so to get a breath of fresh air and escape from his fears.

Conversation abounded between the four, about the

history of the U-boat and its long distance patrols. Captain Janckendorff was delighted to explain that in this ship, and several other ships of similar build, Germany had created the ultimate U-boat at Flensburg and other yards, which were true long-range submarine cruisers. They were of the Deutschland class and this was originally named the Oldenburg before being given the designation U-151, the first of its class.

This submarine was originally built as a blockade-breaking civilian cargo submarine operated by the North German Lloyd Line, and had a cargo capacity of 700 tonnes. She engaged in high-value transatlantic commerce, whilst submerging to avoid British patrols in their home waters. On her first trip to America, she carried dyestuff and gemstone cargoes stored in side bulges outside of the pressure hull, and then nickel, tin and rubber back to Germany.

In 1917, they were refitted to become war vessels and to be used in long-range cruises reaching far into the Atlantic, patrolling the American coast and as far as South America. They were on the lookout for opportune military targets and often, with the bulk-carrying side bulges, they were also able to confiscate valuable cargo which was taken from surrendered shipping.

She had a top speed of 23.0 kph surfaced and 10 kph submerged. A patrol range of 46,000 kilometres at a surface speed of 10 kph, and 120 kilometres at 6 kph using battery power as it submerged. He went on proudly to inform them that she had a test depth of 50 metres. The main armament had twin 150 mm deck guns, 1,688 rounds of ammunition, eighteen torpedoes, and she was manned by a crew of fifty-six , but she had room for twenty more.

At ease with his guests, he then continued to reveal the next phase of her tours. She was in Flensburg for a refit, repairs and changeover of command after five months of cruising over 16,000 kilometres. Three months earlier, she was in collision with a British warship, HMS *Begonia*, ultimately sinking her, whilst under the command of his predecessor. He then mentioned that after this secret rendezvous and journey into the far reaches of the Baltic, where sea trials would be carried out, they were then to proceed on long-range patrols of the American eastern seaboard where pickings were still rich, and he hoped to be on station by the coming May.

Janckendorff continued, pleased to announce the great feat of one of her sister ships, U-155 Deutschland, in 1917. During the summer of that year she made a 105-day cruise, leaving Germany around 24 May and returning on 4 September. During her traverse of the Northern Passage around Scotland and out into the Atlantic Ocean, she was stalked and nearly sunk by one of Germany's own U-19 near Utsira Island, Norway. Far into the Atlantic and home waters, she sank 19 merchant ships, most by either self-scuttling or gunfire. She also attacked nineteen Allied armed merchantmen but only succeeded in sinking nine of them. Upon her return to Germany she had covered 18,930 kilometres, of which 1,150 kilometres had been travelled submerged, one of the longest voyages made by a U-boat during the war so far. 'These are the finest submarines in the world, gentlemen,' he exclaimed very proudly.

Johnson then asked about the general journey protocol for the sailing to Tallinn.

Captain Janckendorff said, 'Generally, when we are in mid-Baltic waters, then we will be submerged by day and on the surface at night.'

He pointed out that they were under total radio silence for the whole outward journey and that they had to avoid contact with shipping at all costs. Minefields had been set by Germany, and they were thus confined to certain free lanes. However, there were further more secret safe lanes which had been disclosed to them, the details of which had come directly from the Kreigsmarine HQ, which they were to locate and use to speed their journey to Tallinn.

One of the biggest threats was contact with a British submarine, of which there were at least four operating in Baltic waters from as early as January 1917. The bigger threat would come from German submarines, of which there were plenty on patrol and doing sea trials and training in the Baltic. They would have no knowledge of the U-151's presence as there was a complete blackout on this mission.

The weather was turning cold and ice could be seen forming on the rails of the conning tower, and it was suggested that they transfer below to the Comm. They soon returned to their cabins and were met by Olga who beckoned them into her cabin.

She had just seen that there was also a very senior German naval officer on board who she had recognized from British intelligence documents she had seen a few years ago. They had briefly met whilst passing in the corridors. She was convinced it was Admiral Alfred von Tirpitz, who had resigned from active service in 1916 due to his unaccepted demands that unrestricted submarine warfare should continue and be increased. She explained that his argument was that if Britain and the Allies were imposing a blockade causing starvation of the German people, then they should break that blockade or starve Great Britain in return. More to the point, they were all to eat dinner together in the officers' wardroom that evening and were sure to encounter the elderly Admiral.

As the submarine was a huge converted long distance merchant vessel, common areas were unusually large, and the dining room was no exception. The dining table, which was also used as a planning and meeting area for officers, was set out with twelve seats and was laid out with the best of finery and tableware. This astonished Michael as he had heard of the terrible and cramped smelly conditions that were commonplace in the submarine service of all countries at war.

They sat around with other serving officers and it was notable that the two top seats were not occupied. During light pre-dinner conversation, the informal atmosphere was interrupted and turned to formality upon the entry into the dining area of a higher-ranking naval officer with Captain Janckendorff at his side. He was introduced as Admiral von Tirpitz. The scene was certainly set for an interesting evening's discussion.

Dinner was served: a four course meal of excellent quality, and eaten amidst generally good-hearted banter conducted in a mixture of German and limited Russian. This proved to be a time of ease and reflection on the perceived good nature and courtesy levels of the enemy at close quarters.

The Admiral was a large and imposing figure who sported a handsome, creatively styled beard which tended to declare the position of leadership. He was courteous, fair-minded and very pragmatic. One of his generous traits was sympathy toward the preservation of life when presented in its immediacy. He did not promote unwonton killing, and influenced his naval commanders to show mercy.

Tirpitz was, by the standards of his time, a modern naval officer. He possessed a sound knowledge of the world, a dedicated mind, and an active interest in technology, and he was a brilliant organiser. He was obsessed by his work; he therefore tended to be biased and, once he had enunciated his principles, raised them to the status of a doctrine. The continuous and steady implementation of the naval laws took priority over other technical, tactical and political considerations. Naval construction and its impact were to determine how the navy was to be used and hence its political value, and not vice versa. With the largest ever German Navy, which under him became the world's second-largest, Tirpitz forged an efficient military weapon that did not see the action for which it was intended in the war.

After dinner, cigars, schnapps, vodka and port were served and the chatter became more loose, especially from Von Tirpitz who felt safe and secure in whatever subject he talked of. He perceived that all the men around the table were pursuing self-serving objectives, with the approval of each of their countries. Von Tirpitz felt enabled to chat amiably about his vision of the outcome of the war, and said he was confident that they would now snatch victory out of the jaws of defeat and starvation, due to the forthcoming peace treaty. Indeed, hostilities at that time between the central powers had ceased in anticipation of the signing of the treaty scheduled for the coming days, and even as he spoke, vast numbers of troops were being refreshed and sent onwards to the Western Front for a spring campaign.

Reilly took the opportunity to reply, as he wanted to control the tenor of the conversation and reveal as much misinformation as appropriate, since he did not trust either Johnson or Michael to discuss matters. Reilly thought the best way to move forward in these opening conversational gambits was to readily volunteer some of the information that they were known to have, in connection with alleged discussions with Admiral Scheer, and to advance in more detail with counter-intelligence subterfuge to add to the importance of their mission and sidetrack Tirpitz into not suspecting anything other than complete support for Germany.

Speaking on Johannsen's behalf, Reilly, explaining his assistance as his language skills were in Russian and Finnish, he addressed Tirpitz concerning the mission to Estonia. He calmly related the story of Johannsen's recent visit to Denmark to persuade the government to deny the British and American naval forces any access to the Baltic Sea. Tirpitz knew something of this thinking and expressed his delight at having more detail laid before him, which encouraged his views of certain victory in the war.

Reilly, now in his stride as master of misinformation, continued with elegance and certainty as he could see Tirpitz was lapping up his story lines. He drove forward with increased energy and conviction, explaining that in his discussions with the Danish Government, he had also gained knowledge of a German support agreement with Denmark, that should the British try to force their way into the Baltic to attempt to engage with the German Grand Fleet, with the help of potential massive naval support from America, then the Danish Navy would, with the assistance of German naval forces, try and stop them. It seemed that the only way Britain could successfully get through into the Baltic was by the occupation of Denmark. The Danish Government would resist this, and so it was necessary that the newly installed provisional Estonian Government should know of the joint German and Danish approach to any hostility from the Western Allies.

He then went on to inform Tirpitz of the details of the meetings he was to hold in Estonia. Johannsen, as a Finnish envoy, knew of the struggle for their independence from Russia and needed to persuade the newly installed leader of the provisional government, Konstantin Päts, to tone down his efforts for independence as Finland was intending to pledge support to the anti-Bolshevik movement after the cessation of war, when Estonia would become part of a unified political settlement with Russia for the independence of both states.

Tirpitz looked quizzically at Reilly and shot a glance toward Olga, mystified at their seeming to be working against their own new Communist Government. Reilly was quick to point out that he and Olga were rampant Bolsheviks, and part of the subterfuge to blindside the Estonian Government into thinking that they would gain independence after the war; but in fact they both knew that Estonia would come under the complete control of the new Communist regime under the terms (hoped-for) of the coming treaty between Russia and Germany.

Tirpitz thought about that. He knew that this would never become a part of the treaty, as his information was that Germany would demand the ceding of the Baltic states from Russian control to Germany, in order to protect their flank when the next war would inevitably break out. This knowledge further added to the concerns Tirpitz had, as he was worried at the rise of Communism in the hands of the Bolsheviks, and the final game in German minds of these moves and countermoves was also the annexation of Poland by Germany. However, he did not comment on this as these were future moves which from a political perspective were too complex to absorb entirely, and he felt that the short-term activities would play out into longer-term gains for the victorious and powerful Germany.

Reilly continued with his explanation of the purpose of this mission, saying that Johannsen would remind the Estonian Government forcibly that they should also be careful at this stage not to become hostile too readily towards Russia, as the German Navy – now strengthened by a pact with Denmark and the pending increase in the size of the German fleet at the expense of acquisitions from Russia. Additionally, there was the threat of German land forces moving into their territory which could, if they were not careful, come under full German occupation. He was to remind the Estonian Government that good counsel should be observed for the preservation of lives in Estonia, as these were complex times.

Reilly also explained that Johannsen also had knowledge of the proposed transfer of some of the Russian Navy assets to Germany after the treaty of Brest Litovsk, and would be travelling back to Helsinki immediately after his meeting in

Tallinn. He would ensure that the Russian ships anchored in Helsinki were held impounded, as based on the terms of the coming treaty, for the safe transfer to the German Navy.

Tirpitz was relaxed and had turned from drinking port to schnapps. He calmly mentioned that he knew every detail of Reilly's plan as he was a party to its approval behind the scenes, with Scheer and the Kaiser. This was not entirely true, as he had become aware from Reilly's delivery of facts previously unknown to him. But for the purposes of seniority and maintenance of his own status and presence, he felt he had to add his own weight of international current and secret affairs.

He then decided that he should announce his role in all this activity. He too was on his way to Helsinki after dropping off the party at Tallinn, and his purpose was to inspect the Russian Baltic fleet and to arrange a handover agreement with Commander Alexander Ravozov, who was the Russian Fleet Commander, as this was a crucial part of the yet unsigned treaty. He would then personally return in triumph at the head of the Russian fleet to the home ports of Germany and Poland, which it was hoped would be ceded to Germany – this was as yet a matter of negotiation, as Poland was showing signs of insurrection against the influence of Russia over its sovereignty.

Tirpitz seemed very pleased with himself, and saw this as an opportunity to end his long career in the Kreigsmarine in triumph and the glory of his noble standing. Tirpitz announced that, as they spoke, German forces were already advancing into Estonia and making efforts to land in Finland to provide a presence there as their part of the treaty to support the Russian Government. Privately, he thought that if it was to be the Bolsheviks, then so be it. But his preference was to see the White Army triumph.

It seemed that Reilly's plan of subterfuge was working well, as a double bluff. The Germans were being of great help to the British cause. There seemed very little chance of them being discovered, especially due to the total blackout of radio contact. The party then retired to their cabins thoroughly exhausted at the complexity of the machination of all parties and the theatrics of the evening and hoped for another interesting day ahead.

Johnson, arriving back at his shared cabin with Michael, spoke to him after they had retired to their bunks and recounted his astonishment at the intrigue and complexity associated with these plans and forthcoming treaties. Would Europe ever be stable? In the back of his mind he yearned for a life in Britain, protected as she was by seas and oceans, with law and order and prosperity in obvious abundance, which he had briefly encountered. And what of Russia? Would the Bolsheviks be denied governance by the coming invasion of Western Allied forces at Archangel? Or would the Bolsheviks triumph, and add to the aggression and agonies of the citizens of mainland Europe? Should Germany triumph in France, then they would inevitably turn their attention to a weakened Russian state, and easily invade and conquer.

Michael agreed, and thinking about the maze of difficulties ahead of him he wondered if he was the right man to take on this mantle of responsibility as proposed by Britain, in the face of so much aggression, secrecy and double-dealings amongst the leaders of the so-called civilised world at war.

The following morning, they awoke and realized that the gentle swaying of the boat had ceased and the throbbing of the twin diesel engines, that were the normal sounds of the journey the day before, was silenced.

Johnson went next door to see Olga and Reilly, who were dressed and ready to go to the dining room. They enquired whether the U-boat had pulled into a port for supplies or for some other purpose. Reilly explained that they were now submerged, and the craft was running on electric power only from the batteries. Johnson suddenly felt sick again at the thought of being in a steel coffin and, ashamed to discover that he was somewhat claustrophobic, retired to his bunk feeling unwell.

Michael got up, and hearing the explanation, thought this was another marvellous experience. He quickly dressed and washed and went off to the dining room, hoping to meet Reilly and Olga.

Reilly was not at the table, and Olga explained that he had been called to the Comm as there seemed to be an incident developing. She decided not to mention what it was, and suggested to Michael that he enjoy the buffet breakfast which had been set out. Other officers came into the dining room and had very little to say. They each grabbed a couple of bread rolls and some cold ham, swigged mouthfuls of coffee, and then returned to their stations. Michael thought that was odd.

Reilly then came in, and reported to Michael and Olga the current position. A British submarine was tracking them. Shortly before they had dived to periscope depth for the day journey, the lookout had spotted a submarine lying astern about 2 kilometres away, and they were tracking its course. The British sub was then observed to be diving to hide herself, and was apparently hoping to gain on them discreetly. As the U-151 had an advanced sonar listening device, they could keep watch on the following sub.

He invited Olga and Michael to the Comm and there they found the Captain and Tirpitz pouring over sea charts and drawing up evasive plans in case they were threatened. They were perturbed to note from their periscope observations that the British sub had only partially submerged, and through this tactic was making more speed and gaining on them.

Then Tirpitz, senior in rank and a great naval tactician, took over and steered a course deviation of 15 degrees to port, to see whether the British had equal sound technology to enable them to alter course in pursuit. After a further fifteen minutes it seemed she had, as was again tracking them from behind and had closed to within 500 metres.

At that point the sonar operator cried that two torpedoes had been released and were bearing down on them from astern. Tirpitz then ordered a 270 degree turn, hoping to meet the British submarine broadside, and thus missing the torpedoes.

After a few minutes, they raised the periscope and found that they had indeed come about sufficiently. The British sub was now on the surface and was tracking the torpedoes it had fired a minute or two earlier.

Tirpitz then announced 'Action stations!' and the U-151 surfaced at 30 degrees astern of the British sub. Quickly the gunners ran onto the decks and opened the covers of the twin 150 mm deck guns, and trained them on the sub.

The British sub was not expecting this tactic and her crew were busily looking forward to see if there was any strike, as they would soon be over the position where they thought the U-151 to be. Tirpitz raced up onto the bridge and ordered full speed ahead, and soon bore down on the sub which was now directly in front of them.

Captain Janckendorff joined Tirpitz and asked him not to sink the sub, as it may well have a lot of valuable information on board. With this element of surprise, they could fire a warning shot to her port and then announce over the intercom loudspeaker that the crew should surrender or be blown out of the water with the twin 150 mm deck guns.

Sure enough, that was what Tirpitz was thinking too. They fired off two simultaneous rounds which caught the sub by surprise and they saw the huge explosions ahead of her port side. Reilly had joined them, with Michael, and asked if he could hail them with the terms of the surrender, as they would clearly understand an English accent and this left no room for mistakes. Also, the clarity of the English voice would act to confuse the Captain.

Reilly then addressed them, saying, 'Now come on, old boy, slow down and tell us who you are and what you are doing in these waters, tracking His Majesty's submarine.'

This was a good ruse, as there were no markings on the U-151 to identify her.

'Heave to and make ready to be boarded.'

With that, twenty seaman tumbled out of the forward hatch of the U-151 and stood shoulder to shoulder with rifles pointed at the British sub's bridge. The two deck guns were re-loaded and ready to fire. There was also an anti-aircraft gun on the bridge which was trained on the sub.

The Captain in total confusion over the orders and the guns which were aimed at him, ordered all engines to be stopped. He was simply mesmerised by the colossal size of the submarine on his flank, and was amazed at its new design, which he at first thought appeared to have come from the British shipyards. Only when the U-151 was alongside did he realise that this was a German submarine – or even Russian, given the unusual naval dress worn by the sailors. It was too late to take any alternative strategy, as he knew he had the lives of his crew at stake.

The boarding party went aboard and held the Captain and deck officers at gunpoint, ordering them to bring all hands on deck. They were then told to abandon ship and step aboard the U-boat now moored aside. The British seaman arriving on deck were staggered at the sheer size of the unknown ship. They wondered, in hope, if it was Russian – as the Russians were still Allies, of sorts. Without any hesitation, they chose to abandon ship and make for the German submarine. The last man off was the Captain, and all were taken below as captives. Then the German boarding party disappeared down into the lower decks.

After they had been gone for no more than two minutes there was a huge explosion astern from the sub, and it was immediately obvious that explosive charges had been set and the sub was taking on water fast. With that the boarding party came quickly out of the conning tower and threw themselves overboard to escape the sinking vessel. Quickly the deck crew cut the fastening ropes so they would not be dragged under and then hauled the boarding party out of the freezing sea.

Tirpitz put a wry smile on his face, and thought

that was exactly what he would have done under the circumstances. Reilly was also pleased, as there was no loss of life and the British Captain had retained his self-respect to some extent.

The sub then quickly sank, and that was the end of that episode of danger and excitement. The U-151 submerged again and continued on its planned course due east.

The captured seaman were searched and all their possessions confiscated. Cigarettes and cocoa was supplied to the grateful submariners, who were only too happy that they had not been killed in the action, but had mercifully been saved. Being blown apart with the boat was the normal end in that theatre of war.

Tirpitz and Captain Janckendorff then went to talk to the prisoners, declaring that the war would soon end, and he was not inclined to kill any further adversaries, who he respected for their brave performance of duty as submariners. He announced that very soon, after the German victory, they would be repatriated to England to join their families once again in a peaceful Europe.

Reilly, who had joined them, was impressed with the humanity that had been shown, even though it was for a failed self-serving excuse to steal possibly very important papers and codes, and so on. However, he felt that this was a chivalrous way to treat the defeated, and was a lesson of comradeship amongst that part of the naval senior service. He also mused over the great propaganda that Tirpitz was producing; he had always felt that battles could be won by the simpler war to capture the minds of adversaries.

The rest of the day passed peacefully and it was interesting to hear that the British submariners were in good voice as they sang sea shanties. Mainly, this was to convince the Germans that their spirit would not be broken, even though they had suffered a defeat at the hands of the U-151 crew. The afternoon passed in a peaceful lull after the tension of the action, and all aboard felt to some degree that it was a good thing there was no loss of life on either side.

Shortly before dinner Reilly came to Michael's cabin to check on their well-being. Johnson was feeling much better and had seemingly got over his fear of being submerged, now that the voyage was continuing in darkness and on the surface. They, with Olga, made their way to the dining room and saw that there were about fifteen members already seated. They were pleased to see that the British Captain and his two senior officers had been invited to join them, and the scene was set for an episode of friendship in adversity.

Dinner was more lavish than usual, to impress the British officers of their high standards, invincibility, and to show that the blockade was having little or no effect. Tirpitz was quick to seize the advantage of being the victor over the defeated, and tried gentle persuasion in his propaganda style to encourage the British officers to reveal a little more about their position in the Baltic, and how they had overcome the very tight defences on the Danish islands, and had been able to navigate through anti-submarine nets and mines.

The British Captain was as familiar with subterfuge as Reilly, and simply said that all the German defences were known to the British Admiralty. Navigation was a very easy trick to pull, and espionage and intelligence were in abundance; they had agents at the highest level in Germany. Each major move was being made known to them and the Germans very far from winning the war. Indeed, the

American presence in Europe was building at such a rapid pace that very soon they would be overcome by massive fire power on both land and sea.

Tirpitz then said, 'May I ask what forces of submarines you have in the Baltic? Unless you ply me with more lies.'

The Captain countered, 'Yes, I am happy to tell you that we have far more than you realise, and we are waiting to strike the minute any of your battleships leave port.'

Tirpitz's face turned very pale and he was stuck for words. He quickly changed the subject and asked if the British Captain played chess or poker. The captain announced that he did play, and that he was exceptionally good at both. He knew that Tirpitz was wanting to reassert his superiority somehow. Tirpitz than became unsure, and said that at some convenient point when his duties became lighter, he would send for him for a game.

After dinner Reilly escorted the Captain back to his quarters with the other captured officers, and mentioned that his friend Johnson was also good at chess and backgammon and asked if he would like to play him.

'Not on your Nelly,' the Captain replied. 'I am bloody useless at both. But I don't think that Mr Turnip will be asking me to challenge him after the bloody nose I gave him about the build-up of our forces which are ready to win the war.'

Reilly took a liking to this guy, as he was as British as himself, although that was a truth he could not speak about here.

The following day and night passed without any further events – other than a near collision with a Russian freighter.

That was accompanied by shrieks over the intercom speaker of a call to 'Action stations!' and 'Dive! Dive! Dive!' The sudden burst of power, and the steep 30 degree angle of dive for three minutes, told the story.

As the journey was coming to a close, Reilly came to Michael and Johnson and advised them to get their things together as they would be disembarking in one hour. As soon as they had docked they needed to make a very quick exit, as at that point radio silence would be broken when the U-151 made contact with Naval HQ in Germany, and it was likely that their plot might well be exposed.

The four of them were now on the bridge as the submarine was mooring alongside an empty berth. Captain Janckendorff looked at them, surprised at how quickly they were wanting to depart without much conversation or farewells. Tirpitz also came onto the bridge to see the four of them climbing down the conning tower, and again was surprised at their hurry. They looked at each other in disgust and thought little of their manners.

Below, in the radio room, the wireless operator was sending and receiving several messages to and from HQ, and was busy decoding. He then climbed up to the conning tower and, ashen-faced, approached Captain Janckendorff with a received message. He could not easily understand the message as it read: 'Apprehend the four travellers on board. They are all British spies. You must find out their real names and use extreme methods as required. Await further guidance and keep the radio frequency open for more information.'

Captain Janckendorff handed the message to Tirpitz, who was equally astounded. As they looked on, he could see the four 'spies' disappearing into the gloom of the winter day. They could just see, them being escorted by Estonian soldiers, boarding a truck.

Now Tirpitz was faced with a very embarrassing situation and was perplexed as to how he could answer the message. Delays would not be acceptable, he was on his way to Helsinki to meet his Russian counterpart. Or was he? This Johannsen fellow had him confused, as he had not had any conversation with him other than greetings. He decided to contact Admiral Scheer himself and discover the whole account of what was reality and fact.

He finally got a direct line of communication with Admiral Scheer in attendance in the wireless room at HQ and he found that he too was writhing in mental pain, as he had been completely deceived by the two Russian Commissars. He had checked with Moscow at the very top and they had no knowledge of these two people, and could only suggest that British spies had trounced the German Navy.

At least Tirpitz did not feel alone in being stitched up. He quickly decided that the trip to Helsinki was a red herring, and ordered Captain Janckendorff to dispatch thirty of his men to search and chase after the spies and hope to recover some semblance of victory in this humiliation.

As soon as the thirty marines disembarked and made their way to the dock gates, they were met by Estonian guards who closed the gates and blocked their path. Tirpitz, now seeing that they could not move through the dock gates, ordered the marines back to the U-151. He was becoming very uncertain of the position of Germany in relation to Estonia, and indeed Helsinki. He was becoming concerned that they would be captured and interned for the rest of the war. A message was sent back to Admiral Scheer in Berlin informing him that it was futile to make any further attempts to search for the spies as they could now be anywhere in Estonia.

26

Tallinn

The truck they had climbed into was driven by members of the Free Estonian Army which was in resurgence due to the collapse of the Russian military and confusion over the future of Europe. They had been helped into the truck by Otto Strandman, the leader of the Provisional Assembly. Otto was a keen activist for Estonian independence and was anxious to help Michael in his endeavours to secure the return of the Romanovs with the active support of Britain and America.

Otto engaged eagerly in conversation with the four political adventurers. He knew from his own counter-intelligence network of agents that German armed forces were preparing to invade Estonia, and was certain they would be as merciless in the prosecution of hostilities and occupation as the Russians had been in the past decades.

He saw the need to reopen an Eastern Front with Germany which would hopefully end the war quicker than had been envisaged.. Indeed, the freed German war machinery from east to west was a great danger to the Allies on the Western Front.

He complimented Michael on his bravery in undertaking his round trip, and for putting himself forward to become the new head of state in Russia should the invasion prove successful.

Otto directed the driver to proceed quickly to the telephone exchange offices in Tallinn. They arrived to see the building crowded with people who were desperate to keep in contact with their loved ones during these very dangerous and fluid times in Tallinn. There they were shown to an upstairs meeting room to meet with Konstantin Päts, the interim Prime Minister.

On arrival, they were pleased to see that breakfast was being served at the boardroom table. The food and atmosphere was Spartan in nature due to both their timetable and the austerity that was gripping Eastern Europe.

Päts, got quickly down to business wanting much more detail on the Allied landings and when they were scheduled to take place. Reilly and Olga took most of the questions and gave a very positive performance. It seemed that the pressure on Estonia was growing much quicker than anticipated, ahead of the hoped-for invasion. Päts announced that the German forces were assembling on the Estonian borders and it would be a matter of days before they entered the capital with very little opposition.

All Reilly could do was promise on behalf of the British Government that shipments of supplies that were held in Stockholm, in neutral Sweden, would be ferried into Estonia immediately. These were ready to be sent as they spoke and it needed only an acceptance by the Provisional Assembly, and then they would be with the Estonian underground forces in three days. They would include rifles, machine guns, ammunition and half-tracked vehicles, with as many field guns as could be put on board. This was not nearly enough, but the Provisional Council had made a resolution to defend the borders as best they could, and were now occupied in preparing defences against the pending German occupation.

Otto Strandman then turned his attention to Michael enquiring on what grounds would he be constitutionally allowed to become the new Tsar of Russia. He reminded Michael that he had refused to accept that mantle in March 1917.

Michael asserted himself and replied that the whole invasion process was dependent on him becoming a rallying point which would subvert the position of the Bolsheviks with the population, and make it very difficult for them to govern. The people of Russia wanted a return to the Monarchy, but under no circumstances would they accept Nicholas being back in the court. Information-gathering over the past three months had indicated that Nicholas should go into exile with his family. There were just too many negative memories of his governance over the last two decades, and the people had no faith in him or his ability to govern.

In contrast, Michael would provide freedom of speech, and new voting rights. A new Constitution would be drawn up which would allow much-needed investment into agriculture and industry. A new Russia would emerge. More to the point, he would seek to approve proper engagement with the freedom movements of those satellite states which sought independence.

Michael then pointed out that the governments of the Western Powers and the people were in unison: that he should be Tsar. He had often spoken out against the ruling of Nicholas and the unnerving influence of Rasputin, but to no avail. He agreed with the popular choice that he should rule, and that Nicholas should be provided for in another country without having any Imperial responsibility. His accession would also be welcomed by the armed forces, as they had grown to respect Michael as a fair and honest person who thought a great deal about the conditions of those forces under his control.

Päts then asked Michael how he would see the establishment of Estonian independence. Michael responded very quickly and told him that he would actively encourage and support it, and that of Lithuania and Latvia, so that the new Baltic states might join a trading partnership where full autonomy, through effective trade deals, would bolster the prosperity of the United Free States of Russia.

There would then come further advantages to old Russian conquests, in that Poland would be free from Russian occupation and would become a key player in these free trade agreements and a coalition bloc to serve the protection of those nations.

Päts was overwhelmed by Michael's vision of the future and complimented him on his foresight. Michael then replied that these were his long-held views, and that his secretary, Johnson, was the major architect of this pragmatic political solution to promote the future peaceful prosperity of Europe.

The only threats could come from a newly arising Germany, perhaps in many years to come, but France and Britain would always want to have standing armies on the borders of Germany to thwart any future ambition of expansionism. They, in combination, would be an economic and military bulwark against any further German and Austrian aggression in this century.

Michael, in the spirit of openness and honesty in declaring his plans, continued by saying that he felt that Ukraine should be divided into East and West, which would solve the ethnic differences and population dynamics. Essentially, East Ukraine would be encouraged toward independence and become a member of the United States of Free Eastern Europe (USFEE).

He was convinced that this was the only route towards a free, and prosperous Europe, through a peaceful evolution, rather than revolution. Let 'Prosperous Peace' become the new mantra for Europe.

This gave Päts and Strandman great hope for the future and convinced them that they should put up the stiffest opposition possible to the Germans, together with a policy of non-compliance with the Bolshevik regime which was increasingly asserting its powers in Estonia. The question was, however, could they gain enough time to wait it out until the Western Intervention in Northern Russia became a reality and extended its help to Estonia in time?

Olga then spoke up to reinforce these feelings of euphoria and hope, and revealed that there would be a massive entry into the Baltic by the Allies and Denmark with the sole objective to seal the fate of the German fleet, finally breaking the blockade which had imposed a 'No Entry' in and out of the Baltic. The smashing of that blockade would regain the freedom of the seas, which would be available to all, and especially the new Eastern Bloc world order.

The meeting broke up with new vigour and optimism, and the whole assembly were very encouraged by each other's offering of information.

Reilly, then taking Michael to one side, mentioned firmly that these interests of a new Eastern Bloc had never been discussed with London, and it seemed unlikely that these would pass agreement without much serious consideration, and probably amendments.

Johnson intervened and simply said, 'You can have eternal war or eternal peace, and if London want to use Michael to create a re-engagement with Germany on the Eastern Front, then these are Michael's terms, and they are not for turning.'

Reilly, faced with the fact of such a stark choice, had to agree with Johnson. He then turned to Olga and simply said, 'Let it be, and let the future take care of itself. It is far too late in the day to start squabbling.'

Olga reminded them of the final part of the journey, which was to meet Patriarch Tikhon at the Cathedral of St Alexander Nevsky in Tallinn. They should start out on that journey immediatley. She then made the expected call from the telephone exchange office they were in and got through to Tikhon's secretary, announcing that they would be arriving in the next thirty minutes.

The truck was brought to the door and again they all boarded. The truck was the best disguise they could have as the town was crawling with various political factions, and German and British informers. They were reliant on the gathering and passing of information to secure small amounts of money to eke out the hard existence they were enduring in Estonia. When they arrived at the Cathedral they drove straight through the open gates and up to the courtyard.

They were met by two very stiff and formal clergymen who took their bags and showed them to a room prepared for all four of them. The room was very cold and unwelcoming with four bunk beds which, when sat on, proved to be as uncomfortable as they looked. Reilly thought that there was some reluctance to see them, and seemed to feel some fear at the association of Russian counter-revolutionaries, lest they be implicated and tortured by the ever-present Cheka, who were on their streets constantly watching the activities of the Church.

Olga was anxious for the meeting to get started as she was aware that time was running out for Michael and Johnson if they were to keep to the schedule which had been worked out within the Reilly Plan. She enquired of the two clergymen what had been planned for the meeting. They replied that lunch would be served at one o'clock, and they would be joined by Patriarch Tikhon and his two bishops.

Olga was very concerned that the patriarch was finding it difficult to resist the power of Lenin and Stalin in wanting to attempt the dissolution of the Orthodox Church in Russia. Lenin and his Marxist ideology held a goal for the elimination of religion in Russia and its replacement with state atheism.

During the rise of Lenin and the Bolshevik revolutionary activities, the Patriarch was widely considered as anti-Bolshevik, and many members of the Orthodox clergy were jailed or executed by the new regime. Tikhon openly condemned these murders and protested against violent attacks on the Church by the Bolsheviks. In response, Tikhon had excommunicated the Soviet leadership, leading to a period of intense persecution of the Russian Orthodox Church which was to be manifested in further imprisonments and executions.

It did seem from intelligence that Tikhon was just barely holding together his resolve and open opposition, and that many of his bishops, clergy and worshippers were coming under attack and their mental resilience was disintegrating. This would mean that the people, upon understanding that their Church was collapsing, would become easier targets for consuming the Bolshevik ideology.

Tikhon arrived at the dining hall just as the four were being led in by the clergy. Again the sparse furnishings of the room and the splendour of the robes of high office worn by the Patriarch were very noticeable. Tikhon was very stiff, formal, and had a distinct lack of warmth, which was unusual for a priest, but this was normal for higher ranks in the Orthodox Church. Tikhon was no exception to this form of protocol.

However, they were welcomed and invited to sit and be served. Tikhon was first to apologise for the sparsity of the accommodation, especially for Michael, of whom he had come to know more about since his recent promotion to the leadership of the Russian Church.

He was most concerned about Michael's brother being held in Tobolsk, especially as the White and Czech Armies were approaching the city. He felt that was a further danger for them, even though there was a view that they may well be rescued. To Tikhon it was very certain that Lenin would never let that happen, even if it meant disposing of Nicholas and his family.

This analysis took Michael aback as he had no idea

that the White Army were gaining ground. He had mixed feelings about a rescue now that Tikhon had put that scenario to him, as he was seeing that it would become a viable consideration to assassinate Nicholas.

Tikhon had been briefed by Olga in November about what was afoot with the Allies and of recent date he had heard senior members of his Church and Bolshevik politicians (who were not yet entirely wedded to the revolution) talk about this possibility. He suggested that these were very uncertain times for all members of society in how they viewed their positions and alliances. The Bolsheviks were increasing the activities of the Cheka, and daily it seemed that many influential people were disappearing. He again reiterated that these dangerous times were not in favour of the survival of Nicholas.

He made a personal recommendation to Michael that he should at the earliest opportunity take himself, his wife and child out of Russia, and make towards Sweden or back to the UK. There, he would be more effective and out of danger, and would then be able to return to Russia when it was safe to do so. He could not understand the British allowing him to journey back to Russia, as it was a strong possibility that Lenin would also imprison Michael, to destroy the Romanov influence at a stroke.

Michael replied by saying that had this offer been put to him, he would have rejected it, as his wife and child needed him back home and their safety would be in peril if he was seen to have fled Russia. More so, the people of whom he was hoping he could become leader would not respond if he was not there to lead and encourage them to support the invasion and rise up against the Bolsheviks.

His own intentions had been thought through, and he intended to collect his family and possessions in Gatchina, and then journey down to the Crimea where there was a strong White Army defence corps and abundant royal accommodation for him and his family. There was also a small loyalist fleet of naval assets which would allow supplies to be brought to the stronghold. That, then, would become the headquarters of the resistance with the White Army, and from there he could become a rallying point. So, when the Allies invaded, the pressure would come from the North and the South simultaneously. Tikhon mused over that thought and wished Michael the best of luck, but said he should not delay his flight from Gatchina with his family.

Reilly then turned up the pressure on Tikhon, who he had noted took a fatalist's view of the demise of Russia, and in particular of his Church. He asked Tikhon what he felt the view of his clergy would be when the invasion started in the late spring of 1918. Would they in fact stiffen their resolve and openly preach through the still popular Church that the people should resist the Bolsheviks, and take to the streets in support of the invasion when it happened? He reminded Tikhon that London wanted to know of his position well in advance, as it was an important factor in the invasion plans. If the Church were to prevaricate and showed no backbone for meeting the Bolsheviks head on, then it could prejudice the invasion plans. He pointed out that the Allies had to be certain of victory as they could not afford to have a prolonged campaign in the East.

Tikhon pondered his response, as suddenly he felt that the whole future of Russia was hanging on his words of truth and wisdom. He then turned to Michael and declared that if it could be shown that Michael was safely installed in the Crimea with his family, and that there was a credible plan and support from the White Army, then he would give his reply to Reilly. In the meantime, he could only say that without Michael being in a safe place, then whilst he would always show opposition to the destruction of the Church, he could not speak of any certainty about the Orthodox people.

Reilly looked at Olga as if to say that was better than his worst fears, but was still not, in his view, sufficient for the Allies. Knowing that he had to relay this information, he quickly left the dinner and went to a local bar where there was a British agent.

He sat down in a corner where he could be plainly seen and pulled out a very unusual pipe that had been made for him by MI6. He began to smoke it and then to twiddle the stalk around his fingers using his left hand. That was the sign that he was a British agent and needed to talk.

After an hour, and when he was beginning to think that this was a disappointing no-show, a dirty and dishevelled dockworker came shuffling in and came to Reilly, asking to buy him a drink. This was the agreed sign. Reilly roughly told him to get lost and the old guy left. A minute later (as arranged) Reilly left too, and turned right and caught up with the accomplice and disappeared down a side alley.

Reilly quickly told him as succinctly as possible: 'The boys in Estonia will happily play ball to win when the manager makes his base away from the opposition.' – Eagle Wolfe (Orlov Volkov).

That cryptic message would leave his accomplice safe as he would not know its interpretation. He was really a communications worker at the telephone exchange and had access to wiretapping and into MI6's communications in London. Reilly felt that the boys back home would easily understand that message coming from Tallinn.

Reilly then rejoined the party to discover that they were ready to leave and return over the border to Russia. 'London will have the messages in the morning.' he exclaimed.

The next part of the journey now needed some planning in travelling across the border into Russia from Narva with the least amount of fuss. For this, Reilly and Olga thought that they would not be able to bluff their way in by using the senior Commissar act, as they had seen that the Germans were hot on their tail and knew that it must have been discovered by now that they were British spies. So this required a different tactic altogether, and it was likely that there would be extra scrutiny at the borders.

It was also now important that they were not travelling as a foursome. Therefore, it was decided that neither Olga's or Reilly's presence in Russia at the moment would serve any great purpose. It was more important that they worked on a plan to get Michael and his family out of Gatchina and into the Crimea, to be in place for the invasion, and to start his campaign from there. Michael should go across the border alone, on foot, as there were plenty of unmanned crossing points, and even open fields through forest and woods; these should be his chosen routes.

Johnson would be given forged papers as an Estonian doctor and be driven over in an Estonian medical car painted white with a red cross on the side. This was the 'plain sight' routine which had proven itself often, in its audacious approach. The border guards would not be suspicious of one man travelling alone, especially as they would have been alerted to a group of three men and a woman as being the foreign spies. Johnson had an average look of insignificance, being a quiet person generally, and would help with any challenges at the border.

Michael changed clothes, disguising himself as a peasant, with a small backpack of rudimentary food and nothing else. He was driven in an old battered farm truck to a remote farm in Karoli, 10 kilometres from the unmarked border of Estonia and Russia. They were met by Anastasia Kosygin, a stout member of the local church and a strong woman of character who ran the farm with her son, who was of a similar age to Michael. He was given the identity card of her son Andrei Kosygin, and shown the direction of the Russian border. His story was that he was the son of Anastasia and that he was going into Russia to look for work, as the family finances were in collapse and they could not afford to feed him any more.

27

Home to Gatchina

It would be dark in a couple of hours, so Michael set off briskly. He was enjoying the brief life he would live as a peasant, and thought how interesting an education this was for him, and for his new Russian Federation.

The distance was around 150 kilometres to Gatchina and he knew that this would be far too long a journey on foot. So, he intended that once he got 30 kilometres from the farm, and well over the border, he should be safe enough to wander on the highway and try and get a lift to Gatchina.

Michael had been walking for six hours, most of it in moonlight, and was exhausted. He was finding it difficult to navigate through the woods and open farmland, so he found a hollow under a tree and settled down for a few hours' sleep. It was not too cold that night, and his peasant's thick quilted jacket and trousers were comfortable enough for him to catch some undisturbed sleep. A piece of bread and dried fish was his meal that night. It made him wonder just how the rest of the country was coping with the serious food shortages.

The following morning, he awoke very stiff and rather

lame feeling once again the gnawing pain in his stomach. He was still suffering from his ulcers and often on the journey around Northern Europe he had been in great pain, and if it were not for Johnson nursing him through and ensuring he was medicated to overcome the worst, then he would have not survived as well as he had.

Calculating the distance he had already covered, he knew it was not too far to the road. He eventually arrived at the main road and found it to be occupied by mostly army trucks travelling the highway. There was also a regular movement of donkey carts and occasional people trekking on the road. Michael felt his luck would be in if he were able to hitch a ride with a truck, and hoped to be able to disguise his Royal accent.

After an hour of luckless attempts to gain a lift he decided to wave down a donkey and cart as he was now very weary. He was in luck, as a peasant farmer stopped for him. The old peasant farmer was happy to give him a ride. He asked whether he could sit in the back of the cart and sleep, as he had been on the road all day. That was an easy ask, and he could escape the boredom of chatting away the hours by just saying he was tired.

Michael was pleased to hear that the old boy was travelling as far north as Kingisepp, which as luck would have it was on the east–west highway directly from Narva to Gatchina. There, he was sure, he would get a reasonable lift from perhaps a passing farm truck. He had no chance of getting a lift in a car, being dressed as a peasant.

It was nearly dark when they arrived at Kingisepp and Michael was relieved to get off the very uncomfortable cart. He thanked the peasant and asked him for his name.

'Joshua,' he replied jauntily and said he was pleased to help. He remarked at how tired he must have been, as he had slept all the way. Michael than announced that he would remember him and make the effort to track him down one day and pay him handsomely for the ride. Joshua thought he was mad to think he would believe such claptrap.

Michael was now on the main road and was visible to the vehicles that were trundling past. It was no more than four hours to his destination, but most people refrained from the dangers of picking up travellers in the dark, but still hopeful that he would get a lift onwards. There was a café at the road junction and he hoped that, as lorries were pulling out, he might get the lift he so badly needed. After two hours, he began to think about an alternative solution as no one was stopping to give him a lift because of his appearance.

28

Stopford! Of All People

At that moment, a rather stately car pulled up and a skinny man jumped out and wandered over to the café and disappeared. Michael thought that this was an opportunity. If the keys were in the ignition, then he would simply steal it. He was in luck: the keys were still in the ignition. Just as he was about to start the car, the driver was reappearing from the café and it was certain he would catch him as he attempted to escape. Michael decided to jump in the back, lay on the floor and hope for the best.

The skinny guy got back into the car and drove off. After about a kilometre the driver became very suspicious as there was a heavy smell assailing his nostrils and he had noticed that the engine response was not as effective. Thinking that he had a stow away he stopped by the side of the road, got out and pulled his revolver, shouting to the occupant in the back to get out, or be shot.

The game was up for Michael and he meekly got out. The driver was standing in front of the car and instructed Michael to join him in the headlights so that he could be dealt with.

Michael observed the man who was tall and elegant and looked faintly recognisable. He then noted that he had a Beretta handgun. He knew this was a favoured hand weapon of the British Secret Service and political envoys in the Embassy. He very quickly came to recognise the unmistakable countenance and voice of Albert Stopford.

Michael then put on his best authoritative voice, and in the best of English said from the shadows, 'Now, my friend I may stink like a pig in season, but I will wager you that my average lotion at £20 a bottle is more or less what you might earn in a good day selling antiques and lifting Romanov jewellery.'

As Stopford was spluttering, lost for words, Michael appeared in the headlights and held out his hand for Stopford to shake, announcing himself as the Grand Duke Michael Alexandrovitch. 'And you would be Albert Stopford, I presume.'

The penny started to drop for Stopford as he had known of Michael's journey out of Russia, but without too much detail. They embraced in comradeship, and Stopford quickly announced to Michael that he would get him back to Natasha as soon as possible, with the least amount of delay. He explained that he had been watching out for Natasha and the household appeared to have been keeping the story going that Michael was in Tallinn and due to return very soon.

Michael enquired what he was doing travelling the road between Estonia and Russia. Stopford simply said that he was doing what he was good at, in aid of the Russian Imperial families. Michael guessed that he was on another trip to save the fortunes of the Romanovs.

Stopford had, on a few occasions, been helpful in deflecting attention away from Michael's absence from Gatchina and Michael's old colleague, Peter Polotsov, who still carried a senior position in the New Russian Red Army, had been active in asserting the story of his treatment for ulcers.

The remaining 80 kilometres of the journey passed very quickly, as they were in long and deep discussion about the events of Michael's journey and the hopes and aspirations of a successful outcome of the current crisis with the coming Allied invasion. As they approached Gatchina they could see that there was an unusual presence at the gate : it was the arrival of a new unit of Red Army soldiers. Stopford drove on by and stopped about a kilometre away, and let Michael out of the car. He instructed him to make his way back on foot and through the rear gardens and staff quarters, and without any niceties climb straight into his bed after taking a bath. Michael thought that the most secure way of entering the Palace was to use the secret tunnel at the Silver Lake which led directly into the state room.

Stopford turned around and drove straight into the gates, sweeping past the new army guard, and with a wave of his hand demanded that they get out of the way or be ran over. He pulled up sharply and jumped out of the car and walked stiffly into the Palace. There he heard loud conversations coming from the drawing room. He walked in briskly and announced himself as a member of the British Embassy staff and demanded to know what the commotion was about. Natasha was there confronting the Commander of the guards and refusing to let him search the Palace as he had not given her good reason to do so. Michael's family doctor was also there, adding weight to the protest against this informal intrusion.

Stopford quickly intervened and asked to see the Commander's papers, and demanded to know on whose authority this illegal entry had been made. The Commander thrust a single sheet of paper in front of him and showed it to be a personal document signed by Lenin to search the house and apprehend anyone who refused him entry.

Stopford then looked coldly at the Commander and said, 'On two counts, this is a fraudulent document. On the first count, this is not Lenin's signature – I know what it looks like – and Lenin has been in Germany for the past 48 hours discussing the peace pact with the Kaiser. On the second count, this has not been countersigned by the still legitimate courts who must give their approval for any warrant for a search. Furthermore, if you were to make any arrest then that would also require a warrant for arrest.'

The Commander was taken aback and was very uncertain of what his next move should be. Stopford, seeing that he had gained an advantage and got his adversary on the back foot, lowered his voice and kindly suggested that he should return to barracks. Stopford could be minded to make an issue of this with Peter Polotsov, the garrison Commanding Officer, and the sitting judges at Petrograd. The forged signature would also become an issue. However, in the interest of good relationships and peace, and because it was very late for the household to be disturbed any longer, Stopford suggested that this event had never taken place. He then showed the Commander to the door and waved him off the premises.

Natasha was so pleased that Stopford had arrived just

in time, and wept on his shoulders, expressing her misery at missing Michael and wondering where he was.

Stopford suggested that she take a bath and go to bed. He said he was positive that she would feel instantly more refreshed and at one with the world. She took his advice and wearily trudged up the stairs to her quarters. After a few minutes, Stopford, stationed at the foot of the staircase, heard an almighty scream and loud cries of joy. He walked out of the house feeling very pleased at the way the evening had turned out, and headed back to the Embassy in his car.

29

Doctor Johnson?

Back at the Cathedral, Johnson waited for a day so that he could be fitted up with a suit, a fully functioning doctor's bag and a white car which would be painted with a red cross on either side. His papers showed that he was an Estonian citizen, Ivan Milankovitch, and a doctor from the Tallinn Institute of Medical Research. In the trunk, there was a 20 litre glass flask full of coloured water which was labelled as a medicinal formula. This should give him credence and right of way on the roads, as he could easily claim an emergency status.

The following morning Johnson set off with a clergy driver who was dressed in a Private's uniform of the Russian Army. Johnson was sitting in the back looking imperious with his doctor's bag on his lap.

After a couple of hours of driving they approached the border. There was a queue, as all the vehicles and carts were being searched, border guards on the lookout for the foreign spies. With that Johnson got out and marched the 100 metres towards the border post and shouted to the guards to get a move on as he waved his false papers in the air impatiently. He shouted that he wanted right of way immediatley as he had to deliver vaccine to Petrograd for Commander Peter Polotsov most urgently.

The border guards had been pre-warned by telephone that there was a requirement to let Ivan Milankovitch through with papers which showed he was delivering urgent medical supplies to Petrograd. The Estonian border guard, seeing the doctor approaching, had been on the lookout for the hospital car. He sent a guard up to the car and waved it through to the front. Johnson asked the clergy driver to keep honking his horn so that they could attract as much attention to themselves as possible.

They arrived at the border gate and immediately the guards opened it shouting to the approaching Russian border guards to let the hospital car through as an emergency. They drove up to the Russian gate and, very slowly, a rather large lady sauntered out of the office, stood in front of the car radiator and in a loud voice told them both to get out of the car. They did so and immediately two guards searched their pockets, and took out their personal possessions.

The guards then asked Commissar Pushkina, who was standing with her arms folded and looking threatening, whether they should search the car. She bellowed at them of course they should. Pushkina came over to Johnson and gave him a very cold stare and asked him what he had been doing in Estonia. Johnson replied that he was working for the Russian Government and was involved in carrying out research in Tallinn at the medical school, developing vaccines for a flu strain which was on the verge of becoming an epidemic, and was known to be emanating from Siberia and emerging in Western Russia.

Pushkina was then taken aback by this as she had known as a child the ravages of untreated influenza. With that, Johnson pulled out a mask and gave one to his driver and put one over his mouth and nose. He then said that she should quickly telephone comrade Commander Polotsov, who would confirm that he was awaiting a delivery of the vaccine as it was vital that the senior staff in Petrograd were protected.

Pushkina then slacked off in her aggression and thought about it. She then brightened up and asked Johnson why he had so few personal possessions on him; this seemed strange to her. Johnson quickly replied that he was woken in the early hours and told to collect the 20 litre jar of vaccine from the medical college urgently, and had no time to collect money or wallet. However, he did have his new-fangled watch, which he showed her, and without changing his tone he then pushed past her and marched into her office and demanded that the operator contact Petrograd.

Pushkina came hurrying after him and agreed that should be done. She then softened her tone and enquired about the vaccine to discover if it was a viable solution to the prevention of flu. Johnson, seizing his chance to disarm her, said that without this being mass-produced in the next six months, the strain would get a hold over too many people and the epidemic could not be stopped, and there would be more deaths in Europe than that had been in the war to date. This shocked her as Johnson was extremely clear and serious about this, and certainly on a mission regardless of her interruption to his journey.

Polotsov answered the phone and asked what the operator wanted. Polotsov had been pre-warned by Reilly in a telephone call whilst he was in Tallinn that this was a matter on behalf of his old friend Michael. Polotsov was a secret supporter of the old regime and a good friend and colleague.

Johnson explained the situation, and quickly thrust the handset towards Pushkina, who was now somewhat nervous and asked meekly if there was a doctor due to visit him from Estonia with medical supplies.

'Yes, damn it! Why have you stopped him at the border? Release the man and his driver now!'

Pushkina then apologised to Johnson and he picked up his doctor's bag ready to depart. As he tried to leave the office she grabbed his arm and swung him into a side office and drew the blind.

She then put her face up close to his and told him that she was a Commissar and that she should not be underestimated. Becoming nasty again, she threatened him that if he did not take the 100 roubles that she had thrust into his hand and give her an anti-influenza jab before he left, then he would never cross that border again in peace and she would give him hell.

Johnson had no choice. Never in his life before had he had to administer an injection. He thought, 'What the hell… this should be fun!' He then shouted for the driver to bring the 20 litre flask and his medical bag containing the box of syringes that was in the back of the car. He brought them in and Johnson asked him to leave. He then told her to drop her pants.

She said, 'I will not.'

Johnson ignoring her, inserted the syringe into the jar of water and drew a larger shot. He then stood in front of her with the syringe three inches from her nose and squirted a fine spray onto her cheek.

He said, 'Get 'em off now or I walk. And be aware that I may well have you dismissed for bribery and theft of government property.'

Her face went crimson and she knew she had to obey. She was terrified of epidemics as one had wiped out a large part of her family in the Urals several decades ago.

She slowly bent over and pulled down her trousers and knickers. Both cheeks were of such a size that he could not miss the target. He was determined to get his own back on this bossy madam and took aim and thrust the needle deep into her flesh. He pressed hard on the syringe full of water. He took rather longer that he should have, as he felt the need to twist the needle around in her flesh a little.

Johnson was a little astonished that she had not cringed, let out a yelp or shown any sign of stiffening up. He withdrew the needle, but she was still in the bent-over position and not moving. Hoping that he had not paralysed her or something worse, he patted her rump and told her to straighten up.

She bent slowly upwards and turned around with such a sweet smile on her face. She gave him a big kiss on his lips and said in a sultry, husky voice, 'Thank you, darling.'

Slowly pulling up her pants was a vision which Johnson was not prepared for, and he felt the blood rush to his cheeks, he turned his back in fear of being accosted again. Packing his bag, he swiftly turned around and strode out to his waiting car, jumped in and was driven off. His face did not return to its normal colour for some time.

After a few hours, they approached the turning off the Petrograd road towards Gatchina. Now Johnson needed to be on his guard again, as he had to try and bluff the doctor's disguise as he drove into Gatchina.

He used the same 'in plain sight' trick again as he entered the small town and the driver started honking the horn and speeded up. He threw his arms in the air a few times as he passed army trucks and foot patrols, to show his impatience. Upon approaching Michaels residence , they drove in at high speed past the four guards at the gate and kept honking the horn.

With that, two footmen came rushing out to see what the commotion was. Johnson jumped out of the still moving car and dashed into the foyer. Natasha was waiting impatiently for his arrival as Olga had got a telegram to her only hours earlier that she should expect her long-time medical doctor friend to arrive that afternoon.

Johnson walked into the drawing room and slumped down in a soft chair and thought, 'Job done!' A minute later, and just as Johnson was finally recovering from all the nervous tension, in walked Natasha. She beckoned to him, saying, 'Dr Johnson, your patient is in the drawing room awaiting your call.'

Johnson broke into a smile and rushed towards Natasha and gave her a huge hug, as a best friend would, which lasted a full minute. Michael had approached the doorway and was looking on fondly at how his wife treasured the friendship of Johnson and how his unswerving loyalty was such a support beam in his life.

'Welcome home, my dear friend!' he shouted, and the men embraced in brotherly love as though years had passed between them. They both declared with great humor and laughter that they had made good time and were home within the prescribed timetable after fourteen days of an amazing adventure which they were confident would be the precursor to Europe's lasting peace.

Johnson, now back in the safety of Gatchina after his dramatic adventure with Michael in Britain, thought that he should find a place to hide the coordinates of the burial site on the cliffs at Filey Bay. He knew it should be in the unlikeliest place, but should be easily retrievable by him at a moment's notice.

Sitting at his desk, he was uncertain of the best place. Glancing at his Woodrow Wilson watch, he hit on the idea of secreting it in the mechanism somehow. As he always wore the watch, it would be easy for him to retrieve the data within and it was a secure place to hide it.

With this solution in mind, he took a cigarette out of the desk box and split it open, discarded the tobacco and straightened out the cigarette paper. Using a sharpened pencil, he then sketched on the very thin paper an outline of the coast with features which Michael had noted, and the numbers of the coordinates. He gingerly opened up the back of the watch with his penknife and inserted the paper carefully onto the mechanism plate, and then securely replaced the back of the watch. He complimented himself on a great hiding place and felt secure in the knowledge that it was an achievement of secrecy 'in plain sight'.

30

Arrest and Exile to Perm

Gatchina was now just a ghost of what it used to be. The Bolsheviks had stripped out most of the home comforts and luxuries and had taken huge amounts of furniture, curtains and tableware for themselves to use in the Party HQ and private homes. The cars were gone, and the half-track Rolls, was now probably in the possession of Lenin, after Michael had used it for the journey north to the White Sea port of Belomorsk. It was now a matter of using horseback or taxis if they wanted to venture outside of the Palace.

However, there was his own Rolls-Royce, which he had secreted in one of the garden sheds which had become overgrown. It had been safely hidden under furniture, blankets and bric-a-brac of no value. Michael had taken this step as another emergency route out of captivity should it be required. He would not use it unless it was imperative.

The petty looting by the guards was a personal attack on the privacy and day-to-day lives of his family, and protests to Lenin were still left unheeded. The only remaining delight in the Palace was the presence of Natasha, the children and Johnson. There were still a few valets and servants, but their duties now were only a shadow of what they were pre-1917.

The household did have in place a free access permit to the Crimea for Michael to live, due to his recurring stomach illness. And of course it was far enough away from the Bolshevik HQ to offer them more peace from direct diktat proclamations regarding their existence. However, Michael was reluctant to leave his beloved Gatchina, the place of his childhood and early years of manhood. Michael was still able to come and go as he pleased but it was always known that he was being continually watched and trailed, which he cared very little about, other than insisting to the detachment Commander that his privacy should be respected.

The war now had little interest for the people of Russia and Michael. There had been hopes that the German intervention, because of the soon to be signed peace treaty and the cessation of armed hostilities, would soon arrive. The household felt that they would be far better treated by the Germans being an Imperial power and the sentiments of the Kaiser might allow them more freedom and the semblance of a return to some normality.

However, in the weeks since Michael and Johnson had returned, it seemed that the German troop movements had stopped short of Gatchina. Soon after the signing of the treaty in March, it would be the opening signal for further civil war and unrest in Russia. Within days of the treaty, the worst was to happen. Michael and Johnson were arrested again.

This was very bad timing, although he had been arrested several times before, and it was to be expected that this might be the order of the day from time to time. However, now that civil war was the major issue in Russian politics and daily life, this could spell disaster, as Michael was hoping for the status quo to prevail at least until early summer, when the Allies would invade Russia.

This arrest was a direct order from the Cheka, run by thugs who seemed to have autonomous powers to wreak havoc amongst their own countrymen. This time it was very serious, as it resulted in imprisonment at the Bolshevik HQ in Petrograd, where Michael was locked up under guard.

Natasha became distressed as she knew that this time Michael was in more serious trouble. Being forthright and persuasive, she marched into the HQ and soon found the room where Michael and Johnson were being kept, and rushed into his arms. A while later, she was able, to negotiate slightly better conditions for them with the head of the Cheka, Uritsky, but she held out little hope of this happening due to his vague promises.

As an alternative, the next day she again marched into the Bolshevik HQ and this time confronted Vladimir Lenin, who was not amused at her bursting into his office in such a manner. Promises were made to Natasha to try and ease her distress over Michael's captivity, but they came to nothing.

Lenin was a diminutive figure, well versed in opportunism and a manipulator of men and circumstances, who would use and betray anybody in his way to achieve control, and was dismissive of entreaties for mercy or fair play – but willing to embrace them if it suited his purpose. Encouraging insurrection during Russia's failed Revolution of 1905, he later campaigned for the First World War to be transformed into a Europe-wide proletarian revolution, which as a Marxist he believed would cause the overthrow of capitalism and replacing it with socialism. After the February 1917 Revolution ousted the Tsar and established a Provisional Government, he returned to Russia to play a leading role in the October Revolution, in which the Bolsheviks overthrew the new regime.

However, the following day there was a major change in the activities of the Bolsheviks. The concern was that the Germans were coming closer in the south, in some form of occupation after the treaty, and there was strong support for the reinstatement of the Imperial Government from the north in Finland. A decision was then taken to relocate the Bolshevik Government to Moscow and establish that as the new Capital.

These concerns and movements were enough to convince the Bolsheviks that they needed to halt any possible activities to rescue Michael as he may become a rallying point, so they decided to move him to central Russia. The chosen location was the city of Perm, close to the Ural Mountains where there was a stronger Bolshevik support platform. Johnson was also to join him.

Both were confronted by Lenin's guards and given a very short time to pack their belongings, and were quickly shipped out to the railway station in the early hours of the following morning.

The journey to Perm began at a very slow pace and became more arduous than expected. The journey time, which would have been no more than two days, was to take eight days, travelling at a snail's pace in a rickety old carriage which had many windows missing and letting in the rain and snow. The conditions were disgusting, the train being bereft of any sanitation. Satisfactory food was scarce to non-existent during the journey, other than meagre supplies brought aboard at the frequent stops. The train was carrying freight, merchandise, and minerals, which were loaded and offloaded as it crawled onwards.

Michael was allowed to send telegrams as they drove into remote stations to take on fuel and water. He showed very little concern for himself in his messages to Natasha, as he was more concerned for her own health and welfare and desired to keep her spirits up. She had some measure of safety as she was not of royal blood, and was seen as being no threat to the revolution. He was very much hoping that she would be allowed to join him, and advised that they should be well prepared for any journey as comfort and sustenance were non-existent if she were to travel. Michael was promised by the Cheka before he left Moscow that Natasha and the children would be allowed to follow onwards, but felt that this would not happen quickly, or even not at all.

Michael and Johnson had long learned the diplomatic lesson of staying quiet and enduring without complaint and this attitude during the long journey raised some sympathy with the several guards who accompanied them. The guards in time softened their approach to their prisoners and started to engage in respectful chat. Michael, having brought his guitar, could play for his captors any request as both he and Johnson were accomplished musicians and had reasonable voices. Their music and the friendships they were building up became a pleasant distraction and often, with Michael just strumming away from his well-stocked repertoire of tunes, kept up the spirits for all the members of the coach during the long hours of boredom on the journey. Johnson was also able to teach the guards chess and brinksmanship at cards, and Michael gave the same fellows tuition on his guitar.

Approximately half way, they made another customary stop and hoped to take on fresh food, as even the guards were becoming agitated at the poor facilities en route. Sergei, who was the most senior of the guards, got off the train and made his way to the food counter in a very rudimentary café in the hope that he could secure supplies for the rest of the journey. After a while, they was concerned that he had not returned. Then suddenly there was a cry of anger and a lot of shouting coming from the café.

The other guards and Johnson got off the train to see what the commotion was about. When they walked in, Sergei was being held by the café owner, who was a very tall and much stronger man, with his arm pushed behind his back and a knife held to his throat. It seemed that Sergei had been refused the quantity of rations he wanted, due to the famine that was spreading throughout Russia. The man was angry that Sergei had attempted to take what he wanted without permission.

The guards were quick to act to save their senior officer and drew their pistols to shoot the café owner.

But given the obvious danger that Sergei was in, they were likely to be the architects of his death and probably the café owner would take out at least another member of the undernourished and weak squad of guards, as it was obvious that they had very little military training.

Johnson was quick to observe that the café owner was wearing part of a tatty military uniform and equally quick to see from the style and flashes that it was of the 'Savage Regiment', which Michael had commanded in 1916. He immediately shouted, and called for a stand down of arms.

With that he marched between the combatants and stood erect in front of the café owner and Sergei, and announced, 'These guards are under the protection of his Imperial Highness Michael Alexandrovitch Romanov, Commander of the Savage Division.'

All parties were entirely confused at this announcement. Johnson then instructed the café owner to lower his knife and unleash Sergei. Sergei fell to the floor and Johnson instructed the guards to take the shaken officer back to the train to recover from his ordeal. His face then broke into a smile and he held out his hand and introduced himself as the secretary of Michael, who was travelling to Perm on the train waiting in the station.

At that moment, Michael walked into the room, tall, handsome and with his usual manner of calm authority. He called out, 'Major Andropov, I am glad to see that you have such a thriving business.'

With that, Andropov recognized his old Commander and stood to attention. Michael walked forward and gave him a long embrace of comradeship. They had fought together on many fronts during 1914–16 and Michael was a very well-loved and respected leader and still inspired an immense amount of loyalty from the army. Andropov was a huge man, with a solid, robust frame, and showed a character of hardnosed confidence whilst having a respect for duty and loyalty. He was a man of few words, but wielding the potential for decisive action when called for.

They chatted for a while over hot coffee. Michael then asked if his guards could come and join them, together with the engine drivers. Andropov was happy to oblige and soon there was a banquet atmosphere amongst the captors and captives and the Savage Division's Major was making a fine host. Vodka soon flowed, and after much rowdiness, there settled over them a calm and drowsy atmosphere as each of the guards collapsed in a drunken stupour.

Andropov had avoided the excess drinking, and after asking much about the outside world and political affairs, started to ask Michael what was the real position he was in. Michael was reluctant to say too much, especially about the invasion plans. This was for the benefit of Andropov, as if they were eventually questioned on any interaction by the Cheka, who had eyes and spies everywhere, then Andropov would be asked to recount all he knew under torture. However, Michael did mention his concern for the future of Russia and the safety of his own family.

Andropov then mentioned to Michael and Johnson that two days earlier there had been a stopover by the express train to Perm, and a foreign couple had got off to stretch their legs and had spoken with Andropov. They had recognised his tatty part uniform and engaged him in a conversation about his loyalty and what he thought of his ex-Commander, Michael. Andropov was very complimentary, and upon their leaving, he asked the couple their names. They gave their names as simply Olga and Orlov Volkov, and bade him good day.

Michael's heart rose in joy and great expectation, as he knew who they were: Olga Bystrovia and Sidney Reilly. He felt safe already. They must have contacted Natasha just after they left Moscow, and she would have told them of their plight. By taking the fast express and using the same stopover, then that would be how Andropov came to know of them.

Michael enquired where these two people were going. Andropov replied that they were on their way to Perm to appear in the theatre, as they were comedians. Michael and Johnson, hearing this, were filled with euphoria and laughter at the sense of humour the British spies still possessed. They were certain that they would be met with friends when they arrived at Perm.

Boarding the train the following morning, much refreshed, the guards nursing hangovers, and with a greatly improved stock of food, the train pulled out of the station without much further increase in speed, thus making the journey a prolonged affair. The comradeship that had been built, and saving of Sergei's life, meant they were in a more protective and friendlier environment with their captors.

31

Perm

A rriving in Perm, they were then taken to a rather second-rate and uncomfortable hotel. They were unwashed and tired, but at least they had better sleeping arrangements.

Whilst out shopping the following day after their arrival in Perm, Johnson spotted Olga and Reilly, but it was only a fleeting glance. Both the British spies had also seen Johnson. They had known where they were staying and it would be a matter of time before they contacted either him or Michael. It was too dangerous to talk yet. However, Olga did approach him to ask the time. Johnson glanced at his trusty watch, and at that moment, when she thanked him and shook his hand, she passed him a note.

When Johnson got back to the hotel, he read it to Michael and simply said, 'Escape plans imminent. Stay alert.' This put them both in good cheer and they were looking forward to the next contact.

Shortly after they had arrived, they were taken to the local jail and imprisoned by the Bolshevik leaders. Michael contacted the Cheka HQ in Moscow and complained at the intolerable situation that had been imposed on them.

Several weeks passed before they were released, and very much at the insistence of Natasha who had been protesting against Michael's intolerable position once again with Lenin in Moscow.

In the meantime, Michael's chauffeur had arrived in Perm with his valet, and had brought many comforting supplies in Michael's Rolls-Royce, which they had travelled in. Johnson was so pleased to see that the Rolls-Royce had arrived in Perm. He had forgotten until now to inform Michael that he had hidden Carl Fabergé's egg in the Rolls. Michael was pleased that he had done so, as its contents could well work for them both for bribery during their stay in Perm and, if they were to stay there in the long term, then it could help to establish a new life, even though it was a very tenuous situation and not a perfect home for him and Natasha.

His valet had arranged some very comfortable accommodation in the best hotel in Perm, and indeed the best room. Full board had been arranged so that they could live comfortably, without too many domestic chores. The valet had also made reservations for himself and the chauffeur to be in the same hotel, where he would be on hand to serve Michael. At least now they could eat and sleep in some degree of comfort. It was expensive, but the valet had also contacted Olga and Reilly, who was providing the main funding for their comfort.

Whilst they were still in effect prisoners, they had been granted freedom of movement and the presence of their Rolls-Royce was a major step in their enjoyment of freedom. They had to report each day to the military HQ, and were still being monitored. They became popular figures around town amongst the townsfolk, who started to appreciate their plight. They knew Michael's reputation as being a man of the people, and that he was quiet, caring and gentle. He was offered gifts of food and minor luxuries and often applauded and greeted with a great deal of respect. This was very helpful to his cause as not only did it make his life more tolerable, but more to the point, should the escape plans of Reilly come to fruition, then he may well be able to count on this popular support.

Natasha had been pressuring the Bolshevik Government in Moscow to be allowed travel to Perm and join Michael. After several weeks, her persistence paid off and she was given a permit for herself only, and not the children. George had been secretly spirited out of the country to Denmark with his English governess. Michael's stepdaughter Tata, now a teenager, did not go into exile with her stepbrother George, but because she was not of Romanov blood then her safety lay in keeping a low profile. Accordingly, then, she would not travel with Natasha to see Michael.

Olga, upon hearing of the removal of Nicholas and his family from Tobolsk to Ekaterinburg, decided that she should go there and create a plan for an escape attempt. MI6 had a small spy network there and she could use that as a foundation for her planning.

After Olga left for Ekaterinburg, Reilly moved into the Korolav Rooms Hotel where Michael and Johnson were staying. He had persuaded the management to give him a room and board in exchange for his reception duties, as he was multilingual, and a good replacement for the previous person who had recently died. One of his duties was as a telegraph operator, which put him in an excellent position to monitor incoming and outgoing messages. There he also had the opportunity to transmit his own messages back to Lockhart, who was still at the British Embassy in Petrograd.

The plans Reilly was making very much reflected a change of pace due to Michael being imprisoned and now out of the way in Perm. It was important to keep a monitoring eye and make him ready for escape as and when he knew of the imminence of the invasion. To get him out now would possibly interfere with the natural progress of matters, and of course would further endanger the lives of Nicholas and his family. It was a delicate and dangerous path of inactivity. At this point he had not made firm plans for Michael's escape, and he would have to react quickly as events progressed.

From time to time Reilly would make discreet contact with Michael and Johnson in the hotel to check on their welfare and provide updates. He calculated the position he must take, which was to keep a low profile and act carefully, but warned Michael of the possible need to react quickly, as unpredictable events may arise.

Michael was conscious of having the Fabergé egg in his living quarters, as they were likely to be searched at any point. So he told Reilly of its existence and suggested that he keep it in his quarters at the Korolav Rooms Hotel.

Natasha eventually arrived at Perm in May, much to Michael's delight. It was such a heartwarming encounter for both as they had naturally feared that they would never see each other again once Michael had been shipped off to Perm. Spring was now literally and lovingly in the air and to Natasha it seemed that their lives could perhaps settle down in isolation for a year or two, in the hope that one day they could return to a more civilised way of life. Natasha was still not aware of the pending invasion and Michael's role in it.

During the first few days, it seemed that life with Natasha and Johnson was settling into a reasonable existence. They often visited the theatre, and had dinner with other moderate society folk who were of a wealthy and somewhat influential circle. They had been making some plans to move out of the hotel and into a small villa, but Reilly advised against that as Michael would lose the protection of his proximity and observational skills in case events came to a point of rapid reaction.

Life for Michael, Natasha and Johnson, who accompanied them on most occasions, was becoming more pleasant as the warmer weather was gaining momentum and as spring and summer took over from the harsh winter. All three were often seen walking in the parks and enjoying picnics by the River Kama. Their visits to the marketplace and shops were always greeted with respect from the local townsfolk. They were delighted to understand that Natasha was a commoner like themselves and saw the pair as being of no threat, and more so as being worthy of help.

Towards the end of May there was news breaking in the city that was most pleasant to hear of, but did pose a greater danger to them. It transpired that the Czech Army, which had taken up arms against the Bolsheviks, had joined with the White Army and they were now taking over the provincial city of Chelyabinsk which was some 500 kilometres from Perm.

This event meant that the outcome of the civil war put the Bolsheviks under a greater existential threat; this was now a more dangerous war for them as they were not ready for a battle on two fronts. Whereas the imprisonment of Nicholas and Michael in the east had been a safe option, it was now seen that the Bolshevik Army could be overrun in the east and this could lead to the freedom of the Romanovs from captivity.

Michael was warned of this by his friends in Perm and by Reilly, who was now seeing that he may have to react very quickly to changing events. He advised that Natasha should leave immediately, as it would be difficult for him to carry out an escape if she were with Michael.

Within a few days, it seemed that the situation was escalating. There was growing unrest from the militia, who were annoyed that Michael had been given so much freedom and felt that he and Johnson had created their own fiefdom. They were enjoying so many benefits that they, the revolutionaries, were not able to, and his use of the chauffeur-driven Rolls-Royce was an annoyance. The revolutionary council, knowing the threat of Perm being attacked by the White Army, insisted that Michael be put under more stringent control. The Cheka in the city now took more control over Michael and he was watched wherever he went. They feared that he might be sprung now that Natasha was gone.

The presence of the Czech Army, and rumours of an invasion by the Allies to remove the Bolsheviks, were of major concern. Perm was now a city besieged, as it was becoming a bottleneck for travellers on the railway because there was now no route to Vladivostok due to the Czech Army controlling the railway.

Reilly was now preparing plans for an escape as to avoid the risk of Michael coming to any harm. He had sent for help from the British Embassy via MI6, and within a few days two gentlemen arrived who described themselves as Americans. They were O'Brien and Hess. But they were secret service personnel and the cover they had adopted was American tourists, with some attempt at trying to imitate the accent.

They checked into another hotel so as not to arouse any suspicion, and it was of benefit to their cover that they were seemingly trapped in Perm together with thousands of other east-bound travellers. That was a perfect scenario for Reilly to arrange an escape plan. Reilly was busy at night sending coded messages to London and making subtle arrangements for the plan of action.

Perm was now declared as being on a war footing, and the militia were training townsfolk in the art of defending the city and battle skills. There had been the arrival of a monstrous new Cheka leader, Myasnikov, who would shoot any adversary or suspect without explanation or recourse to trial. Reilly knew that it was now only a matter of time before they imprisoned Michael and he had to act whilst he still had relative freedom. The aim was for 8 June to be the day of escape, and Reilly was perfecting his plan to get them both to the safety of British controlled Archangel.

Michael was to attend the ballet at the theatre with his wealthier friends as usual, so not to arouse any suspicion of his whereabouts. He would be driven there in his Rolls-Royce by Reilly, disguised as Michael's chauffeur and Johnson hiding in the rear. Michael would take his usual seat in his theatre box, at floor level, with his small circle of theatre-going friends. He was to vacate his box just after the interval, and at the start of the final Act. One of his

MI6 colleagues, Hess, was to replace him as he had similar features and height. Tuxedos were a dress requirement at the ballet, and most menfolk looked similar in the semi-darkness.

Michael would then go to the toilet and meet Reilly, who had a change of clothes for him: a doorman's uniform. They would then disappear out of the theatre stage door to be met by the other MI6 man, O'Brien, who was in the dress of a Russian Air Force officer. Once in the car, Michael would change into a similar uniform, but carrying a higher rank and with Johnson still hidden in the back.

Then they would drive west to the city outskirts and go to the airport. There waiting for them would be a Sikorsky Ilya Muromets four-engine heavy bomber.

The Ilya Muromets aircraft, as it appeared in 1913, was of a revolutionary design, intended for commercial service with its spacious fuselage incorporating a passenger saloon and washroom on board. The plane was designed to take 16 passengers and the cabin was heated from the exhaust pipes of the four engines which ran through the interior. This Sikorsky plane was ahead of its time and broke many records in its early guise. During the war with Germany, it became the first four-engine bomber to be equipped with a dedicated strategic bombing unit, unrivalled at that time.

The pilot, who worked for the Imperial Air Force, was secretly sympathetic to the Romanovs and found this a perfect excuse for himself to be liberated from the Bolshevik regime. He would be waiting with engines running to fly to Archangel, an eight-hour journey with a stopover for refuelling and a rest period at Kotlas on the banks of the River Dvina. The cabin was comfortable, to some extent, and food would be stocked on board for the journey. Extra fuel tanks had been added, but the plane would easily take Michael, Johnson, Reilly and O'Brien, especially as the armour had been stripped out. Hess would be left behind to monitor the events unfolding in Perm.

However, on the morning of 8 June, Johnson got a message to Reilly that Michael was in serious pain with his stomach illness and was too ill to stand up. It would not be the best plan for Michael to be carried into the theatre – that would be very suspicious. The plan had to be put back. This was a blow to Reilly as the main problem was the facility of the Sikorsky. However, he had no option but to cancel it and had to replan and work it around the next availability of the Sikorsky returning on some pretext.

The return of the four-engine plane, Reilly was informed, would be on the evening of 13 June at 11.30 p.m. So, it was hoped that Michael would recover enough to make the journey to the theatre again. It was risky, as there was now chaos in the streets and at any moment Michael could be put under close arrest. It seemed that there were now partisan mobs who were wanting the death of Michael.

32

Plotting to Assassinate

As the days rolled on towards 13 June, Myasnikov was becoming more militant, and he had declared martial law on the streets as it seemed the Czech Army was coming closer to Perm. He was of the opinion that Michael was more the target of the White Army, and a plot had been rumored, which had a lot of credence, that many of the townsfolk wanted to raise Michael up to promote the White Army Cause.

There had been a failed and publicly undisclosed attempt to free Nicholas in Ekaterinburg, so Myasnikov was moved to act. He decided that it was now far too dangerous to allow Michael to be rescued, and so he had to be assassinated, together with Johnson. On 12 June, he recruited a squad of four men who all were hardened criminals and had served hard labour prison sentences with him under the Tsarist regime. They were close friends of Myasnikov and were trusted to keep quiet about the assassination and to do the job without fear, as the written order, seemingly coming from Lenin, would have to be a forged document.

Myasnikov explained to them that if Michael was freed,

there would be a bloodbath within the Bolshevik revolution, and his friends would certainly be targets for arrest and execution. Their safety, then, lay in assassinating Michael at the earliest possible moment. The plan would be very simple and secret; there could be no leaks. They were to carry out the deed immediately.

In the early hours of the morning the four armed, aggressive henchmen went to the hotel where Michael was staying with Johnson and rushed inside. Reilly was on the night duty desk at that point and was pushed to one side with a threat of instant death if he tried to stop them. They found the room where Michael was staying and banged on the door. Michael's valet opened the door and they marched in and demanded that he and Johnson get dressed, as they were being moved out of town due to the impending invasion of the city by the Czechs. Michael protested and demanded to see the orders to that effect. One of the assassins brought out the proclamation signed by the local Cheka Commander under the orders of Lenin.

Michael protested for some time, but losing patience, the assailants grabbed him and pushed him and Johnson out of the door, then led them out of the hotel demanding they get into one of two horse-drawn carriages waiting in the street.

In the meantime, Reilly had gone to his room to get his Beretta handgun and went to the assistance of Michael. He had to act fast and without fear. Simply, he had to shoot as many of these thugs as possible, as he guessed the fate that awaited Michael. If he got the surprise jump on them, it just might be possible if he was calm, and aimed carefully at the chest of each assailant. He was hopeful that the chaos and noise in the streets would disguise the sound of his gunfire. His plan was then to secrete Michael and Johnson in the loft space in his attic room, which he had boarded out in secrecy in the event that he needed to hide them both.

Reilly quickly became unsure, however: he was now in two minds, and thought it might be better to follow them and try to rescue them with the aid of his two MI6 colleagues. He rushed out of the back door and made his way to the hotel where his two colleagues were staying, and demanded that they get dressed and arm themselves. In the meantime, Reilly remembered that he had custody of the Fabergé egg, and returned to his room to retrieve it as events were turning for the worse and it may be that he would not be able to return, due to the developing crisis.

They had the use of horses from the hotel stables, so they made their way there and saddled up three horses. Entering the street, Reilly saw a vagrant fellow who he had befriended some weeks ago, and paid him to inform of the activities of the local militia and any stories that were circulating. He asked if he had seen any carriages at the hotel in the last ten minutes.

The man quickly informed Reilly that he had, and that two carriages had gone South. With that information, they headed off in the hope of catching up with Michael and the assailants. After a short while, and galloping at speed, they had no sight of the carriages and concluded this was proving to have been a mistake, or perhaps deliberate misinformation given to them. They turned around and headed back to the hotel. Reilly saw his informer skulking around and, sliding off his horse, dragged him into a side alley, drew his derringer and threatened him with his life if he did not now tell the truth.

The trembling vagrant soon relayed the truth that the two carriages had headed north over the bridge towards the northern district of Motovilikha, and admitted that he was told to misinform Reilly who was under close surveillance by the Cheka. Reilly shot him in the skull, knowing that he, O'Brien and Hess could not return as they were in danger of being exposed as spies, and it was necessary now that they remain totally lost to the Cheka.

There was a lot of commotion in the street outside the hotel and the talk was that Michael had escaped. Reilly knew the truth to be different and that Michael had been kidnapped and was facing execution. Moments later Reilly joined the other two and they set off at speed through the town and over the bridge towards the district of Motovilikha.

In the meantime, the journey with the assailants, whilst uncomfortable, was a silent affair. Michael and Johnson, having been given no time to pack any substantial personal clothing or belongings, were more than concerned as to their safety at the hands of these aggressive captors. They did not believe their main luggage would be sent onwards to a destination still unknown.

Having travelled over the River Kama bridge they became concerned that they were heading into the northern districts where there was no railway station and little sign of urbanisation, the area being mainly forest. The carriages approached a small square, and pulled up. The driver got out and entered a large residential building and reappeared a few minutes later and drove on. After a further five minutes the carriages pulled up in a small clearing in a wooded area.

Michael and Johnson were ordered to get out. They did so without complaint, as they assumed that it was a stop for toileting.

Reilly, O'Brien and Hess were hard on their heels, riding at racing speed. They caught up with the two carriages, which were showing lit driving lamps and were entering into a woodland clearing. Reilly and his companions dismounted and approached on foot for the last 50 metres, in order to remain undetected. As they got within 25 metres they saw Michael and Johnson being pulled out of the carriages and thrust into the clearing.

They were then quickly shot by two of the assailants. Both were wounded and not killed outright. Michael, still standing, rushed over to Johnson who was faltering, and with outstretched arms pleaded with the assassins to let him at least say goodbye to his dear friend. Further shots were fired at their heads and they were left for dead in a heap.

Reilly and the two MI6 fellows were shocked into silence. They had just seen the worst of their fears become a reality. They then lay low to see how this event would turn out. There just might be a chance that Michael and Johnson were somehow still alive.

The bodies were stripped of clothing and personal possessions before being hidden under a light covering of branches. The misty dawn was showing in the sky and the assassins made their way back to Motovilikha to show the Cheka Commander their stolen items to prove that the murders had taken place. During the stripping of the bodies, a watch was wrenched from Johnson's wrist, and was taken as a personal trophy of the murderous deed that evening by Andrei Markov.

Reilly clearly heard the discussion of the assassins, who were talking in loud voices as they were all pumped up with relief over a job well done. They agreed that they should leave now and return later that evening to bury the bodies properly.

Reilly was contemplating his next move. He thought there would be an uncertain outcome if they brought the assassins to quick justice, and tried to eliminate them now. The risk was too high.

The assassins left in one of the carriages, returning to Perm to bring the news to the Cheka and Bolsheviks of the great patriotic duty they had carried out. The other carriage was left behind, with the horse tied to a tree.

Places of Interest

Gatchina Palace near Petrograd

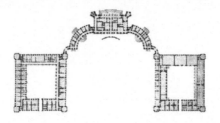

Design and construction began work in 1766, and took fifteen years to complete the imposing castle-style building

The work of two of St. Petersburg's greatest architects, this impressive, fortress-like building was the family home of several generations of Romanovs.

The concept of the project was to create a 600-room palace in the style of a knight's castle, with elements of a royal hunting lodge and an English stately home. Using weathered limestone, the architect, Rinaldi designed a building that is both imposing and welcoming, presenting a sweeping semi-circular facade of classical simplicity on one side, and a more fanciful rear, with two slim hexagonal towers creating the atmosphere of a medieval castle

The Grand Palace at Gatchina is perhaps the most unusual and individual of St. Petersburg's suburban Imperial palaces, although the modesty of its architectural decorations makes it far less striking at first glance than the brightly coloured, stucco covered facades at Pavlovsk and Tsarskoe Selo.

During the Revolution and Civil War, Gatchina was the site of two major events - the final fall of Kerensky's Provisional Government in 1917, and Trotsky's defeat of the final advance of the White Army from Estonia in July 1919.

The palace and park were opened to the public soon after the Revolution, and served as a museum until occupied by the Nazis in 1941. As elsewhere, occupation brought severe damage to the palace and park, and restoration work is continuing.

Gatchina was the main family residence of Alexander III. Michael and his siblings were raised there and when Michael returned from exile in England in 1914, he from time to time went back with Natasha in an attempt to make this their family home.

Michael had many pleasant memories of Gatchina and was hoping to realise those same past days of comfort and joy with his new family. Sadly, Gatchina became a prison on several occasions whilst under house arrest. In 1918 the palace was under Bolshevik rule and quite often was broken into by marauding looting mobs.

Michael left Gatchina for the last time in the spring of 1918 when he was arrested again and sent to Perm in Siberia, from whence several weeks after that, the Bolsheviks murdered him.

Vladimir Palace at Petrograd

Situated on the banks of the Neva River, the palace of the Grand Duke Vladimir Alexandrovich and his wife, the

Grand Duchess Maria Pavlovna is one of the finest preserved residences of the Russian Imperial Family in St. Petersburg.

Like the Winter Palace and the Marble Palace, the Vladimir Palace is situated on the Palace Embankment overlooking the Neva River and the Peter and Paul Fortress. The construction of residences along the banks of the Neva was extremely prized by both members of the Russian Imperial family and the Russian aristocracy.

The palace and its outbuildings contain some 360 rooms. Each room of the luxurious apartments of the palace are all decorated in disparate historic styles.

Until 1917 the palace was one of the main centres of social life in St Petersburg, the venue of countless musical and literary nights and balls. Grand Duchess Maria Pavlovna was regarded as one of the most illustrious socialites and renowned for her musicality.

This was the Palace in which Albert Stopford snook into during 1917 after Maria had left for the Crimea to escape the Bolsheviks. Her personal wealth was rescued from a safe and below stairs.

The Alexander Palace at Tsarskoe Selo in Petrograd

The Alexander Palace was the last home of the Russian tsar, Nicholas II.

Nicholas and his young spouse came to Tsarskoe Selo a week after their wedding and settled down in the rooms of the right wing of the Alexander Palace, where the heir-tsesarevich spent his childhood. For Nicholas, it was an inexpressible pleasure which no words could describe at to leading a quiet life without meeting anyone, being day and night together with his family.

From that time, the Alexander Palace would always be a special place, where the family of Nicholas II would settle permanently several years later and up to the time when they were forcibly removed and sent to Tobolsk in Siberia under house arrest. A year later they would be murdered along with the whole family and pets.

The Grand Hotel in Scarborough, England

This Scarborough Hotel is one of the earliest purpose built hotels in Europe when construction started in 1863. The Grand Hotel, overlooking the South Bay, is a well-known nineteenth-century landmark in this English seaside town. The hotel's heydey was arguably during Victorian times, when wealthy holidaymakers made up the establishment's clientele.

When opened the fashion was for salt water that was believed to be good for the health, hence the Victorian love of bathing in the sea. This is reflected in the hotel plumbing that could pipe both drinking water and sea water.

The building is designed around the theme of time: There are four towers to represent the seasons, 12 floors for the months of the year, 52 chimneys symbolise the weeks, and originally there were 365 bedrooms, one for each day of the year. The hotel's 7million distinctive yellow brickwork was made locally in Hunmanby.

Knebworth House, Hertfordshire, England

The home of the Lytton family since 1490. Knebworth House was originally a red-brick Late Gothic manor house, built round a central court as an open square. In 1813-16 the house was reduced to its west wing, which was remodelled in a Tudor Gothic style and then was transformed in 1843-45 into the present Tudor Gothic structure.

In 1913-1914 it was leased for £3,000 per year by Grand Duke Michael Alexandrovitch of Russia and his morganatic wife Natalia Brasova. Michael had been exiled by his brother tsar Nicholas and had chosen England as his new home. They settled in very well and was prepared to become an Anglophile and live in contentment with his wife and son George. His secretary Nicholas Johnson also joined him together with his house staff from Gatchina. Before his one year lease was to expire his secretary, Johnson created a lease for an alternative mansion in Paddockhurst in Sussex.

Paddockhurst House, Sussex, England

Paddockhurst was once the home of Robert Whitehead, inventor of the torpedo. He sold the estate to the 1st Viscount Cowdray in 1898. This private estate consists of 6,000 acres.

In September 1914 Michael was due to move into Paddockhurst from Knebworth. Furniture was moved down to the new property in readiness for the move. However, before the move could take place, war between Russia and Germany was announced and Michael was recalled to enlist and command a battalion of troops on the western Front. Natasha, George, and Johnson moved back with him and most of his staff. Not thinking that it would be a long war and peace would soon prevail in common sense, their thoughts were that they may perhaps return to England. In the meantime, Johnsons mother Louise stayed behind to look after much of the furniture and private possessions they had left behind.

Shortly after that, it seemed that the war might drag on, so Johnson arranged with the British army for them to take over the building during the war to use as an intelligence gathering HQ. The war was turning out to be a disaster for Russia and the Bolsheviks were coming to prominence once again, so it was decided that Louise Johnson would stay in England until the certainty of safety could be guaranteed.

They never returned to Paddockhurst, and eventually Louis moved on at the end of the war and took with her the furniture and possessions to a new location in nearby Wadhurst.

The Korolav Rooms in Perm, Central Russia

 Michael and Johnson were kept under house arrest at the Korolev Rooms in Perm. The Grand Dukes' room was directly above the main door at the right. In March 1918. It was from here that they were taken to an undisclosed location and shot dead by the Bolsheviks on the night of June 12th, 1918.

Their remains have never been found. The SEARCH Foundation, which is dedicated to finding their remains, return to Perm each summer to search for the remains of Michael and Johnson.

PART II

MICHAEL'S SECOND LIFE

33

Barely Alive

It was now becoming much lighter as the sun was breaking, and once they were left alone, Reilly and his companions approached the bodies in the hope that there may be some way of reviving them. They were shocked to see their body wounds and the shots to their heads.

Hess, who was a trained medic, examined the victims and was elated to find that Michael still had a weak pulse. But Johnson was clearly dead; the bullet wound to his head was conclusive. Michael had two wounds. One was from a bullet which had gone clean through his shoulder and had caused some bleeding. Hess ripped off his shirt and tore it into strips and bound the wound tight to stem the flow of blood. This shoulder wound was not life-threatening and could be dealt with at the right time. The second and more serious wound was to his head. It appeared that a bullet had struck his jaw and lodged in his skull. There was very little bleeding, so this aspect could be coped with. However, the bullet in his skull could very well have a long-term consequence in the form of permanent damage to his brain.

Both Michael and Johnson had been stripped down to

the waist, and Michael would soon suffer from the morning cold. He was still breathing very slowly, but unconscious. It was essential to keep him warm so they gently wrapped him in the carriage rugs and placed him in the carriage in an upright position. With him being so tall, this was the only way they could make him comfortable.

Reilly thought for a while and decided to at least create some mystery and confusion, so Johnson's body, with some ceremony, was laid on the carriage floor with the intention of taking it to an alternative burial site. Reilly mounted the carriage and drove off to rebury the body at a distant point, and Hess and O`Brien followed behind on horseback.

Fortunately, there were two shovels and picks in the rear of the carriage trunk, which Reilly assumed would have been used by the assassins to bury the bodies.

Arriving at a suitable site they dug out a 1 metre deep grave and with little ceremony, they laid Johnson to rest. Reilly, conscious of still having the small box containing the Fabergé egg, thought the best place to hide it would be with Johnson in his grave. Perhaps he could return one day after the invasion to give Johnson a proper burial and retrieve the egg and its contents. O'Brien had a compass and thought it would be a good idea to record the position as best they could for their records, and in case they ever needed to prove the facts of witnessing the murders.

The time was recorded and the position of the rising sun was assessed from due south. There were certain rocky features on the road which were noted, and an agreed estimate of the distance they had covered from the outskirts of the town of Motovilikha. Then they accurately paced the position of the grave in relation to a rocky feature on the main road. Another feature which would help to identify the new burial site was that it was adjacent to a series of lagoons off the Kama River which was flowing to their east. They were very fortunate that there was no traffic on the road at that time, so they were completely unseen in what they had done.

The only option now was to make their escape that evening on the plane that would be waiting for them at 11.30 p.m. at the Perm landing strip which was in a remote area to the West of the city.

It was important now that they did not go back to Perm as it would be certain that with rumours now rife that Michael had escaped, they would be the first suspects. It was of great help that because these murders had originated from the Cheka, there would only be a half-hearted attempt to search and arrest; they could rely on the fact that the Bolsheviks would be feeling very pleased with themselves.

So, they said goodbye to Johnson with a prayer for his salvation, and then mounted up, with Reilly driving the carriage with Michael on board. They decided that the best route was over the River Kama as this was the shortest distance to the landing strip. They made their way to the river bank, where there was a small settlement. Knowing that there were no bridges in that area, they found a rowing boat on the bank. It was a matter of theft, but they felt that by leaving the carriage and horses, that would be payment enough for the boat.

It was large enough to lay Michael down and make him a little more comfortable. They launched the boat and rapidly made headway towards the other side, which was some 750 metres away, with O'Brien and Hess working hard at the oars. The sun was now higher in the sky and they could feel the pleasant heat of the day penetrating through their clothes. Hess was particularly thankful to see the sun as he was shirtless.

During the crossing, Michael started to regain consciousness. He could not speak, but was moaning and his eyes were open. Hess spoke gently to Michael and asked him to use his eyes in a yes/no conversation. Michael was lucid enough to understand this solution.

First Hess explained as best he could, with a full account of what happened at the woodland clearing and the attempted murder. Michael listened in silence, seeming to be recalling for himself those fearful moments before he had passed out. Hess broke the news which Michael's eyes were imploring him for, and when he told him that Johnson had not survived the gunshot wounds, then his eyes closed for a good five minutes of remembrance. Silence filled the boat in respect for Michael and his thoughts.

Michael then came back to reality as his thoughts turned to Natasha, and his will to live became an emotional exertion of strength and determination as he suddenly stood up in the boat. Hess gently sat him down again and then explained to him what the next part of the journey entailed and what their destination would be. Michael seemed to understand, now recalling clearly the plan Reilly had made with him two weeks ago.

Hess asked Michael to respond to a question: there would now be a trek overland to meet the plane on the runway, did he think he would be up to that task? Michael blinked his eyes twice very quickly, which was the sign that he understood and would comply.

Reaching the opposite bank, they then had to journey through the forest south-west towards the landing strip, which was a trek of some 12 kilometres. They should easily do this by nightfall and the time available would mean that they could carefully pick their way through the forest with the aid of the compass, and then lie low until the aircraft landed at around 11.30 p.m.

It was obvious now that Michael was weakening and they had to stop several times to allow him to rest and recover. After about 8 kilometres, Michael could walk no longer, and as they laid him down he fell into a state of unconsciousness. The only option now was to make a rudimentary stretcher from thin branches and stripped bark to make a latticework covering. This was a useful creation and held Michael quite well as his lean stature meant his weight was evenly spread.

Time passed quickly and all three became hungry and very thirsty in the heat of Russia's summer sun. They reached their destination and then lay low in a wooded thicket on the edge of the runway. They desperately hoped that the pre-arranged plan would go smoothly and that the four-engine plane would arrive on time.

Around 11.15 p.m., as the summer daylight had faded, they heard the thunderous roars from distant aero engines. They were now filled with hopes that the rescue mission could be accomplished.

Soon they saw a sight which was quite amazing: none of them had seen such a large and cleanlined aircraft before. The very noisy aircraft approached the aerodrome and landing very smoothly, taxied to the end of the strip. Reilly raced towards the aircraft and signalled the pilot to open the side hatches. Hess and O'Brien picked up the stretcher with Michael still laid out unconscious, and gently slid him into the floor of the plane quickly. They jumped aboard and told the startled pilot to get out fast.

He enquired why there were only four instead of five, to which Reilly replied, "Unfortunately Michael's secretary, did not survive the assassination attempt made on both him and Michael as he beckoned the pilot to take a look at Michael on the stretcher. 'But Michael is alive. Long live the Tsar.'

The pilot made haste as he was inextricably linked now with the theft of a Russian military aircraft whilst seeking refuge in another country. Without further ado, he turned the plane around and started his run to take-off. As he gunned his engine Reilly shouted to make haste as he could see an army truck leaving the aerodrome shack and heading towards them at speed.

The engines, now at high revs, threw the plane forwards and it soon gained speed, but the oncoming truck, now in line with the aircraft, was heading for a collision. The pilot shouted a warning to everyone that he was not going to stop and that they should prepare for a possible crash.

It seemed the truck was not going to stop and the pilot could see the flashes of gunfire coming from the truck with bullets whistling around the plane and ripping through the canvas cladding. One of the bullets struck the pilot in the leg, at which he screamed in pain. Reilly shouted at him to keep going and lift the ailerons. With that the huge plane gained height and just as it seemed there would be a collision, the truck veered to the right avoiding contact which would have resulted probably in their own deaths.

Shots were still being fired but quickly the plane gained more height and they were now safe from further harm.

34

Flight to Archangel

Hess quickly looked at the pilot's leg. The loss of blood was serious so he applied a tourniquet to his upper thigh to stem the flow. He then turned his attention to Michael and decided that he would be better cared for if he were laid on the bunk. There were body wraps on the plane and Michael was cocooned in these to provide maximum comfort and warmth. The loud drone of the four engines would not have bothered him as he had drifted back into unconsciousness.

The pilot then reminded them that the flight plan was to land at Kotlas which was on the confluence of the Dvina and the Vychegda Rivers and half way to the final destination at Archangel. This a forward base of the British which had vast supplies from the depot at Archangel. It was also occupied by White Russian forces at that time. From there they could take on board another pilot who could fly the aircraft on the final leg of the journey.

The instruments and on-board compass were sufficient to guide the plane at low-level flight, aided by a bright moon. This, with the help of dead reckoning, would aid their journey due north-west. By the time they reached Kotlas, the summer dawn would be in its full glory and they would be set for a reasonably safe landing.

After flying for three hours the pilot, was becoming more stressed with the pain. Hot coffee and heated soup from the small improvised galley were now losing any comforting affect, and it was obvious that he could not continue any longer. He was a small, thin man and seemed an unusual match for such a large plane. Reilly, without any further discussions as to his plight, asked Hess and O`Brien to gently remove the pilot to the rear and said he would take over the flight to give him a rest. He had not flown such a large aircraft before but had taken the opportunity to carefully watch the pilot over the past three hours to understand and learn the rudimentary operation in straight-line flight. Fortunately he did not have to negotiate any mountains and had the compass bearing set at north-west.

The pilot was then made as comfortable as possible in the back of the aircraft and kept warm from the internal exhaust pipes of the four throbbing engines. His time would come again, if he were conscious, to relieve Reilly and take the plane in to land at Kotlas.

About an hour later the glint of light from the wide confluence of two rivers came into vision. Reilly was now hopeful that the pilot had recovered enough to take the plane into land. He was in luck, and Hess and O'Brien carried the pilot to the controls as Reilly gingerly moved out of the way. The pilot was much more stable, and adjusted course towards the landing strip which appeared in the distance. He turned the aircraft through a

360-degree circle to see more of the runway and calculate his best entry line. This also gave notice to the ground crew that he would be coming in with a huge plane and that they should clear any obstacles out of the way. He knew the landing strip was a field of compacted earth and would be a bumpy landing which he was very nervous about due to his leg being inactive, and meant he would have to use one foot to operate two pedals.

Making the final approach the pilot shouted to make ready for a crash landing. All the passengers except Michael who was still unconcious, curled up into a ball and waited for the oncoming lumpy and fearsome crash. There was still fuel on board and there could be a disastrous explosion. However, the landing was far better than expected, and the plane glided in and to a halt close to the landing strip control tower.

Reilly made his way quickly to the tower with Hess to discover whether there were any medical supplies. The base Commander, Major Fox, gave them what they needed. He was very helpful and allowed Reilly to contact Archangel and report on the situation. The message simply said: 'One Turkey dead. Three Mignonettes need transplanting.'

There was a small medical unit at the base, who gave the best advice they could. Under the circumstances that Michael was unconscious, there was morphine available for him should he come out of unconsciousness and require pain relief as his protection up to that point had been shock. If he awoke, the shock protection would be rendered useless and it was unimaginable the pain that he would have to endure. It would be better, then, to leave Michael as he was, comfortable and warm, as to disturb him could cause too much damage. Hess brought out bandages and anti-infection creams and dressed the wound to Michael's shoulder, ensuring that he was not unduly disturbed.

The base Commander then arranged for another pilot to report to duty and within half an hour he had arrived and was ready to take them on the rest of their journey to Archangel. The pilot who was injured on take-off from Perm was taken to the local infirmary.

Reilly, O'Brien and Hess then made ready for the next part of the journey. The plane took off into a brightly lit morning sky on its way to Archangel and they were soon sleeping away the trials and tribulations of the past forty-eight hours. After a further four hours of uneventful flying, they landed at Archangel where Michael was rushed to the hospital with a dedicated team of medics who would take care of him, and hopefully nurse him back to health.

Reilly, leaving Michael in the care of the medical team, made his way to the control tower so that he could send a wire to MI6 and make a full report of the whole situation concerning Michael, and discuss the next move. He was told to return to Moscow to liquidate his affairs and to travel to Petrograd and do likewise.

Accomplishing this, then he was to return back to England. After a difficult journey via Finland, using yet another false name and papers, he arrived back in July.

35

Michael, a British Subject

Reilly, after arriving back in Britain was soon attending a meeting with Churchill and other members of the War Cabinet at Admiralty House.

The whole tone was very different from past meetings when there had been high hopes of a seamless plan of action for the coming incursion into Russia to bring about the defeat of the Bolshevik regime. Churchill lead most of the conversation, and brought Reilly up to date. He announced that with the Russian Government firmly under the control of Lenin, and with a working peace treaty with Germany, he was now left with a different view of the plans he had drawn up only months earlier.

Reilly enquired then, 'What of Michael?'

Churchill replied that Michael was very much out of the equation in terms of his being used as a figurehead for the coming actions, as he was still in Archangel in intensive care and was in a coma. Recent reports were that his life was in the balance and they should be aware that he may not survive. Lenin's Government had put out a statement that Michael had escaped and it was feared that he could become an instrument for an uprising against the new Bolshevik state.

He went on to argue that it was better to be known that Michael indeed had escaped. To support that, a tight screen of security had been placed around his whereabouts and the events which had befallen him. As soon as he had been made stable, and was fit enough, then he would be carefully transported back to Britain at the earliest opportunity and placed in the safety and care of the British Government.

It was essential at this stage that this secrecy extended to his wife Natasha, as if it were known by the Bolsheviks that Michael was still alive and in Archangel, then it was certain that the Cheka would make moves to try and finish Michael off.

In conclusion, Churchill announced that the Russian Government should remain content in thinking that Michael had been murdered, and was officially an escapee. The same should also apply to Natasha, and no information to the contrary should be given to her. The invasion plans would still go ahead and the Russian people should be of a view that Michael was ready and able to show up at that moment of invasion.

Reilly then asked Churchill how he proposed to rehabilitate Michael. He replied that Michael would be given a new name and papers to show that he was a serving member of the British Government MI2 department. From there he would come to Britain and start a new life until he was declared fit enough to return to Russia, should circumstances change for the better. However, there was a very real possibility that he may never recover to full fitness, physically or mentally, which would then mean that he should remain anonymous in respect of his rightful position as heir to the Russian throne.

Reilly was then instructed to return to Russia under his usual disguises. He was informed that there was only a skeleton staff in the Embassy and it was cared for by Commander Cromie. Cromie had reported that the Germans were establishing their power and influence in Russia and were of a similar view as the British that the throne should be re-established with Michael as the head, as he was the only one who would be recognised as suitable and able. It was also imperative that he should try to contact and protect Natasha and her daughter Tata and if possible get them to the UK. It was known that the Germans were trying to rescue her from imprisonment by the Bolsheviks. Natasha was the bait they were hoping to use to get Michael to come out of hiding and thus persuade him to their own cause and crown him as Emperor of Russia.

The whole position, with Michael believed still alive by the people, but Lenin believing he was dead, was arousing so much rumour, speculation and sightings of him that the confusion was working well for the British Government. The Germans, whilst wanting a return of the Monarchy, wanted control over Michael, and of course so did the Western Allies; both had the same intention of returning him to the throne, but under the so-called puppet control each was aspiring to.

Reilly's remit, then, was to sow as much subterfuge and propaganda as he could in all the right places where he knew how. The myth of Michael heading up armies in various parts of Russia was to be promulgated as far and as wide as possible. In addition, he was to confirm the belief that the Allies and Japan were to invade Russia, and thus put the Germans into confusion and at least ensure that they would keep some forces on the Russian borders. Therefore, it was imperative for the Germans to find Michael and persuade him to be their man, and thus rely on the support from the Russian people. If Michael was to be known as the puppet of the Allies, then Germany would suffer further. So, until some certainty had developed in the war, and now that America was gaining a winning foothold, it was imperative that no one should ever know of Michael being in the UK.

Finally, Churchill brought to Reilly the tragic news they had received days earlier. Nicholas had been assassinated together with his whole family. There was no further information available at that point. Also, he was informed of the latest news on Natasha: that she had been imprisoned just after the alleged escape of Michael in early June in the Cheka headquarters.

Michael had stayed as a patient in Archangel until January 1919 whilst undergoing treatments and attempts to arouse him from his coma. He had been coming in and out of consciousness, and as of January 1919 he was now stable. With some difficulty, he was able to speak, since the damage to his jaw and mouth had slowly healed. However, it was very difficult to understand his speech. It was clear that there was severe brain damage, as he appeared to have very little memory of the past, and his current attention span was poor. His knowledge of languages was uncertain and he was encouraged to only speak in English as it would be too confusing to converse with him in Russian. He clearly needed a lot of care and rehabilitation.

He was now ready to travel, and in February of that year he arrived in London, disembarking from a British destroyer at London docks. From there he was transferred to St Katherine's Hospital, located in Regents Park, for treatment in neurology and speech therapy. The hospital was a special unit catering for brain-damaged patients and especially those with the newly diagnosed 'post-concussion syndrome'. The facilities were better than anywhere else and had every means to help reconstruct people's lives. There Michael was provided with a 24-hour nursing regime in a small apartment on the ground floor and when fit enough, he could sit and enjoy the park and its flora and fauna.

There was also a 24-hour guard placed on the premises to deter any prying eyes and, more to the point, to provide security in case Michael became threatened by the Bolshevik spies who were in evidence in London. The fear was still that Michael might be found by the Cheka and assassinated (again). Security for Michael did not end until 1922, when it was clear that the White and pro-Royalist armies were defeated and he no longer posed any threat to the Russian Bolshevik Government. Indeed, sightings of Michael were common right up to 1920.

36

Natasha's Exile to England

Natasha, a prisoner of some ten weeks in Petrograd, was desperate to escape and had persuaded one of the guards to help, who she had been cultivating for this special purpose under the guidance of Reilly. He would often bring her food of some quality provided by Reilly, in exchange for money which was passed to him by her daughter Tata. Reilly had gained employment working as a chef in the prison kitchens, and was in a perfect position during the imprisonment of Natasha and also for his subterfuges in the political misinformation that he was disseminating.

The plan was that she would feign an illness of extreme chest pains, using her best dramatic abilities. The prison doctor had been bribed by Reilly and it was to be declared that this was an emergency. Because she was of value to both Russian and German intelligence, she was given priority status and was rushed under guard to a nursing home.

Because the security was weak, Reilly contacted Natasha the following day and it was arranged that he would arrive with transport in a few days' time in his Commissar uniform, and take Natasha back to prison, whilst using his myriad of skills in bribery and the forging of false documents.

Natasha was very nervous as she waited for her rescue, as if it went wrong then she almost certainly would be summarily executed without trial. Reilly turned up at the door with a loud voice and a swagger of self-importance. He ordered the duty nurse to bring Natasha to his waiting car, regardless of how she was feeling or dressed. Moments later Natasha was brought to the courtyard, feigning illness and the inability to walk properly.

They then escaping the clutches of the Bolsheviks, sped off to a secret hiding place he had arranged. Natasha was to stay at an apartment where her brother-in-law had been living, and Reilly had bribed him to leave without notice. He was heavily in debt, and the money was useful to him.

Reilly urgently instructed Natasha to put on the clothes he had provided in the back of the car, which was a disguise at which Natasha was very amused. She changed from her hospital gown into very common clothes that befitted a prostitute, and a wig of a clashing ginger. A basic make-up bag was provided and she was told to apply the make-up in a very heavy, provocative, and common style.

Assisting Natasha out of the car they then went to the first-floor apartment where Reilly had provided changes of clothes, a good stock of food and clean bedding. The apartment was reasonably furnished and would be a place of some comfort and safety until he could arrange the transfer of Natasha to Britain and safety.

Reilly informed Natasha that he too would be staying at the apartment for a short while and their cover was that they were a married couple. Natasha was not shocked, as she trusted Reilly and knew he would be a great bodyguard, and on hand to provide the next step of the escape plan.

Reilly's plan to get Natasha out of Russia was outrageously simple, but very dangerous. He explained to Natasha that there was no effective support in Russia from the British Embassy. The Acting Consul, Commander Cromie, had been murdered by the Bolsheviks in the Embassy and those privileges were at an end. His power had become very limited as many members of his spy network had been apprehended and exchanged between governments. Therefore, his own identity was under threat of exposure, and his resources in Russia were now at an end.

Reilly being a master spy and of great daring, told Natasha that the German Embassy, which now had a strong presence in Russia, would aid her escape. He explained that the Germans wanted to protect Natasha and find Michael as they too wanted the Imperial Crown to be reinstated. Natasha was astonished. She did not want to live in Germany, especially as she was hearing that the German Army was near to collapse on the Western Front.

Reilly held her arm and quietly told her it was for that very reason that the German authority should be used, and that once she was out of Russia and in the safe hands of the pro-Royal Germans, it was a fact that by Christmas there would be victory in Europe over the Germans. At that point then the British Government would rescue her, as she would no longer be of any benefit to the German Empire and its machinations of returning Michael to the throne. They would be under complete Allied control and it would be a formality to get her to Britain.

The following day Reilly, still in his disguise as a convincing Commissar, was in contact again with German secret service spies and effectively gave them access to Natasha. Natasha was very wary, but she trusted Reilly to the point that she would accompany him to the newly established German Embassy for discussions on her extrication. Her disguise was perfect, as she was seen as a prostitute and was ignored by the Cheka.

With that introduction out of the way, and convinced now that his plan would work, Reilly left Russia and travelled to Kiev. This was where Natasha would be taken. Her daughter Tata was also under German control and she was to arrive in Kiev shortly before her mother.

In early October, Natasha arrived in Kiev and was reunited with Tata who had travelled there earlier with the help of German secret agents. They felt safe once again, especially as Natasha could reveal that their German 'friends' would soon be replaced by the British.

However, Tata told her mother of all the bad news which was circulating in Kiev, about the desertion of hundreds of thousands of German troops on the Western Front, and the impending collapse due to overwhelming firepower and manpower being used now that the Americans were in the war. Natasha was not able to reply to that as she would have liked, as Reilly had told her to be silent so as not to compromise her safety whilst in German hands.

Still in the disguise of a Commissar, which left him with sweeping powers, Reilly was now close to what was going on in Kiev. There the British did have a semblance of a spy network which was working at high intensity.

Reilly contacted Natasha to assure her that he was

still in control of her destiny, by the fact that the German surrender would be imminent. He prepared her for his next contact of importance which would be in the second week of November: by that time the Allies would have control of Kiev politically, as he was now certain that the war would be at an end by then.

Tata asked her mother why she seemed so happy and upbeat. Natasha then told her to keep her silence, but that in fact they were to be rescued by the British Government and taken to England. She was so overjoyed at this; it suddenly made her life full again, and she was looking forward to living a new life of freedom.

On November 11 a message was sent to Natasha to be ready and packed, as a car would be waiting for them at their apartments the following day in the early hours. On November 12th Olga Bystrovia, Reilly's co-agent, dressed in her best outfit of elegance and self-importance, went to the apartments where Natasha and Tata were staying and with an air of authority brought them to a large car parked at the kerbside.

Natasha was shocked in not seeing Reilly, but instead, this very beautiful Asian woman dressed like a princess. Olga quickly noticing the look of despair on the face of Natasha, brought her the good news. She explained that she was Reilly's boss, that he had left for England. The next stage was best conducted by her. They loaded up the car and sped off towards Odessa.

Arriving in Odessa, the following day Olga took them to an apartment in the Hotel London which she had prepared for them. Also, a pleasant surprise was awaiting them. On arrival, they were delighted to be met by Natasha's brother-in-law, whom Reilly had earlier made arrangements for, to travel to Odessa where he hoped to build a new life.

Contact with London was now regular and Olga was informed that there would be a rescue ship for Natasha within days. Two days later, and just in time, as law and order was breaking down with a great deal of looting taking place due to the Red Army advancing, two British warships arrived in the harbour.

Olga took them aboard one of the ships and introduced herself, Natasha and Tata to Lieutenant Commander Wylde of the destroyer HMS *Nereida*. Olga would be accompanying them on the journey to England. Two days later they departed on a long and circuitous journey to England, disembarking at several ports and changing ships. The final leg of the journey was through the south of France and on to Paris, where they stayed for a few days. Finally, they travelled onwards to London.

Natasha arrived in London in March 1919 without her daughter Tata. When they had stopped off in Paris she was able to arrange schooling for Tata in a French convent. Much to her relief, she now felt safe and under some limited care of the British government. She now hoped for a more settled lifestyle.

Olga had been busy in advising Natasha and helping with the long journey to England. She had also arranged, via MI6, accommodation which had been prepared for her with Johnson's mother, Louise, whom she knew well in a beautiful Tudor house in Wadhurst in Sussex.

Louise had left Paddockhurst where she had lived in the early war years and moved to Wadhurst as the war came to an end. All the furniture and possessions of her son Nicholas

Johnson and the Grand Duke Michael, previously stored there, were transferred to her new home in the hope that at some point they would return to Britain to reclaim them.

They were so pleased to meet again, as it was some five years ago since they had last seen each other at Knebworth House in 1914 on the day that Natasha, Michael and Nicholas Johnson had departed to return to Russia.

Louise made Natasha so very welcome, and assured her that she could stay in the house as long as she needed, and she would welcome her son George to join her. She mentioned that the house was big enough to accommodate Tata as and when she decided to return from France during school holidays.

After a few hours of settling in with her limited baggage, they sat down and had a talk that went on into the small hours. The main subject was the whereabouts of Michael and Nicholas. Both had heard so many rumours of sightings, and many stories were exciting to the point that Michael would become the saviour of Russia and defeat the Bolsheviks. However, there was a certain dread in the voice of Natasha, who thought that the worst may have befallen them. She had experienced at first hand the ruthless nature of the Revolution and the attitude of Lenin and Stalin. Louise then remarked that they now had each other to offer personal comfort and advice as matters progressed in the news, or lack of it, with son and husband.

That following morning after Natasha's arrival, Louise took her to the stable behind the house and told Natasha to close her eyes. Then she opened the stable door and said, 'You can now open them.' Natasha let out a squeal of delight as she clasped eyes on Tata's pony and her 1913 Rolls-

Royce, which Michael had bought for her when they lived at Knebworth House. This brought back happier memorises and she rushed to hug the pony, then jumped into the Rolls to feel the safety and comfort of her past life.

Natasha then sent for her son George to join her in Wadhurst. He had been living with family members in Denmark. Several months earlier Natasha had sent George there for protection against the marauding thugs who were bringing chaos to the streets of Petrograd.

Natasha had several family members and friends living in London and from time to time they made regular trips to Sussex to visit her. At every opportunity, she went to see them in return, and the topic of conversation was always geared around money, valuables left in Russia, the safety of other family members still trapped there, and of course the constant rumours of the whereabouts and fate of Michael. Life settled down to a pattern of dinner engagements with family and new friends, and her duties to her children George and Tata, who were both away at boarding school.

Money was now becoming a serious consideration for Natasha. Her spending, whilst curtailed, was still above her means. There was still a reasonable amount of jewellery in her possession, so it was more of a cash flow problem. She sought to retain her valuables, but was faced with the unwelcome and only option that she would now have to start selling off her treasures. A year later she had to cut expenses further and called Tata back from France and enrolled her in a boarding school.

That same year the lease on the Sussex home came to an end and she moved to new premises in Richmond on the outskirts of London. She was faced with the inevitability of having to sell off increasingly more of her treasures as she continued to lead a lifestyle which would in time soon deplete her wealth. However, she was an eternal optimist and thought that those severe economic times would pass, and was hopeful at some point of receiving some monies from Michael's estate, or from himself should he reappear.

Life in London for Natasha was becoming too expensive and so in 1927 she moved to Paris. A year later her son, now having finished his education in England, joined her. This was now an excellent location for Natasha as she had plenty of friends and family who had re-located to living there, and it was considerably cheaper.

George was now a strapping young man with a penchant for cars, bikes and speed. He had the same gait as Michael as well as his height and looks. He was very eligible and a star attraction for the most beautiful and well-connected women. He was hopefully due to inherit the throne in Russia, as it seemed it was only a matter of time before the Communists ruined the country and the people called for the reinstatement of the Monarchy. Tragedy struck George in 1931 when he was killed in a car crash in the south of France along with his close friend, who was driving the car.

Natasha was extremely distraught, and wondered how her life could be damaged any more. George was her darling and favourite, and his loss was alomost unbearable. In public, she kept control of her emotions and displayed a grand stiffness befitting her position as Dowager Empress, a title she clung to but which was not used by many people. However, in private she wept, and could not be consoled. This did indeed seem to be the end of the direct line to the Russian throne. The loss of George was mourned for a long time by the remaining members of the Romanov families.

Tata was now self-sufficient in her life and unfortunately this became a great problem to Natasha as she slipped from one marriage to another via graceless affairs. She now had to contend with her own life and made the best of her looks and position even though money was always a problem for her.

Over the years she fought many battles to obtain monies from Russia and other countries where she and Michael had estates, but most claims came to nothing, especially as she could not hire effective lawyers due to her poverty. Life was a daily drag for Natasha now, and the Second World War came and went without her seeing much of her daughter. After the war, contact was made again, but it was pitiful as Natasha was living in a small attic room now paid for by friends, and with a little help from Tata. She was ever pale, thin and undernourished. Natasha died in 1952 of cancer in a Paris hospital, and was buried there. Her gravestone said simply, 'Wife and lover of the Grand Duke Michael of Russia'.

37

1919: Michael's New Life

Several months after Michael arrived at St Katherine's Hospital, in February 1919, Reilly and Olga paid him a visit. They had become close to Michael during the adventures of the past two years, and they had been asked to visit the hospital by a senior member of Michael's care team, as they were to meet another gentleman who was connected with the care of Michael.

They met Professor Nick Jones at the main entrance, where he invited them into his office to talk and gain a picture of how Michael had progressed and what the prognosis was for his recovery. Professor Jones had a rather bright look on his face as he began to explain that Michael's bodily health was now in great shape, bearing in mind what he had been through a year ago, notwithstanding the old matter of the possibilities of reoccurrence of ulcers in his stomach. He was mobile and alert and had regained some speech, although it was slurred and sometimes incoherent. He had to think carefully before he answered questions, but a dialogue was possible and he was improving day by day.

Olga enquired whether he knew what had happened

to him. Then the professor became sad, and told Olga that Michael's memory was almost non-existent. His life seemed to have started when he awoke from his coma in Archangel, and through early therapy there they had discovered that he could recall only glimpses of his past.

When arriving at St Katherine's, the team concluded that they should not at this stage try to delve into his past and awaken his memories. They felt that part of his life should remain untouched as it would cause too much trauma if he were to revisit his past. Jones explained that if Michael's mind opened up that past life, then they would deal with it.

Life in hospital had settled down into a rhythm of peaceful coexistence alongside the daily care and treatment regimes. He had a dedicated team of psychiatrists to help him manage the confusion he was encountering about why he was there, and who he was. His personal health was restored through daily light exercise, and gentle feeding with a nurse in attendance at each meal time. The left-hand side of his face and jaw was badly disfigured where the second bullet had entered, and most of his teeth were missing or damaged. His shoulder wound was now healed, and other than a limp arm which needed weekly physiotherapy, the doctors were confident that he would regain adequate use for the medium term. Full use, however, was limited as motor dexterity with his right hand was impaired, meaning that he would need to be trained to use his left hand for writing and handling domestic items in his daily life.

Professor Jones then mentioned the other reason for their visit, which was to meet a gentleman from the government who wanted to see Michael, Reilly and Olga, together. He showed them to another office and there they came face to face with Sir George Mansfield Smith-Cumming, Head of the Secret Intelligence Service, the SIS.

'Hello boss,' Reilly quipped, 'I guessed that you would be involved with Michael's health. What have you got planned for him next?'

Olga intervened as she could see that Reilly was becoming confrontational. She gently smiled and took a seat, and gestured to Reilly to do the same. 'Hi Boss,' she said with a wry smile on her face, genuinely glad to see that he was involved with Michael somehow.

Cumming was not perturbed by Reilly's off-hand engagement, and welcomed them both, expressing his gratitude that they had shown concerns for Michael's welfare. He went on to congratulate them both on their endeavours in Russia, and welcomed them back to Britain.

He wasted no time in bringing to them up to date with the current and future position of Michael whilst under the care of the British Government. He went onto explain that Michael had been given a new identity, and it was best to mention only a vague past in conversation, for him to remain comfortable. If they forced the issue of turning his memory back to a life in Russia, then it would put him at risk, through possibly another assassination attempt. Also, they were very unsure as to how his wife and son could react to his facial disfigurement and memory loss. Natasha and her son George could also be a target for the Cheka if they were to hear that Michael was still alive. It had become clear that Lenin was still in the throes of a civil war, and the last thing he would want would be to hear of Michael and his family's survival as one unit again.

Reilly then asked Cumming to what extent Michael's new identity had been created. Cumming then spun the story of Michael being in a motoring accident in northern Russia in June 1918 and Michael was lucky to be alive. He had been in a coma for a few months, and when he had recovered, he had been transported back to Britain and was now undergoing physical and mental therapy to restore his life. He worked for the British Government as a cartographer and was doing a photographic survey for MI2.

'Why so elaborate?' Reilly enquired.

Cumming responded by saying that Michael had from time to time talked of a Russian life, but was very unsure and sometimes inaudible through his mumbling due to the gross disfigurement to his face. 'So, if we give him a Russian connection, then there were some truths mixed up with fantasy, which might quell his inquisitiveness into why he has memories of Russia.' He admitted it was a game of uncertainties, but it was being as fair to Michael as was dared, knowing that it was essential now to create a new identity for him to go forward with in some safety.

'So what is his created past?' enquired Olga.

Here Cumming was confident in the ploys which had been designed. He explained that he was born on the correct dates, his name is Michael Alexander and was a clerk working at MI2 in London which handled geographic information for the secret services. It was a mundane back office job to which he was apparently suited. He was a bachelor and lived in an apartment overlooking the Thames in Deptford. He was educated in East London and had been to university at Cambridge, where records had been created for him.

Michael was an only child. His parents had emigrated to Canada when he attended university. There had been no contact details left with Michael and he had never seen his parents since the day they left. As far as he was concerned he was alone in the world. There was no trace of who his friend was who died in the car crash.

Reilly thought for a moment and declared he could see the cleverness of the past life that had been created for Michael, as it explained why he was now alone. Olga pointed out that it was a good cover as his connection with MI6 through MI2 was like a mother figure to him and if he ever wanted to return to work, then MI6 was his home, so to speak. There he could be kept an eye on and supported. Cumming confirmed that his treatment costs and immediate needs for Michael's rehabilitation would be funded through Government sources. This ensured a future for Michael.

Reilly declared that the British Government, whilst being very fair to Michael due to the fact that they had created a dangerous path for him in the plot to overthrow the Bolsheviks, was right in showing responsibility for him. He also reminded Cumming that he had another agenda. If at any point they needed to parade him for the benefit of the Government as, Michael Alexandrovitch Romanov, then they had power and control over Michael.

Olga then pointed out that this new life was very unfair to Natasha, as she had been completely excluded from the future of Michael.

'Sadly, this is the case,' Cumming replied. He underlined the danger to them both if Natasha knew of Michael being alive, and that they would inevitably become targets for assassination by the Cheka. It seemed that she was now becoming resigned to his death at the hands of the Bolsheviks, but was still hopeful as it seemed that rumours were still being put around as to his whereabouts. He went on further to explain that it would be unfair to try and engage them a future together, not only due to these circumstances, but because Michael needed so much care, and his gross disfigurement, loss of memory and very uncertain future would be a massive strain on them both. It would appear that the SIS protection and care for Michael may cease if Natasha were to become involved in his life.

Olga asked Cumming if there could be some compromise so that Natasha could be trained in a way to deal with Michael at a distance, as it surely would benefit her and her son to know that he was living, even if it was in some cocoon. Cumming shook his head and expressed that this was a 'Red Top Secret'. However, he did offer some hope that in the coming years this may change.

The meeting broke up and cordial departing comments were exchanged between the three of them. Olga and Reilly now wanted to see Michael and went back to see Nick Jones in his office and asked to be shown to Michael's room.

Olga, seeing him for the first time since February 1918, rushed over with outstretched arms to hug and embrace him. The doctors had warned them that he may not remember them, as his memory was by and large a total loss.

Michael was rather confused at the attention this beautiful and kindly lady was showing him, but all he could say was, 'Hello. And you are…?' in an unrecognisably slow and slurred voice.

Olga, not put off by this lack of memory as to who she

was, still hugged him and gave a reassuring look which told Michael that this lady cared for him.

It was a beautiful summer morning and the three comrades sat down on the patio overlooking the garden, and tea was brought to them by the personal carer for Michael. Reilly introduced himself and reminded Michael that he and Olga were old friends and were visiting London, and thought it was a good idea to say hello. Michael was delighted to understand that they were friends and he enquired where they were from and how they had met. Olga thought for a few seconds, signalling Reilly not to speak. She announced that Reilly had met him at university in Cambridge when they were close friends. Olga then explained that she was Reilly's girlfriend.

Michael was interested to learn what Reilly knew of his past life. Reilly was happy to engage in this fantasy and explained that he had met Michael in 1896 during his first year, and had only known him for a short while as he was in his final year.

It took a time for this information to sink in, but then Michael enquired as to what he was studying, and what type of person did Reilly recall him being.

Reilly thought this a good time to inculcate some self-worth into Michael. He explained that as far as he could remember he was studying geography, and Reilly was studying psychology. He described to Michael how he was such an energetic guy with a huge desire for adventure and sports. He liked fast motorbikes and was a superb horseman. He was very well liked and preferred to be a gay bachelor rather than a married man. However, he had only known him for a year at university, but they did keep some contact on and off during Michael's time there. The last time he had seen him was on his graduation day in 1900. Sadly, he explained, they had lost touch since then.

He had just recently secured a job as a translator for the foreign office in London, and had heard of Michael recently in the gossip of the walls of Whitehall, and remembered his name from his past days of study at Cambridge. So here he was to say hello again, and to be on hand if he could be of any future help in Michael's recovery.

Michael asked Reilly for more information about his past life, which he had no recollection of other than what had been told to him by MI6. All Reilly could add was that Michael had become withdrawn at the end of his graduation and it seemd that it was due to him being effectively abandoned by his parents after the ceremony when they went to live in Canada. All he knew was what Michael had told him all those years ago: that they were going to live in Calgary, and a year had passed and he had not heard from them. He wondered indeed if they were still alive. Since then, as he had explained, they had lost touch and he knew nothing of Michael's life until recently when he discovered that he was here in hospital after a serious accident.

Olga listened with a warm heart as she could see Reilly was creating a nice storyline which Michael would be comfortable with, and he was showing the hand of friendship and support. It also kept Michael close to him just in case Cumming tried to use and abuse Michael whilst he was in this delicate state of recovery; but more so for his welfare in his future life. She also could see that she and Reilly could keep in contact with Natasha and be a form of caring partnership for both as they progressed their lives separately.

The next hour passed in eloquent discourse which was designed to try and normalise as much as possible the life of Michael. They broke up with a firm hand of friendship and assured Michael that they would visit him as often as possible.

38

1926: From Hospital to a New World

Michael had not progressed much beyond his early years at St Katherine's Hospital. He was in effect kept there under surveillance, especially as his memory might return and that would have mounting consequences for the British Government. Olga made a visit to Michael at least two or three times a year, and it was a great time of bonding and friendship. Occasionally she brought Reilly with her.

On Christmas Day 1924 Olga visited Michael. She walked straight into his room as was now normal, carrying presents and a small Christmas tree. They hugged for what seemed like a couple of minutes and sat down for the usual chat and news.

Olga then put her arm around Michael's ever hanging head – these days he had developed a stoop – and whispered that she had some bad news. Michael looked at her intently as he was always wanting to hear of news from the outside world. She whispered that Reilly was dead.

Michael suddenly felt that he had lost the only link with his past and became distressed. He burst into tears holding his head in his hands. Olga kissed his forehead and held him until he could come through his ordeal. He asked her what had happened. She decided not to tell him the truth – that he was murdered by the Cheka in Russia whilst visiting the British spy network – and simply told him that he had died very quickly and peacefully in hospital of pneumonia.

Michael looked morose and asked Olga what was now to happen in his future as she was the only friend he had, other than his old boss from the government department he used to work for, who would visit him once every year.

Olga reassured him that for as long as he was alive, she would be there for him as often as possible. Olga told him that she had resigned from her job at MI6 and had taken up a teaching post only 5 miles away from St Katherine's Hospital. She told him with a happy smiling face that this meant that she would be available to visit him far more often.

Michael's eyes brightened with gladness and he was now certain that his life would become more bearable compared to the isolation and loneliness he had endured for the past five years.

Olga complimented Michael on his progressive recovery and how well he was looking, and said that his speech was becoming more coherent. They walked in the gardens for a while, holding hands and talking about the sweet things of life.

Olga now started to think more about Michael and his rehabilitation into a more fruitful lifestyle. Meeting Nick Jones the following week, just before she went in to see Michael, she asked him if his release could be fast-tracked, with limited supervision, back in the community.

Jones gave her some good news: that Michael had

been put forward for some pioneering treatment in the reconstruction of his face. He had passed all the critical tests and was due to undergo facial surgery in two months.

Olga excitedly hugged Jones, they had become friends to some extent, and asked him about the best possible outcome. Jones was delighted to tell her that it may well produce facial features that were within 80 per cent of what Michael had looked like before the accident. It would improve his speech and his self-worth and be at least a two-year process and be in bandages and some pain for most of that period.'

With that news, she jumped for joy and rushed in to see Michael. Michael was already standing up expecting her as he had seen her taxi draw up to the main entrance. Both upon seeing each other rushed forward, and they embraced and both started talking at once about the good news.

Michael progressed through the traumas of four operations and in early 1927 he was released into the care of Olga, knowing that the treatment plan still had further to go, but that he was now an outpatient. She had prepared a flat for him overlooking Richmond Park and had secured the lease through the British Government who, through Olga's insistance, were still prepared to give financial support to Michael. The apartment was pleasantly furnished in the new Art Deco style. Michael marvelled at the style and grace of the new world.

He asked Olga whether, in all the time he had been in hospital, he had contributed to any of the costs. He was now concerned that, with no job, he could not pay for the hospital care and the new apartment.

Olga put her arm around his waist and looked at him with affection, and told him that when Reilly had died, he had left a sum of money which would see to all his accommodation needs for the rest of his life. Reilly had become so fond of Michael and so involved in his plight, that he felt it an honour to bestow upon him that support, for as long as it was needed. Reilly's estate was considerable. Michael once again broke down in tears at how someone who he felt he hardly knew, could be so kind and generous.

Michael then enquired how the hospital bill was to be paid. Again, Olga explained that the Foreign Office, where he had worked, had a generous health scheme and had paid all his bills.

The best news she announced – and here she jumped up and down with joy – was that his job was waiting for him to return to. Michael was excited and was now seeing a new life ahead. But he suddenly stopped and exclaimed that he had not a clue of what to do, as whatever he had learned in the past years of employment, he had simply forgotten. Olga squeezed his hand said that was a minor detail, and life for him would now be wonderful.

After Olga left, and Michael had settled in to his flat, he was anxious to explore the area. Richmond Park was a beautiful vista of green grass, trees and flower beds. More so, there were wild deer roaming through the park, which had a road running through it with benches spaced at around 100 metre intervals. He decided to stop for a while and sat on a bench to take in his new surroundings.

Traffic was light and was moving at a respectful speed due to the roaming deer. As he was enjoying the peace, a car drove by and he noticed its occupant staring wildly at him through the rear window. The car screeched to a halt, reversed and stopped by the bench where he was sitting.

Michael was perplexed, and more so as a small and beautiful lady jumped out and stood staring at him. Michael stood up too and enquired whether he could help her.

She cried out at him that she was his beloved Natasha. Michael stood back and became alarmed as she tried to hug him. He then asked her to return to her car as she was obviously mistaking him for someone else.

Natasha was bewildered and confused at this rebuff and took a closer look at Michael. His face, whilst being very familiar, was different and had a strange twist. His voice was entirely different, and he was stooping. She stared at him for a few moments more and then gently and sincerely apologised for the inconvenience. She had been convinced he was her Michael, yet she had to accept that if this were so, then he would surely have recognised her.

Mystified and embarassed she climbed back into the taxi, and asked the driver to proceed. She could not take her eyes off him as they slowly began to drive away. Suddenly, she leaned out of the open window and shouted to Michael, 'What is your name?' Michael shouted back that his name was Michael. Natasha froze and was of a mind to go back, but she knew that he could not be her Michael as this man seemed to be quite different. As the car gathered speed she again shouted out of the passenger window, 'And your second name?' Michael announced it to her, raising his voice, but Natasha could not hear him clearly. She was horror-stricken as she thought he said it was 'Alexander'. She was so perplexed that by the time she had come to her senses the taxi had left the park and was engaged in some heavy London traffic.

Michael was also confused as he was struggling to make

sense of the incident. He had a weird feeling that he had recognised the voice, and the face seemed familiar as a person who he had known in the past. She could have been a university student who he had met many years ago. He felt a strange sensation of love towards this lady but could not understand how that could be. In a quandary, he got to his feet and crossed the park to head home.

Natasha was overcome with grief and could not put the encounter to one side. She demanded that the taxi turn around and re-enter the park, urging the driver to increase his speed. When she arrived at where the encounter had taken place, she was devastated to find that the bench was occupied only by a middle-aged lady, who kindly smiled at her as she drew up.

The lady enquired if she could be of assistance. Natasha beseeched her to know if there was a tall gentleman sitting on the bench when she arrived, and which way he had gone.

She replied that there was no one on the bench when she had arrived two minutes ago.

The taxi driver cautioned Natasha that they were running out of time if she wanted to get to Dover by eight o'clock to catch the ferry to France. Natasha was on her way to Paris, leaving England for the last time. She slowly sank back into the rear seat of the taxi and told the driver to make haste.

39

1934: Michael and Olga

Michael and Olga had become close friends since his discharge from hospital in 1927 and the monthly visits to his apartment in Richmond were proving to be of great help in him being able to settle into life as an Englishman. He enjoyed his job working for MI2 and had a very focused interest in his section which was handling geographic information on Russia and Scandinavia.

Over the years, Michael was showing a keen interest in Russia especially. His work and apparent knowledge of the Russian landscape was remarkable, and he often confounded his colleagues with the reports he drew up with such great accuracy. This was proving invaluable to MI6 operations as Michael was an effective resource to the whole SIS machinery.

It was June 1934 and on one of Olga's regular visits to Michael at his home, she found him quite distressed. She sat him down seeing that he was very agitated. He announced tearfully that he wanted to go home. Olga was wondering what he meant, since as far as she was aware, Michael had settled into his English lifestyle very well and had made a few very good friends in the area and was a happy man.

She enquired what he meant by that. Michael just said that he had this strange feeling that he was not in the place of his birth, and he felt that he belonged somewhere else, but could not determine in his mind what this meant to him.

Olga now became more concerned as she realised Michael was starting to recall his past, which had eluded him for the past sixteen years. She had been thinking for a long while that his post at the SIS HQ, and the MI2 department he was working in, may one day trigger a more detailed recall of some description. She thought it best to listen sympathetically rather than reject his idea of a past life somewhere, and emphasised to him that he was English, and was born in London in 1878. Michael seemed to calm down. He trusted Olga and now seemed happier, and during her visit he eventually put his concerns to one side.

40

1936: Fear of War

Two years later, in 1936, Olga was recalled back to the services of MI6. She had been in the reserve force since leaving several years earlier, and now that there were threats of a German invasion to extend its borders in Europe, she was to become again a key member of the team.

She needed to tell Michael of her new appointment back with SIS as it would mean that she could be out of touch with him for long periods. She was told that from then on she should not visit Michael at his home as, it would soon come to the attention of other European secret services, and Michael's identity could be compromised if she was seen visiting him at home.

So, being in the same building, she called into see him and found him at his desk. She was shocked to see that his small office was full of maps and sketches and the oak-panelled walls were covered with maps of Russia. Michael exclaimed with great delight and surprise to see her at his office. Olga hugged him and showed how impressed she was at the collection of files, maps and books. He showed her around very quickly and was eager to tell her how much he enjoyed his job and how expert he was on Russian affairs and mapping.

Her eye caught a huge scaled plan drawing of Gatchina Palace laid out on his desk. She enquired why he was studying it, peering over his shoulder, to focus on the many jottings he had made and comments on certain rooms.

Michael explained that he could not put together a good reason why he was always drawn to that plan. All he could say was that he seemed for some unknown reason to be fully aware of all the rooms and the landscape around the Palace. He commented that he had discovered much of the history of the building and its occupants over the years, and was planning to visit Russia in three months' time and to stay in Leningrad. He commented to her that it had been renamed from Petrograd to honour Lenin. He excitedly then said to Olga that he had been preparing this as a surprise, and that he dearly wanted her to accompany him on a two-week excursion.

She had to think very quickly how to respond to this lovely invitation. She explained that she was now working back with MI6 and her future movements were unclear, and she was very much bound by the Official Secrets Act, and so had to be careful of who she met and what she said. Michael understood, as he too was aware, due to the amount of work which was piling up on his desk, that affairs in Europe were turning for the worst with the rise of the Nazi regime.

Olga came close to Michael and looked him straight in the eyes and gently said to him that she was unsure of any future meetings due to her position, but assured him that she would always, at every opportunity, meet with Michael in the SIS HQ and share some quality time in the café and the building's gardens. This was a blow to him: not only the loss of regular contact with his dear friend, but it seemed that he would have to travel to Russia on his own.

Olga guessed that Michael would still be determined to travel to Russia, and she suggested that it might not be a good idea and that he would need clearance, as politics and free travel in Russia were becoming more restrictive.

41

Michael's Awakening

ichael declared with a darkening face that he would go whatever the circumstances, and became a bit more open with Olga. He reminded her of a visit at his home in Richmond two years ago, when he had broken down and could not understand why he felt ill at ease in London and had thoughts that his home was elsewhere. He now confided with her in that those feelings never went away, and as the months passed he was becoming more certain of his intent to discover his roots, now not believing that he was born and raised in London.

'Where do you think you were born, Michael?' she enquired.

Without any hesitation, he said in a firm voice, 'Russia. I want to go home.'

Olga was struck dumb as she had had no idea he was harbouring these thoughts, from all the visits and closeness they had shared over the past two years. This was now a matter of SIS importance, since if Michael did go without proper authority, and then suddenly on his visit to Russia he became aware of who he was, it was likely that he would make his presence known. Then there was a certainty that he would never be allowed to travel back to the UK and, most probably, that he would be disposed of by Stalin.

Now she knew the importance of humouring him and trying to discover as much of his plans as possible, to keep a close eye on the developing situation. She bade him goodbye and promised that she would try and pop in to see him in his office as much as possible, after explaining again that it would not be a good idea for her to visit him at home due to security risks.

The following morning, when she reported back to her desk at MI6, she arranged a meeting with Admiral Sir Hugh Sinclair, who was head of operations. She explained in full detail the whole history of Michael. Sinclair was nodding during the whole conversation and declared that he too knew the full details, especially as the 'Michael factor' had been on his watch since his appointment in 1923.

Sinclair had always known that at some point they might have to deal with a situation of Michael recovering of his memory. Now, because Michael was, regardless of all costs, going to visit Russia, then he was a potential loose cannon. He said to Olga that the situation had to be dealt with as a top priority, since if he did travel, as Olga had pointed out, then this could have massive repercussions on the relationship with Russia and for the British public. He got up and said very firmly to Olga, 'You must keep close contact with him and report back to me any suspicions of his regaining his memory and of his activities.' He told her that from now on there would be surveillance of all his movements at home and around the city.

Olga was taken aback by the firmness and control that

was now being directed towards Michael. She then asked Sinclair if she could be given the task of his surveillance personally, together with two other MI6 operatives whom she would choose. She explained that she was intimately aware of all his habits and movements and she would be best placed to monitor him and his thoughts.

Sinclair thought this was an excellent idea and instructed Olga to disengage from her current activities; from now on she was given control of this new project, and must report to him regularly. Leaving her with that best of news under the circumstances, and insisted that she must at all costs keep a lid on it, advising her that she should not reveal to any of her chosen aides the background of Michael. With that Olga left his office, and was now happier in the knowledge that she would have him under her control.

It was now time for her to work out various strategies which she could implement to suit the developing situation. The minor strategies concerned her ability to dissuade Michael from any visit to Russia, and handling him should he not make any or much more recovery in his memory. The main plan, however, was to look at the question of him becoming a loose cannon and insisting on his visit. This would mean him going to Russia with Olga, and under her supervision. If then, during that visit, he came to a full recollection, then she would be on hand to deal with it and bring as much comfort as possible to him as he assimilated all the past traumas in realising who he was.

Making visits to his office two or three times a week, Olga and Michael settled down to a routine, and she became seemingly supportive towards his excitement in arranging a holiday, while also gently advising him of the dangers now that Europe was in political turmoil once again. If it turned out that the best thing was to let him go, and under her supervision, it was important to deal with it now whilst the borders were still accessible.

As the weeks rolled on, and it was coming closer to the two-week holiday which Michael had arranged with SIS, his resolve was becoming more firm, and it did seem that his recollections of Russia were becoming more implanted in his mind.

Olga now thought it was time to open her plan to Sinclair. Arriving at his office for the weekly briefing on Michael she announced to him that the only way to deal with this was sooner rather than later, and that he should be allowed to visit in the next few weeks. She advised Sinclair that if the worst happened, and he came to full recollection, she was certain that she would be able to deal with it.

'How?' said Sinclair abruptly.

'I have a very close relationship with him, on a purely platonic standing. He trusts me more than anyone in the world and he absolutely knows that I am the only one who has his best interests at heart.'

'Go on,' he said impatiently.

She explained that there was no one left of his family in Russia, the rule of Stalin was evil, he had no wealth left in the country and his sole comfort would be memories, and no more. She would easily convince him, if he became aware of who he was, that he must keep this quiet or he would never get out of Russia alive; and at best, would be transported to a concentration camp in Siberia.

'That seems very plausible,' Sinclair commented. He realised that if Michael became aware of his past sooner rather than later, then he would no longer be a loose cannon. He remarked also that Michael should show some gratitude to MI6 and Reilly for saving his life and bringing him back to Britain to start a new life under the safety of a pseudonym.

'Good!' he exclaimed. 'What is your next step, Olga?' he enquired.

Continuing with her plan she proposed that she and Michael should travel within the next two weeks before winter set in and whilst the weather was still reasonable in Russia. It would be best, she added, that they go with diplomatic immunity and reside at the Embassy in Moscow. It would be easy to create diplomatic paperwork as they would be on a cultural mission and both could have academic qualifications in fine art. The Russians were still disposing of much of their cultural wealth and artistic creations from the Imperial times, and they would be welcomed for their expertise, and as possible new sources of disposals. The rest of the time would be spent in travel into and out of Russia.

One of the main destinations to visit would be Gatchina Palace. She explained that this was a major focus of Michael in his quest to unravel his lost memory. He seemd captivated by the building and it absorbed much of his thoughts of Russia. Sinclair added that he knew a great deal about Russia and was aware that Gatchina was where Michael was raised as a child and that he lived there prior to his imprisonment in Perm.

'Excellent, Olga.' he declared. 'This is a perfect answer to this dilemma. If not controlled as you have outlined, then we will all be in real trouble.' He went on to say that the world media and spin on the situation would be very detrimental to the British interest worldwide, if the true position were ever known of the past eighteen years of Michael's life in England.

42

To Russia with Love

Olga was delighted at this latest development regarding Michael, and went to see him at MI2 immediately. She was soon in conversation with him about arrangments for her to join him on his trip to Russia. Michael hugged her and thanked her for the care and interest she was showing in this phase of his life.

Olga confirmed the travel plan and assured him that all the costs would be borne by the British Government, and that as he would travel as a government officer, his entry in and out of Russia would be quite simple. It was clear that if he travelled alone, and with his papers showing he was working for MI2, then it was likely that he would not get a visa. This way, she confirmed that there was no requirement for a visa as it was under diplomatic status. She reminded him that there was a security issue in Russia, and there had been instances of British tourists being abducted and imprisoned, accused of spying.

This trip, she assured Michael, would deal with his quandary over who he was, one way or the other. She then asked Michael what convinced him most of all that he was Russian.

He replied that he had discovered that he could speak perfect Russian, and that was why he was so affective in his job, pouring over Russian documents. Not understanding how he was able to speak Russian became a driving force in him now wanting to make the visit in the hope of unlocking that mystery.

This revelation now convinced Olga that it was only a matter of time before he discovered his past.

Olga now asked Michael if he minded that they should travel as intimate partners, as it was essential to show as much confusion as possible among any Cheka who might be still on the lookout for Michael. Michael would not know of her real reasons to obscure his identity. He was very happy to agree.

The plan was to leave in late September and to travel on a tourist ship to Leningrad with a change of shipping line at Denmark. Olga made all the arrangements.

Now that Michael was using his fluency in Russian, she altered her plans a little. Michael would be known on his papers as the person he was in England, so his existing papers would suffice, and his work would be given as a Cartographer for the Government's Ordnance Survey Department. He would be travelling on holiday with his girlfriend Hannah Chudasama, who took on the guise of a wealthy art collector. The reversion to Hannah's real name was suitable, as it was not appropriate to use her undercover name of Olga Bystrovia. (However, the use of the name Olga Bystrovia was such a constant for Hannah that eventually she chose to be known as Olga for the remainder of her real life.)

They were under the invitation of the Embassy, with the express purpose of reviewing certain Russian treasures with a view to buying. This was an arrangement (through the SIS) of the British Ambassador Viscount Chilston with Boris Legran, the previous Director and Curator of the Hermitage Museum in Leningrad. He had certain items still to dispose of which were not ideologically suited to the Russian revolutionary education process, and the financial gain to the Soviet Union would outweigh the cultural loss.

Olga only new a little of classical art, but was very able in the art of subterfuge and convincing trickery in seeming to be a serious collector of art. However, if she seemed gullible then that was all for the good, as it would encourage the seller. She also advised Michael that they were travelling in some disguise, and that Michael could use his Russian as an aid to her subterfuge of being an art collector. However, she explained that he should not show too much of his fluency, as he would be expected to be rather faltering in his knowledge of the language.

It was late September when they set off from Southampton docks, and Michael became very excited at the prospect of going home, as he now saw it. Where his home was in Russia, he knew not, but he was hopeful that the trip would raise some certainty in his confused state of mind.

He had remarked with great mirth on Olga's disguise. She was dressed in typical Russian winter fashion with high-knee boots, and a very expensive-looking coat with sable fur on the collar. This was topped off by a sable hat of Russian fashionable design. Her jewellery was abundant and matched her very expensive-looking handbag. He could also see that she was wearing a tiara under her hat, and that her hair was bleached blonde. This was a strange mix for an Indian lady, and displayed some vulgarity, as was now becoming common in the styling and taste of British dress. This would help her be rather more convincing that she was of a defined Western culture and had poor taste in displaying her wealth.

Michael and Olga arrived at the British Embassy in Moscow. Whilst there had been a recent increase in the Russian guards at the Embassy gates, due to the Cheka taking a keen interest in those who presented themselves there, they were of little concern as they were on official business.

The Ambassador welcomed them both and found them suitable quarters in the staterooms. The following day they were introduced to Boris Legran at a lavish dinner hosted by Viscount Chilston. Legran came with a gift for Olga which she greatly admired and accepted. It was an ikon of Patriarch Tikhon, which was seen to be of little or no value to the Russian state, which had effectively banished any religious activity in Russia, and was not seen as suitable Russian art.

Michael was an effective aide to Olga as it was purported that he had studied the Russian language at university. During the conversations, and especially as Legran's English was poor and Chilston spoke very little Russian, Michael took up a key role in the conversations as they moved from subject to subject.

The outcome of the meeting was that Legran would come to the Embassy and take them to a warehouse close to the State Hermitage Museum in Leningrad, where they had stored most of the despised state treasures which were now for disposal. Legran finished by asking if any of the party had any difficulties over flying, as he wanted to make the 600 kilometre journey as quick as possible.

Michael suddenly became very enthusiastic and declared that he would love to fly. It seemed for a moment that he was going to announce that he was a capable pilot. Hannah stepped in very quickly to avoid that, as it might put Michael into a difficult position. She declared that they would both be able to fly, and then rose and began to take their leave.

Two days later they gathered at Moscow airport and boarded the daily internal flight to Leningrad. Michael was delighted to see that the airline had been supplied with the new American DC-3 Dakota which was introduced earlier that year. Olga had to keep a careful watch over Michael as he was displaying concern on his face, and often he would screw up his face in concentration. She knew he was experiencing flashbacks. She held his hand tightly and tried to open conversations that would draw his mind away from his past flying days.

When they had landed and disembarked from the aircraft, a large car was waiting for them at the airport and once they were on board, it quickly sped off into the city. Leningrad was a beautiful city of culture and held many palaces of the past Royal Family. This was a most dangerous time for Michael, as the vision of the streets and buildings would surely evoke disturbing thoughts for him.

To distract Michael, and engage him in translation, she spoke with Legran at some length about Leningrad and the fantastic architecture. Legran was most happy to oblige, it seemed, and so she left them chatting happily as he explained the grand scenes that were passing them by.

Michael suddenly ceased the conversation and was staring at the Vladimir Palace, which had suddenly appeared to his right. He asked the driver to stop, and he obliged. He got out of the car and observed his surroundings, slowly turning around. His face was in awe of what he was seeing. Olga managed to persuade him back into the car, but his face was transfixed. Legran was a little worried for Michael's health as he looked very pale. Olga then assured him that he was OK, and that he often suffered from losing his bearings. He knew that the best remedy was to stand and walk about for a minute or two to regain his presence of mind.

Michael then came very close to Olga and whispered that he was home, and had visited the Vladimir Palace before. Olga quietened him down and asked him to now refrain from any further chat about his concerns as he could well expose them both, and especially Hannah, being Olga Bystrovia the British spy. She then comforted him and said that she would have a long talk with him that evening.

The rest of the journey was in silence, with Michael avidly looking out of the window. It was plain to see on his face that he was now coming into a state of understanding of his home town. He glanced at her from time to time with a knowing look on his face, and he pointed out buildings in silence to let her know that he was coming to a state of realisation.

The journey ended, and they got out and were invited into the warehouse for an inspection of the treasures. They were amazed at the storehouse, as it was full of treasures and junk furniture. Olga was shown several paintings of religious style and some jewellery which depicted religious ornamental designs. Legran then was quick to mention that he would only accept US dollars, and in return he would ensure that the prices were very competitive. The Russian economy was going through a depression again and the value of the rouble was at an all-time low against the American dollar.

Olga was fascinated at the array of items, and of such a varied assortment. She got rather carried away and was doing deal after deal with a very pleased Legran. Michael had wondered off and was busy looking at furniture. In his mind, many of the items were recognisable to him, and of an old Russian Imperial style.

An hour later, after Olga had bought far more than she ever imagined she would, and being aware that the first principle was just a cover to settle Michael's mind, she now would have to arrange the shipping of all this great assortment of 'worthless' Russian treasures. The deal she had done amounted to $2,000, which in Russian hands when converted to roubles was several years' salary for an average worker. Legran was pleased.

Olga then became concerned that in her shopping spree she had forgotten about Michael. She and Legran went in search and he was found at the end of the building looking at a pile of very dusty and damaged furniture. Legran asked Michael why he was interested in that junk. Michael replied that it reminded him of similar furniture he had grown up with. Legran was quick to exploit his interest and asked him if he would like to buy some and have it transported to England with Olga's purchases. Michael looked at Olga and she gave an approving nod. She then took Legran to one side and asked him if he would do a deal in view of all the items she had had purchased. Legran was more than happy to do so, as he was thinking that much of it would otherwise be given away as it was now seen as decadent and too old-fashioned.

Olga called to Michael and told him to make a list of whatever he wanted and that she would buy it for him. An hour later Michael had sorted out a great deal of furniture, enough to furnish a five-bedroom house on Richmond Hill. He had often admired the graceful five-storey buildings and was always keen to own one in the future.

Olga then whispered to Legran that she would only pay $50 maximum. Legran was delighted at her offer. She gave him the $50 for Michael's furniture in cash and also $200, and told him to arrange the shipping for that cost and to keep the change. She arranged to get a banker's draft to him the following day for 50 per cent, and would pay the balance with a draft when it arrived at the London docks. She informed him that she wanted it to land in London by the end of November at the latest. The deal was agreed.

Michael was now so happy, and his love for this country was becoming clearer to him. He had an inner yearning to return one day and live there. Then he would be able to understand more clearly the confusion which was now becoming a burden for him.

They left the warehouse and travelled back to the airport talking excitedly about the purchases they had made. Legran had invited them to dinner that evening, but Olga respectfully declined as she was tired and needed to catch up on paperwork and her diary.

The plane journey again for Michael was such a joy and Olga could see that he was itching to go into the cockpit to speak with the pilots. She relented and suggested that he did so. Michael was off like a shot and was soon in detailed discussion with the pilots.

Legran became a little suspicious, as he could hear Michael's conversation. His Russian was much better than he had thought whilst in conversation with him during the day. He remarked to Olga that Michael had a rather interesting countenance and posture and when he spoke he reminded him of someone he had met twenty years ago, in the army. Olga mentioned quickly that would be an impossibility as she had known him for thirty years and he had never left England before in his life.

Back at the Embassy they spoke with Chilston over dinner and told him of the day's work. She asked if he would ensure that Legran kept his word and made the transportation arrangements. She also gave him two signed banker's drafts, each for $1,000. He would give Legran one when the goods were on board ship, and the other when it reached the London docks.

Olga then asked Michael if he would excuse her for the rest of the evening, and for the whole of the next day, as she had other business with Embassy staff. Michael was a little disappointed as he wanted to have a long conversation with Olga, to relive the exciting day he had had. Olga assured him that it would be a certainty the following night, but asked him to stay in his room and not leave the Embassy building. His reward was to be a visit to one of the grand Imperial Palaces and was a surprise, as it was now an art gallery of distinction and was open to the public.

This brightened Michael up and he nudged Olga excitedly. 'Please let it be Gatchina!' He explained that he had so much love for the place as he had often read of its history and thought the photographs he had found in the Library in London were so evocative. She left him with a wry smile on her face.

43

Michael Awakes

Michael awoke in great excitement, as he was visiting Gatchina with Olga, and he instinctively knew that he would be facing his past in one shape or another. Olga was already up and about and brought him a coffee and toast in bed and lay down on the bed beside him.

Michael was charmed by her kindness and they cuddled for a while. Michael then asked Olga to talk to him about his life, and asked if there was anything else about his past which she could help him with to piece together his life. He had thought it strange for many years that he was somehow being controlled with care and kindness, and it seemed such a strange environment that he was working in, for the British SIS. He knew this was against his basic instincts to be working for an agency like that, but had accepted all that was offered, as not having a past memory, he could only see Reilly, Olga and their S.I.S as 'Mother', and it would be unwise for him to break that tie.

'Now the time has come,' she thought. It was important that she had him in a relaxed state of mind as this was going to be a massive shock for him. Starting off the process would

353

be so difficult, and she had no real idea of where to start. Should she play it off-handedly and let him pick away at the facts as they unrolled, and only answer questions as they arose? Or should she go for the big opening and deal with the shock at first stroke. She held his hand very tight and told him to be prepared for some shockingly good news.

'I am ready to hear whatever you say to me, and have prepared myself for this time.'

Looking lovingly into his eyes, Olga carefully said, 'Your name is Michael Alexandrovitch Romanov, and your title was Grand Duke, the brother of Tsar Nicholas II.'

Michael's face froze and he stayed silent, just looking ahead. His hand left Olga's and he got up from the bed and sat down in the chair by the well-lit fire. After a moment, he called to Olga to join him.

Michael told her that for many years working at the SIS, he had immersed himself in Russian history and had made himself aware of the current and past politics. He continued that he was now quite an expert on the geographical and industrial nature of Russia, and had a fascination for the past Imperial Royal Family. He had studied intimately the destruction of the Imperial Dynasties and the rise of the Soviet Union.

He looked at her in anger and asked her why she was being so cruel: he knew exactly what had happened to Grand Duke Michael and his secretary Nicholas Johnson in 1918. 'The man is dead, for goodness' sake! What are you talking about? The only clue as to you having that notion is that you have noted that I have some resemblance to him, and you have come up with a cocked-up story based on that.'

She walked over to her suitcase and withdrew a picture

for Michael to look at. He took it from her and Olga asked him to look at it and let it dwell in his mind for any clues. The photo was of him, Natasha and young George taken in early 1917, and it was on the steps of Gatchina Palace.

After a full five minutes of stunned silence, Michael looked at Olga and said that he knew the lady, as she had stopped to talk to him in Richmond Park several years earlier. 'She exclaimed at the time that she knew me and shouted my name in a distressed state. She was convinced I was very dear to her, and could not readily accept that I had never seen her before. She was more upset when I told her it was a case of mistaken identity and I asked her to leave. I did have a vague recollection somewhere in my mind that I had seen her somewhere before, but I put it to one side. Who is she?' he demanded.

'This lady is your wife, Natasha Countess Brasova. The little boy is your son George' Olga replied.

Michael's face slowly screwed up, showing his mental pain, and tears rolled down his cheeks. His head sunk slowly to his chest and he started sobbing. Olga could do nothing but wait by his side and watch to see how his distress would develop.

After a while he raised his head, and told Olga that he believed her. They hugged for a few moments and Michael then asked her to tell him all the details of his life that she knew, leading up to the accident, as it was obvious to Michael that this was the catalyst of his new identity.

Olga was pleased at Michael taking a pragmatic view of a careful unrolling of his past. She thought that in the next few days in Russia, this would be an ideal environment to gently bring back his past with sights and sounds which hopefully would bring some joy to counter his distress.

'There are a few major things I need to tell you right away in your story board so that you can build around these events as we talk over the next days whilst in Russia.'

She listed them in a pragmatic order without showing too much emotion. 'Your life was saved by Sidney Reilly in 1918 when the Bolsheviks tried to assassinate you. You were brought to Britain after losing your memory, to keep you safe. You married Natasha in 1912 and came to live in England for two years before you were recalled by Nicholas to join the army and fight against the German invasion. Your son George was born on 6 August 1910 and tragically died in a motoring accident in France on 21 July 1931. Your wife Natasha lives in France and knows only that you were murdered in Russia in 1918. If you can absorb these major facts over the next few hours, Michael,' she said, 'then that will be a good platform for me to help fill in more details around that framework.'

Olga decided that the rest of the day should go as planned, and that Michael should be kept occupied and go to visit Gatchina Palace. Gatchina was not far from Leningrad and so the same flight was taken as the previous one. Michael was so busy asking about and discussing his past with Olga that he thought no more of his desire to get into the cockpit again. Fortunately, the plane was half-empty and the roar of the twin-engine Dakota drowned out any details of their conversation.

Michael was astounded at the life he had led during the first part of 1918, and his journey to Britain, as Olga revealed in detail the great adventure he had undertaken on behalf of the restoration of Russia, and his proposed Manifesto to bring a fair and prosperous life into Russia for the first time in its history. Olga noted how proud he seemed to know what a critical role he would have played. He mentioned to Olga that he was so disappointed in how Russia had progressed and said to her in an imploring manner, 'What if!'

Olga then asked Michael for his thoughts of Natasha, as he had not mentioned her since the opening conversation back at the Embassy. Michael replied very simply and in a matter-of-fact way, that he had never known love in his new life, and the evidence of Natasha as shown in the photo did not stir him into any romantic emotion. That was his past, and there was nothing he could do to change it. He did not feel inclined to find her in France, as their lives had changed so much in the past eighteen years, and it would be a trauma for both of them, and could result in a very difficult outcome.'

Olga mentioned that it was a very difficult position he was taking, but it was the only way in which he could enjoy and make a success of his new life. She pointed out that Natasha would never be able to accept why she was never informed of his survival, and if she were told then this would put them both in great danger. The media hype would be intense and their lives would become unliveable.

Olga asked him about his thoughts on George. He replied that if, as she said, George was dead, then what could that mean to him in real terms? He would like to discover where he was buried, to pay his respects, but he would rather not know any further details of the lives of Natasha and George.

She enquired further, 'If Michael was remembering

anything of his life in Russia?'

He replied that he was, and several things were coming back to him; most of it was about his childhood. Those seemed to be the best of his memories, and he wanted to dwell on them much more than exploring his memories into adulthood. He felt that there could be difficult thoughts lying there, and at this time he needed as little disturbance as possible.

Olga was so pleased at the way he was handling these revelations. She thought that she may never find out exactly how he was feeling as he seemed to be developing a steel shell around him, and it may well turn out that he should only be told what he wanted and needed to know, and it would be best to let this wall he seemed to be building be his own protection.

Arriving at Leningrad, they took a taxi down to Gatchina, and arrived in the town. Michael was silent all the way and Olga could see clearly that he was taking in all the scenery and fine detail of his surroundings. His life was clearly changing, and she was noting a very mature manner and a sharpness in his authority and agility of mind. He was visibly becoming a different person. Gone was the often childlike dependency on his surroundings, and his uncertainties. His smile was becoming natural and engaging, and it seemd as though the 1918 Michael was re-emerging. Michael remarked how the scenery had changed, and that the roads were much better. Gatchina was, however, still a charming and beautiful town and even looked better than he remembered.

As the taxi wheeled into the Palace gates, he let out a squeal of delight as they joined the other cars and horse-drawn carriages in the car park. He slid his hand into Olga's and whispered to her, 'We are home, darling.'

She replied without any thought, 'I am so glad to be here with you, darling.'

Olga was shocked and delighted that he had used such warm words. In all the time she had known him as a friend, they had never exchanged such warmth. They both instantly realised what they had said, and with warm melting eyes, they both giggled, and had no thoughts of apologising or retracting what they had said.

Wide-eyed and now laughing, Olga and Michael walked hand in hand into Gatchina via the main entrance. Olga shared the joy with Michael, who now was visibly so happy and wanted to share in his excitement. The grand house which had been the home of several tsars had undergone a great deal of change since its forced abandonment by Michael in 1918. Gone was much of the finery and furnishings, and very little other than the structure would be there to remind him of the halcyon days of his childhood and early years of being a gay bachelor.

The house had been beautifully converted into a museum and had retained all the wall panelling and ceiling decorations. Michael squeezing her hand said he was remembering much of his happy childhood, and could see himself with his sisters and parents living there so comfortably and having so much fun.

Michael had very little interest in the artwork which was displayed on the walls, as he was rushing from room to room and taking them all in. Olga cautioned him not to make any comments which might draw attention to themselves.

Suddenly Olga was aware of an old lady who was

seemingly one of the assistant curators, sitting in a chair and knitting in an abstracted manner. It was a job of boredom but was necessary to have a presence in the halls with expensive works of art on display. She noticed that the old lady was looking at Michael with her mouth open, and obviously speechless. Olga was aware that, whilst in Russia, there was a high possibility that someone would arrive at thoughts of how Michael was so much like Grand Duke Michael Alexandrovitch, even though he was dead to the world. She saw the signs on this old lady's face and knew she had to react quickly. She left Michael, who was gazing at the ceilings and decorations, and walked up to her with a smile. She asked her a question in English as if she was a real tourist.

The lady was brought back to her senses and replied in very good English to the banal question. Olga remarked on her English and the old lady was happy to reply that she had lived here for many years up to 1918 and was a Nanny to the Romanov children. She went on to say that in the closure days the Palace became derelict and forgotten; however, she was pleased to see it being reopened a few years ago as an art museum. She applied for the job, which was on a residential basis and came with a couple of small rooms to live in. She was an excellent choice as she knew the house intimately and had very good English, which was useful to tourists.

'I am very old now,' she explained, 'so I have a comfortable life sitting, knitting and being on hand to guard against any theft, but more so to speak to tourists.'

Olga enquired why she was taking an interest in her partner, as she had noticed she was transfixed by him. She giggled a little and mentioned that he was the image of her little Micha, who she had cared for through his early life at Gatchina. She introduced herself as Michael's 'Nanny'.

Suddenly Olga realised that Michael had come over, hoping to prise her away from the conversation and explaining that there was so much to see. He then asked the old lady to be excused and bade her farewell using his best Russian.

The old lady stood up and screamed aloud, 'Michael! My Misha, can it be you?'

Quickly Olga knew that it was time to take control. She sat the old lady down and quietened her with comforting tones.

Michael was shocked into silence. After a few moments, he gathered himself and realised very quickly the situation. He also recollected who this old lady was. He bent down on one knee and clasped her hand and put his arms around her confirming that he was her 'Misha'.

Nanny started weeping on Michael's shoulder, not believing what she was hearing, let alone seeing. Olga then took over and asked Nanny to calm down a little as she quickly mentioned that if Michael was recognised he would be arrested and imprisoned. Nanny quickly understood, as she knew the antipathy between the Soviets and the Romanovs.

Michael comforted her and said he wanted to see her in private so that he could explain to her how he was still alive amidst all the stories of his murder. Olga backed him up in this and told her she must be very quiet, and that they would plan to meet her for the following day. Nanny, now more alert and enthused at the thought of spending more time with Michael, mentioned that was her day off and that they should visit the Palace again, but this time go to the rear entrance of the west wing staircase. From there she would take them to her room and they would be free to talk. She explained that the west wing was deserted and locked up from the public, and she had the only access to that part of the Palace.

Michael confirmed to her that he knew exactly where she meant, and that was where the children and tutors had lived, as he recalled the several playrooms and bedrooms he and his brother and sisters shared. He asked her to watch out for their arrival from the windows, it would be around 10.30, and they would saunter around the outside of the west wing as tourists and then knock four times on the door. Nanny gave him a loving wink, knowing that he was definitely her Misha.

With that exchange of plans, Michael got up and shook her hand. He could not hug her again, as there were now other people watching and any further display of love and affection would raise suspicions. Olga shook her hand, and whispered that this was a great day for both her and Michael.

They continued with their tour around the Palace, but it was now half-hearted as this meeting with Nanny had mentally blown Michael apart. Now he had to sit down, as Olga could see that his memories were flooding back and he needed some time for it all to slowly sink in as the realisations of his past were all coming back to him.

They decided to leave the Palace earlier than planned. The best move now was to get a hotel in Gatchina, and not bother going back to the Embassy in Moscow, but they would perhaps get a flight back to Britain via Paris to London from Leningrad.

A hotel room was easy to find, but because of the strict attitudes of these times in Russia, they were not able to present themselves as man and wife so they checked into rooms side by side. That amply covered them in their ruse that they were tourists, and especially at Gatchina, which was visited by cultured people from around the world.

The following morning after a very good breakfast by Russian standards, they got a taxi back to Gatchina. Arriving at the car park they walked hand in hand, very slowly looking and marvelling at the building. They caught sight of Nanny at the window and she waved a handkerchief very briefly in acknowledgment. Michael tipped his hat in recognition. Michael did not have to knock four times as the door was half-open, and they slipped inside.

Nanny threw her arms around Michael and he swept her off her feet, and they both broke down in tears of joy. Olga was so pleased and was smiling at them both to how much they loved each other's company. She was also alert to anything which might happen unexpectedly.

Michael led the way up the staircase as he knew perfectly well the route to the vast network of rooms in the children's wing. Olga and Nanny followed as Michael raced ahead. Olga enquired whether they were safe, as she could not contemplate them being caught in that part of the building. Nanny gave an assuring smile and told her that no one dare set foot in that part of the deserted building, which was full of ghosts from the past. They were fearful of being cursed by the Romanov dead. There had been incidents in 1919 and 1920 of unexplained and horrible deaths in the Palace by anyone who ventured in without cause. Nanny explained to Olga that she was also the caretaker of that wing and had worked on the idea that she should announce from time to time that she had seen horrible apparitions of ghosts and had heard moaning and crying in the wing. This ensured that she would be left alone.

Michael excitedly came running back and beckoned the two ladies to hurry so that he could show Olga the fantastic surroundings they had lived in. Olga remarked that it was rather drab and severe.

'Michael agreed and said. 'That was exactly how he was brought up, by his very strict mother and father. Life was made austere for them so that he would never become fat and lazy and would always respect how the rest of the Russians were living, in cold, severe surroundings.'

Nanny was now leading the way and she walked the full length of the wing and arrived into a room on the corner which had dual-aspect windows. Michael was delighted to see that this was in fact a small apartment, with a living room, kitchen, bathroom and two bedrooms. It was nicely furnished and Michael recognised the furniture as being from the rooms the tutors had lived in. It was warm, pleasant, and had great views of the lawns and park beyond.

Nanny sat them down and poured the coffee she had made in anticipation of their arrival and begged Michael to tell her of all the past events.

This conversation lasted for two hours and Olga just sat back, admiring how Michael had matured and was seeing the full man of yesteryear.

Nanny was so pleased at hearing of Michael's adventures and how he had settled into a free and useful life in England, and how he had now come to understand exactly who he was, in full knowledge of his past life. She cautioned Michael that he should stay in England and never come back to Russia. She knew how much harder life was under the authoritarian rule of Stalin, and every week she would hear about purges of innocent people being executed, and others being carted off to the Gulag and on to slave labour in Siberia. Olga reinforced Nanny's view and warned Michael that his fate would be just the same if he were caught.

Nanny then took Michael by the hand and led him down the corridor to his childhood bedroom and the playroom which was adjacent. Michael knew exactly where she was leading him, and was full of expectation as they entered his playroom. To his amazement, it was full of his old toys and personal effects from his childhood. He had always kept them in that room. When he grew up, he had chosen to live in the other wing, which was reserved for him and visiting guests.

He also recognised the items as belonging to his sisters, Olga and Xenia. Michael quickly delved into his childhood possessions and, rummaging around, with a cry of excitement he pulled out his three stamp albums. He spent the next few minutes leafing through them with the odd shout of joy. There were other books too, and some were his old exercise books which he had used during his years of private tuition. There were many old photographs too. After a few more minutes of searching, he suddenly went quiet and looked rather sad. He was holding a photo of his beloved friend, Nicholas Johnson.

He asked Nanny if he could take some of these precious mementos back to England with him. Nanny agreed and Olga approved, so long as they were not too bulky, as this might arouse suspicion when they went back through customs control at the airport.

Nanny had a bright idea. She went into Michael's bedroom, and returned with a Gladstone briefcase which had been Michael's during his schooling days.

Olga, ever watchful, agreed that it seemed the perfect choice. She told him that he could put in some of his personal items from his other suitcase, and some of his travelling papers. If they were questioned, then he could simply say that he had bought the old books and stamp albums from a market stall in Moscow. None of these had any value and they were not in any way politically compromising papers.

They returned to the comfort of Nanny's room and had another coffee and conversation. Olga enquired about the ghost stories and the tragic deaths of some people all those years ago. Nanny`s face turned crimson and she rather falteringly explained that they were ghosts of Bolshevik thugs who were ransacking the building and met an untimely and horrible death. After Michael left in 1918 she had stayed on with the permission of the Cheka, as she had nowhere else to live. They thought that she was harmless and would be useful to keep some sort of visual security and be on hand as an on-site keyholder. From time to time the premises were broken into, and the Cheka were rather uninterested in its security. Nanny was more concerned for her own safety as she was then living on the ground floor in the old laundry rooms. In 1919 and 1920, she was sheltering an old friend of Michael's from his days in the army, Peter Polotsov.

Michael interrupted enquiring what became of him?

Nanny explained that he had been accused by the

Cheka of being a White Army sympathiser. He was hunted and would have been arrested and executed had they caught him. She explained that he stayed with her for two years, hiding in the Palace. One night in December 1919 there was another break-in and this time Peter was caught in the corridor. He knew these to be two Cheka thugs, and they also recognised Peter. Peter had to act decisively and he pulled his revolver first and threatened them.

She had come out to see what the commotion was about and Peter quickly told her to get some thin rope to tie their hands and feet. When they were securely tied he turned them on their bellies. He went to the kitchen and brought out a rope which he used as a garrotte and strangled each one of them. The men made such a loud screeching noise, begging for help and mercy. Peter would have none of it, and despatched them to hell. Nanny paused and enquired if she should continue as it got worse.

Michael encouraged her as he was enjoying this tale of retribution by his old pal.

She continued, saying that 'Peter then made two hangman's nooses and put one round each of their necks, and carried the bodies up to the main staircase. He untied the bindings from their hands and feet. Then he tied the ends of the nooses around the staircase rail and pushed each of them over.

The best part was that, before he had garrotted them, he had struck a bargain for their lives and persuaded them to write notes in their own hand. The words were written in Latin, "*Mia Culpa Mia Culpa Mia Maxima Culpa*". They did not know what they were writing as neither of them were educated to the point of knowing Latin. He then, stuffed the notes in each of their mouths. It looked perfectly reasonable to assume that they had had an extreme experience with an invasion of supernatural conscience and committed suicide.

It was arranged then that Nanny would use the phone in the main building early the following morning, and contact the Cheka offices in Gatchina Town in a screaming panic. She would explain that whilst doing her daily round of security checking of doors and windows, she was confronted by these two men hanging from the staircase railings.

She went on to say that, the Cheka came and interrogated her. It was obvious that she could not have committed such a murder, so they soon concluded that there must have been another person in the building who had committed that act. They searched everywhere and found no trace of any other person who perhaps may have been in hiding.

Peter had hidden himself in a secret room that Michael knew of very well, from when games of hide and seek were being played in the Palace. It was under the staircase and behind a false wall. She explained that for five days he hid there, and each night Nanny would provide food and let him out when it seemed safe, to stretch his legs. After that she felt it was safe to hide him back in her private rooms which was not far from the staircase. Should the house be broken into again, then he could quickly hide.

The stories soon spread that there was an entity dispensing supernatural revenge in the house. Nanny added to the stories, as from time to time she told people that she had heard weeping and crying, which suddenly turned into a cacophony of sound and then suddenly stopped.

Six months later, there was another night-time break-in. This time it was a lone intruder and Peter was alert again to the same tactics. Once again a body was found hanging on the staircase, with the same note in the man's mouth. Peter this time thought that he had better leave the protection of the Palace as it was pushing his luck to have got away with it twice. That evening he left, and Nanny had never heard from him since that time.

The Cheka tried to cover up the new event, but it did leak out and the whole place took on a fearful aspect and no one would go near it. That was when she was evicted, and they boarded up the Palace.

She went to live in Gatchina town and was given accommodation by an old friend. She worked in the local school teaching maths after that. She was given great respect as many people thought she had some sort of divine quality to have withstood so much spiritual chaos and the ghostly presence which was now known of in great detail as the stories of Gatchina were expanded. Michael was delighted to hear of these stories as he could see it had thrown up a ring of defence around his home and he was thankful that it was being left alone.

Nanny then explained that she was glad to have come back, and perhaps because of the past events, she was the only one eligible and brave enough to live on site. Michael laughed wholeheartedly and hugged Nanny once more.

Olga was keen to know who Peter was.

Michael replied that he was a good friend and officer in his Savage Division during the war, and had gained a powerful position as a Commander in Petrograd. He had been instrumental in providing travel documents for Michael in early 1918 so that he and Natasha could travel to Finland and freedom. But the journey never got beyond Petrograd due to the mobs and was returned to Gatchina.

Michael finished by saying he was a good man and friend during his army days. He was keeping himself safe whilst being drafted to the Red Army. But his sympathies to the Whites and Romanovs would soon have exposed him and it was only a matter of time before his conscience would lead to a trial of inquisition.

Olga then announced that they should go, as they needed to catch the flight from Leningrad and they would need a taxi as soon as possible. They gave each other hugs and kisses, and Nanny shooed them out of the door and hoped they would both have a great life in freedom.

They left and started to mingle with the crowds of tourists. They soon got a taxi from the car park to the airport. Arriving at Leningrad airport, Olga bought the tickets and after an easy customs clearance with their diplomatic immunity, they were soon taking off and on their way back to London.

Michael said to Olga, 'Let's go home, darling.'

She slid her hand into his and said, 'Yes, darling, let's go home.'

She was now perfectly content that Michael was aware of his past life; he had successfully dealt with the trauma, and they both knew that England was home, and perhaps a new life of love would entwine them in a long-lasting relationship.

44

England... Home!

Arriving in England after the Russian trip, it was now a matter of finding a home to live in as partners. Marriage was not a first requirement. Both being in the service of SIS, that may have had some security issues, especially for Olga as she was now engaged in a deeper role in espionage. It was certain that she would at some point be sent to Europe to work within spy cells, as intelligence-gathering was becoming a very important part of the security of Britain.

Michael wanted to live on Richmond Hill in one of the grand townhouses which overlooked the park. Olga shared his vision and they decided to buy a home on the hill. Within a few weeks, they had sourced a new home and were preparing to move in together. They had recently collected the artefacts and furniture they had bought in Russia, and now were excitedly planning the move and establishing a home furnished with rich antiques from Michael's past life.

45

1939: The Second World War

In July 1939, Olga was posted to Madrid and she was given the job of CEO to the network which was being rapidly expanded. Her role was to oversee all activities in mainland Europe and be the key to disseminating all the intelligence and then transmitting this back to Bletchley Park, which was just being set up as the British HQ for counter-intelligence and code-breaking.

Michael was posted to that department in Bletchley in December 1941, at the height of the war and on the announcement that America had joined the war. His fluency in Russian and German were of great advantage and he was a key member of staff in translation and in supplying false information and counter-intelligence. He particularly enjoyed the subterfuge in creating confusion among the German defences in the Normandy area prior to the D-Day landings in June 1944. His enthusiasm, though, was the intelligence and interpretation on the Russian front. He was keen to help the Russian covert operations and prepared many reports of significance in the movement of troops, as he knew very well the geographical perspectives of the country.

Fortunately Olga's work was not in the field and it did not represent any real threats to her safety at the British Embassy in Madrid, especially as Spain had stayed out of the war as a neutral country.

Michael was also safe from any harm in his post in England. However he was becoming rather frustrated in his work and at the start of 1944 yearned to be more involved in translating his ideas and creativity into action. He made his feelings known to his fellow agents and shared some of his ideas with them from time to time. As a result of this Michael was called to the office of Sir Stewart Menzies, head of SIS and MI6, in May 1944 to explain his impatience in wanting to become actively more involved in the war, and to contribute his skills towards the growing MI6 internal movement to assassinate Hitler. Menzies had become aware of his feelings for some time from his MI6 colleagues and at his work at Bletchley Park.

Menzies opened the conversation very abruptly and announced that Churchill had instructed him to give Michael an audience to explain his interest in the assassination of Hitler. He was still circumspect about Michael, and when he was promoted to the head of MI6 he had gained the knowledge of his hereditary past position in the Imperial Royal Family and knew that he still needed to be personally managed, as he was a potential embarrassment.

Michael was excited that he was to have an audience with Sir Stewart so that he could explain his own reasoning and possible contribution of a plan which he had been formulating during the winter of 1944. He explained that he had grave misgivings about the forthcoming post-war era, which was anticipated to start around the end of 1944, and just months after the proposed landings in France. The power of the Soviet Army, which he felt would overwhelm the Allied forces and their aspirations if they failed to get a foothold in Europe, was a real option and could simply exchange one dictator for another.

His own feelings against the Bolshevik Soviets were tainted by the events of 1918 when they murdered his secretary Johnson and the Romanov Imperial families. He wanted not only revenge, but also to assist in the neutralising of the advances they were making in the east. He knew from his work at Bletchley Park, in interpreting transmissions via Colossus, that the Soviets were intent on world domination, just as Hitler had been pursuing since 1933. He had become aware from the XX Committee and his connections in MI6 that plans were being developed, known as Operation Foxley, to assassinate Hitler at the Berghof using SOE agents in a sniper attack as Hitler walked in some security in the surrounding forest.

He knew the area well, being located on the Austrian, German and Italian borders, as he had been staying at the small town of Berchtesgaden, which was close to the Berghof, when he visited Italy in 1912 shortly after his marriage to Natasha. He made another visit to the area in 1930 when he took a mountaineering holiday in the Alps and had based himself there for four weeks. So, he was in a good position to be able to support the small team, and could speak four languages fluently, German, Italian, English and, of course, Russian. Working for MI6 as he did, then he was able to apply support services and felt that he should be inserted into the region with the assassins.

Sir Stewart thought for a moment, as it did seem to

make a lot of sense. Additionally, it did cross his mind that if Michael was shot, or captured, then it would get rid of a problem which MI6 had been dealing with since 1918 and was a thorn in their side, as Michael's new life was always a hot potato politically. Even if Michael was to convince the Germans that he was Grand Duke Michael Alexandrovitch Romanov, in the hope of his life being spared, they would still undoubtedly get rid of him.

Michael then produced his well-thought-out plans for the ensuing vacuum which would arise if Hitler was assassinated. This was not his remit, but because he had a great understanding of the secrecy, current political map, and the undecided future of post-war Europe, then his views could be considered alongside any other plans. More so as there had been little attention paid to the post-assassination European picture and any plan to secure a rapid end to the war.

He had a key ally in this interest, who was no other than the British Prime Minister. Churchill was a keen advocate of killing Hitler, but there were other senior members of the War Cabinet who felt that he should be kept safe as, being a poor strategist, mad and unpredictable, then this was a recipe for a speedy conclusion to the war, should an invasion of Europe succeed. Michael declared to Sir Stewart that in his recent meeting with Churchill, who he had met previously on the HMS *Iron Duke* in 1918, was keen to promote his views and interesting plans.

Michael had become aware, through coded German intelligence-gathering traffic and members of the XX Committee, that Colonel Claus von Stauffenberg of the German Army was plotting with other high-ranking officers to assassinate Hitler in the summer of 1944, and very much based on the supposition that the coming Allied landings in France would be a success.

He then opened a short dossier of ten points and reasons to promote his thoughts on a post assassination picure:

The Plan

1. *Prepare a plan to be submitted to the German army officer Colonel Claus von Stauffenberg, who it is known is planning the murder of Adolph Hitler, and to gain traction with his co-conspirators, to agree an end to hostilities with Germany and to install Field Marshall Rommel as interim leader pending elections at the end of the war.*
   - *He is popular in Germany and seen as a clean pair of hands.*
   - *He is honest, reliable and a hero.*
2. *To engage in pre-planning with Germany and other Allied powers the freedom of France and reinstate a .friendly government in Germany with essential postings of allied political and armed forces within Germany and remain in occupation until the end of total hostilities.*
   - *This would then save an enormous amount of lives on both sides.*
   - *It would show goodwill and not weakness in the new German Government.*
3. *To allow the Allies to have a northern corridor to the Eastern Front and conclude a peaceful end of hostilities with Russia at the Polish border. The corridor would be*

via the freeing of Holland, Belgium and 50 kilometres wide along the northern coastline of Germany and Poland.

- *This at a stroke would free these countries and they would come under the protection of Allied powers.*
- *Russia would see that it had two potential adversaries at its own borders and would become well advised to cease hostilities with Germany.*

4. *Should Russia not conclude these end of war terms then the German Army would form a bulwark against Russia at that border and resist, together with the Allies, any further armed confrontation.*

- *This would then provide the German and Allied forces an excuse to press home the huge advantage they would have and possibly lead to the demise or restraint of Communism, which has always been the goal of Germany and the Allies.*

5. *The German armed forces to withdraw to the northern Italian border and leave Italy a free nation.*

- *Italy has no strategic importance for Germany and it would free up armour and troops.*
- *Italy would once again within a short period of time be able to attain freedom of speech and political reform from dictatorship.*

6. *An immediate release of all racial and political prisoners from the camps.*

- *This would enable the German peoples to gain some legitimacy as being able to apportion the whole blame on the racist masterplan of the defeated Nazis.*
- *This would minimise atrocities, saving lives and*

*the ongoing persecution of Jews, political prisoners
and forced labour.*

7. *Allow all occupied territories to determine their own
political futures in alliances with either the Western
Powers or Russia. Those choosing the Western authority
would come under the immediate protection of the
combined Allied and German forces.*

- *This would be a clear message to all states that
Western freedom is better than incarceration by
the Soviet system.*
- *This would unify most of Europe into free states to
determine their own futures.*
- *Germany also would become a free nation once
again.*

8. *Formal negotiations to be carried out in Paris with the
Allied powers to formulate a long and lasting peace
treaty and determine alliances for the future.*

9. *After the cessation of all resistance then a peace treaty
could be worked out with the hope that there could be
a return to the post-1918 borders for all countries.*

10. *The Nazi Party to be immediately disbanded and
the control of the Interim Government to be under a
martial law.*

- *War crimes trials would commence and the Nazi
Party would be outlawed.*

The estimated number of lives saved would be enormous,
and could number millions on all fronts of a war which
could become protracted for years to come, especially as it
was known that Hitler was years ahead in the design and
implementation of super-weapons which could turn the tide

of any war. The fear of Hitler's atomic power research and development was real within MI6 circles.

After spending twenty minutes reading the proposal, Sir Stewart was of two minds. As it was not his remit to introduce policy, he was free to add his own views. He announced to Michael that this was a preposterous fairy story and would gain no acceptability amongst the Allies, and would certainly be rejected by the Germans. In his view, if they got rid of Hitler then it would be worse for the Allied prosecution of the war to defeat Germany.

He looked quizzically at Michael and asked if he understood just how much of an ally Hitler was. He explained to an astonished Michael, 'We can more easily defeat a madman running an asylum than an intelligent, bold and hardened hero warrior with 100 per cent support from his people – such as Erwin Rommel, who would most likely succeed Hitler. Under martial law with leading and respected German armed forces intelligentsia, then our chances are far worse than if we left Hitler to self-inflict the damage.'

He challenged Michael to think about the adverse effects of Hitler's assassination. The pro-Hitler movement, who had been brainwashed for the past 15 years, would only raise him to martyr status, with a subliminal link to deity in their minds. The German citizens would become fanatics, and much more so than they were today. The German people would fight on, and effectively to the last breath.

Michael countered that the German armed forces had far more to gain by the implementation of his plan, and that the art of politics was far superior to the art of war, as many a pen has blunted a sword.

Sir Stewart then complimented Michael on his perception and how he had engaged with him on the subject. He ended the meeting by saying that he would suggest that Michael became an associate member of the XX Committee, and be an advisor to Operation Foxley as it was now gaining some ground in political circles.

He went on to say that if the plan was to be commissioned by the War Cabinet – and probably by Churchill, as this seemed to be his baby – and if Michael was considered a worthwhile choice for becoming a member of the SOE insertion team, then he would support his application. He also advised Michael that the deputy head of SOE's German Directorate, Lt Col Ronald Thornley, was firmly against the plan for the reasons he had just told Michael

Michael left the room elated, and now felt that he had an important part to play in the ensuing war. He knew he could make a huge difference to the success of the operation as and when it was to be given the go-ahead.

Sir Stewart was relieved that he had been able to deal with Michael in a sensitive and political massaging manner. He knew that the pro-life views on Hitler were stronger than the pro-death views, and that his plan would never see the light of day. He was convinced that regardless of the saving of life versus loss of life issue, the unconditional defeat of Germany was imperative. He had seen action in the First World War, and to allow Germany to rise again in defiance of defeat that would cause more chaos and even be the start of a so-called Armageddon with new and fantastic super-weapons.

However, he was shrewd enough to realise, as he had access to much intelligence information that the real and final enemy was Russian Communism, and that the help of Germany would be needed in the end if only to protect themselves from Stalin's enslavement. But only on the terms of the Allies.

46

1945: Life of Bliss

At the end of the war, in July 1945, Michael and Olga were discharged from the service as most operations came to an end. Michael returned to Richmond and a week later Olga was also repatriated and joined him. Life now could begin again, although for many returning forces it seemed to be a different world, especially as industry was turning away from the war effort and now returning to peacetime production and reconstruction of the infrastructure. Life for Michael and Olga was settling down and they both applied for and started new jobs. Michael's job was in teaching: a post in the languages department at a local grammar school. Olga took an administration job in local government.

Christmas 1945 was a special occasion, and even though austerity was now in full flow, they could still have a lavish time together. Their joint incomes were well above the average, so they could indulge in luxuries. However, on Boxing Day, Michael became ill with his long-suffered stomach pains again. He attended the outpatients department at a London clinic, and it was confirmed that he would need an operation to remove the ulcers which had blighted his life for the past thirty years. He had undergone this type of operation just before his discharge whilst at St Katherine's Hospital in 1926, and for ten years he had been free from any reoccurrence, and with diet and medication he had been able to control any potential ill-effects.

They planned a New Year celebration for three days in York as it was a special place of cultural interest which they both enjoyed. It was also to be a time for Michael to take it easy and get over his recent ulcer problems. His diet was now strict, and Olga was always on hand to insist that he keep his medication up to date.

Arriving in York, Olga had secured some luxury rooms in a historic building close to the Minster. The New Year was a special time for them and a memorable occasion. As they were not far from the coast and the winter was so far not too cold, they hired a taxi for the day and drove east to Scarborough.

When they arrived, Michael suddenly started to remember all the events of 1918. The sights and sounds came streaming into his mind and he became full of nostalgia. He recalled very clearly the Grand Hotel, and later his flight from Filey Bay in the seaplane. After lunch in the Grand, Michael asked Olga if she would like to take a trip to Hunmanby Gap to see if his old pal Robert Blackburn was still living in his bungalow on the lower cliffs. The day was bright and sunny and she agreed, as they could take in the sea air with a walk on the clifftops. Unfortunately, the tide was coming in so a beach walk was out of the question.

After thirty minutes' drive, they arrived at the village and turned left onto the road which led down to the small settlement. They drove down the very steep hill to the lower cliff top, and there on the left was Roberts home. However, it was a long shot to expect to see him still living there, and that turned out to be the case, as the house was deserted and boarded up for the winter.

Looking beyond, Michael could also see that the concrete slipway had gone; it seemed that it had been deliberately destroyed. He assumed that this was part of the coastal defence work, as should a German invasion have taken place, then this would have provided them with a good access point onto the mainland.

Michael whilst looking out at the beautiful bay with the winter sun behind them, suddenly had a massive recall of information. He grabbed Olga's arm and shouted aloud, 'My jewels! My treasures! My heritage!'

Olga was shocked by this sudden shout of enthusiasm and wondered what he was talking about. Michael then took her out of earshot of the taxi driver, and babbled out a story of incomprehensible detail about treasure on the clifftop. She thought he was pleasantly mad, and did not believe anything he was saying. Perhaps it was just a jumbling in his mind. All she really took on board was 'buried treasure' in 1918.

Michael exclaimed to her that he would have none of her assumption that he had gone loopy, so he grabbed her hand and marched her back to the waiting taxi.

'Drive on my good man. Drive.'

'To where?' he enquired with a strange look on his face, seeing that this quiet gentleman was now wide-eyed and very agitated.

'I don't know,' Michael replied, 'but I will direct you as best as I can.'

The taxi driver thought that this was an interesting adventure and made a change from the humdrum of daily driving. Approaching the main coast road, Michael told the driver to turn left. They drove southwards for about 2 kilometers and Michael started to recognise the scenery again. He saw a line of white cliffs ahead and asked the taxi driver to slow down. There on the left was a road which he recognised, and the nameplate said Sands Road. Now he was on familiar territory and recalled that he had made a serious attempt to remember this road back in 1918. They soon encountered the series of mini bumpy hills which gave a great childlike pleasure like being on a rollercoaster. Michael and Olga enjoyed that brief sensation, with Michael requesting the driver that on their way out, he should take the bumpy folds in the ground at top speed.

The taxi then came to the end of the road, where there was a small carpark on the cliff edge. Michael was amazed to see how the scenery had changed. There was now a large settlement of bungalows, and even a small shop, which was closed, facing the car park. However, it did have a little fish and chip shop attached to the left-hand side, and it was just opening for the evening trade. Michael giggled as he looked at the flag above the shop, which had written on it, 'When the flag is flying, the fish are frying'.

Now Michael could barely contain himself. He rushed over to an old bench which he recognised as being the one he had sat on in 1918 whilst Johnson was busying himself burying treasure. He sat down with Olga, as he had now got her full attention.

Michael recounting the whole story which was now clear to him from when he left Gatchina in 1918 on the start of his journey to Britain. He told her of the immense wealth he had brought with him, which was given to him from Nicholas with the help of Albert Stopford. He also told her that there was also a cache which had been taken from the Vladimir Palace for safe-keeping on behalf of his Aunt Maria, who used to live there. Then the treasure haul had been increased when he visited Knebworth House and Paddockhurst in Englad to retrieve his valuables which were left behind when they returned to Russia in 1918.

He explained about the journey on the Royal Train back to Scarborough and how he took a ride in an old prestigious sports car, a Vauxhall Prince Henry, to Filey Bay, before flying the seaplane to Denmark. The vehicle had been owned by the RFC. He and Johnson realised that it would be foolish to take the treasures with them back to Russia, so the idea was that they should bury them on the cliffs of Filey Bay.

'Where did you bury them?' exclaimed Olga in an equally excited manner.

'I don't know,' was Michael's reply. He explained that he had sat on this very bench for a while, and Johnson was entrusted to do the burial. All he knew was that he was gone for about an hour and returned with a story that he had marked the two spots and had taken readings using a sextant which he had found in the RFC Prince Henry. Any further detail of that event was a blur in Michael's mind.

Olga then asked, 'Where are the coordinates?'

Then Michael realised that his old friend had told him he had secreted the readings in his Woodrow Wilson watch.

'What is a Woodrow Wilson watch?' she mused.

Michael explained that it was a campaign watch for the Presidential election in 1912. 'The watch had been given to

Johnson and it was supposed to have been given onwards to me. Because it was a bit of a cheap gimmicky watch, then I told Johnson to keep it. I do recall that he wore it constantly right up to the time he was murdered in Russia.'

'That was unfortunate,' she exclaimed.

It had a very deflating effect on their excitement, as there was no telling where the watch was now, or even if it still existed. Michael then looked very sad and it dawned on him that they may well never recover the items. After nearly thirty years, there would be no trace of anything, and the area was just too huge to search.

Olga mentioned that there were devices now which could detect mines in the ground and would make a high-pitched sound transmitted to earphones when metal was detected.

'That would not work,' said Michael, 'as they were buried in sealed earthenware pots and the detectors would not have a chance of picking up a signal.'

'Oh,' said Olga. 'Then they are lost for good.'

'Yes,' said Michael. 'Unless the watch was to be discovered and in the hope that the piece of cigarette paper which he wrote the coordinates on was still in the back of the watch, then there would be a possibility, in providing a reasonably accurate area. Even then it could be a long and fruitless search, as Johnson being gone for a fair length of time could have walked some distance either way from this bench.

They were both crestfallen. Olga then stood up and announced to Michael, 'It is for the best, as it would be too big a deal to be able to handle that fortune, and it would only expose you to the Russians and be a great embarrassment to the British Government. It is for the best that they are lost.'

Michael then stood up and embraced her saying, 'You are right, darling. The best treasure in my life is you, and that is worth more than money can ever buy.'

They hugged for a while. It was now getting dark and they both gazed at the rising moon over the horizon of the sea. They stood awhile, hand in hand, and took in the glorious sight as it arose and sent shimmering reflections onto the sea below, lighting up the bay.

'Time to go home,' shouted the taxi driver.

They walked back to the taxi arm in arm. The driver enquired as to the reason why they needed to visit the cliff tops. Michael replied, in quite an amusing tone, that they were looking for lost treasure.

The driver then went pale. He was now a man in his sixties and had a vague memory of a tall gentleman coming into the café which he and his wife ran just down the coast, around the end of the First World War, and selling him four earthenware pots. He remembered he had asked the guy what he wanted them for as they were leaving. The reply came flooding back to him now: that they were wanting to use them to bury treasure in.

They now saw that the fish and chip shop was open so they decided to have dinner in a newspaper on the way back to York. Whilst they were in the shop, the taxi driver was becoming more convinced that he had seen this man before and was certain it was he who had bought the earthenware pots.

When they returned to the taxi, and after a half an hour into the journey back to York, the taxi driver was still pondering on this story. He tentatively mentioned that he seemed to have met Michael a very long time ago, when he ran a small café on that coast near Hunmanby.

Michael replied simply saying. 'Perhaps we did meet.'

Olga smiled at Michael and both knew that this could be the start of a rumour which could go on for years. Michael bellowed out a huge laugh which kept them giggling for the next half hour. They cuddled in the back seat, and fell asleep in total contentment.

47

1946: Union and Heir

The New Year in 1946 was a dismal time of cold winds and storms. This type of weather was upsetting for Michael as his stomach pains were becoming uncontrollable and were now beginning to tell on his general health. The advice that he had received just after Christmas was that he needed an operation.

Olga was very concerned for him as she had not realised that Michael had been suffering in this way for most of his adult life. She and Michael decided to visit St Bartholomew's Hospital in east London, which had a very good reputation for a wide range of medical needs, and its facilities were amongst the best in the capital.

After a week, they returned to the hospital in February to receive the prognosis. It was as Michael had feared: the ulcers had returned with a vengeance and there were multiple lesions which had showed very clearly on the several X-rays which had been taken. The surgeon, Professor Willingham, told them that an urgent operation was required to give him any chance, as these were now becoming life-threatening and the open wound would become a danger to the condition of his blood.

He went on to explain in more detail. Peptic ulcers can lead to gastro-intestinal bleeding, which if sudden and serious (because of eating into a blood vessel), can cause imminent death.

Michael recognised this prognosis as reminiscent of what he was told in 1925 whilst at St Katherine's. There he had had an operation to remove them, which had been successful, but only up to the last few years when the stomach problems increased again. The diet and medication had worked to some extent, but because of the sudden increase in the number of lesions, then it was an urgent situation.

Michael was told to stay at home and be at perfect rest with no stress, and he should only eat a prescribed diet. Olga arranged a date for surgery, and due to the emergency, it was planned for the end of February.

They both returned to Richmond in a resigned mood, but Olga was very hopeful of a full recovery after the operation. Michael shared with her that he felt he was on borrowed time. 'Nonsense!' Olga declared. Olga lit a fire and it was soon blazing and warming up the day room. She invited Michael to lie down on his favourite Gatchina chaise lounge, and made him a warm glass of milk into which she put his new powder medication.

Michael was comfortable and knew how much he owed to Olga, who had been the only pillar of sanctuary and security in his whole life. Olga joined him and took his hand.

She lowered her voice and gave him one of her spectacular smiles. 'I love you so much and I want to be your wife. Will you marry me?'

Michael looked at her with so much pride and love, as tears rolled from his eyes, his mouth quivered with emotion. It took several seconds for him to be able to reply. He replied in such a humble tone, which Olga had never heard before, but it was a simple 'Yes', which carried so much weight of love and devotion. Michael then said to her that he would like to marry her immediately and not wait for any formalities, other than was necessary. Olga was delighted, as she would prefer a civil ceremony with just the two of them, and of course a witness.

There would be just enough time to catch the Register Office in Kensington before it closed for the day. Olga left Michael comfortable and then went into the hall and phoned the office to make an appointment. She then rushed out to get a taxi and went to the Register Office to collect all the required forms and book a date and time. When she returned a few hours later, Michael was sleeping peacefully and had the most amazingly happy look on his face. She knew how much this meant to him.

The next thing was to find a suitable witness. The first person she thought of was her old boss at SIS, Sir Stewart Menzies. He knew both Michael and Olga very well and had a close relationship with Michael in his time at Bletchley Park. In fact, when he expanded the service after taking over in 1939, he interviewed Michael and recruited him in December 1941. Olga had worked under his watch as Chief Intelligence Officer in Madrid and also knew him well. Menzies was intimately aware of the story of Michael, and he would be best suited to create the right pathway, should it become sticky.

It was essential that Michael did not return to work until

after the operation, once he was fully fit again. That evening, seeing Michael so tired, but very peaceful, Olga brought down the eiderdown from his bed and put it around him. She stoked up the fire and settled down on the sofa to keep watch over the only person she had ever come to love in her whole life.

She drifted into thoughts of herself and Michael now that they would become husband and wife. She was fifty-eight years old and Michael was ten years her senior. Michael should be retired, but he was still mentally very agile and with his language skills he had been snapped up by the local grammar school a few months earlier on a three-year contract. It was strange to have found this kind of love so late in her life. She had never thought about marriage before and never contemplated having a family, as she had been a career woman. The dangerous profession she was in would have been entirely unfair to a husband. It was true that she knew how stunningly beautiful she was, and she had had several suitors seeking her affection. But none had ever come to know her intimately and she had always kept a respectful distance. She laughed to herself as she thought of the nicknames which she had been given in the SIS. 'Posh Totty' stuck out as the one which gave her some pleasure. The 'Hot Totty' name, whilst being complimentary, was a little near to being rude.

Olga woke up early the following day and roused Michael. He apologised for sleeping on the couch and went to have a shower. Olga told Michael that she was off to see Stewart Menzies, to ask him if he would be a witness to their wedding at the Register Office.

Michael shouted back as he disappeared up the stairs,

'Fantastic idea, darling. I could not have thought of anyone better.'

Olga had another reason to go out. Before she arrived at the SIS offices, she called in to see her doctor. When she arrived in his consulting room, her doctor, Chris Smith greeted her with his face lit up like a Christmas tree and sat her down.

'I hope that, by the look on my face – may I call you "young lady"? – you can guess the result of the pregnancy test.'

'Oh, wow! Goodness gracious!' she blurted out, and stood up and hugged the doctor.

He was only too pleased to reciprocate with warmth as he had known Olga for many years and knew how delighted she was, and how much this meant to her at the age of fifty-eight.

They both sat down again and the doctor now turned to a more serious conversation. He reminded her that childbirth could be difficult, as she was at an age when births were generally seen as very dangerous and mother or child may not survive. He advised her that during the pregnancy he wanted to see her every week and she should be put on a substantial diet packed with vitamins and minerals. He asked her how she was coping with the morning sickness, as that had been the reason why she consulted him. Olga was finding it unpleasant and hoped it would soon pass.

'Great!' he said. 'I will see you next week, same day, same time.'

Olga left the surgery with an unbelievable spring in her step. She knew everything was working out just fine and could only see a future of bliss in front of her.

She made her way straight to the offices of SIS to see Menzies. At the reception, she was met by his personal assistant, Kathleen Pettigrew. They had been good friends over the years and she was so glad to see her.

'Can I see the boss for five minutes? I have some fantastic news and I want to tell him first.'

Her face lit up, as she suspected it was something to do with her and Michael. She called Menzies on the intercom, and in his gruff voice he said, 'Speak.'

'Mr Menzies I have a lady here who I know you will want to see. She has some fantastic news to tell you.'

He was taken aback but could not refuse such an interesting prospect.

In Olga waltzed and strode over to Menzies, smiling and laughing stretching, out her hand to shake his. He rose and came around his desk, pushed her hand to one side and hugged her instead.

After a short exchange of niceties and updates, she came to the point. 'Stewart, I want you to be witness at my marriage to Michael and also to be a godfather to our love child.'

Menzies nearly fell over, and had to steady himself on the desk. His face was such a sight to see. Olga could not believe how thrilled he was: in her long years at SIS, she had never known he had it in him.

'It will be my eternal pleasure, Olga. And this is the best news I have had since VE Day! I am at your disposal and whenever the dates are fixed, then I will cancel everything. Even if that pain in the neck Churchill calls, I will simply tell him I have far more important business to attend to than meeting with him.'

'I think we have a problem, though, Olga said quietly. Michael is also married to Natasha Countess Brasova. She may be still alive.'

Menzies replied, 'You must be mistaken, Olga. Michael is a British subject born in Deptford and it is impossible for him to have married this lady you have mentioned.'

He was grinning, and Olga knew that Menzies would ensure that all the formalities were in his capable hands. The day was becoming more perfect.

Rushing home to see Michael she quickly pulled him out of his chair and took him over to to the bay window with one of the best views in town, overlooking Richmond Park. This was the most memorable place to tell Michael all the news. They stood side by side and held hands.

Michael broke the tranquil silence of observing the park in winter. 'Tell me of your day, darling,' he said.

She said very quietly, 'We will be getting married on the 14th of February, Valentine's Day. Stewart Menzies will be our witness. Our child is due to be born on the 14th of September, and Stewart will be Godfather.'

Michael said, 'Please repeat that again. I thought you said something about children.'

She repeated it very slowly as they exchanged a mutual gaze. Michael's face was surprise and expectation, Olga's was pure love and warmth.

'A baby!' he screamed in delight. 'How can that be? We are old people, and old people do not have children, how did you manage such a wonderful thing?'

Olga pressed into his arms and said, 'Darling, you did it, not me. I am here to love you and serve you for ever.'

After absorbing all this fantastic news, Michael suddenly

realised that after all there could be an heir to the Russian throne.

Valentine's Day, 14 February 1946, dawned to produce a bright and crisp morning. Michael looked at Olga as they were being driven to the Register Office at Kensington and told her this was the best day of his life so far, and 14th September would equal this day too. He told her he had never felt so happy and complete as now, in his new home and country. Life was just so perfect. Olga listened and said nothing, the tear in her eye reciprocated all Michael's thoughts. The service was to be the last of the day at 4 p.m.

Menzies was waiting at the steps of the Register office and dutifully walked over to the taxi which had just pulled into the kerbside and opened the door. He announced to the bride and groom that on this day it was his pleasure to serve them. 'Madam, Sir, please step forward to enjoy the best day of your lives.' With that the three of them walked slowly up the steps and into the chamber hall.

They were amazed to see the whole place decked out in flowers, and many of their old colleagues from SIS HQ in London and Bletchley Park. They all started to clap and cheer and came forward with hugs and well-wishing.

Olga's good friend and old MI6 colleague, Xenia, a Russian exile from Odessa, whom she had not seen since she left Madrid, walked towards her with a small posy of daffodils and a little souvenir of a chimney sweep doll. The chimney sweep was a traditional gift of good fortune. Another came to give her a blue garter which she wrapped around her wrist. Another stepped forward and gave her a new copy of *War and Peace*; and finally Michael gave her his old stamp collection to borrow. Michael was in on this surprise for Olga, as he and Menzies had colluded the previous week.

Olga was stunned into silence and by now her tears were flooding down her cheeks. Michael took his handkerchief from his top pocket and dabbed her eyes. Menzies led them into the ceremony chamber and all the 33 invited guests followed to loud cheering and singing, 'For they are jolly good fellows, For they are jolly good fellows, For they are jolly good fellows… and so say all of us!'

This chamber again was decked in an abundance of flowers of all types and colours. Olga was dressed in a slim black dress, and wearing a floppy black-brimmed hat, and wore around her neck a three-stranded pearl necklace, and a wrist bangle with five rows of pearls. Michael was dressed in a smart tuxedo and black tie. When they arrived at the ceremony point in front of the Registrar, Xenia came forward and gently took off Olga's floppy hat and placed on her head a beautiful tiara. She whispered that it was her treasured possession from Russia, and was made by Cartier, and it was her wedding gift. Now she looked like a princess and mused at the unlikely title of the future Empress of Russia in waiting.

After the official parts in the wedding, they all exchanged hugs, kisses and hand-shakes. The office was filled with much chatter and laughter, which went on for some time. It was now past closing time, but this was a special occasion, and the usual strict protocols were ignored, which probably had much to do with the Chief of Staff of the SIS being there as witness.

Leaving the great hall and walking down the steps, Olga and Michael were taken aback by the very unexpected group of paparazzi who were waiting for them by the kerbside, keeping a respectful distance. The invited guests were duly on hand to shower them with multicoloured rice, and the whole scene came to perfection when the nearby bells of St Luke's Church, where Charles Dickens was married, opened into a crescendo of the traditional after-wedding tune. This was a truly spectacular situation and it had all been arranged by Stewart Menzies.

To cap the whole experience of surprise after surprise, gone was the London cab, and in its place was a pre-war Daimler DB18 with a special Ritz sports body shell. This was Michael's surprise wedding present to Olga.

Menzies opened the doors for the bride and groom and settled them comfortably into the rear, which was bedecked with flowers and cosy rugs. Menzies got into the front seat and directed the driver to Claridge's for a late tea. Arriving at Claridge's, they were met at the door by the maître d' who showed them to the tea room where they sat in comfort and splendour.

Olga had never seen such splendour, as she gazed around the room. In the centre, there was a very large ornate chandelier and underneath it a grand piano. On a nod from Menzies, the pianist played his own creation of various wedding themes cleverly woven into a montage of joyous sounds.

They were sitting underneath several pictures of the British Royal Family. Olga remarked that perhaps certain members had visited from time to time. Menzies remarked that indeed it was so, and they were sitting in the Royal seating area where, many times during the year, the hotel would entertain Royalty.

Tea was served to the delight of everyone and it was a lush mixture of the most perfect sandwiches with exotic fillings, fancy cakes and delicacies accompanied by an array of types of tea which were so tantalising in their richness of choice.

After an hour or so of warm conversation and relaxing music from the pianist who had been joined by Evelyn Laye, a British international singing star, excusing himself for a few moments, Menzies disappeared. After ten minutes, Michael became a little concerned at their being left alone for so long. He knew he was taking a big risk in promoting himself in such a way, and perhaps the paparazzi photographers did not help, as it would be an extra pressure on SIS to keep Michael's identity secret.

To Michael's relief, a few minutes later Menzies returned and asked if they would follow him as he wanted to introduce Michael and Olga to two special people. Menzies led the way and they entered a very beautiful and cosy room with a roaring fire in the centre of the back wall. There were five chairs around the fire with two people were sitting there. As they entered, they rose and turned to greet Michael and Olga.

48

King George VI and Queen Elizabeth

Michael and Olga were absolutely stunned, and shocked to the core. They could not move and stood there with their mouths open in awe. Menzies introduced King George VI and Queen Elizabeth. The King and Queen, realising that their guests were rendered immobile, walked over to them with smiling faces which put them at some ease.

The King held out his hand and Michael, trembling, took it and shook it politely. The Queen then addressed Olga who, with her usual agile mind, curtsied.

The King was, in a way, an undecided and hesitant man, was led much by public opinion and Government pressure, rather than his own judgement, but he was ably assisted by his wife, Queen Elizabeth, who whilst appearing a stern, authoritarian person, also possessed great charm and warmth. When faced with personal matters, he would reflect in an honest way, and was not afraid to become contrite where it was required. His outward demeanour, however, was very formal, as it should be seen by his subjects and how the Government would wish him to be.

The King announced that it was his great honour to meet the last Tsar of Russia and his wife Olga. Menzies then bade them all to take a seat by the fire so that they could engage in pleasant conversation. Michael then slowly became aware of who he was and all the memories of his own Royal Family came flooding back to him. The King made him more relaxed and talked of Michael's valuable war effort and proposed the same acknowledgment to Olga in her service to the security of Great Britain for so many years.

Engaging for a while in a relaxed tone of conversation which covered several subjects of personal interest and their professional work. The King then changed the tone slightly and became rather contrite as he talked to Michael of his own family connections in pre-communist Russia, not knowing how Michael would engage with him in that area. Michael was happy to follow his lead.

The King's sorrow was over the fate of Michael's brother and family back in 1918, and he talked of his own family not acceding to the wishes of Nicholas in wanting asylum. He felt this was an indelible stain on his father's reign, and asked for Michael to accept his apology.

Michael was magnanimous in his reply, simply saying to the King that it was three decades ago, and that part of his life was too long in the past for him to have any untoward feelings. He explained that he had an audience with the King's father in 1918 when he visited Britain, and he was satisfied that King George V was equally sorrowful, although the outcome of the imprisonment was not known at that time in February 1918. Michael did accept, though, the explanations he was given and knew just how much of a difficult position his father had been in. He went on to say that he had regained his memory, and over the years he had become thoroughly Anglicised and was now enjoying his life to the full with Olga as his crowning glory.

With these words, 'crowning glory', Queen Elizabeth had since they arrived been looking with interest at the tiara Olga was wearing. The Queen was a keen historian of Royal Russia, and was convinced that she had seen that tiara long ago. Olga could not provide any provenance for her tiara as she told the Queen that she had just been given it by her long-standing friend from SIS whom she met in Madrid. She did however say that she was a Russian émigré who arrived in Spain in 1919, escaping the Bolshevik revolution.

Their whole conversation had lasted for around an hour, which was a long audience with a Monarch. At the end, the King stood up and embraced Michael as a family member, and told him of his pleasure in beholding the last Tsar of Russia. Michael reciprocated the honour and told the King that it was a wonderful experience to meet him, and that he felt very close to the British Royal Family.

The Queen, still intrigued by the tiara Olga was wearing, mentioned as they were leaving that she would hopefully remember where she had seen the tiara, which perhaps might reveal itself in some of her old photos.

Finally, the King said, 'I am about to ask you a question in a very unusual manner.'

Michael stood to attention at this request. The King asked both Michael and Olga if they would accept, on behalf of the British nation, an Honour each . The King supported the offer by saying that Michael would be recognised in his new name, for his services to the country.

This was an unbelievable recognition of achievement for Olga and Michael and they both gratefully accepted to be put on the Honours List for the New Year of 1947.

It was now time to leave as Menzies seemed to have another surprise. The King and Queen were insisting on escorting the newly-weds to the front foyer of Claridge's to bid them farewell. Walking past the piano, Evelyn Laye made a deep curtsy. Queen Elizabeth stopped in recognition, smiled, and gently bent over Evelyn, whom she and the King knew very well and said 'My dear Boo, (her society nickname) you must not do that as you are older than I am'. Boo replied with a serene smile showing her fun side, 'But only by a few days Your Majesty'. The King joined in the mirth, laughed and gave his favourite singing star a hug and a kiss on the lips, and winked at her privately.

Leaving the presence of the King and Queen, Olga said to Menzies, 'What more could be added to a perfect day?'

Menzies replied with a twinkle in his eye, 'How about one of the best seats at the Royal Opera House in Covent Garden?'

'Oh, my God!' Olga screeched, 'You are a wizard of wizards.'

'I think you will like the performance,' he said.

'Tell me, tell me, tell me!' she prompted in such enthusiasm that Michael had never seen before in Olga.

Menzies joyously cried out, '*Romeo and Juliet!*'

Michael and Olga held each other, weeping with joy.

49

An Heir

In early March Michael and Olga arrived at St
Bartholomew's Hospital for the lifesaving operation to
remove the several ulcers which Michael had suffered
from recently. The consultant surgeon was waiting for him
at reception and guided them both to the waiting room.
Michael embraced Olga and then he went with the surgeon
to the operating rooms, leaving Olga, who was showing
signs of distress.

After two hours, the surgeon came to the waiting room
with a smile on his face and assured Olga that it had been
a complete success, and that the lesions had been removed.
'Not a moment too soon,' he added. He assured Olga that
Michael was comfortable in a recovery room and was now
being revived and she would soon be called to the ward to
see him.

After a further hour of waiting, she was led to the private
suite and saw Michael sleeping peacefully. She stayed by his
bedside for another two hours, when he awoke with a smile
on his face which told Olga he was comfortable and pleased.

August was drawing to a close and Olga's pregnancy was now approaching full term. She had carried their child comfortably during the pregnancy period and had taken great care of herself under the watchful eye of her doctor.

In the first week of September she was feeling uncomfortable and it was advised that she should go into the maternity hospital at Queen Charlotte's in Chelsea. Michael took her by taxi and had packed several bags of essentials. Olga had added some glamorous clothes for when she was released from hospital including her essential cosmetics bag. Upon entering the hospital Michael called for a wheelchair as she was now looking a little pale and exhausted. He wheeled her into the prepared private room and settled her into her home for the next two weeks.

Later that day the senior surgeon came to see them with the midwifery team and they exchanged cordial greetings. The surgeon explained the various procedures for when the time came for the delivery of their child. He was confident that the pregnancy term had gone very well to date and it was natural that she would be feeling a little unwell as this was a big event for a middle-aged lady, and not least because there were concerns for a successful delivery. But he assured Michael and Olga that they were under the best of care possible in the whole of the United Kingdom, and all would be well.

Michael visited Olga each day in the pre-delivery period, and he could see that she was far more relaxed in Charlotte's than at home. The days passed uneventfully, and Michael was a great comfort to her in spending several hours a day at her side.

On September 13th, Michael had decided to stay with

Olga in the adjacent visitor bedroom to be on hand when the birth signs appeared. The morning of 14 September dawned and Michael was awoken by one of the delivery team members, who mentioned that Olga had just been taken to the delivery room as her waters had suddenly broken.

Amidst the excitement, Michael got dressed and went to the waiting room. He was brought a coffee by a team member and was grateful for it. He then asked if he would be allowed to be at Olga's side during the birth. This was a very unusual question, which she was unable to answer. The nurse disappeared into the delivery room and a minute later the surgeon came out to Michael and beckoned him to join them.

Olga, on seeing Michael, stretched out her hands in welcome and told him how pleased she was to have him at her side. They clasped hands and Olga at that point went into labour. Before long and with much of the usual stress and groaning which was expected at all births, Olga produced their love child.

Michael fainted and was caught by two nurses who were standing behind him. They had noticed how unsteady he had become and were prepared for the inevitable.

About thirty minutes later Michael came round, seated in a wheelchair next to Olga's bed. He awoke to see her holding a baby in her arms wrapped in warm woollen swaddling blankets. Michael was astounded at seeing his darling wife look so radiant and holding their child. He arose immediately and sat on the bed, giving her a very tender and long kiss.

Then, seeing an expectant unspoken question in his face, Olga looked at their baby and whispered that they had a son. Michael was visibly shaken with joy and he felt he had to sit down again in the wheelchair lest he fall over. Notwithstanding the joy of being a father at this late time in his life, he was very aware of his dynasty and that he was seeing before his eyes, the heir to the Russian throne.

Olga remarked that is was Saturday and the old rhyme spelt out "Saturdays child works hard for a living" and hoped that through hard work and dedication that their love child would become prosperous and enjoy a fruitful life.

They had never discussed any names beforehand as there was the real possibility that Olga could have miscarried due to her age. Olga asked Michael what his thoughts might be now that they had a son. Michael had not thought about names, in all honesty, and put the question back to Olga. She replied that she had given a lot of thought to that question over the past several months, and she asked Michael what he thought of George Michael.

Michael thought for a few moments and realised just how caring a person Olga was. She had chosen to honour Michael's dead son George, who had died 15 years ago in a car accident. He stood up and bent over giving her a long and loving kiss, saying, 'I think your choice, darling, is as impeccable as you are a perfect lady.'

Life was good at Richmond Hill and baby George was in excellent care with Olga who was as remarkable a mother as she was a wife and (ex-)British Government spy.

In November Michael was feeling unsettled as his stomach was again giving him pain. He saw the consultant and was given a different medication to see if that would help. It did, and life returned to normal again, but his diet had also been altered again and now it was a tougher regime for him. The diet had a complete absence of anything that had spice or acid in the ingredients.

His birthday arrived on 4 December, and they both went out to enjoy a meal in Chelsea, leaving baby George in the care of Xenia, who had remained a close friend of Olga. The evening was, as usual, a wonderful time of happiness for them both. Michael, breaking from the tradition of him receiving presents, took Olga's hand, and slipped on a glorious deep blue sapphire ring with a surround of hardened ebony in a casing of clear glaze.

'I want you to have this as a personal gift from me as an eternity ring to show you each day the love and romance I see in your presence in my life, every day.'

Olga slipped her hand into his and said in her most wonderful loving voice, 'Thank you, darling Michael. It will never come off my finger from this day forward.'

Then she brought out her own gift to Michael. She asked for his hand and she too had the same idea of buying an eternity ring. She slipped onto his finger a large gold ring which had a beautiful circular ruby set in the centre within a ring of ivory forming a cultural bond of ebony and ivory.

50

1947: Michael's Battle Continues

hristmas passed in a more subdued way as Michael was again feeling ill. Olga took him, under protest, to St Bartholomew's and insisted that she see Michael's surgeon. It was New Year's Eve and he was leaving early to enjoy the rest of the day in celebrations. Although he was just going off duty, he saw the concern on Olga's face and knowing of the immediacy of the last operation, due to it being a life-threatening condition, he examined Michael on his office couch. He could detect the lesions within Michael's abdomen and knew they had appeared again from the pain on Michael's face. He quickly called for an X-ray.

The developing process would be several hours and he advised Olga to return in the morning, as in the meantime he wanted to admit Michael to the hospital ward close to the intensive care theatre, just in case things got worse. For the first time Olga became afraid, and thought his ulcer problems must be far more serious than she had ever realised.

She had to return home to relieve Xenia who had rushed round, dropping everything, to look after George while they went to hospital. The following morning, New Year's Day,

Olga and Xenia returned to the hospital. Baby George had been left at Richmond with a nanny. Michael seemed to be in a stable condition and there was hope that the medication would quell the ulcers.

A few days later, on the daily morning visit with Xenia at her side, they were met in the corridor by Michael's team leader. He had a worried look on his face and announced that they were just in time, as Michael had taken a turn for the worse two hours earlier.

They went straight to the ward and enquired how Michael was. She was told that he was going in to surgery due to complications which had occurred earlier in the morning. The surgeon had been called out as an emergency, even though it was his day off. Michael was now in the process of a pre-med and there may be just enough time to see him before he was taken to the operating theatre. A nurse was called and Olga was taken to the pre-med room.

Michael was laid out on a trolley and as Olga called to him he lifted his head with a huge smile on his face. He cried out that he was so pleased to see her before he went into theatre, and she hugged him and started crying. He consoled her and mentioned that it was just standard procedure and he had won all previous battles with his ulcers, and this was just another occasion of little concern. She did not believe him, but did not let him know what was gnawing at her mind. She felt this was a very critical time in Michael's life. They waved goodbye until the swing doors of the theatre engulfed Michael.

After two hours, the surgeon came to see Olga in the waiting room. His face was dark and tearful.

'I am so sorry,' he said.

Olga pushed past him and went straight into the theatre, despite gentle protest from the medical staff. Michael was laid out on the operating trolley with a sheet over his head. She cried aloud, screaming Michael's name. She managed to get to his body despite being constrained, now more firmly, by the team. She pulled the sheet away and kissed Michael on the lips, calling for him to revive. The team then thought it better to let her grieve, and left them alone.

The sobbing and crying slowly died down. When they went back in, Olga was silent and holding Michael's hand. She had come to the realisation that he was gone. As she let go of his hand she slipped the ring off his finger that she had given to him on his birthday a month earlier. This was now to be given to baby George as his eternal gift from Michael.

51

Natasha Completes the Circle

During the war years when Xenia and Olga were posted to Madrid with MI6, they had become good friends. One of the commissions Xenia was given by Stewart Menzies was to occassionaly monitor the activities of Natasha in Paris at the end of the war in 1945. This was to ensure that Natasha would not discover the new life of Michael. Xenia knew of her activities and movements, and had met her on several occasions under a different guise. She had become very sympathetic to her position and the difficult financial circumstances she had been living in for many years. Indeed she had become a confidante and adviser to her, and had listened with understanding to her talking about the events of the last period of her life and times with Michael. She was still in contact with Natasha from time to time in the post-war years, and now more so as a friend.

Xenia had shared this with Olga as she felt that it was a betrayal of their friendship if Olga was not kept up to date with the events in Natasha's life. Olga had understood these arrangements completely, as she herself being part of MI6, was aware of all the consequences and had the integrity to be able to handle the matter of Natasha being still alive.

As Michael's condition had become very serious in the days before his surgery, Xenia had realised that there was a very good chance that Michael's life was in danger, and as Olga had indeed been told by the surgeon to prepare for the worst in the forthcoming surgery. Xenia had discussed with Olga that it would be appropriate to break the security and protocols of the secrecy of Michael's new life with Natasha as they both felt that it was a humane act of love to allow Natasha to share Michael's end.

Natasha had gone through the occupation of France and experienced very hard times. The likelihood of that improving were unlikely as she was now sixty-six years old and living in an attic room in Paris. Her only form of income was from gifts from certain Romanov relatives and her granddaughter.

Olga had in particular been very thoughtful about Natasha but had never wanted to meet her whilst Michael was alive. But she did understand her poverty and her past traumas of dealing with the loss of Michael. In some ways, she had confirmed to Xenia, she felt a moral responsibility of care and comfort, as was Olga's supreme nature.

In that openness, Xenia had, on knowing of the dangers to Michael's life, travelled to Paris to carefully discuss the revelation of Michael being alive. Natasha was so shocked, but delighted too. As Xenia explained the loss of memory and Michael's new life in full detail, Natasha began to understand, and knew it was of no fault of Michael, and that he had himself been through some terrible trauma.

She wished him the very best for a full recovery, so that he could continue with his own life. She recognised that, at his age of sixty-eight, then he too was facing an old age of memories and would not want the presence of Natasha in his life, which would undoubtedly cause so much commotion in both their lives and such public concern that neither of them would be able to handle any fallout, which would be inevitable. She swore herself to secrecy and to take the revelations of Michael's life to her grave. Natasha was particularly pleased to hear that Michael's wife was Olga Bystrovia, whom she had met for the first time in Kiev in 1918 and who had taken excellent care of her and her daughter Tata in bringing them to Britian on behalf of MI6.

Xenia's guesswork had been correct and she was relieved that Natasha was so brave in handling this information. More so she was very appreciative of being given a last chance to share the knowledge of the second life of Michael.

Back at the hospital, Xenia was waiting for Olga in the waiting room and quickly rushed over to her to comfort her when she appeared from the operating theatre. She hugged Olga tightly for a full minute and shared her tears as they sat down.

After half an hour, Olga was now in full control of herself and had come to accept the loss of Michael which she had privately feared would be the outcome of the life-long struggle with his stomach ulcers. She had prepared herself some time ago for this event. She now could undertake the love and care of George and prepare her life going forward into the future.

They left the building and stood at the entrance for a few moments. There, standing at the bottom of the entrance steps, was Natasha. Olga knowing that she was due to arrive that morning from Paris, walked towards Natasha with her arms outstretched in welcome and shared distress. Olga's containment of her loss of Michael broke, and tears were streaming down her face as she cried uncontrollably in an embrace with Natasha. Natasha was surprisingly brave and comforted Olga in the way in which only friends could do. This surprised Xenia and she saw the scene as one great moment in time of humanity and love of mankind. Xenia left them both as they sat on a bench holding each other's hands, as they talked and talked for an hour.

After a while Xenia returned and suggested that they might want to return to Olga's house for lunch. Both agreed readily. Xenia went to the car park and brought the Daimler to the bench and both Olga and Natasha sat comfortably in the rear, now chatting like old friends with a common bond.

Natasha was surprised when they got out of the car at Richmond. She remarked to Olga that she herself had lived in that area before deciding to relocate to Paris. It then dawned on her: she recalled the day she was leaving and was driving through Richmond Park and felt sure she had encountered Michael sitting on a bench in the park. Olga remarked that could be the case as Michael had moved to Richmond in 1926, and always had a daily walk in the park.

Arrivng at the house, they were met by the nanny who they employed to look after George. They settled down to lunch which was made for them. After lunch the Nanny made her departure and Olga thanked her for stepping in at a moment's notice. Natasha asked why there would be a nanny in the house.

Olga took her by the hand and led her to the nursery. Natasha's eyes lit up when she saw George lying asleep in his cradle. She looked at Olga in sheer delight as she realised that she was seeing Michael's baby. Olga invited her to pick up baby George. Natasha took faltering steps towards the cradle and gently picked up the child. She told her it was a boy. As tears rolled from Natasha's eyes, she asked what his name was. With a bright smile told her his name was George Michael. Seeing more tearful joy on Natasha's face she put her arm around her and they both looked lovingly at the heir to the Romanov throne.

The rest of the day was a peaceful ending after the earlier distress of the last moments of Grand Duke Michael Alexandrovitch. Now they were both seeing, in a way, the rebirth of Michael in the life of George.

It was now time for Xenia to take Natasha back to the hotel and then onwards to Paris via the Channel port of Dover. As they were saying their goodbyes, Olga thought for a moment how nice it would be to give Natasha a gift which she hopefully would find useful to help sustain herself. She went to her bedroom and brought out the tiara which Xenia had given to her on her wedding day. Olga asked her to take it with her deepest love, as a gift from her and baby George.

Natasha was shocked at seeing the tiara. It was with certainty that she exclaimed to Olga that it had once belonged to her, and that she had sold it to Albert Stopford whom she had met in Paris in 1930. Olga was taken aback and so pleased at this revelation, as it was now being returned to its original owner.

'How on earth did you come by this?' Natasha enquired.

Olga looked at Xenia, who herself was as surprised as anyone. Xenia could see the whole circle was completing in closure and repeated the story of how she had met Stopford in 1937 in Paris and they had become good friends. On the announcement that Xenia was being posted to Madrid in 1939, he had given her a farewell gift and token of friendship on New Year's Day. Albert was not in good health and he may have realised that his death was imminent. He died a month later in February 1939.

Olga then remarked that when she had met the Queen at Claridge's a year ago, she had mentioned that she had seen the tiara before and was puzzled as she could not remember exactly where. Natasha then told Olga it would have been at a charity dinner in 1923, at which she wore the tiara and was introduced to Elizabeth Bowes Lyons, as she was then.

Olga then announced to Natasha with great joy, embracing her in a manner of warmth, love and friendship that she had never felt before for another woman such love and that this was a very auspicious day in the lives of them both.

As Natasha departed with Xenia to return to Paris, Olga gave Natasha an envelope and asked her to open it when she got back to Paris. It contained money, and three photos of baby George and Michael. Natasha left with Xenia for Paris with treasured memories and reminders of her past life with Michael.

Michael had lived.

Michael lives on in George.

The tiara became Natasha's treasured possession from her past life at Gatchina.

The circle had closed.

Postscript: In closing the circle, it has been noted that George had become the rightful and legal ascendant to the Russian Imperial Throne. Therein lies a story yet to be told.

APPENDIX III
Assets Used in the Journeys

Imperial Royal Train...
last goodbye before the journey to exile in Tobolsk.

A selection of photos of the luxurious personal train of Russia's last tsar, Nicholas II. The Emperor appears in pictures with his wife, Empress Alexandra, and members of the Royal Family. The train was built originally in 1894 and by 1902 it consisted of 10 cars, with space enough for the staff. Nicholas II's reign ended with the Bolshevik Revolution in 1917.

1914 Rolls Royce Ghost Kegresse conversion

This is an Alpine Eagle conversion designed for Russian winter roads for nobility and equipped with the 'Kregresse drive' a hang-on device converting any car to a halftrack 'Kegresse audosledge'.

The name comes from the system's inventor Adolphe Kégresse, who designed the invention while working for Tsar Nicholas II of Russia between 1906 and 1916. He applied it to several cars in the Royal garage including Rolls-Royce cars and Packard trucks.

The car still exists and is kept in one of the still-numerous Lenin museums. The RR Silver Ghost was a very popular vehicle amid the motorized Russian nobility, being a well-built and tough chariot, quite capable of withstanding awful running conditions in winter.

A Kégresse track is a rubber or canvas continuous track which uses a flexible belt rather than interlocking metal segments, and the propulsion and suspension system incorporates an articulated bogie, fitted to the rear of the vehicle with a large drive wheel at one end.

The Imperial Royal Yatch `Standart`

Elegant style yachts were once the norm among many of the world's most important rulers. But few of these highly specialized ships can compare with the Standart, reserved exclusively for the use of Tsar Nicholas II of Russia

This handsome ship was a graceful seagoing vessel and was built to the Tsar's own specifications, she was constructed in Copenhagen in 1895.

The Standart was a superb, black-hulled 5557-ton yacht measuring 401 feet in length and 50 feet wide, making it the largest private ship in the world and reaching speeds of up to 40 km/h. She combined elegance and comfort and met all the requirements of a floating palace. A large bowsprit, covered with gold leaf, hung forward from her bow and three tall masts towered above her two white funnels. Also on the main deck was a huge dining saloon that could seat up to seventy-two guests at one long table for luncheon or dinner. The Imperial Yacht even had its own chapel for the private use of the Imperial Family.

When the Standart sailed, she attracted attention wherever she went. The yacht was manned by a crew from the Russian Imperial Navy. Also on board was a platoon of marines as well as a brass band and. In order to communicate with the mainland and other ships of the Russian Imperial Navy, the Standart was also equipped with radio, a novelty in 1912.

The officers were certainly in an exceptional situation as most days, the Tsar invited them to dinner and after the meal liked to play billiards with them or enjoy a game of dominoes. In return the Imperial Family accepted invitations to tea in the mess.. "We form a united family," the Empress used to remark.

After the Revolution, the former Imperial Yacht was destined to be stripped of all its former elegance. In 1917, the Standart was renamed Vosemnadtsate Martza. (Meaning eighteenth of March) and was refitted as a drab, grey minelayer for service in the Soviet Navy. She was scrapped at Tallinn in Estonia in 1963.

HMS Iron Duke

HMS Iron Duke was a dreadnought battleship of the Royal Navy, the lead ship of her class and was commissioned into the Home Fleet in March 1914 as the fleet flagship. She was armed with a main battery of ten 340 mm guns and was capable of a top speed of 39.36 km/h. Iron Duke served as the flagship of the Grand Fleet during the First World War, including at the Battle of Jutland. In January 1917, she was relieved as fleet flagship in favour of HMS Queen Elizabeth. She participated in both the Allied intervention in the Russian Civil War in the Black Sea. She was broken up for scrap in the late 1940s.

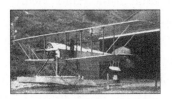

Blackburn Type L Seaplane

After failures with monoplanes construction, there was a move to biplanes. The Type L, 2 seater seaplane was built specifically as a candidate for the Circuit of Britain Race sponsored by the Daily Mail with a £5,000 winner's prize. Assembled at Blackburn's Olympia Works in Leeds. The Circuit of Britain race was due to start on 14 August 1914. When the First World War was declared on 4 August. All the aircraft were impounded by the Admiralty. During this time, some modifications were made to it, aimed at cooling and control problems: At some point, it carried a 8mm machine gun.

Vauxhall Prince Henry Tourer

Known to Vauxhall as their C-10, three specially prepared cars were entered in the 1900 km long 1910 Motor Trials named in honour of Prince Henry of Prussia. All the Vauxhalls which ran in the Prince Henry Tour, did about 65 miles an hour in the speed trial, which was really quite good for that engine with a four-seated body and a full complement of passengers.

Replicas of the trial cars sold quickly and became known as Prince Henry Vauxhalls. Prince Henry cars also competed in other international trials including the 1911 St Petersburg to Sebastopol Trial and so two cars were sold to Tsar Nicholas II.

The engine was of 4-cylinder with side valves and a capacity of 3054 cc giving 40 bhp output. In 1913 the engine capacity was increased to 3969 cc. Cars produced in 1914 have flutes in the bonnet that fade out a short way behind the radiator.

GNR Atlantic 251

This is the first engine, No. 251, introduced in 1902, with eighty more being built at Doncaster Works between 1904 and 1908. The Atlantics were generally very successful, and remained in front-line service for many years, sometimes being called upon to haul trains of over 500 long tons.

They were often called upon to take over trains from failed Pacifics and put up some remarkable performances with loads far in excess of those they were designed to haul. One once took over the Flying Scotsman from a failed A3 at Peterborough and not only made up time but arrived early.

Royal coaches in use in 1918

In 1902, Edward VII commissioned knew Royal coaches saloons to add to those in use from his mother, Queen Victoria. Two saloons were provided, one for the King and one for the Queen. The Kings saloon had a smoking room in mahogany, with inlays of rosewood and satinwood, a day compartment in the Colonial style, in white enamel. The saloons included electric heating.

King George V 1914 Daimler

This Royal car was a modification by Hooper Brougham to enclose the drivers compartment. Its 7.4 litre engine would produce 45hp which for that time in the evolution of cars was excellent power. The car was used extensively during the WWI years and was eventually replaced in 1922 with another Daimler.

U-151

Germany created the ultimate World War I U-boat which was a true long-range submarine cruiser. Boats of this class were 213 feet long, about 1500 tons with a speed of 23 km/h on the surface, and a range of 46,000 km at a speed of 10 km/h. Armament was twin 150 mm deck guns, eighteen torpedoes, and manned by a crew of 56 with room for twenty more.

https://www.youtube.com/watch?v=QPecQaraLpk

One of the first of the Deutschland class was built as a blockade-breaking civilian cargo submarine operated by the North German Lloyd Line. She had a cargo capacity of 700 tons. She engaged in high-value trans-Atlantic commerce before being taken over by the German Imperial Navy where she started her war service on 27th. July 1917. and finished on 11th. November 1918 after sinking 37 ships.

Her most successful mission was a long range cruise to the Eastern American seaboard where she had considerable success after leaving Kiel on 14th. April 1918. On one day she sank 6 American ships in the space of a few hours. One of her tasks on that journey was to lay mines and cut telegraph cables on the seabed. *U-151* returned to Kiel on 20 July 1918 after a 94-day cruise in which she had covered a distance of 20,215 km. Her commander reported that she had sunk 23 ships totalling 61,000 tons and had laid mines responsible for the sinking of another four vessels.

At the end of the war *U-151* surrendered to France at Cherbourg. The French Navy sank her as a target on 7 June 1921.

A Russian Drosky early 1900s, Phaeton Carriage

A Phaeton was a form of sporty open carriage popular in the late eighteenth and early nineteenth century. Drawn by one or two horses, a phaeton typically featured a minimal very lightly sprung body atop four large wheels. With open seating, it was both fast and dangerous, giving rise to its name, drawn from the mythical Phaëton, son of Helios, who nearly set the earth on fire while attempting to drive the chariot of the sun.

With the advent of the automobile, the term was adapted to open touring cars, also known as phaetons.

Sikorsky S-22 Ilya Muromets 4 engine Bomber

Full-scale replica of Sikorsky S-22 Ilya Muromets in Monino Air Force Museum. This is a replica of the worlds first four engine bomber. It was originally designed as a luxury airliner and the series was named 'Ilya Muromets' after a hero from

Russian Mythology. 73 aircraft of this type saw military service between 1913 and 1918. It was also the first type to carry out bomber raids, night bombing, and photo bomb damage assessment.

Daimler DB18 Ritz Body 1939

The Daimler was the last production car just before WW2 and iintroduced in 1939. Powered by a smooth 2522cc OHV straight-six engine allied to a four-speed pre-selector transmission was capable of 76mph and 22mpg. Built to a standard that befitted the holders of a Royal warrant, by Mulliner. Recommencing after WWII, DB18 production continued until the early fifties after some 2,500 examples are thought to have been sold.

Credits

Attributions

All material derived from, or adapted through, copyright material found on en.wikipedia.org has been so used in compliance with the terms and conditions of the Creative Commons Deed, which can be found at https://creativecommons.org/licenses/by-sa/3.0/" https://en.wikipedia.org/wiki/Wikipedia:Text_of_Creative_Commons_Attribution-ShareAlike_3.0_Unported_License

"The Copyright Works used in creating this book, from en.wikipedia.org, and the authors of these relevant works can be found at the following web address: https://en.wikipedia.org using the search button. Please note that this original work has been adapted for use in this book, the author of the original work in no way endorses any of the views, facts or any other expressions made in this book."